CONTENTS

"You're engaged?"

Tommy couldn't help his shock. He felt gutted. She hadn't been engaged the nights they'd spent together and that was only a couple of weeks ago, or had she? *"Since when?"*

"It just happened," Bella said, clearly avoiding his eyes.

He shook his head, trying to make sense of this. If there'd been someone special in her life, she would have told him the weekend they were together, wouldn't she? He thought they told each other everything. Or at least used to. *"Who?"*

She cleared her throat before she spoke. He caught the slight tremor in her lips before she said, "Fitz."

He laughed and said, "That's not even funny." Of course she was joking. They'd grown up with Edwin Fitzgerald Mattson the Third. Or the *turd*, as they'd called him. Fitz had been two years older and the most obnoxious kid either of them had ever met.

B.J. Daniels is a *New York Times* and *USA TODAY* bestselling author. She wrote her first book after a career as an award-winning newspaper journalist and author of thirty-seven published short stories. She lives in Montana with her husband, Parker, and three springer spaniels. When not writing, she quilts, boats and plays tennis. Contact her at bjdaniels.com, on Facebook or on Twitter, @bjdanielsauthor.

Books by B.J. Daniels

Harlequin Intrigue

A Colt Brothers Investigation

Murder Gone Cold
Sticking to Her Guns

Cardwell Ranch: Montana Legacy

Steel Resolve
Iron Will
Ambush before Sunrise
Double Action Deputy
Trouble in Big Timber
Cold Case at Cardwell Ranch

Visit the Author Profile page at Harlequin.com.

B.J.

NEW YORK TIMES BESTSELLING AUTHOR

DANIELS

STICKING TO HER GUNS & SECRET WEAPON SPOUSE

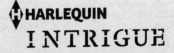

HARLEQUIN
INTRIGUE

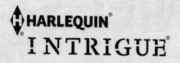

ISBN-13: 978-1-335-46291-6

Recycling programs
for this product may
not exist in your area.

Sticking to Her Guns & Secret Weapon Spouse

Copyright © 2022 by Harlequin Enterprises ULC

Sticking to Her Guns
Copyright © 2022 by Barbara Heinlein

Secret Weapon Spouse
First published in 2006. This edition published in 2022.
Copyright © 2006 by Harlequin Enterprises ULC

For questions and comments about the quality of this book, please contact us at CustomerService@Harlequin.com.

Harlequin Enterprises ULC
22 Adelaide St. West, 41st Floor
Toronto, Ontario M5H 4E3, Canada
www.Harlequin.com

Printed in U.S.A.

STICKING TO HER GUNS

This book is number 115!
I dedicate it to all my loyal readers. Thank you
so much for making it possible. I always wanted to
write stories when I grew up. It took me a while to
grow up, LOL, but this is what I love doing. What a joy
it is that I can share these stories with you.
I hope you enjoy this next Colt Brothers Investigation
book. Welcome to Lonesome, Montana.

Chapter 1

Bella Worthington took a breath and, opening her eyes, finally faced her reflection in the full-length mirror. The wedding dress fit perfectly—just as he'd said it would. While accentuating her curves, the neckline was modest, the drape flattering. As much as she hated to admit it, Fitz had good taste.

The sapphire-and-diamond necklace he'd given her last night gleamed at her throat, bringing out the blue-green of her eyes—also like he'd said it would. He'd thought of everything—right down to the huge pear-shaped diamond engagement ring on her finger. All of it would be sold off before the ink dried on the marriage license—if she let it go that far.

As she studied her reflection though she realized this was exactly as he'd planned it. She looked the beautiful bride on her wedding day. No one would be the wiser.

She could hear music and the murmur of voices

downstairs. He'd invited the whole town of Lonesome, Montana. She'd watched from the upstairs window as the guests had arrived earlier. He'd wanted an audience for this and now he would have one.

The knock at the door startled her, even though she'd been expecting it. "It's time," said a male voice on the other side. One of Fitz's hired bodyguards, Ronan, was waiting. He would be carrying a weapon under his suit. Security, she'd been told, to keep her safe. A lie.

She listened as Ronan unlocked her door and waited outside, his boss not taking any chances. He had made sure there was no possibility of escape short of shackling her to her bed. Fitz was determined that she find no way out of this. It didn't appear that she had.

In a few moments, she would be escorted downstairs to where her maid of honor and bridesmaids were waiting—all hand-chosen by her groom. If they'd questioned why they were down there and she was up here, they hadn't asked. He wasn't the kind of man women questioned. At least not more than once.

For another moment, Bella stared at the stranger in the mirror. She didn't have to wonder how she'd gotten to this point in her life. Unfortunately, she knew too well. She'd just never thought Fitz would go this far. Her mistake. He, however, had no idea how far she was willing to go to make sure the wedding never happened.

Taking a breath, she picked up her bouquet from her favorite local flower shop. The bouquet had been a special order delivered earlier. Her hand barely trembled as she lifted the blossoms to her nose for a moment, taking in the sweet scent of the tiny white roses—also his choice. Carefully, she separated the tiny buds afraid it wouldn't be there.

It took her a few moments to find the long slim silver

blade hidden among the roses and stems. The blade was sharp, and lethal if used correctly. She knew exactly how to use it. She slid it back into the bouquet out of sight. He wouldn't think to check it. She hoped. He'd anticipated her every move and attacked with one of his own. Did she really think he wouldn't be ready for anything?

Making sure the door was still closed, she checked her garter. What she'd tucked under it was still there, safe, at least for the moment.

Another knock at the door. Fitz would be getting impatient and no one wanted that. "Everyone's waiting," Ronan said, tension in his tone. If this didn't go as meticulously planned there would be hell to pay from his boss. Something else they all knew.

She stepped to the door and opened it, lifting her chin and straightening her spine. Ronan's eyes swept over her with a lusty gaze, but he stepped back as if not all that sure of her. Clearly he'd been warned to be wary of her. Probably just as she'd been warned what would happen if she refused to come down—or worse, made a scene in front of the guests.

At the bottom of the stairs, the room opened and she saw Fitz waiting for her with the person he'd hired to officiate.

He was so confident that he'd backed her into a corner with no way out. He'd always underestimated her. Today would be no different. But he didn't know her as well as he thought. He'd held her prisoner, threatened her, forced her into this dress and this ruse.

But that didn't mean she was going to marry him.

She would kill him first.

Chapter 2

Three weeks earlier

Bella smiled to herself. She'd just enjoyed the best long weekend of her life. Now sitting in a coffee shop with her closest friend, Whitney Burgess, she blurted out the words she hadn't even let herself voice before this moment.

"I'm in love."

Whitney blinked. They'd just been talking about Bella's new online furnishings business she'd started. "You're in love?" her friend repeated. "With the new line?"

Bella shook her head. "With a man. The man I want to spend the rest of my life with." This was a first so Bella was sure it came as a surprise.

"Love? Marriage?" Whitney laughed. "Seriously? Anyone I know?"

"Maybe. I just spent a long weekend with him in that luxurious hotel downtown. It was amazing."

Her friend shook her head. "And you aren't going to tell me his name?"

"Not yet."

"Well, at least tell me about your weekend," Whitney said, dropping her voice and leaning closer. "Don't leave out a thing."

"We watched old Westerns, made popcorn, ate ice cream, ordered the most wonderful breakfasts in the mornings and had hamburgers and fries at night."

"Wait, you skipped the best part," her friend joked.

"We didn't even kiss." Bella laughed. "It was the most fun I've had on a date in forever."

Whitney sat back. "Sorry, you didn't even *kiss*? So you didn't…for a whole long weekend together?" she asked incredulously.

Bella shook her head. "It was *perfect*."

"Not my idea of the perfect date, but clearly it has you glowing. Come on, who is this amazing man?"

Bella hesitated. "Tommy Colt."

"That wild boy your father ran off the ranch with a shotgun when you two were teenagers?" her friend asked in surprise.

Laughing, Bella nodded. "I think I've been in love with Tommy for years, but I never admitted it, even to myself, until now. We were inseparable from about the time we were five, always sneaking away to see each other. Our ranches are adjacent so it was just a matter of cutting through the woods." She smiled at the memories. "We built a tree house together at ten. That's about the same time we became blood brothers, so to speak." She held out her finger and touched the tiny scar.

Whitney was shaking her head. "You're really serious?"

"I am. It feels right," she said. "I wanted to wait before I said anything."

"Wait. He doesn't know how you feel about him?"

"Not yet," Bella admitted. "But I think he might suspect. Maybe."

Her friend laughed again. "Why didn't you tell him?"

"I'm waiting for the right time, but I will soon. My dad called. I have to go back to Lonesome. I told Tommy that if he was around…"

Whitney was shaking her head again. "You amaze me. When it comes to business, you don't hesitate. But when it comes to love…"

"I'm cautious."

"No," her friend said. "You're scared. And truthfully, I didn't think anything scared you. Are you worried he doesn't feel the same?"

"Maybe."

"Tell him! He's a rodeo cowboy, right?"

"He's on the circuit right now. I think he has a ride in Texas coming up."

"You could meet him there, surprise him," Whitney suggested, clearly getting into this.

"I could." Bella smiled, the idea appealing to her. "I definitely could." Her smile faded. "But first I have to go to the ranch and see what my father wants." She didn't add that there had been something in his tone that worried her. She just hoped this wasn't another ploy to try to get her to join his business partnership. She didn't trust his other two partners, Edwin Fitzgerald Mattson senior and his son, Fitz.

"I am going to tell Tommy how I feel about him," she

said, the decision made. "I'm glad we got together today. I think I'll surprise him in Austin." She just hoped he felt the same way about her.

Tommy couldn't believe he was home in Lonesome—and for good.

"Okay, Davey and Willie are gone," his brother James said after the others had cleared out. The four brothers had gotten together for the weekend, but now Davey and Willie were headed back to the rodeo circuit, leaving Tommy and James alone.

"Why are you really here, Tommy?"

They were in the upstairs office of Colt Investigations, what would soon be Colt Brothers Investigations, if Tommy had his way.

Before answering, he walked to the second-story window and looked out on the small Western town of Lonesome, Montana. It was surrounded by pines and mountains and a river to the east. He'd grown up here but had been gone for years on the rodeo circuit.

"I told you. I'm done with the rodeo and living my life on the road. I want to join you in our father's private eye business and stick around here."

"What's her name?"

Tommy laughed and turned to smile at his older brother. "So like you to think it has something to do with a woman. Speaking of women, how is Lorelei?" Lori, as they all called her, was his brother's fiancée. They were in the process of having a home built for them on the Colt Ranch.

"Lori's fine. Don't try to change the subject." James leaned back in the old high-backed leather chair behind the marred oak desk. Four years ago it would have been their father sitting there. James looked enough like Del that it still gave Tommy a start. They all had the thick dark hair, the same classic good looks and a dark sense of humor. They all had loved rodeo for as long as they could remember.

Thinking of their father, Tommy felt the loss heart deep. They'd lost their father way too soon. Worse, none of them believed Del's death had been an accident. Tommy had known that coming back here would be painful.

"I want to be part of the business," he said. "I can do this. I know I can."

"You don't know anything about being a private investigator."

"Neither did you," Tommy said. Everything about this room reminded him of their father and the Colt legacy. "But look at you now. A major cold case solved and business picking up."

James shook his head. "I never thought you'd ever quit the rodeo. Not you."

He could feel his brother's gaze on him as he moved around the room. "I used to dream of following in our ancestors' footsteps," Tommy admitted as he studied an old Hollywood poster featuring his great-grandfather Ransom Del Colt. Ransom had been a famous movie star back in the forties and early fifties when Westerns had been so popular.

Their grandfather, RD Colt Jr., had followed in Ransom's footprints for a while before starting his own Wild West show. RD had traveled the world ropin' and ridin'. Tommy and his brothers had grown up on the stories.

He could see himself in their faces as well as his father's and his brothers'. They shared more than looks. They were all most comfortable on the back of a horse—even when it was bucking.

"So what happened?" James asked.

Tommy shook his head. "Recently rodeoing just didn't have that hold on me anymore."

"Uh-huh," his brother said. "You going to tell me about her or not?"

He smiled and continued around the room, looking at all the photographs and posters. The Colts had a rich cowboy history, one to be proud of, his father always told them. And yet their father, Del Colt, had broken the mold. After being a rodeo cowboy, he'd had to quit when he got injured badly.

Del, who'd loved Westerns and mystery movies, had gotten his PI license and opened Colt Investigations, while he'd encouraged them to follow their hearts. He'd taught his sons to ride a horse before they could walk. Their hearts had led them straight to the rodeo—just as it had Del and the Colt men before them.

Tommy had thought that he would never stop living and breathing rodeo. That love had been in his soul as well as his genes. But he didn't need to get hurt like his father and brother to quit as it turned out. He was home—following his heart.

He was the third-oldest behind Willy and James, and like his brothers he had enjoyed life on the road and made enough money to put quite a bit away. But for a while now he'd been feeling the need to grow roots. It had made him restless. When James had taken over their father's business back here in Lonesome, Tommy had felt the pull.

But that wasn't what had made the decision for

him, James was right about that. He turned to face his brother. "Did you hear that Bella is back?"

James swore. "I thought you'd lost your nerve bronc riding in the rodeo," he joked. "Instead, you've lost your mind. Not Bella Worthington?"

"Afraid so," Tommy said. "She and I ran into each other in Denver a couple of weeks ago."

James opened the bottom drawer of the desk and pulled out what was left of the bottle of blackberry brandy and two paper cups. "If this conversation about Bella is going the way I suspect it is, then we better finish this bottle." He poured. Tommy took his full paper cup, stared at it a moment before he downed it.

His brother laughed. "So maybe you do realize that what you're thinking is beyond crazy. Do I have to remind you who her father is? Not a fan of yours or the rest of us, for that matter. I'm sure he has aspirations of her marrying some biz-whiz with big bucks."

"It's not up to him," Tommy said as he smiled and traced the scar on his right temple. The scar was from when they were kids and he'd made the mistake of suggesting that Bella, being a girl, shouldn't try to cross the creek on a slippery log. She'd picked up a rock and nailed him, then she'd crossed the creek on the log. He smiled remembering that he'd been the one to slip off the dang log. Bella had come into the water to save him, though. It was what best friends did, she'd told him.

"The woman can be a firecracker," Tommy agreed. "Maybe that's why I've never gotten over her."

James shook his head. "What are you going to do? I suspect you won't get within a mile of the Worthington ranch before the shotgun comes out if her father is around." He shook his head and downed his brandy.

As he refilled the cups, his brother asked, "How'd this happen? You wake up one day and say, 'Hey, I haven't been kicked in the head by a bucking horse enough lately. I think I'll go home and see if Bella wants to marry me'?"

Tommy shrugged. "Something like that. I can't explain it. I guess I did wake up one day with this feeling." He met his brother's gaze. "I think it's meant to be. Running into her again in Denver, I suddenly knew what I wanted—what I've always wanted."

James studied him for a moment. "I just have one question. When she sends you hightailing it, are you planning to tuck your tail between your legs and leave Lonesome and Colt Investigations?"

"Nope," he said. "I'm serious about going into the business with you." He glanced around. "The way I see it, you need me maybe even worse than she does."

His brother laughed. "You're serious about the job—and Bella?"

"Dead serious," he said.

James shook his head. "Dangerous business going after Lady Worthington. That is one strong, determined woman."

Tommy grinned. "That's what I love about her. I can't seem to quit thinking about her. I think it's a sign."

"It's a sign all right," James mumbled under this breath, but he smiled and raised his cup. "Fine. You start work in the morning."

Tommy looked down at the paper cup full of blackberry brandy in his hand. But this time he took his time drinking it. Tomorrow, he would learn as much as James could teach him, start an online class and apply for his private investigator's license. He hadn't seen Bella yet, but he wanted to accomplish something before he did.

When he went out to the Worthington ranch to see her, come hell or high water, he planned to ask her to marry him. He had the ring in his pocket. As terrified as he was, he was doing this.

Bella couldn't help being worried as she drove out to the ranch. She'd heard something in her father's tone when he'd called her in Denver and asked her to come see him at the ranch. There'd been an urgency that surprised—and concerned—her.

Maybe this wasn't about trying to get her to go into business with him. He often made her feel guilty for striking out on her own, but he knew why she'd declined. She didn't like his other partners, Edwin Fitzgerald Mattson and his son, Fitz. As generous as her father's offer had been, she'd also wanted to start her own business.

Her father had started his from the ground up. She thought he should understand why she wanted to succeed on her own. But the more she thought about it, she wondered if this visit would be about something different entirely.

"I need you to come home," her father had said.

She hadn't been back to Lonesome River Ranch in months because of her business. When he'd called, she'd given legitimate excuses as to why she couldn't come home right now.

"Bella." His voice had broken. "I have to see you. If you'd prefer that I come to you—"

"Are you sick?" she'd asked, suddenly frightened. Was it possible he was worse than sick? It seemed inconceivable. Her larger-than-life father never even got a cold.

"No. It's not that. I have to see you. I wouldn't ask, but…" His voice had broken. "I'm sorry."

"I'll come right away," she said and then hesitated before asking, "Are you there alone?"

"Except for the staff," he said, sounding both annoyed and resigned. He knew that if Edwin and Fitz were there she would refuse. The last Christmas she'd spent at the ranch had been so miserable because of the two Mattsons, she'd told her father that there would be no encore.

Parking, she got out of her vehicle in front of the ranch house and took a deep breath. The Montana summer air was ripe with the smell of pines and river. She'd missed this, another reason she was ready to make some changes.

As she started up the steps to the wide front porch that overlooked the river, her father stepped out and she felt a jolt of shock. He'd aged. While still a large, imposing man, Nolan Worthington appeared beat down, something she'd never seen before. She was instantly taken aback. He had to be sick. Her heart fell.

He quickly ushered her into the house, going straight to his den. This had always been his favorite room in the ranch house with its leather furniture, huge oak desk and small rock fireplace.

"What's wrong?" she asked, her pulse thundering with fear.

Tears filled his eyes. "I've been a fool," he said and broke down. "I'm in terrible trouble and the worst part is…" He looked up at her. "I'm afraid that I've dragged you into it."

Chapter 3

Present Day

Tommy Colt woke to sunshine—and as usual, a good strong jolt of reality. For days now, he'd been learning the investigations business from the ground up. And each morning, he'd awakened with a shock.

He'd come back to Lonesome, Montana, for a woman. A woman who had no idea how he felt and might not feel the same way. Not only had he blindly returned home for love, but he'd also quit the first and, for a long time, *only* love of his life. The rodeo.

Because of that, he'd thrown himself into a new job with his brother as a private detective for Colt Investigations. The two of them were following in their father's footsteps, both knowing the job had gotten Del killed.

In the light of day each morning, the whole thing

seemed pretty risky on his part. But his brother James, as Jimmy D was going by now, had already solved his first case, gotten his PI license and was making money at it. Tommy had jumped in feetfirst with no training.

But then James had learned on the job when he'd decided to take over their late father's agency, he reminded himself. Clients were now pouring in.

Maybe more like trickling in, but enough so that his brother could use the help. Tommy told himself that he wanted to prove he could do this before he went out to the Lonesome River Ranch and told Bella how he felt about her. He was planning to go out to her family ranch as soon as he got settled in. He wanted to make sure he had a job and a place to live first before he asked her out on a real date, told her how he felt about her and asked her to marry him.

He had to have some experience under his belt before he told her what he'd done, quitting the job he'd had and taking on one he currently didn't know for beans. All he knew was that she'd returned to Lonesome to her family ranch—after that amazing long weekend in Denver with him. It had been platonic. That was another crazy part of this.

Tommy was planning to ask a woman he'd never even dated to marry him. What was the worst that could happen? She could say no.

James had agreed that him learning more of the business before going to see Bella was a good plan.

"I'd like to get some work out of you before you go out there and her old man shoots you," James had said. "I doubt his feelings about you have changed."

Tommy doubted it, too. Nolan Worthington had his

own aspirations for his daughter. None of those aspirations included one of the wild Colt brothers.

Since moving home, he'd found a place to live in a cabin down by the river that he could rent cheap for a while. He'd saved most of the money he'd made rodeoing. But to say his life was up in the air right now was putting it mildly.

Forcing himself out of bed, he showered and changed for work. It was an alien feeling. Could he really do a nine-to-five job?

"More manuals?" Tommy asked as he came through the door of the office later that morning. This was the most studying he'd done since college when he'd also been on the rodeo team. He figured James would start him out doing something like filing once he finished with his studies.

"I have a skip for you," James said now, shoving a sheet of paper across the desk at him without looking up.

Tommy couldn't help being surprised. "A real job?"

"What were you expecting, a soft, cushy desk job?" James laughed. "It's an easy one, Ezekiel Murray."

"Wait, *Zeke*?"

"I would imagine you'll find him downtown at the Lariat."

The Lariat bar was one of three bars in Lonesome. Like a lot of Montana towns there were more bars than churches, more pickups than cars, more Stetsons than baseball caps.

Tom checked the time as he picked up the paper, folded it and stuffed it into pocket. 8:45 a.m. If Zeke were already at the bar, it would mean one of two things—he'd been there all night, or he was starting earlier than usual. Either was trouble.

"Is this like my initiation? Bringing in Zeke?" Tom asked half-jokingly.

"I hear that he's mellowed," his brother said, still without looking up from his desk.

Tom laughed doubtfully. Even Zeke mellowed would be wilder than probably any bronc he'd tried to ride.

James looked up. "If you can't handle it…"

In the Colt family, those words were tossed out as a challenge at best. At worse, foreplay for a fistfight.

"I'm on it," Tom said as he headed for the door. This was definitely a test—just not one he'd expected. But there was no turning it down.

Colt Investigations was housed in an old two-story building along the main drag. Their father, Del, had bought the building, rented out the ground floor and used the upstairs apartment as an office.

But James was currently working on moving the office to the ground floor now that Tom was joining the business. The upstairs would remain an apartment where James was living while his house was being built on the old Colt Ranch outside of town. He and Lori, who owned the sandwich shop next door to Colt Investigations, would be getting married on the Fourth of July weekend.

"What did Zeke do this time?" Tommy asked, stopping just inside the office door before leaving.

"Drunk and disorderly, destruction of property, resisting arrest. The usual. His mother put up the bail. He missed his court hearing yesterday."

"Great," Tom said. "So all I have to do is walk him over to the jail."

James chuckled as he looked up from what he'd been working on. "Easy peasy for a guy like you."

Tommy grinned, nodding. "I knew you were jealous of how much bigger, stronger and tougher I am than you. Better looking, too."

"Yep, that's it," his brother joked. "The longer you stand here giving me a hard time, the drunker Zeke will be. Just a thought."

"Uh-huh." He put on his Stetson and strode on out the door.

It was only a little over a block to the Lariat. The town was still quiet this time of the morning. Not that there was much going on even later. Lonesome was like so many other Montana towns. Its population had dropped over time, but was now growing again as more people left the big cities for a simpler lifestyle. That was Lonesome. Simple.

He pushed open the door and was hit with the familiar smell of stale beer and floor cleaner. In the dim light, Tommy thought that this could have been any bar, anywhere in Montana. There were mounts of deer, elk, antelope and rainbow trout on the knotty-pine walls. The back bar was a warbled mirror with glowing bottles of hard liquor under canned lights.

At the end of a long scarred wooden bar sat Ezekiel Murray. His massive body teetered on a stool, body slumped forward, his huge paws wrapped around a pint of draft beer that he had just dropped a shot glass of whiskey into—shot glass and all. The whiskey was just starting to turn the beer a warm brown. Tommy would bet it wasn't his first boilermaker and would win.

In Lonesome, Zeke was known as a gentle giant—until he got a few shots in him. Tommy tried to gauge how far gone Zeke was as he approached the man.

Chapter 4

Other than Zeke, the bar was empty except for the bartender, who was busy restocking. A newsman droned on the small television over the bar, with neither man paying any attention.

"Hey Zeke," Tommy said as he joined him.

A pair of unfocused brown eyes took him in for a moment before the man frowned. "Which one are you?"

The thing about the four Colt brothers...they all resembled each other to the point that often people didn't bother with their first names. They all had the same thick head of dark hair that usually needed cutting and blue eyes that ranged from faded denim to sky blue depending on their moods.

They were all pretty much built alike as well and all liked to think that they were the most handsome of the bunch. Close in age, they'd spent years confusing their teachers. They were simply known around the county as those wild Colt boys.

Having been gone on the rodeo circuit now for so long, Tommy wasn't surprised that Zeke might not remember him.

"I'm Tommy Colt."

Zeke nodded, already bored by the conversation, and lifted his glass to his lips.

"I need you to take a walk with me," Tommy said standing next to Zeke's stool.

The big man looked over at him before the drink reached his lips.

"Your mother... She posted your bail."

"I don't want any trouble in here," the bartender called from a safe distance.

"Won't be any trouble," Tommy assured him. "Zeke doesn't want his mother upset. Do you, Zeke."

He wagged his big head and started to put down his drink, but then thought better of it and downed the whole thing. The shot glass that had been floating in the beer clinked against the man's teeth and rattled around the beer glass as he slurped up every drop of the booze before setting it down with a loud burp.

Okay, this probably wasn't going to go easy peasy at all, Tommy thought as Zeke got to his feet. Even at six foot four, Tommy had to look up at Zeke. And while in good shape from years of trying to ride the wildest bucking horses available, he knew he was no match for the big man.

Zeke pulled a few bills from his pocket, slapped them down on the bar and turned to Tommy. "Ready when you are."

They left the bar as the sun crested the mountains to

the east. It was a beautiful summer day filled with the scent of pine from the nearby forest and that rare smell of water, sunshine and warm earth that he loved. There was nothing like a Montana summer.

Tommy couldn't believe his luck. Was it really going to be this easy? The courthouse was kitty-corner from the bar. Tommy was tempted to jaywalk, but Zeke was insistent that they walk up to the light and cross legally.

Lonesome had begun to wake up, a few cars driving past. Several honked, a couple of people waved. Tommy could just imagine what he and Zeke looked like, the gentle giant looming over the cowboy walking next to him.

The light changed. They were about to cross the street when Zeke seemed to realize where they were headed. "I thought we were going to see my ma?"

"But first we need to stop by the courthouse." The jail was right next door. Once inside, Zeke would be the deputy's problem.

"This about what I did the other night?"

"I suspect so," Tommy told him. "But once you go before the judge—"

Zeke turned so quickly Tom never saw the huge fist until it struck him in the face. He stumbled back, crashed into the front of the electronics store and sat down hard on the pavement. He could feel his right eye beginning to swell. Blinking, he looked up at Zeke.

"You realize I'm going to come after you again if you don't go peacefully with me now. Next time I'll bring a stun gun. If that isn't enough, the next time I'll bring a .45. I'm working with my brother James at Colt Investigations now and my first job was to bring you in. So, sorry, Zeke, but I gotta do it."

"I didn't say I wasn't going," Zeke said. "But I have to at least put up a fight. How would it look if I just let you take me in?" With that the man turned and walked on the crosswalk toward the courthouse.

Tommy got to his feet, only then starting to feel the pain. This was worse than getting thrown off a bucking bronco. He hurried after the man.

Once Zeke was in custody, Tommy headed back toward the office. He'd taken a ribbing from the deputies, but growing up with three brothers, he was used to abuse. He'd known this job wouldn't be easy, but so far it wasn't making him glad he quit the rodeo.

Worse, he could well imagine what James was going to say when he saw him. *Gentle giant my ass*, Tommy was thinking as he looked up and saw her. Bella Worthington.

She'd just come out of the bank and was starting to put on her sunglasses. She was crying.

"Bella?"

She hurriedly wiped the tears on her cheeks and lifted her chin, defiance in her gaze, before covering those amazing more-green-than-blue-today eyes with the sunglasses. He'd known her since they were kids playing in the woods together since their family properties were adjacent to each other.

Bella had been defiant even at a young age. Her father had forbidden her from playing with any of the Colt boys, but she'd always snuck out to meet him at the tree house they'd built together. They'd been best friends. The kind of friends that would let the other take a splinter from a finger with a pocketknife. The kind that would fight the town's worst bully even knowing the linebacker was going to kick your behind bad. The kind of friend the other would lie to protect.

"You all right?" he asked, thinking of the last time he'd seen her—just weeks ago. She'd been laughing, her head tilted back, the look in those eyes warm with emotion. They'd spent a few days and nights together, curled up on the couch in her suite at the hotel and watching old movies until they both fell asleep. They'd ordered room service breakfast and drank champagne promising that they would do it again soon.

He thought about the sweet scent of her, the way her long dark hair shone like a raven's wing, floating around her shoulders as she moved. He thought of the way she threw back her head when she laughed, exposing the tender pale flesh of her throat. And that laugh... He smiled to himself. But it was her voice he heard at night when he closed his eyes. A conspiratorial whisper next to his ear.

He and Bella had always been best as a team. Best friends for life, he thought, touching the tiny scar on his finger that they'd cut with their pocketknives to take their blood oath. It was as if they'd both always known how it would end, the two of them falling in love and getting married. Together forever.

Or at least that was what he'd thought, especially after their weekend in Denver. While they'd spent the time only as friends, he'd seen the promise in her eyes when she'd given him her cell phone number. "Call me. I've missed you, Tommy." She'd hesitated. "If you're going to be in Lonesome..."

He'd been surprised that she was going to the ranch and said as much. "Dad" was all she'd said with a shrug, as if it explained everything since he knew Nolan

Worthington only too well. It would have something to do with business. He was always trying to get her to join him in the partnership he had with the Mattsons.

"Maybe I'll see you there," he had said, not realizing that within the next few weeks he would completely change his life for a woman he hadn't even kissed yet.

"I'm fine," Bella said now, looking embarrassed and not all that glad to see him. Even as she said it, she shook her head, denying the words out of her mouth. As her hand went to her cheek to snatch away the last fallen tear, he saw the ring and felt his eyes widen, the right one widening in pain.

"You're *engaged*?" He couldn't help his shock. He felt gutted. She hadn't been engaged the nights they'd spent together and that was only a couple of weeks ago, or had she? *"Since when?"*

"It just happened," she said, clearly avoiding his eyes.

He shook his head, trying to make sense of this. If there'd been someone special in her life, she would have told him the weekend they were together, wouldn't she? He thought they told each other everything. Or at least used to. *"Who?"*

She cleared her throat before she spoke. He caught the slight tremor in her lips before she said, "Fitz."

He laughed and said, "That's not even funny." Of course she was joking. They'd grown up with Edwin Fitzgerald Mattson the Third. Or the *turd*, as they'd called him. Fitz had been two years older and the most obnoxious kid either of them had ever met. His father was the same way. Edwin Fitzgerald senior was Bella's father's business partner along with his son.

Because of the business arrangement, both Fitz and his father often came to the Worthington ranch. Whenever they did, Bella's father always insisted that she spend time with Fitz. But he cheated at games, threw a tantrum when he lost and told lies to get Bella into trouble if she didn't let him get his way.

Often when she knew Fitz and his father were coming to the ranch, she and Tommy would take off into the woods. They could easily outsmart Fitz as well as outrun him. Spoiled rotten, Fitz loved nothing better than making the two of them miserable. Bella had always despised Fitz, who Tommy had heard hadn't changed in adulthood.

He stared at her. "You wouldn't marry Fitz."

Anger flashed in her gaze. "Why not?"

"Because he's a jerk. Because you can't stand him. Because you can do a hell of a lot better."

"What? With someone like you?" She raised an eyebrow. "Run into a doorknob, Tommy?" she asked, indicating his right eye, which was almost swollen shut now.

"Zeke punched me, so it could be worse. Don't try to change the subject. Were you engaged when we met up in Denver?" She shook her head. "So you got engaged in the past week or so?"

She pushed her sunglasses up onto her long, dark hair and stared at him. "I don't want to talk about this with you, all right?" Instead of anger, he saw the shine of tears.

"Why would you agree to marry him?"

"Maybe he was the only one who asked," she snapped.

Tommy shook his head. "Come on, you aren't that desperate to get married or you would have asked me."

She bit her lower lip and looked away. He saw her swallow. "And what would you have said?"

"Hell yes. But that's only if you had gotten down on

one knee," he added in an attempt to get things between them back like they had been not all that long ago.

Bella shook her head. "What are you doing in Lonesome? Don't you have a ride down in Texas?"

He glanced down at his boots and sighed. This certainly wasn't going the way he'd seen it in his dreams. "After we saw each other again in Denver, I came home." He met her gaze. "You said you were going to be here. I left the rodeo circuit."

"Why would you do that?" she asked, her voice breaking. She knew he'd loved being part of the family legacy. He'd been on the back of a horse from the time his father set him in a saddle while he was still in diapers and told him to hang on.

He'd grown up looking at the old Hollywood poster of his great grandfather Ransom Del Colt, the Hollywood cowboy star; his grandfather, RD Colt Jr with his Wild West show; his own father, Del Colt. Rodeo was in his blood and if anyone knew how hard it was for him to give up, it would be Bella.

He met her gaze. "Maybe after I saw you in Denver, I wanted more."

She looked away and he could see that she was fighting tears again. "You're a fool. So now you're jobless?"

Her words felt like the flick of a whip and smarted just as much. "I'm working with James at the detective agency. The eye? I brought Zeke in after he skipped out on his bond. I've applied for my PI license. I'm staying in Lonesome."

She let out a mirthless laugh. "Great job. Bucking horses trying to kill you wasn't enough? Now you're going into the detective business? Look where it got your father."

He let out a low curse of disbelief. She knew how much he'd idolized his dad, who'd started Colt Investigations after his injury. Del had never made a lot of money but he'd helped a whole lot of people.

"I can't believe you would really go there, Bella, especially after all these years of being contemptuous of your father using money to control you."

"I'm supposed to be happy about you going into a business that got your father killed?" she snapped, sounding close to crying. "But it's your life."

"Right, and you're marrying Fitz, so what do you care?" Her chin rose in defiance. "What exactly is he offering you?"

"You wouldn't understand," she said and shifted on her feet as she slid the sunglasses back over her eyes and looked down the street away from him.

"Looking for your fiancé?" he asked. "I suspect Fitz wouldn't want you anywhere near me."

"You're right, Tommy. The best thing is for you to stay away from me." Her voice broke and he saw her throat work as if she'd wished she'd swallowed her words rather than let them fly out like she had.

"Wow, the difference a couple of weeks can make," he said as he took a step back. "I sure misread that weekend with you. Maybe a whole lifetime spent together. Guess I didn't know you as well as I thought. I take it back. Fitz is perfect for you." He started to turn away.

"Tommy?"

He heard the tearful plea, felt her fingers brush his sleeve and he stopped to look back at her. What he saw in her expression nearly dropped him to his knees. Just then he saw Fitz appear behind her, all decked out in a three-piece suit that probably cost more than Tommy's horse. The man didn't look happy to see him talking to Bella, but Fitz's displeasure was nothing compared to Tommy's.

"Good luck," he said to Bella and turned away before he put his fist in Fitz's face. He felt shock and disappointment and an unbearable sense of loss as he walked away. He and Bella had had something special. He was sure of that. Why would she agree to marry Fitz? It was inconceivable, especially after the two of them had been together just like the old days merely weeks ago. It wasn't possible that in that period of time she'd gotten engaged. And yet he'd seen the large diamond on her finger. He'd heard the words come out of her mouth.

So why was he still unable to believe it?

He slowed his steps. He kept thinking about the last look that Bella had given him in Denver. Could the woman change her mind that quickly? Especially a woman he'd known all his life. He thought of the hours they'd spent in their tree house. They'd shared their secrets, they'd shared their desires, they'd even shared their blood with their prized pocketknives. He thought of the two of them together in Denver. That lifetime connection was still there—only stronger.

He stopped and looked back. Fitz put his arm around Bella, but she pulled away only to have him grab her hand and jerk her roughly back toward him. Lovers' quarrel? Or something else?

He caught a glimpse of Bella's face. Something was wrong. He knew this woman. She wasn't acting like a woman in love.

Chapter 5

Bella was still shaken when she reached her car after seeing Tommy—only to be accosted by her so-called fiancé. Fitz. She hated everything about him. The way he brushed back his blond hair with that arrogant shake of his head. She really hated that smug expression that marred an otherwise handsome face. He was strong and fit. No doubt he had a trainer who kept him that way. But he wasn't agile. Even as a kid, he couldn't climb a tree or jump a ditch or run fast enough to catch her.

He'd always been a bully and that hadn't changed. She shoved away that image of the pudgy Edwin Fitzgerald Mattson. The man she was dealing with now was much more formidable.

Looks were everything to Fitz. Like his car, his fancy condo in the city, his gold jewelry he seemed so fond of. She'd caught the glint of a few inches of gold chain at his neck. It must have been new because he kept reaching up to touch it as if to make sure it was still there.

But it was that self-satisfied look on his face that had made her want to attack him on the street, her hatred of him growing by the hour. The problem was she didn't know how she was ever going to beat him at his own game. He had her neck in a half nelson and wasn't about to let go until he got what he wanted.

She warned herself that she had to keep her cool and pretend she was going through with this ridiculous wedding that Fitz was planning. He had invited everyone in the county. He was so sure that there was nothing she could do to get out of it.

The only way she could keep from losing her mind was by telling herself she was merely stalling for time. She would get this sorted out. She would see that her father's name was cleared so Fitz could no longer blackmail her—or die trying.

Just the thought of Fitz made her stomach roil. Worse was the thought of Tommy Colt because that made her want to sit down and bawl her eyes out. He was right. She was in love with him. She'd been from as far back as she could remember. He'd been her bestie. He'd been her everything growing up.

Her father had been immersed in his business. When Nolan was around, so was his partner and Fitz. It was no wonder that she preferred the company of wild boy Tommy Colt and his equally feral brothers. They'd been her true family.

Now, as she drove toward the ranch, she knew that feeling sorry for herself wasn't doing her any good. She had to figure out what to do next—and quickly. She'd never felt more alone. Or more scared. The clock was ticking, the wedding coming up fast.

Looking down at the pretentious huge diamond ring on her finger, she wanted to rip if off and throw it out the window. But what would that accomplish? She had to help her father. Losing her temper would only make matters worse.

Tommy watched Bella and Fitz part at her vehicle. Clearly angry, Fitz drove off in an obnoxious mustard-yellow sports car, the tires smoking. Bella sat in her SUV for a few minutes before leaving as well. He recalled that she'd been crying as she came out of the bank. He knew what it took to make Bella cry.

What had happened inside the bank? Was it about Fitz? Or something else? He had to find out what was going on and felt better as he turned back to the bank, even though his right eye was now almost swollen shut. He'd finished his first job for the detective agency. Now it was time for him to start believing that he could do this work.

Having grown up here, Tommy knew most everyone. One foot in the door of the bank and he spotted a young woman in one of the glass-wall offices. Carla Richmond had long black hair and large brown eyes. One of his brothers had dated her for a while, though he couldn't remember which one.

He stuck his head into her office doorway. "Have a minute?"

After her initial surprise, he could see her trying to figure out which one he was. "It's Tommy," he said as he stepped in and closed the door behind him. "I could use your help."

It was clear that Carla thought he'd come in for a bank loan. She started to reach for an application form, but he stopped her as he took a chair in front of her desk.

"This is awkward," he said, leaning forward. "I wouldn't ask but it's important. It's about Bella. Bella Worthington?"

She nodded and carefully replaced the form she'd been about to hand him. "You realize that I can't talk about—"

"She left here crying."

"I'm sorry to hear that," Carla said carefully.

"I don't want specifics, okay? I just need to know what might have caused the tears." He saw her jaw set. "Her father's rich. I would think she would come out of a bank all smiles." He caught that slight change in her expression. Something in those dark eyes. He felt a start.

"Tommy, you know I can't talk to you about bank business." She started to stand.

"Please, just tell me if you know why Bella was crying." He put his hand over his heart. "She means everything to me."

She sat back down and shook her head, but he could feel her weakening. "How is your brother Davy?" she finally asked as if changing the subject.

So it was Davy she was interested in. "He's still rodeoing, but I suspect it won't be long and he'll be coming home. You want me to let him know that you asked after him?"

She started to shake her head but stopped. "I suppose. If it comes up. We dated for a while in high school."

He smiled at her. "That's right. Look, how about you say nothing and I just run some thoughts past you." Before she could argue, he went on. "I doubt Bella is having any financial problems. Her business is going great guns from what she'd told me."

Carla's expression confirmed it.

"So who does that leave?" Again, that quick flicker in her eyes. He frowned. "Her father? Is he ill?" Tommy would have heard. Bella would have mentioned it. It dawned on him what Carla was *not* saying.

He let out a curse. It was a bank, not a hospital. "It's financial to do with her father." She looked past him again, clearly nervous. He could tell by her pained expression that he'd guessed it. "He's in financial trouble?"

She avoided his gaze as she rose and stood with her palms pressed to the top of her desk. "As I said—"

"I get it. You can't tell me." Tommy stood up. "I'll take one of those loan forms if you don't mind."

Carla looked relieved as she pulled out one and handed it to him. "I didn't tell you anything. Not a word."

He nodded. "Thanks." He held up the form. "I'll tell Davy I saw you."

Was it possible that Nolan Worthington was in financial trouble? If so, it would certainly explain what Bella was doing back in Lonesome at the ranch. With a curse, he realized it could also explain why she had agreed to marry Fitz. He thanked Carla and left her office.

He had to see Bella again.

But first he needed his brother's help.

James looked up from his desk and grinned as Tommy came into the office. "Nice eye. Zeke?"

"Good guess." He pulled the signed, delivered form from his pocket and tossed it on his brother's desk.

James picked it up, saw what it was and blinked. "I thought that might be your resignation letter."

"I told you, I'm in this all the way. We have a new case."

His brother lifted a brow. "A paying case?"

Tommy shrugged and pulled up a chair in front of his brother's desk. "If you don't agree it's a case we should take, well then I'll pay for it as your new partner."

"I'm not sure you understand how the business works," James said as he leaned back in his chair, but Tommy could tell that he was intrigued. He quickly told him about running into Bella as she was coming out of the bank crying.

"She's engaged to Fitz!" James shook his head. "I thought you said you and she—"

"Exactly." He told him about their conversation and then about Fitz showing up and the two arguing on the street. "I could tell something was wrong so I went into the bank. Did you know Carla Richmond works there?"

"Davy's old girlfriend. They were pretty serious back in high school."

"Right, anyway, she couldn't divulge anything about bank business…"

"But you got it out of her." James was sitting forward now, clearly interested.

"It's Nolan Worthington. He's in financial trouble."

James blinked. "Bad investments?"

"I don't know. It still doesn't make any sense. Why would a self-made man who went from nothing to filthy rich be so stupid as to make bad investments?"

"Is the partnership in trouble or just him?" James asked.

"No idea." He hadn't even thought of that. Maybe his

brother was a better investigator than any of them had thought—and the one big cold case he solved wasn't a fluke.

James opened his computer and started to type, then abruptly stopped. "Wait. You were just with her in Denver. She didn't mention any of this, including the engagement?"

"She wasn't engaged but she said she'd gotten a call from her father and was headed for the ranch. She didn't sound happy about it. Something is wrong for her to even consider marrying Fitz." James looked away. "What?" Tommy demanded, knowing the look all too well.

"I didn't want to be the one to say it, but…" James looked up. "Maybe she's marrying Fitz because her dad's in trouble financially."

"I already thought of that, but we're talking about Bella. She isn't like that."

When James raised a brow, Tommy swore, wanting to cuff his brother upside the head for not believing him. "Then how do you explain it?" James finally said. "Did you ask her?"

Tommy sighed, got up and walked over to the Hollywood poster of his grandfather. Her being engaged to Fitz made no sense. Was it possible this woman he'd loved for so long was that shallow? Had he been a fool to quit the rodeo and come back here?

He turned back to his brother. "She said Fitz was the only one who'd asked."

"You think she's just trying to get you to step up?" James asked.

Tommy shook his head. "She knows how I feel about her. Even if I haven't spelled it out, this engagement is too sudden. Knowing what I do know about her father, I have to help her."

"That's just it," James said. "You don't know anything for certain. You need facts."

"You're right," he said as he came back over to the desk. "I need to find out the truth—with your help, bro. I need a quick course in PI."

"Then pull up a chair and let's see what we can find out about Nolan Worthington and his business and partners, Edwin Fitzgerald Mattson and his obnoxious son, Fitz."

That first day back at the ranch, Bella had been forced to drag the sorry tale out of her father. He'd said he hadn't been paying enough attention to what was going on with the business. Edwin had him sign papers all the time. He hadn't thought anything about it.

"What did he get you into?" she demanded. She'd never trusted Edwin Mattson let alone his son Fitz, who was now invested in the business.

Her father shook his head. "I'm in trouble. The Feds are involved. I have no proof that I didn't do any of it. But these businesses it says I bought? They're money laundering operations." He broke down, dropping his face into his hands. "I sold them as soon as I realized what I'd apparently done, but I lost so much money and the Feds are even more interested in me now."

She had to pull every sorry word out of him, but she quickly got a picture of what Fitz had done to him. He'd tricked her father, who hadn't realized that at least Fitz—and maybe his father as well—had set him up to take away the business Nolan had started. Of course, if he were arrested on a felony, he would be forced out of the business he'd started.

"It's worse than even that," her father said. "Fitz says he has proof that I've been embezzling from the company for the past six months for my drug habit. I'm sure that if any money is missing, it's been going into his pocket. But while none of that is true, added to the mistakes I've made…"

"You look guilty." He was also acting guilty, she noted. "So basically they're about to fleece you," she said and frowned. "You've hired a good lawyer, right?"

He looked at the floor. "I made a bad investment. I'm afraid I'm broke. It's all gone. Everything but this ranch and now I'm headed for prison."

Her hatred for Edwin and his son had her pacing the den in fury. "Surely you have some recourse."

He lowered his head, shaking it slowly. "The judge usually goes easy on a first-time offender—if I agree to pay back the money, but that's impossible. On top of that, now with the Feds… Edwin and Fitz have been setting me up for months." He met her gaze. "They have our investors believing I have a drug problem. A few months ago at a restaurant I was drugged and appeared…" He broke down again. "There'd been ru-mors going around about me, I guess, started by them. I found drugs in the glove box of my car and got rid of them, but I never know where drugs are going to turn up. They have me tied up. There is nothing I can do."

Her blood boiled, but she knew she had to keep her head. One of them had to be strong right now. "There must be a way to prove that this is all a setup." She stared at her father. It couldn't be possible. There was no way the man she'd known all her life was taking this lying down. Nolan Worthington had gotten where he'd been by being smart and doggedly determined. He'd built the business that Edwin and Fitz were now stealing from him. "There has to be something we can do."

His gaze lifted to hers. She caught hope in his green eyes so much like her own. "Fitz said he can make it all go away."

She waited, knowing that whatever her father said next would be bad. She just didn't know how bad. "What do you have to do?" she asked in a whisper.

"Fitz has been taking over his father's part of the company for some time now. He's the one who's in control, according to Edwin. If so, Fitz has me right where he wants me. You know he's always been jealous of what I built, this ranch—"

"What is it Fitz wants?" she demanded, fear edging her voice. She knew Fitz, knew the kind of boy he'd been, the kind of man he'd grown into. "What?"

Nolan Worthington held her gaze tremulously. "You. He wants you."

She shook her head and took a step back, too shocked to speak for a moment. "Well, he can't have me."

Her father nodded in resignation. "I can't say I blame you."

They both went silent for a long moment. "What happens if he doesn't get his way?" she finally asked, remembering the deplorable child she'd known.

Nolan Worthington looked away. "It doesn't matter. I can't ask you—"

"Tell me." She waited.

He finally looked at her again. His eyes filled with tears. "This isn't your problem. I got myself into this and—"

"Tell me what happens if he doesn't get me."

"He'll send me to prison," her father said. "He'll plant more drugs. He'll see that I get the maximum time. Twenty years."

Twenty years. A life sentence at his age. She swallowed and said, "Fitz is going to have to say that to my face."

"You won't have to wait long. He said he plans to meet you here at the ranch." Her father pulled himself together. "I need to tell the staff. He's replacing them all and basically kicking everyone out but you—even if you agree to marry him. I'd rather let them go than have him do it."

"Wait, he can't just take over the ranch. You said it's in my name."

Her father stared at the floor. "He said he plans to stay here until the wedding and if you didn't like it, you could discuss it with me in my jail cell."

Bella was unable to speak. If Fitz thought he could bully her... But even as she realized it, she knew that it wasn't an idle threat.

Her father stumbled to his feet and reached for her. "I knew I had to tell you what was going on. I'm so sorry, but I can't ask you to—" He hugged her and she felt him trembling.

"And if I do this?" she asked, her anger making her blood thunder through her veins.

He let go of her to step back so he could see her face. She saw a glimmer of the father she'd known flash in his eyes as anger. "Then he will produce evidence that proves I'm innocent. He said he'd even buy my share of the business. I'm sure he will do it for pennies on the dollar, but at least I won't be in prison."

She wasn't able to believe this. "How can he make this all go away just like that?" she demanded with a snap of her fingers.

"Apparently he has another scapegoat."

Bella stared at him. "His father?"

"I don't know. Maybe this was Edwin's idea."

She shook her head wondering if her father really believed that. "So what do you get if I go along with this?"

"I'd be out of the company," he said. "But Fitz will pay me enough that I could live comfortably, but only if I left the country since my reputation is ruined, thanks to the two of them. Even with proof, no one will believe I wasn't guilty."

Chapter 6

As threatened, Fitz had arrived a few days after Bella's return to Lonesome. He'd driven up in his expensive yellow sports car—one that verged on ridiculous in this part of Montana. He'd be lucky if he didn't break an axle on the ranch road. Come winter, he'd high center the car in the deep snow and freeze to death. She could only hope.

Bella had warned herself not to lose her temper. It wouldn't help her father even though she knew it would make her feel better.

Fitz shook back his mop of blond hair to expose small blue eyes the color of twilight. He had that same haughty look on the classically handsome face that he had as a boy. It said, *I'm spoiled rotten and hateful and there is nothing you can do about it.*

She feared this time he was right as she opened the

door before he reached it. She'd called him days earlier, wanting him to confirm what he'd told her father—and record the conversation. He'd ignored the calls.

He stopped, a smirk coming to his lips as he pushed his sunglasses up onto his head and met her gaze. Bella thought she could have started a fire with the heat radiating out of her eyes. For a moment, he didn't look quite so sure of himself.

"I'm assuming you talked to your father," he said as he looked around, clearly avoiding her laser gaze.

"My phone messages weren't clear enough for you?"

His gaze came back to her along with the smirk. He raised an eyebrow. "You called me?"

She said nothing, waiting. Let the bastard admit what he'd done. She had her hand around her cell in the pocket of her pants, her finger hovering over Record.

He finally looked at her again. "I suppose he told you. Damned shame. Your dad should have known better."

That she could agree on. She'd never liked him going into business with Edwin Fitzgerald Mattson even before Fitz got involved. There was something about the man that she hadn't trusted—even as a child.

"So now what?" Fitz asked, getting visibly annoyed to be left standing outside the lodge. Had he really expected to be invited in?

"You tell me."

"At least invite me in. After all, pretty soon this ranch will be mine." He laughed and started up the steps toward her. "Excuse me, *ours*. It will all be ours."

"Over your dead body," she said, making him stop in midstep.

He raised an eyebrow, his mouth quirking into a

smirk. "I thought your father would have told you how much trouble he's in. I hope you have the money for a good lawyer for him. He's going to need it. My father and I were shocked when we found out what he's been doing behind our backs."

She couldn't believe Fitz would lie like this to her face. Then again, she knew she shouldn't be surprised. She said as much, daring him to tell the truth for once. His expression suddenly changed as if he realized what she was up to.

He came at her, grabbing her arm and pulling her hand from her pocket with the cell still clutched in it. With a laugh, he pried the phone from her fingers. "You said you wanted to talk, when you left me all those messages."

"So you did get my messages," she said. "Too bad you didn't take any of them to heart."

"Threatening my life?" He shook his head. "You are only adding fuel to the fire. Like father, like daughter."

What made her even angrier was that he was right. She needed to keep a clear head and find a way out of this. Threats were a waste of time. But it would be next to impossible not to want to claw his eyes out.

"If anything, you should be nice to me," he said smiling broadly. "It's to your advantage."

"I wouldn't count on that," she snapped, unable to hold her tongue.

His blue eyes, a deep navy, darkened even further as he gave her a push back into the open doorway.

It was all she could do not to physically push back. She feared what would happen though if she could get her hands around his neck. But he was right. He had the upper hand. At least for the moment. She took a step back and then another, afraid of what she would do if he shoved her again. She needed time to try to find a way out of this. She wasn't letting her father go to prison. But she also wasn't marrying this fool.

Once in her father's study, Fitz closed the door. "I could use a drink. How about you?" he asked as he walked to the bar.

"A little early in the day for me." He went to her father's bar as if he owned the place. Apparently he would soon enough unless she could stop him.

"Where's the help?" Fitz asked as he turned from the bar, a full drink in his hand. "There's no ice in the bucket."

Since her father normally lived in an apartment near his office in Missoula, there had been only part-time staff at the ranch except during the months he came here to stay. "My father let the staff all go as per your instructions apparently," she said. It was hard to be civil to this man. But she'd try a white flag of surrender first. If she didn't get the information she needed, she'd resort to all-out war.

Fitz chuckled. "I think that is the first time Nolan has ever done anything I asked him to do." He smiled. "How times change."

She watched him take a slug of his drink, lick his lips and settle his gaze on her again before she asked, "Your idea of a marriage proposal is to frame my father?"

He had the good grace to drop his gaze to the floor for a moment. "Over the years, I've tried other approaches."

"I recall. Slamming me against a file cabinet to grope my breast. Cornering me in the kitchen and spilling your drink down the front of my blouse as you forcibly tried to kiss me."

"'Forcibly' is a tad dramatic," he snapped. "I've tried nicely to get your attention. I decided on a different approach after you rebuffed my every advance."

"You could have just gotten the message and backed off."

His gaze hardened to ice chips. "I don't want to back off. In case you didn't get the message, I want you and I will use any measures to have what I want."

She nodded. "Just like when you were a boy and didn't get your way. This is just another form of tantrum." She turned and walked to the window so he couldn't see how hard she was shaking. None of this was going to help her father. If anything, Fitz would tighten the screws.

Bella turned to look at him again. It was all she could do not to gag at the sight of him slurping down her father's expensive bourbon. She could never let him win, for her father, for the ranch she loved, but mostly for her own sake. She swore right then, she would kill him before she ever became this man's wife.

"What now?" she asked trying to keep the tremor out of her voice.

He smiled as if he thought she'd finally accepted the inevitable. "We get married. Didn't your father tell you that I want the whole package? A big wedding. I've already sent out invitations to most of the county. It's going to be in the barn here at the ranch. It's going to be till death us do part."

She nodded, thinking she could live with the death part. "I really can't see you married to anyone, let alone me."

He put down his empty glass and stepped toward

her. She stood her ground even as the floor seemed to quake under her. Reaching into his pocket he pulled out a velvet box and shoved it toward her.

She didn't take it, didn't move. Instead, she looked down at the floor. Fitz was simple and spoiled, but he wasn't entirely stupid.

He let out a sigh. "Fine. We can do it your way if that's what will make you happy." She watched him drop to one knee and thought since he was already on the floor how easily it would have been to end this right now. One good kick with her cowboy boot and he would be helplessly writhing on the floor. But it wouldn't help her father if she went to prison as well right now.

"Bella Alexandria Worthington, I'm asking for your hand in marriage," he said with a sigh and opened the box.

The diamond engagement was gaudy and ridiculously ostentatious. She looked from it to him. "It looks exactly like something you would choose." If he caught the sarcasm, he didn't show it.

"Only the biggest and best for you," he said and took the ring from the box and reached for her hand.

She thought of her father and tamped down her fury. Was she really going to let this man blackmail her into becoming his fiancée? If she hoped to stall for time to figure a way out of this, she had to at least let him think she was.

She stuck her hand into his face and he put the ring on her finger. It surprised her that it almost fit. He must have found out her ring size. She met his gaze, wondering what else he'd found out about her. That she'd been with Tommy recently for an entire weekend? It wouldn't matter that they hadn't made love. Fitz had always been jealous of the closeness she and Tommy had shared over the years.

As Fitz awkwardly got to his feet, she realized how dangerous this man was. What he'd done to her father was diabolical. All because she'd spurned his advances?

Bella looked down at the ring on her finger. Maybe this was just a show of power. He wanted her to know that he was in control. He didn't really want to tie himself to a woman who couldn't stand the sight of him, did he?

"Why would you want to marry me?" she asked quietly.

The question seemed to take him by surprise. "Have you looked in the mirror lately?" he asked with a laugh. "I want other men to look at me with naked jealousy."

"I saw your sports car. You can have any woman you want, women who are better looking than me. So why me?"

"Because I can and because you and I are the same." She instantly wanted to argue against that, but he didn't give her a chance. "Bella, you go after what you want. Look at the way you turned your father down when you had a chance to go into business with him."

"With you and your father you mean."

He smiled. "Yes, with me. That was a mistake. You should have joined the partnership and not forced me to take other measures." He was blaming her for this? "You and I could own the world."

"I don't want to own the world," she said and swallowed back the bile that rose in her throat. The conceit of this man, the hollowness of his desires, his all-out criminal behavior, and for what? Just to feed his ego?

"Well, you'll be with me soon and I want to own the world any way I can get it," he said.

"I can see that." He seemed to take her words as a compliment until he looked into her eyes.

"You may not like my methods. Fight me all you want, but I'd hate you to have to visit your father in prison. That is, if he doesn't overdose before then. Or jump out a window from our office building. Desperate men do desperate things."

Her hands knotted into fists at her side. She heard the threat and knew it wasn't idle. It was all she could do not to lunge for his throat.

"As your fiancé I'll be moving into the ranch right away since the wedding is going to be here and it's coming up soon. Your large new barn is the perfect place for the wedding, don't you think?"

She shook her head. "You're not moving in here."

Fitz moved swiftly for a man of his size. "When are you going to realize that you no longer have a say in anything?" He grabbed her by the waist and pulled her into a kiss. She bit his lip, making him howl. He took a step back and slapped her so hard her ears rang, but he didn't try to touch her again.

As he'd gone back to the bar, Bella had promised herself that Fitz would never be her husband. One way or another, she would stop this marriage.

Chapter 7

Tommy pulled up a chair as his brother began to type at his computer. "Let's see what we can find out." He watched James go to a variety of sites, taking notes, determined to learn as much as he could quickly.

"This is interesting," James said. "Six months ago, Nolan bought some small businesses. During those six months, he'd gone through a lot of money on top of what appears to be several bad investments."

"So he is broke?"

"This does not look good. Car washes are cash-heavy businesses like casinos and strip clubs. Simply owning businesses like that is a red flag for the Feds. This could get him investigated for money laundering even though it appears that he turned around and sold them quickly at a loss, which frankly I would think makes him look even more guilty."

"You think he's involved in money laundering?" Tommy asked in surprise.

James lifted an eyebrow and shrugged. "The thing is, in most business partnerships, if one of the partners is arrested for a felony, the remaining partners can buy him out for pennies on the dollar."

"So you're saying that Nolan Worthington could lose everything."

"It certainly looks that way," his brother said. "I always thought he was a smart businessman. Didn't he start the investment business from the ground up? No wonder Bella's upset." James began to type again on the keyboard. "But at least it looks as if the ranch is in her name. That's good."

"Until she marries Fitz," Tommy said. "Then he'd own fifty percent should there be a divorce." Tommy thought about the ranch that Bella loved. She wouldn't jeopardize it to save her father, would she? "How did this happen?" He knew he was asking why Bella would have ever agreed to marry Fitz under any circumstances.

"Greed? The business with Edwin Mattson seems to be doing fine," James said. "Maybe Nolan wanted to make more money. Maybe he got involved with the wrong people." He seemed to hesitate. "I did hear a rumor that he might have gotten involved with drugs."

Tommy shook his head. "Nolan? That's not possible."

James shrugged. "Fitz started his own business no doubt financed by his father. He's doing fine. Didn't Bella start her own business?"

He nodded. "But she's barely gotten it off the ground. She wouldn't have the funds to bail out her father."

James closed his computer. "Could explain why she's agreed to marry Fitz, though."

Tommy wanted to argue that James didn't know Bella the way he did. She'd never marry Fitz under any circumstances, let alone marry any man for money. But there was that huge rock he'd seen on her ring finger. Not to mention the words out of her mouth. He stood and shoved back the extra chair. "I've got to talk to Bella."

Bella knew that she had to move quickly after Fitz's visit. The wedding day he had chosen was coming up fast. She realized that her father hadn't really explained how Fitz had left him so bankrupt. Conning him out of the partnership was one thing. What about her father's other investments? He shouldn't be this broke.

She called Fitz's father, wondering what kind of reception she would get. Edwin senior had always been kind to her even though she'd never trusted him. But when it came to Fitz, Edwin had almost been apologetic. Had that changed? Surely he was aware what Fitz was up to.

"Edwin, it's Bella," she said when he answered his phone at the office. For a moment all she heard was silence on the other end. "I'm sure you know why I'm calling. There's a few things I need to know. Starting with my father's finances."

There was a deep sigh. "This is something you should be asking your father."

"I'm asking you," she said, hating that underlying regret she heard in the man's voice as well as the pleading in her own. "Please. There is so much going on right now with Fitz… Tell me why my father's broke." She could understand Fitz and Edwin using the clause in the partnership to get him out of the business. But there had to be more going on here.

Edwin cleared his throat. "Apparently you are un-
aware of your father's indiscretions."

"Indiscretions?"

The man sounded embarrassed. "You really should
take this up with your father."

"I would but I don't know what *this* is," she said losing her patience.

"Ask him about Caroline."

The name meant nothing to her.

"That's all I can tell you. I'm so sorry." Edwin disconnected.

Bella knew he could tell her much more, but he
wasn't going to. Apparently she would have to hear it
straight from the horse's mouth. How much more had
her father kept from her?

He had gone back to his apartment in Missoula,
which was only blocks from his office. She'd been so
busy starting her online Western wear business that she
hadn't been to his apartment since he'd first rented it.
Instead, what little she'd seen of him had been at the
ranch—usually at his request. Now she wondered if
that was because he kept this Caroline at the apartment.

On the drive to Missoula, she had too much time to
think about all of this. As she reached the new high-
rise apartment house and parked, that stupid engagement ring on her finger caught the light, winking at
her as if in on the ruse. She took it off and tossed it
into her purse.

Her father's SUV was in the lot, but when she
reached the reception area on the lower floor, the man
behind the desk wasn't going to let her go up.

"He's had movers in and out all day," the man dressed

in a security uniform told her. "Other residents are complaining about him tying up the elevator."

"You can take it up with him," she said. "I'm his daughter and I'm going up to see him."

The man looked as if he wanted to argue. "Fine, but please tell your father that the movers he hired need to use the service elevator."

Her father was moving? So much for her theory that he was keeping this Caroline woman in the apartment. But where was he moving? Surely not back to the ranch. Or was he preparing for prison? she thought with a sense of panic as she took the elevator up to his floor and rang his doorbell.

Her father opened the door, clearly surprised to see her after their discussion at the ranch a few days ago. She was equally surprised to find him in such disarray. He hadn't shaved for a couple of days and appeared to be wearing the same clothes he'd had on the last time she'd seen him.

Past him, the apartment was filled with boxes. She caught the scent of old takeout and saw the food containers discarded on the breakfast bar along with several nearly empty alcohol bottles before she closed the door behind her and stepping past him. Her father never drank much, just a nightcap of his precious bourbon—not the rot-gut stuff that had been in the discarded liquor bottles she was seeing.

"I haven't had time to pick up," he said, stepping to the breakfast bar and beginning to toss items into the trash.

She moved deeper into the apartment. "What is going on?"

He stopped cleaning up, seeming surprised. "I already told you."

"You apparently left out a few things," she said. "Who is Caroline?"

All the blood drained from his face. He planted a hand on the breakfast bar as if to steady himself. "Who...who told—"

"It doesn't matter who told me."

"Fitz? Or his father?"

She'd never seen Nolan Worthington look more defeated. She wanted to reach for him and assure him that they would get through this. Except she didn't know the extent of what this was. But from the look on his face, this was even worse than what he'd told her before. "What have you done?"

He bristled and straightened taking on the stature of the father she'd always known. "I'd appreciate you not using that tone with me." She waited. "Could we at least sit down?"

She looked around for a place to sit, moved a couple of half-packed boxes and sat. He went to the breakfast bar. Picked up one of the almost empty bottles of bourbon and poured what there was into a dirty glass.

"I'd offer you one but..." He drained the glass, then came into the living area, moved a box and sat down some distance from her. The alcohol put a little color back into his face. "I made a mistake. It happens."

Bella sighed. How many mistakes had he made? Even more than he'd admitted to so far. "Just tell me so we can deal with it."

His Adam's apple bobbed for a moment before he spoke. "I met a woman. Caroline Lansing. I... I fell in love with her."

"She took all your money." It was a wild guess, but she saw at once that she'd hit a bull's-eye on the first try even as she told herself that her father was too smart to be swindled by a gold-digging woman. But he'd been alone for years since her mother's death. Lonely men could be easy prey for a female with criminal designs.

And Bella hadn't been around. "How bad is it?" She knew it had to be very bad.

"She... I...thought we were getting married. She let me believe that she had money, but that it was tied up in real estate, so I..." He shook his head. He didn't need to continue.

"She's long gone?" He nodded. "With your money?" Another nod. "None of that matters right now," he snapped. "Fitz is trying to put me in prison."

When she said nothing, he added, "Go ahead and say it. I was stupid. I was played for a fool." His voice broke. "I was in love for the second time in my life."

Bella didn't know what to say. There really wasn't anything she could say. "Is there nothing left?"

"Just the ranch."

She had a feeling that her father would have probably raided the ranch for this woman if he hadn't legally put it in his daughter's name. She would bet money Caroline, whoever she was, had wanted every last cent he had and would have gotten the ranch if she could have.

"So this is why you're broke, this woman? Do you have any way to get your money back from her, legally or otherwise?" she asked.

He shook his head. "It's gone. She's gone."

"How long did you know her?"

"I met her six months ago," he said. "I was...distracted and Fitz took advantage."

Six months. Was that when Fitz began plotting to

destroy both her father and her? Bella glanced around at all the boxes. "Where are moving to?"

"Everything is going into storage." He met her gaze. "My life is so up in the air, and I can't come back to the ranch. I know Fitz is moving in."

"That's what he says." She had much bigger problems. If she didn't marry Fitz, her father would be going to jail and then prison. Even if she did marry Fitz, her father's future was still uncertain. He was broke. Fitz was threatening to enforce the breach of contract clause in the partnership so that her father would lose everything, including his reputation.

"How did you meet this woman?" Bella asked.

"She came to the office, wanted advice on an investment," he said sheepishly. "One thing led to another."

She didn't doubt that Fitz had taken advantage of her father being distracted by this woman. But she couldn't help being suspicious that he'd been set up, and not just by Caroline. It seemed odd that the woman just happened to be sent back to her father's office.

"Do you have a photo of her?" Bella asked.

Her father looked surprised. Who kept a photo of the woman who had fleeced him? A man who'd truly believed he'd been in love. He started to reach for his cell phone.

"Send it to me and everything you know about her." She got to her feet. Her father looked better than when he'd opened the door. He had raised a strong, resourceful, smart daughter. However, she doubted even she could save him from himself. But she would try because he was her father.

She kissed him on the cheek as she left. The tears she'd seen in his eyes made her hate Fitz even more than she thought possible because all her instincts told her that he'd had something to do with everything that Nolan Worthington was now going through—and her as well.

Fitz stood on the steps of the ranch house, considering what he would do with the place once it was his. Once Bella was his. He touched his tongue to his lip where she'd bitten him. Anger made him see red. Once they were married, she was in for a rude awakening.

He'd moved up the wedding from the original date he'd planned, anxious to teach her how things were going to be. That was if he could wait that long. She would soon be his in every way whether she liked it or not.

Smiling to himself, he realized that he wouldn't mind if she fought back. It might make taking her all the more enjoyable. He knew it would be an even bigger thrill to get her on her knees than the excitement and joy he felt when he took over businesses and crushed the life out of them.

A truck pulled up out front. He saw it was from the locksmith shop in town. An elderly man climbed out. "You the one who needs the locks changed?" the man asked, glancing around. "Where's Nolan?"

"He's away on business. He asked me to take care of it. Unfortunately, I'm locked out."

The locksmith looked wary.

"I'm Edwin Fitzgerald Mattson the Third. My father and I are Nolan's business partners." At least for the moment. "Bella's my fiancée."

The man didn't move. "Where's Bella? Going to need either her or her father before I change the locks."

Fitz was about to let out a string of curses when he heard a vehicle approaching. With relief he saw it was Bella. He wondered where she'd been. He was going to have to clip her wings. She couldn't just come and go without a word to him about where she was going, but one step at a time. Clearly, she needed more convincing about who was in control here.

"Here's Bella now," he said, seething inside at how she'd locked him out of the ranch house. He really needed to bring this woman to heel and soon, he thought, narrowing his eyes at her as she climbed from her SUV. And he knew exactly how to do it.

"I understand you want the locks changed," the elderly locksmith said to her as she approached.

Bella glanced from the man to him. Her look was so defiant that for a moment Fitz worried that she would embarrass him in front of this old man.

"Oscar," she said, turning to smile at the locksmith. "I appreciate you coming all the way out here." She turned to Fitz. The challenge in her eyes sent a spike of pure fury straight to his gut where it began to roil. So help her, if she defied him on this—

"Let me open the door, Oscar, so you can get the work done and be on your way. I know that you like to have lunch with your wife. How is Naomi doing these days?"

"She's fine, thank you for asking, Bella." Oscar grabbed his toolbox from his pickup and started up the steps after her.

As the man passed Fitz, he didn't even give him a glance. "I have some wedding arrangements to take care of," Fitz said from between clenched teeth. "I'll see you later." Not that either Bella or Oscar was listening. Bella was busy offering the locksmith a glass of iced tea for when he finished the job.

Fitz was almost to town when he realized his mistake. What were the chances Bella would give him one of the new keys? He swore, slamming his palm against the steering wheel. He should have stuck around until he had the key. She thought she was so much smarter than him and always had.

He considered what he would do if she locked him out again. It was time to teach that woman how things were going to be from now on.

He pulled out his cell phone and made the call.

Chapter 8

Oscar had just finished changing the locks and given her the new keys when her phone rang. She didn't recognize the number, but something told her to take the call anyway. "Hello?"

"Bella." She could barely hear her father's voice, but she immediately picked up on its urgency. "I've been arrested. I need you to get me a criminal lawyer. I'm so sorry." There was noise in the background. "I'm about to be booked on a drug charge. I got pulled over. They found drugs hidden in the door panel on the passenger side of my car. He put them there." His voice broke. "I have to go." The phone went dead.

She clutched her phone, closing her eyes and trying hard not to cry. Fitz. She'd childishly locked him out of the ranch house and this was how he was getting back at her. When they were kids, he'd been sneaky and vengeful. She knew better than to taunt him.

The new keys in her hand, she threw them across the floor, angry with herself. If she was going to do something to him, then she had to be more careful. She had to be smarter. Taunting him would only make him tighten the screws on her father.

She had no idea how bad the drug charge would be— depended on how much was found in his car. While her father probably wouldn't get any time as long as it didn't appear he was selling the drugs, this would only add to the story Fitz was concocting against him.

Opening her eyes, she looked around the ranch. She and her father loved this place. She'd missed it desperately being away as she started her business. Now they were about to lose it. Her father was going to have legal fees, she thought as she made the call. Because of Fitz.

There had to be a way to stop the man before this ridiculous wedding. If she were stupid enough to marry him, he would find a way to take the ranch, she knew that, and her with it.

She spoke for a moment with a prominent criminal attorney a friend had used. As she hung up, she heard the sound of a vehicle pulling up. She took a deep breath. If it was Fitz, she feared what she might do that would only make things worse yet again. But it didn't sound like his sports car.

Bella stepped to the entryway, picked up the new keys from the floor and opened the door. Tommy Colt was climbing out of his pickup. Her heart leaped to her throat. He stopped to look up at her and she felt tears of relief fill her eyes. She'd never been so glad to see anyone in her life. He'd always been there for her— even after what she'd said to him on the street in town.

Propelled by nothing but raw emotions, she rushed down the steps and into his arms—just as she had in Denver.

This was not the reception Tommy had expected. Far from it. He breathed in the scent of her, the feel of her in his arms and held her tightly. She smelled wonderful, felt wonderful. He didn't want to let her go.

When she finally pulled back to look at him, he saw that she'd been crying. Again. "I'm in so much trouble, Tommy."

"I know. At least I suspect. That's why I'm here." He let her go as she stepped back and wiped her eyes.

"If Fitz catches you here—" Her voice broke. "There is so much I need to tell you. But not here." She seemed to be trying to come up with a place that was safe. Her green eyes widened. "Meet me at the tree house in ten minutes and I'll tell you everything."

He didn't want to leave her, seeing how upset she was, but quickly agreed.

"Take the back road out of here. Fitz can't see you," she said.

He could see how frightened she was and, while he didn't like leaving her alone, he had to do as she asked. Clearly, she was afraid of the man. Tommy had never known her to be afraid of anything. What had Fitz done to put this much fear in her? He drove out the long way before circling back to the ranch's adjacent property— Colt Ranch property.

The road in wasn't as bad as the last time he'd seen it. They'd had a mobile home on the property to stay in when they were home from the rodeo circuit but one of

James's girlfriends had rented it to some meth makers and had gotten it blown up. James had had the debris hauled off when he and Lorelei began building their house on another section of the property. Each brother had his own section to build on, if they ever decided to settle down.

Tommy parked and hurried through the pines toward the back side of Bella's ranch. He was scared for her, worried Fitz would come back and keep her from meeting him at the tree house.

But as he came through an open area, he saw her standing at the bottom of the ladder waiting for him.

The tree house looked as if it had weathered the years fairly well considering. "You'd better let me go up first," he said to her, seeing how nervous she was. He doubted her worry though was about the wooden structure the two of them had built together all those years ago.

One of the steps felt loose as he climbed up and pushed open the door. It looked as if some critters had made themselves at home in one corner, but other than that, the space looked better than he'd expected. He wondered if some area kids had discovered it and been keeping it up. There were several wooden crates someone had brought in. He dusted off one of them.

Turning he started to hold out a hand to help her up, but Bella was already coming through the door. He moved back to let her enter and handed her a crate to sit on.

For a moment they simply looked at each other, then she put down her crate and sat. He grabbed the other one, shook off the worst of the dust and sat down as well. The wooden crate creaked under his weight but held. He couldn't help but think of the hours he and

Bella had spent here together, and the weekend they'd spent together recently. They had a bond that couldn't be broken, he told himself.

"A little different from that suite we shared in Denver," he said to break the silence. They'd watched movies, played cards, ordered room service and gone for long walks. They'd reconnected in a way that had made him realize that he no longer wanted to live without this woman by his side.

"So you're engaged?" he said even as he knew it couldn't have been her idea. He couldn't have been that wrong about her. Or how they both felt about each other.

Bella gave him a wan smile, tears sparkling in all that green before she dragged her gaze away. "I don't even know where to begin." He said nothing, waiting. "I told you that my father had called me and that I was headed home?"

From there she spilled out a story that shocked and infuriated him. "I'll kill the son of a—"

"No, that's just it. If either of us do anything, he'll just send my father to prison. He isn't bluffing. He planted drugs in my father's car and just had him arrested because I locked him out of the ranch house."

"You aren't seriously going to marry him," Tommy said, trying to tamp down his fury. He'd felt such relief when she'd told him that she'd been coerced into the engagement. But he hadn't realized how serious it was until now.

"I'm not marrying him," she said with a shake of her head. "But unless I can find evidence that proves my father is being framed…" She met his gaze. "I want to hire Colt Investigations."

He blinked. He had little PI experience. The skin

around his eye was still bruised from taking Zeke in. "Bella, I appreciate your confidence in me but—"

"I'm so sorry for what I said on the street—"

"No, what I'm saying is that you need to hire an experienced investigator."

She shook her head. "You and your brother are the only people I can trust right now. I'll help. I know enough about my father's business and I have a key to his office—if Fitz hasn't had the locks changed. Will you help me?"

"You know I will," he said. He'd do anything for her. He realized sitting there, a shaft of sunlight coming through a slit between the old boards and lighting her face, that he would die trying to save her because he was crazy in love with her.

"But we can't be seen together," she said. "Fitz can't know that we've even talked after seeing us together in town. You probably shouldn't call me on my cell, either."

"I'll get us burner phones. I'll find us a safer place to meet." He grinned. "We grew up here. We know all kinds of places where we can be completely alone."

She smiled and let out a sigh. "I feel better than I have since my father called me. We can do this. We have to."

He nodded. "If you need to reach me before I can get the phones, call Lorelei and she'll get a message to me." He considered the trouble she was in and wished he could do more. Nothing like diving into a new job headfirst and blindfolded. But he was a fast learner and James would help from the sidelines.

She reached across the space between them and held out her pinkie finger. Tommy laughed at their old ritual they'd enact before leaving the tree house. He hooked his pinkie with hers.

"Best friends forever," she said and met his gaze.

Till death do us part, he thought.

Chapter 9

Bella hoped she hadn't made a mistake by dragging Tommy into this, but she needed help and he was the only one she trusted right now. She'd left the ranch house front door unlocked and was glad she had when she returned.

Fitz's sports car was parked in the drive. She circled around so it would appear she'd come from the trail along the river—rather from the woods that led to the Colt property.

"Where have you been?" Fitz demanded when she walked in the front door.

"For a walk along the river." She met his gaze. "My father's been arrested."

He nodded and smiled. "Drugs, huh. Such a shame. I see you left me a key to the house." His look said he hoped that she'd learned her lesson. He looked way too pleased.

But she had learned her lesson, she thought, heart pounding. It still took all her control not to attack him with her words let alone her bare hands. She warned herself to be smarter as she started past him toward the kitchen.

He grabbed her arm. She froze, telling herself to play along—but only so far. Glancing over at him, she gently pulled her arm free. "Unless you've hired new staff, I was just headed for the kitchen to see about dinner. I don't know about you, but I'm hungry."

He seemed surprised that she could cook. Let alone that she might cook for him. "What are we having?"

"I'll surprise you." Before she started away, she saw the wary look come into his expression and smiled to herself. Let him worry about her poisoning him.

In the kitchen, she turned her thoughts to Tommy Colt. She'd made the right decision telling him. He was her bestie. She'd realized how much he meant to her in Denver. The feelings had always been there, but she'd never acted on them. Neither had Tommy.

It was as if the two of them were giving each other space, knowing that one day... She shook her head at the thought. No wonder he'd been so upset to see the engagement ring on her finger. She couldn't bear that she'd hurt him. But everything had been happening so quickly.

Tommy. Just the thought of him made her heart ache. Once this was over... Right now she needed her best friend more than ever. Tommy was the only one she trusted with this news. With her life. He might be new to PI work, but he was smart and resourceful. Together, she had to believe that they could outsmart Fitz. They had to, because the clock was ticking. Fitz had already sent out the invitations to the wedding that was just over a week away.

Back at the office, Tommy told his brother everything that Bella had told him. His gut reaction had been for the two of them to find Fitz and beat him senseless.

"Not an option," James agreed.

"But definitely what I want to do. Not that it would do any good. He's really set up Bella's father bad. We have to stop this before the wedding."

When he told him the wedding date, his brother groaned. "Nothing like a challenge. Are you sure about this? Bella is strong-willed as you already know. You sure she won't refuse to marry Fitz?"

Tommy shook his head. "She won't let her father go to prison. And neither of us think it's an idle threat. Fitz just had Nolan arrested in a drug bust. He planted the drugs. He did it because she locked him out of the ranch house. He's serious."

James shook his head. "He wants Bella that badly?"

Tommy looked away. "Maybe we should have been nicer to him when we were kids."

"Come on, I remember the kind of kid Fitz was. He's just grown up into a meaner adult. He sees Bella as something he can't have so he's determined he will have her," his brother said. "She's probably the only person who's ever said no to him."

"So what do we do?" Tommy asked as he banked his anger.

"We need to get the proof. The truth will be in the real bookkeeping," James said. "Which means it's on a computer somewhere. Didn't the partnership have an accountant? I'd start with him." His brother thought a moment. "You've got to hand it to Fitz. He came up with the drug addiction as a way to show where the embezzled money went. Otherwise, there would need to be evidence of large expenditures like boats, cars, big vacations."

Tommy had a thought. "If you were her, wouldn't you demand to see the evidence he's holding over her head before she agreed to marry him?"

His brother beamed at him. "Very smart. That way we know where it is and how hard it will be to get. You think Bella will do it?"

He laughed. "We're talking about Bella, remember? She has more guts than anyone I know. But that doesn't mean that Fitz will go along with it."

As Bella came in from the kitchen, she saw Fitz nervously rearranging the salt and pepper shakers, straightening the cloth napkins on the table and shifting his chair to put himself directly in front of the place setting in front of him.

She frowned as she put two plates of food on the table, one in her spot and the other in front of Fitz. She realized this wasn't the first time she'd seen him do something like this. When he was a boy, he had to have everything just so from his clothing to his room.

As she started to sit down, he suddenly grabbed her plate and switched it with his. She looked over at him and smiled as she picked up her napkin and laid it carefully in her lap. "Have you ever seen the movie *The Princess Bride*?"

"Of course. It's…" Fitz frowned and then quickly switched the plates back, making her laugh. He looked miserable. Did he really want a lifetime of this?

Picking up her fork, she took a bite of her dinner. She'd had a lot of time to think while she was cooking. She would have to tread carefully. He'd proven today how vindictive he could be. Anything she did could have major repercussions for her father.

Bella looked up. Fitz hadn't touched his meal. "Is something wrong?"

He scowled at her. "I'm hiring a cook. You won't be allowed in the kitchen," he said angrily.

She shook her head. "Whatever you want, but I made that meal especially for you." She reached across the table, purposely knocking over the saltshaker as she did, and jabbed her fork into a piece of the sweet-and-sour chicken dish she'd made.

Gaze locked with his, she brought the bite to her lips, opened her mouth and popped it in. As she began to chew it she watched Fitz pick up the saltshaker and put it back exactly as he'd had it before. She reached over, this time just moving the saltshaker a fraction of an inch out of line, and skewered a piece of pineapple.

She'd barely gotten the bite to her mouth when he grabbed the saltshaker, his hand trembling as he squeezed it in his big fist. She recalled how Fitz had always had to control things when he was a kid. Apparently, he hadn't changed—only gotten worse because now he thought he could control her.

"There is nothing wrong with the food on your plate," she said. "Cross my heart." She made an X over her heart and smiled.

Angrily, he shoved back his chair, knocking it over as he rose. "You like messing with me? Tormenting me? You should know better. Have you learned nothing today?"

"I haven't done anything but leave you an extra set of keys to *my* house and make you dinner." She reached over and stabbed one of the sliced carrots on his plate and popped it into her mouth. "You can't blame me if you're paranoid."

He was breathing hard, his face flushed. "I can't wait until we're married. I will make you pay dearly. Nolan always held you up as an example. 'Look at Bella. Isn't she amazing? So smart, so talented, so independent.'"

She looked into his eyes, feeling his hatred like a slap. "Just because my father loves me and is proud of me—"

Fitz let out a bitter laugh. "He put you on a pedestal and stood next to you, just asking for someone to knock you both off."

"I'm sure he didn't mean to make you feel—"

"Like I could never measure up?" Fitz grabbed the chair up from the floor. For a moment, she thought he was going to hurl it at her. But he seemed to catch himself. He slowly lowered it to the floor and gently pushed it in. She could see him trying so hard not to reposition it perfectly.

"He was just proud of his daughter," she said again, quietly. But Fitz had seen it as her father comparing her to his partner's son. "With my mother gone—"

"Well, soon I will have his daughter and then we'll see how proud he is of you when he has to watch what I do to you."

Bella felt a shudder move through her. She had no doubt he would make good on all his threats. Now at least she had some idea why he was doing this.

"I'll be back with my things and a new staff, including a cook, first thing in the morning," he said.

"I wouldn't suggest you do anything to stop me. Once we're married…" He sneered at her. "You will be mine to do with as I see fit in every way and there won't be anything you or your daddy can do about it." With that, he turned and left.

She felt a sob rise in her throat and tears sting her eyes. He planned to tear her down, dominate her, destroy, her and all to prove that he had always been smarter, more talented, more everything. He was fool enough to think it would make him feel better about himself.

Taking an angry swipe at her tears, she made a solemn oath that he wouldn't beat her down no matter how hard he tried. Nor would he destroy her because she was never marrying him.

She finished her meal, although she'd lost her appetite, but she wasn't going hungry because of Fitz. His hatred for her and her father scared her. She regretted involving Tommy and Colt Investigations. It terrified her, what Fitz would do if he found out.

Yet a part of her needed Tommy for support, needed his help. After their time in Denver, she'd missed him. Something had happened between them during that long weekend. Not that either of them had acted on it. But their feelings for each other had grown into something special that she hadn't anticipated. Or maybe she had, she thought with a laugh. Maybe that was why she'd looked up his rodeo schedule and made sure they'd crossed paths.

Given the way she felt about him, she told herself that once she got the burner phones he was picking up, she should fire him. This was her mess. She shouldn't have dragged him into it. Knowing how cruel and heartless Fitz could be, what would he do to Tommy if he got the chance?

She shuddered at the thought. But even as she thought it, she knew that Tommy would keep trying to help her even if she did fire him. The thought warmed her. The truth was she needed Tommy on so many levels. She couldn't do this without him. She'd just have to make sure that Fitz never knew.

When she finished dinner, she took their dishes to the kitchen. She was loading the dishwasher when she remembered something. About a year ago, she'd been home to the ranch and overheard her father on the phone arguing with Edwin. He'd been upset about some deal Edwin had made with a company called Mammoth Securities Inc. Her father had warned Edwin not to do it. She was pretty sure the man had gone ahead.

There might be something there she could use. With a sigh, she knew she'd have to ask Tommy to look into it. But with luck, they might be able to fight fire with fire.

She turned on the dishwasher and left the clean kitchen. She had no idea where Fitz had gone or when he would be back. She didn't trust anything he told her. She called Lorelei, James's fiancée. "Can you get a message to Tommy? Also, could you pass on a photo and some information I have for him?"

Chapter 10

Tommy had spent the day finding out everything he could about Edwin Fitzgerald Mattson the Third. Fitz looked good on paper, but the more he dug, the more questionable behavior he found.

He'd been reprimanded at boarding school for bullying. He'd also gotten into a cheating scandal at university. His father bought him out of both by making donations to the schools.

But Tommy had tracked down one of the former administrative assistants who'd been involved and gotten fired over it. The man had been most happy to give him the dirt on Fitz.

Unfortunately none of that would help the current situation, though. They already knew what kind of man Fitz was. What he discovered more recently was that Fitz had fired the partnership's long-time accountant

six months ago. He felt that might be important since
it was about the same time that Nolan Worthington had
met the mysterious Caroline Lansing.

"How do we find this woman when we can't even
be sure she gave Nolan Worthington her real name?"
Tommy asked his brother.

James considered that for a moment. "Remember that
kid in school, Lance Black's little brother?"

"Ian?" Tommy nodded.

"He's FBI. I think you should give him a call. Didn't
you save his life that time in the river?"

Tommy laughed. "It wasn't quite that heroic. I did
haul him out of the water, that much is true. But if you
think he might help, I'll give him a call."

Ian sounded glad to hear from him. When he told
him what he needed, Ian promised to see what he could
find out. Tommy sent him the photo of Caroline and
what information Nolan had given Bella and she'd sent
to him through Lorelei.

"It's good to hear from you," the FBI agent said. "So
you and your brother have taken over your father's PI
business. Congrats. Probably safer than riding bucking horses."

Tommy wasn't so sure about that. "It's been interesting so far." He thanked him and then left to meet Bella.

He was already waiting for her at the abandoned old
fire tower high on a mountain outside of town when she
drove up. He could tell something more had happened
even as she tried to hide it.

"You can talk to me," he said after they climbed up
the four floors and took a seat on the landing. From
here the view was incredible of the river valley and the
mountains around them. They used to come here and

drink beer with a friend who manned the tower during fire season. Now it was an empty locked shell that hadn't been used in years.

As the sun sank in the west leaving the sky blood orange, Bella nodded without looking at him and told him what Fitz had said to her. "I'm sorry I involved you. Fitz is dangerous. I can't let anything happen to you."

Tommy fought his anger, knowing, as James had said, if they did what they wanted to the bastard, it would only make things worse for all of them. He reached over and took her hand. "Nor can I let anything happen to you. I'm helping you no matter what you say. That's what we do, you and me."

She looked at him, those green eyes filling. "Tommy."

He put his arm around her and pulled her close. She felt warm and soft in his arms. He pulled back a little to look at her. All around them, darkness began to fill in under the towering trees. The air felt cool and crisp, scented with pine. The beautiful summer night filled him with memories of the two of them—and such love for this woman.

Tommy leaned closer, slowly dropping his mouth to hers. He brushed his lips over hers. He'd dreamed about kissing her from as far back as he could remember. He'd always feared that it could spoil their friendship. He was way past that now.

Her lips parted on a sigh as she leaned into him. He pulled her closer, deepening the kiss. She wrapped arms around his neck and drew him down for an even deeper kiss. Their first kiss to the music of the summer night was everything he'd known it would be.

He drew back slowly and looked into her eyes. "The marriage isn't going to happen. We're not going to let it."

She nodded and snuggled against him as they looked out over the darkening land. After a while, he took one of the burner phones out of his jacket pocket and handed it to her. "Keep it close. My number is the only one in there."

She nodded and took the phone before telling him about the conversation she'd overheard between her father and Edwin Mattson.

"We're going to need to get into his office and Fitz's."

"I have the key to the main office door."

Tommy smiled over at her. "If Fitz is moving into the ranch tomorrow, I think we'd better break in tonight."

"I know the security guard should he stop by. He won't think anything about me being there. I just can't make things worse for my father. I got him a lawyer. He should get out on bail. At least for the moment. We discussed what he should do until his hearing and he's signing himself into rehab even though he doesn't have a drug problem."

"Smart. But I'm worried about you alone in that house with Fitz," Tommy said.

"There will be staff. I can hold him off until the wedding." She didn't have to mention that the wedding was coming up fast. He knew that Fitz had moved it up from the original date. The man certainly was in a hurry.

"There isn't going to be a wedding," he said again. "Let's go see what we're up against at the office. More than likely he wouldn't leave any evidence lying around. It's probably in a safe. Know a good safecracker?"

"No. I know a good locksmith, though," she said. "I

also know Fitz." Then she leaned in and kissed him. "For luck," she said smiling.

The office of Lonesome River Investments was in the older part of Missoula on the river. The partnership had bought the narrow two-story brick building. It had a vintage clothing store on one side and a coffee shop on the other side, both leased to the businesses.

Bella used her key to open the outer door. They stepped into a stairwell and she locked the door behind him before they started up the stairs to the second-floor offices.

This floor had been completely remodeled with lots of glass and shiny metal. Her father, who'd originally started the business, had been content with the original exposed brick and worn hardwood floors. But Edwin had insisted appearance meant everything when dealing with other people's money.

She used her key to open the door off the landing and quickly put in the security code. She felt Tommy's worried gaze. Wouldn't the first thing Fitz would have done be to change the code?

No alarm sounded. Bella let out the breath she'd been holding, but grew more wary as she neared the separate offices. Edwin's was the first along the hall across from her father's. Fitz's office was behind his father's with storage and a conference room at the end of the short hallway.

She passed Edwin's dark office and headed straight for Fitz's. She told herself that while Edwin had to be in on this scheme, Fitz would keep the evidence close— not trusting anyone—including his father.

As she reached the door to his office, she was only

a little surprised to find it locked. She and Tommy had expected this.

"I've got this," Tommy said and pulled out his lock pick set. "Thanks to my misspent youth." It took him only a few moments to get the door open.

"Nice job," she said. Both of them had gotten quite good at picking locks as teenagers. It was a skill though that they'd never imagined using at this age, she thought.

Once in his office, she turned on the overhead light knowing it would be less suspicious from the street to alert security. Her father paid for a security patrol in the area.

Bella went right to Fitz's desk. It was too clean. No desktop computer. No laptop, either. Which meant that Fitz always had it with him in that large briefcase he carried.

She wondered what he actually did for his pay here. She opened each drawer. All too neat. The bottom drawer was locked. She motioned to Tommy that she needed his lock pick when he was finished.

Tommy had gone to the filing cabinets against the wall, picked the lock and was now going through the files.

She was rusty at this, but the desk drawer lock was simple enough it didn't take her long. She opened the drawer. Empty except for a single folder. She pulled it out and placed it on the table. As she did, photos fell out and spread across the table.

Tommy was at her side in an instant, having heard the shocked sound she'd made. Every photo was of Bella. They appeared to have been taken over the years, most with a telephoto lens from some distance. Tommy was in many of the photos.

"What the hell?" he said as he went through them. "Sick bastard."

"He's apparently been spying on us for years," she said, surprised her voice sounded almost normal given the trembling inside her. She'd become the man's obsession long before she had any idea of what was going on in Fitz's mind.

"Has he been planning this for years?" Tommy said more to himself than her. He started to throw the photos in the empty trash can under the desk, but stopped himself. "This could be evidence if things go south." He pulled out his phone and spread the photos across the desk next to the calendar with "E. Fitzgerald III" on it and snapped a half dozen shots.

She put the photos back into the file and locked them in the drawer again. She felt uneasy and realized why. Had Fitz known she would break into his office? Had he put them in the locked drawer for her to find?

"Did you find anything?" she asked Tommy.

He shook his head as he started around the room, peering under the artwork until he found what he'd been looking for. Removing the painting that had been covering the safe, he took a photo of the safe. "You really do know a locksmith who might be able to open it?" he asked as she joined him.

"Maybe." Bella thought of the single file in the locked drawer. Fitz had known she would break into his office, break into his desk. She couldn't shake the feeling that he'd wanted her to find it.

She touched the dial on the safe and slowly began to turn it.

"Bella?" Tommy said next to her.

Not answering, she finished putting in her birthday. Something clunked inside the safe and the door popped open.

Tommy let out an oath. "What the—"

The safe was empty except for an envelope addressed to her. She hesitated before she pulled it out. It wasn't sealed. Taking out the folded sheet inside she read:

Did you really think I would leave anything here at the office, Bella? You think you know me so well, but the truth is I know you better. I've been watching you for years. That's why I can predict your every move. Speaking of moving, you should get out of there. The moment you opened the safe a silent alarm went off. Security will be all over this building within four minutes.

She crumpled the note in her fist even as she and Tommy quickly exited the building. They had planned to look around Edwin's office. Another time, she thought. Except next time, Fitz would have had the locks or the security code changed.

They were a block away when they heard the sirens and saw the lights as security descended on the Lonesome River Associates offices.

They would have already called Fitz.

Fitz smiled to himself as he hung up the phone. Bella thought she could outsmart him. He couldn't wait to see her face. But not tonight, he thought as he turned back toward the woman lying in bed. She was waiting for him, the covers pulled back, exposing her lovely breasts.

Bella was right. He could have most any woman he wanted, like this classic beauty waiting for him. He could do anything he wanted to her. That was what money and power got him.

Yet even as he had the thought, he felt his desire fade. There was only one woman he wanted. Bella. He told himself he would have her soon.

"You should go," he said, turning away to reach for his robe. "It's late."

"Are you sure?" She sounded disappointed even though he'd already had his fill of her.

For a moment, he reconsidered. A bird in the hand… Or in this case, a breast. He dropped his robe knowing this woman would do anything he asked her and come back for more.

"There's something I would like," he said and opened the drawer next to his bed. Her eyes widened and she drew back a little. "Is there a problem?" he asked as he pulled out the device.

She shook her head as he tossed her a gag and watched her put it on with trembling fingers. All he could think about was seeing that kind of fear and then pain in Bella's green eyes. She would learn soon enough who was in charge now.

"I hate the thought of you out at the ranch with that man," Tommy said when they reached the fire tower where they'd left his pickup earlier.

She'd turned off her engine, letting the summer darkness and quiet in. For a few moments, they sat in silence. "He thinks he knows me."

Tommy saw her shift her gaze to him in the darkness of the car. Overhead the sky was splattered with stars, but down here in the pines there were deep pockets of darkness.

"I'm afraid he proved tonight that he knows me better than I know him," she said, her voice breaking. "He's been one step ahead of me."

He reached for her, drawing her to him. She rested her head against his chest as he smoothed her hair. "He won't win. We won't let him. We can beat him, the two of us."

She nodded against his chest and pulled back, biting her lower lip for a moment. "What now?"

"James said you might want to demand to see what he's got against your father. That would let us know where he's keeping it. You could also demand an audit of the books. If Fitz wasn't expecting that move—"

"But if he is expecting it, that would alert the IRS of the embezzlement."

Tommy nodded. "It would mean calling Fitz's bluff. If the auditor suspected at all that there was a second set of books…"

She shook her head. "I don't know. So far Fitz seems to have thought of everything—the drugs in my father's car, the embezzlement, the setup at his office. Clearly, he's been planning this for a long time."

Tommy nodded. "It's a risk, but it could buy us time."

"Let me think about it," Bella said. "Maybe I'll talk to my father. I don't know that Fitz showed him the doctored books. You could be right and they don't even exist."

Tommy nodded and said, "Exactly," but he thought she was probably right the first time. Fitz had planned this. There would be doctored books. What if an audit only put her father in even more jeopardy with the law?

"What did you find out about Mammoth Securities Inc.?" she asked.

"Edwin dumped it at a loss," Tommy said. "That's all I've been able to find out."

Bella started the car. "I'll call you tomorrow the first chance I get."

He wanted to warn her to be careful. But she knew better than anyone what was at stake—and how dangerous Fitz was. "I did want to ask you to marry me." The words just came out as he reached for his door handle and looked back at her.

She smiled. "Is that right?"

Tommy nodded. "I still plan to." With that he got out and headed for his pickup. Had he looked back he would have seen her smiling.

Chapter 11

Bella had seen the vehicles pull up in the ranch yard last night from her bedroom window. As she watched a half dozen men exit the vehicles, Fitz drove up and got out of his car before leading the men into the house. Even from where she stood watching, she could see that the men were armed. Several of them looked like thugs. She noticed that those two were the ones Fitz had pulled aside to talk to.

Fitz was preparing for war, she thought, imagining the ranch becoming a fortress to keep only one person in—her. After that, she'd had a fitful night, sleeping little. This morning she'd showered and dressed, determined not to let Fitz get to her.

Her cell phone rang and she saw it was Whitney. She hadn't spoken to her since they'd gotten together after her weekend with Tommy. "Hey," she said as she picked up.

"What is going on? I just heard that you're engaged to Fitz and getting married in a matter of days?"

"It's a long story. I can't get into it right now," she said, wondering if one of the guards was listening outside her bedroom door. "Needless to say, things have been a bit complicated since I returned to the ranch."

"What happened with Tommy?" her friend asked, sounding sad.

"I still feel the same and I'm pretty sure so does he. It's going to work out." Her voice broke. "It has to." She hoped she sounded more positive than she felt right now. "Think good thoughts for me."

"You know I will. I'm a hopeless romantic."

She disconnected and started down the hallway to the stairs. As she did, she heard Fitz's raised voice coming from the guest quarters. Glancing around, she checked first to make sure none of his security was around before she moved down the hallway. Stopping at his door, she listened. He was angry with someone. She didn't catch a lot of his words. He seemed to be walking around with the phone.

"I don't care what you think," Fitz snapped. "I want this and damned if I won't have her."

Bella felt a chill as she realized that he was arguing with someone about her.

"You will back me on this or I'll take you down with him," Fitz yelled. "That's right, you don't think I didn't see this coming?" The laugh made her shudder. "That's right, you did teach me everything I know. Thanks, Dad. But if you bail on me now you'll wish you hadn't."

At the sound of footfalls coming up the stairs, she hurried down the hall before she turned and pretended to only just now be leaving her room. Her heart pounded so hard she thought for sure the security guard who appeared would be able to hear it.

She gave him a smile, but he barely gave her a glance, confirming what she'd suspected. They'd been told not to interact with her in any way. Of course Fitz would want them only loyal to him. The rough-looking guard continued on down the hallway toward Fitz's room. She heard him knock and Fitz open the door and call him by name. Roman. Fitz asked about Milo.

Roman said Milo was on his way. Then the door closed and she could no longer hear their voices. She swallowed, straightened her spine and went downstairs, but had barely reached the first floor when she heard someone coming. The men he'd called Ronan and Milo exited the house without a word.

Right behind them was Fitz. He saw her and he gave her that annoying smirk. It had changed little from the time he was a boy. But now she saw satisfaction in his eyes. They were dark, brooding, so different from Tommy's sky blue eyes that spoke of summer days and sunshine.

"Have a nice night?" Fitz asked as if he'd secretly put spiders in her bed. She could imagine what he'd been like at camp—if he'd ever gone.

"Actually," she said, thinking of Tommy's last words to her, "I did." She smiled, turning his smirk into a frown. "I see you *bought* some friends."

He started to correct her when he realized she'd purposely not said *brought*. She watched him grind his teeth for a moment. "I want you to be safe so I've hired some men to make sure you are."

They had lined up in the living room as if waiting for

assignments. Bella knew it was Fitz's idea, a show of force. None of them scared her as much as Fitz himself.

"One of them is a cook?" she inquired. "I hope so because I haven't had my breakfast yet." She knew that needling Fitz wasn't smart, but she couldn't stand how self-righteous he'd looked when he'd entered her house last night with his soldiers as if it were his own. It would be soon enough if he got his way, she reminded herself.

"Roberto," Fitz snapped. "You're in charge of the kitchen. I don't want Bella to lift a finger in there. In fact, I don't want her in there at all. Can you make sure she has no reason to enter?"

"Yes, sir," Roberto said and looked toward her. "Just tell me what you would like for breakfast, Miss Worthington."

The man showing her respect clearly grated on Fitz. She could see him struggling to keep from saying something.

"It's Bella and thank you, Roberto. Surprise me."

As if he could take no more, Fitz barked orders to the five other men to act as security for the ranch house and her. She realized he must be putting them up in the bunkhouse, which meant they would be on the property 24/7 until the wedding.

Bella took a seat at the table in the dining room to wait for her breakfast even though the thought of food made her sick to her stomach. But she would eat every bite even as her stomach roiled. It was clear what Fitz was doing. How long before he ordered the men not to let her leave the house?

Roberto made her huevos rancheros. When she told him that she loved Mexican dishes, he promised to order chorizo, pinto beans, all kinds of peppers and tortillas to make some dishes she might like.

She thanked him and ate her breakfast, which was delicious and seemed to calm her. Her thoughts ricocheted back and forth from dark ones of Fitz to happier ones of Tommy. When she finished, she knew better than to take her plate to the kitchen. She unhooked her shoulder bag from the back of her chair and headed for the front door.

Her burner cell phone was hidden in her car. She'd felt it would be safer there than in her purse or even in her room. Fitz had already shown how low he would stoop. She knew it wouldn't be long before he started going through her things.

She had just reached the front door when she heard Fitz behind her.

"Wait!" he called, his footsteps heavy on the stone floor. Her skin crawled as he came up behind her. "Where do you think you're going?"

She took a deep breath and let it out slowly before she turned to face him. "I'm going into town to get my hair trimmed and my nails done. Do you have a problem with that?"

"I don't think it's safe, you running around with that big rock on your finger," Fitz said. "I'd prefer you take one of our security guards with you."

"I'd prefer not." She pulled the ring from her finger and dropped it unceremoniously on the entry table. It rattled as it skittered across the glossy top, coming to a stop on the edge before almost plummeting to the stone floor. "Problem solved," she said and reached for the door handle.

He grabbed her arm and jerked her back around to

face him, squeezing her wrist until she let out a cry. "Haven't you caused enough trouble for your poor father? You don't want to underestimate how far I will go. You will do as I say."

"So you think," she spat over the pain as he continued to grip her wrist nearly to the point of breaking it. "But you will keep your hands to yourself and I will do as I please. You take it out on my father again and I will slit your throat while you sleep. Try me, if you don't believe me."

Fitz let go of her, flinging her arm away. "Once we're married—"

She didn't wait to hear the rest of his declaration as she held back tears of pain, turned and walked out the door. She figured he would station a security guard at his door tonight—and probably one at hers as well.

Tommy had been expecting Bella's call. "Hey," he answered, relieved. Every moment she was in that house with Fitz she was in danger. "You all right?"

"Fine."

He heard too much in that one word. "What's happened?"

"Just Fitz being Fitz," she said, brushing it off. "I'm on my way to Edwin Mattson's office. I heard Fitz arguing with him on the phone this morning. He might help us."

"I'll meet you outside of town at Four Corners. We can leave your car there," Tommy said and disconnected. Four Corners was an old café and gas station where two county roads crossed.

On the drive into Missoula, he broached the subject. "Maybe you should move off the ranch."

"Even if I would give him the satisfaction, he wouldn't allow it. He's made it clear that he'll do even worse to my father. Last night he moved a half dozen security guards onto the ranch. Earlier…" She seemed to hesitate and he saw her touch her wrist. "He tried to keep me from leaving."

"If he hurt you—"

"I told him that until the wedding, he wasn't to touch me and that I would do as I pleased."

"And he agreed to that?"

"*Agreed* probably isn't the right word, but he didn't try to stop me." She turned to look at him as he drove. "Don't worry about me. I can hold my own."

He didn't doubt that under normal circumstances. But this was Fitz. And now he had security guards at the ranch?

"We just need to get our hands on whatever he tricked my father into signing. Maybe Edwin will help us."

Tommy had his doubts, but he didn't voice them. Edwin and Fitz had always seemed a lot alike, two peas in a pod. But if Bella was right and Edwin was against this, then maybe he would help. Unless he was just as scared of what his son was capable of doing as the rest of them.

"Did you know that six months ago, your father and Edwin's company changed tax accountants?" She shook her head. "I suspect it was Fitz's doing. He didn't want their old accountant to catch any red flags."

"So six months," she said. "That at least narrows it down."

He nodded. "Which means past tax returns won't help until we have the current records. I'm wondering if it would do any good to talk to the former, fired accountant."

Bella smiled over at him. "I knew coming to you was the right thing to do."

Tommy took her hand and squeezed it, hoping she didn't regret it. "But first we see Edwin. Fitz already knows that you broke into the office. I don't think it hurts for him to know that you're not alone in this, that I'm doing everything I can to help you."

She nodded but he could tell she was worried. "Just be careful."

"I will. I don't think he'll do anything more to your father at this point," Tommy said, hoping that was true and glad when she agreed.

There was no one at the front desk when they entered the main office. He saw Bella glance at the empty assistant's desk and frown. The nameplate on the desk read Dorothy Brennan, he noticed as they passed.

They walked down the same short hallway they had the other night. Edwin's door was slightly ajar. Bella pushed it open.

The white-haired man behind the desk looked up. Tommy hadn't seen Edwin Mattson in quite a few years and was shocked by how much he'd aged. He seemed surprised to see them. Not just surprised, but nervous.

"What are you…" He looked at the landline phone on his desk as if wanting to call someone for help. Dorothy? Or Fitz?

Tommy closed the door behind them and locked it.

Edwin's eyes widened. He stumbled to his feet. "Bella, what… If this is about Fitz… None of this is my doing. You have to understand—"

"I do understand," Bella said as she stepped into the

room and took a chair. Tommy continued to stand, his back to the door. "I heard you on the phone this morning with Fitz. He's got something on you as well as my father."

Edwin slowly lowered himself back into his chair. "I don't know what to say."

"I thought you and my father were friends," she said. "You really won't help him?"

The older man wagged his head. "I can't, even if…"

"What is Fitz holding over your head?" she asked. "Mammoth Securities?"

His eyes widened. "How did you know about—"

"I overheard my father telling you not to get involved with them."

Edwin looked sick. "I should have listened to him."

"Which is also why you can't let my father go to prison for something he didn't do. Fitz has no conscience but I'm hoping you do."

The older man reddened as he looked up at her. "It isn't like your father is completely innocent. He's embezzled money from the partnership before."

"That's not true," she snapped.

"I'm afraid it is. That time, I caught it and we remedied the problem before it was discovered. I would imagine though that it is where Fitz got the idea to use it against Nolan."

Tommy could see that Bella was shaken. "When was this?" she asked and listened as Edwin gave her the details. "But this time?" she asked, her voice breaking.

Edwin shook his head. "I don't know. Fitz swears Nolan's at it again. Are you aware that he has a drug problem?"

"Fitz or my father? My father definitely doesn't. It's

all part of this web of lies that Fitz is spinning to control me. That's why I need to prove that Fitz is trying to frame him," Bella said.

"It isn't that easy," the older man said with a sigh.

"Why is that?" Tommy asked.

Edwin seemed to recognize him then. "You're one of those Colt boys."

"Tommy Colt. I'm working with my brother at Colt Investigations."

The man nodded, looking sicker, as if things had gotten even worse. "You realize that if Fitz finds out you came to me..." Edwin shook his head. "You'd be wise not to cross him. Either of you. You have no idea how far he'll go."

"Oh, I have a pretty good idea," Bella said. "Surely you can see that he'll take you and my father down as well. He can't be trusted to keep his word—even if I did marry him."

"If you don't marry him..." Edwin looked terrified at the thought of what his son would do. "I wish I could help, but my hands are tied. You coming here with..." He glanced toward Tommy again. "You're only making matters worse for yourself. Once Fitz has made his point—"

"You don't believe that. He's determined to destroy me and my father. It sounds like he plans to do the same to you."

Edwin started to come around his desk. "I'll see you out."

Tommy shook his head as he unlocked the door. "Don't bother. You made this monster. You need to take care of it."

"Tommy's right," Bella said. "You're just as guilty as he is if you don't do something to stop your son."

"Don't you think I would have stopped him a long time ago, if I could?" Edwin demanded and followed them to the door to slam it behind the two of them.

As they were leaving, Bella slowed at Dorothy's desk and picked up what appeared to be a dead potted plant before heading for the door.

"Are you all right?" he asked once they were outside. She was hugging the pot with the dead plant, looking close to tears. "Edwin could have been lying." He didn't believe that and he knew she didn't, either, but she looked as if she needed a little hope. He glanced at the pot. "I hate to even ask."

"Dorothy. Her plant is dead." Bella met his gaze. "Which means she not only got fired, but also left in a hurry without her plant."

"Sounds like Fitz is cleaning house," Tommy said. "First the accountant, now the administrative assistant. You thinking what I am?"

Bella glanced at her cell phone. "I want to talk to her, but I can't be gone any longer today. I'm hoping to get into Fitz's room when he leaves again."

"Please be careful," Tommy said.

"Believe me, I am," she said. "How are you doing on tracking down the company's former accountant?"

"Working on it." He hated to tell her that the man seemed to have disappeared.

Chapter 12

Fitz was waiting for her when she entered the ranch house. "Roberto has made us a special dinner."

"I'm not hungry," she said.

"Please join me. I have something we need to discuss," he said. "Unless you no longer care what happens to your father." He started to take hold of her arm, but then seemed to think better of it even though clearly she wasn't really being given a choice about dinner.

"Why don't you lead the way," he said and stepped to the side to let her pass. "We're having steak, my favorite. As I recall, you don't like steak. Probably because you had so much of it growing up. There was always beef in your freezer, wasn't there."

"I was raised in Montana on a cattle ranch," she said as she stepped past him. Even though they hadn't touched, she still felt her skin crawl. But what Edwin had told her about her father's earlier embezzlement had her shaken. If true, could it also be the case this time as well?

"Yes, growing up on this ranch," Fitz said. "That's probably why you didn't appreciate it and why you looked down your nose at me when I always asked for steak when we visited here."

"Stop pretending you were some poor kid who went without food. If I looked down my nose at you, Fitz, it was because you were as rude, obnoxious and demanding as a boy as you are now as a man," she said as they entered the dining room, where Roberto was ready to pour the wine. "I see you've gotten into our wine cellar as well as into our freezer," she said under her breath.

Fitz seemed to clamp his jaw down as he took his chair and Roberto helped her with hers. The wine poured, Roberto went into the kitchen, leaving them alone. Bella watched Fitz straighten everything before settling back in his chair. She could imagine what life would be like married to this awful, self-absorbed man. She felt sorry for any woman innocent enough to marry him. It certainly wasn't going to be her.

"Did you have a nice day?" she asked as she took a sip of her wine. He wanted to play at being husband and wife? She'd play along—to an extent.

"Very much so," he said. "And you?"

"It could have been better," she said and put down her wineglass after taking a sip. It was one of her father's expensive wines, which came as no surprise. Of course Fitz would help himself to the best. But she had to keep her wits about her.

Out of the corner of her eye, she noticed that the door to her father's den was open. But it was what she saw inside that made her momentarily freeze. Her father's gun safe stood open. There were no guns inside.

She looked at Fitz, who was smiling. She smiled back. Was he so afraid that she might shoot him? Was he going to hide all the knives in the kitchen as well? She would have found it amusing under other circumstances, she thought, as Roberto brought out their meals.

"Your father made bail, I heard," Fitz said. "I suppose you've talked to him. I hope he's doing all right. Maybe we should have him committed to rehab—at least until the wedding. What do you think?"

She met his gaze and laughed. "Actually, he committed himself. He needs a good rest and it will look good when he has to go before the judge."

Fitz's surprise that he'd been outmaneuvered was wonderful to see. She took pleasure in it, wanting to gloat. She and her father had anticipated what Fitz would do next and had beaten him to the punch.

He picked up his knife and fork and began to hack at his steak with angry jabs at the meat. "You didn't get your hair trimmed or your nails done."

She said nothing. He wanted her to know that he'd checked up on her. That he would be checking every time she left the house—if not having her followed. She'd never been fond of steak but sliced a bite off and put it in her mouth.

Moments before, she'd been gloating—a mistake. If she thought she could beat this man at his game, she'd better think again. She chewed and met his gaze head-on. "No, I didn't go. I changed my mind. I was too upset after I left the house."

"So what did you do?" he asked as he took too much time cutting his steak. He knew she'd posted her father's bail. She should have seen it in his smugness the moment she saw him before he'd insisted she join him for dinner. But he'd gone straight to rehab.

"I'm curious," she said, not answering his question. "Is your plan to marry a woman who you're determined to make hate you to the point that she would kill you in your sleep?"

He looked up from his steak. "Do you really think I care how you feel about me?" He laughed. "This won't be a real marriage, Bella. Once I completely destroy you and your father, once you're flat broke and broken, I'll dump you in the street. I'll sell your precious ranch and I'll move to some exotic place where I can have any woman I want—just as you said."

His words shocked her more than they should have. Wasn't this exactly what she'd thought he would do? He'd never wanted her. This was about humiliation. He'd felt small around her and her father. Apparently he couldn't live with that unless he brought her down and her father with her. Which meant even if she agreed to marry him, he would still send her father to prison.

"You do realize how pathetic that makes you sound, don't you?" she asked and took a bite of the twice-baked potato on her plate.

Fitz bristled, slamming down his knife and fork. Both clattered to his plate. A piece of steak flew off and onto the tablecloth. "I know you went to see Edwin. You and Tommy Colt. Did you really think my father wouldn't tell me?"

Bella considered that for a moment. She'd seen how scared Edwin had been of his only son. She should have known he'd tell Fitz, fearing that Fitz would find out and punish him even further.

She could see that Fitz was having trouble leaving the bite of steak on the tablecloth. Grease had started to leave a stain. She leaned forward, warning herself that she was taking this too far, but unable to stop herself. She snatched up the piece of steak from the table and tossed it back on his plate.

"You know what I think?" she said at his horrified look. His gaze kept going from the stain on the tablecloth to the piece of steak balancing on the edge of his plate. "I think this has something to do with your mother leaving you when you were five." All the color drained from Fitz's face. "I heard your father tell mine that you cried for days. I can't imagine how traumatic that must have been for you. I think it explains a lot about why you're acting out now and why—"

Fitz shot to his feet, overturning his water glass and knocking his chair backward. It crashed to the floor. "If you ever mention my mother again—" The words spewed from his mouth along with spittle.

"I'm just trying to understand where all this hate comes from," she said. From the look in his eyes, she'd taken it too far and yet it didn't feel like far enough at all. Look what the bastard was doing to her family.

For a moment, she thought he might have a heart attack. He stood swaying slightly as if trying to speak, but no more words came out. He heaved, each breath labored, his eyes poison-tipped darts aimed straight for her. When he did start to move, she realized he might launch himself across the table and go for her throat.

She picked up her knife. *Let him come.*

"Mr. Mattson? Can I get you anything else? Dessert is almost…" Roberto realized he had interrupted something. "Ready."

It took a moment for both of them to acknowledge that they were no longer alone. Fitz seemed to take a breath, his gaze shifting from her to the table and finally to Roberto standing in the kitchen doorway.

"Clean up this mess," Fitz snapped and shoved away from the table to storm out of the room.

Bella slowly put down her knife. "I think we're finished, but thank you, Roberto." She hated to think what might have happened if the man hadn't interrupted them.

"I will see that some dessert is sent up to your room, Miss—Bella," Roberto said.

She smiled at him as she put down her napkin and rose. "Thank you." She almost warned him that being kind to her would get him fired. But her heart was still in her throat. How would she survive this? Unless she could find a way out, she wouldn't.

Chapter 13

To Bella's surprise there wasn't a guard outside her door the next morning. She'd had a fitful night filled with nightmares. As she made her way down to breakfast, she wasn't looking forward to seeing Fitz after last night. She told herself she would try to be pleasant. Even as she thought it, she found herself grinding her teeth.

But as she approached the dining room, she heard the sound of his sports car engine rev. When she looked out, she saw him speeding away.

Was he going into Missoula to see his father? She wondered if she should call Edwin to warn him. Then again, Edwin had told Fitz about their visit and had refused to help, so she figured he was on his own. After all, Fitz was his son.

"Good morning," Roberto said as he came into the dining room. "I have a special breakfast for you. Please have a seat."

She felt as if she were in a fancy restaurant rather than at the ranch. Her father had a cook who made meals when they were here at the ranch and had company. The rest of the time, they did for themselves.

"I have for you this morning quesadilla frita," Roberto said with obvious pride. "Two crispy tortillas topped with black beans, layered with fried egg, ham and cheese, and topped with my special spicy sauce. Served with a side of fried plantain."

"This looks wonderful," she said, admiring the dish. She asked about this family and if he'd always enjoyed cooking.

"I would spend time with my grandmother in Mexico," he said. "We would cook together. Everyone loved her cooking. I hope you enjoy your breakfast," he said and retreated to the kitchen.

Bella dug in, surprised by how hungry she was before she realized that she hadn't eaten but a couple of bites of dinner last night. After she finished, she stuck her head into the kitchen doorway and thanked him.

Then she'd hurriedly gotten ready to leave before Fitz returned. Her first stop was the rehab center her father had checked himself into. It was small and expensive and more like a spa than rehab, but money well spent if it helped should this ever go before a judge.

She found her father sitting out in the garden. He heard her approach, his expression brightening at the sight of her. She joined him on the bench and let herself breathe. Her father looked good, although she could still see fear in his eyes.

"I can't stand the thought of you having to deal with Fitz alone," he said, glancing around to make sure no one was listening. They were alone in the garden except for a man trimming a hedge in the distance. The buzz of his saw sounded like a swarm of bees.

Bella turned her face up to the warm sun. She took a deep breath and caught the scent of freshly mown lawn and pine from the nearby trees.

"I'm not alone," she said. "I've hired Colt Investigations."

"You aren't serious?"

She turned to meet his gaze. "I trust them. They are about the only ones I trust right now. You didn't tell me that this isn't the first time money has gone missing. Only last time, you paid it back."

"Who told you that?" her father demanded.

"Edwin."

Nolan Worthington slumped a little on the bench and turned his face away. "I'd made a couple of bad investments. You were in college. I couldn't borrow any money from the bank without worrying clients… So I borrowed some from the business."

Bella shook her head. "Is there more I don't know about?"

"No," he said, turning back to her. "I swear. But that's probably what gave Fitz the idea. It was stupid, but fortunately Edwin caught it and I sold some assets over time and paid every cent back."

"How do I know that this time is any different?" she asked.

His face reddened. "I didn't take the money." Her father shifted on the bench. "But no one is going to believe me if my own daughter doesn't."

She said nothing for a few moments as she tried to breathe. The sky overhead was cornflower blue, dotted with cumulous clouds that morphed in the breeze. She loved Montana summers. They always reminded her of Tommy. Back when they were kids the summer seemed to stretch out before them with so many possibilities.

Now she could feel the days slipping past, headed for the train wreck of a wedding that she wasn't even sure would save her father if she was stupid enough to let Fitz force her into it.

Her father spoke, drawing her out of her thoughts. "About six months ago, I was considering retiring. I'd had enough of Fitz. Edwin was cowed by him. I wanted out of the partnership, but Fitz wasn't having it. He made me an offer for the ranch." Her father hurried on as he saw her horrified expression. "I told him he'd never have the ranch, that I had my lawyers put it in your name. He got really upset."

She stared at him. "You think that's when he decided to force me to marry him for the ranch?"

Nolan shrugged. "I doubt it's that simple. Fitz probably doesn't even know what he wants. It's just something he doesn't have. Maybe he thinks if he had you and the ranch, he would be happy."

She laughed. "Is he really that juvenile? I would make his life a living hell and enjoy every minute of it." Bella couldn't believe this. The ranch was safe as long as she didn't marry Fitz—if she did, under Montana law he would own half of it. But she thought her father was right. It wasn't the ranch Fitz wanted so badly. He wanted revenge for feeling less around her and her father and the ranch.

Nolan reached over and took her hand. "I got myself into this mess. You need to let me get myself out even if it means going to prison."

She sighed. "You know I won't let that happen."

"I'm not sure either of us has a choice," he said, letting go of her hand. "But if you marry him—"

"Don't worry," she said, getting to her feet. "I'm not going to marry him. I'll find a way out of this for both of us."

Her father still looked as scared and worried as she felt. She touched his shoulder. "I'll think of something."

As she left, Tommy called.

"I got an address for Dorothy Brennan, but we need to hurry," he said. "Her landlord said she gave notice and is in the process of moving out." He rattled off the address. "I'll meet you there."

Dorothy Brennan had been with her father's company from as far back at Bella could remember. A tall, thin, serious woman, she'd kept small treats in her desk for when Bella visited her father at work. The one thing she knew about Dorothy was that she loved plants. The one on her desk had been started from a cutting her grandmother had given her.

While she'd never married or had children, Dorothy had kept this plant alive for decades. That was why when Bella had seen it sitting on the woman's desk dead, she'd known something was terribly wrong. Dorothy wouldn't have left that plant behind.

Tommy was parked down the block when Bella arrived. She parked and got out as he joined her. They walked up the driveway to where Dorothy was loading boxes into the back of her SUV.

When she saw Bella, she started and glanced around as if expecting...who? Edwin? Fitz? Or the cops? The woman looked haggard and scared. Her gaze lit on the pot Bella was carrying and hope shone in her eyes.

"Miss Brennan," Bella said, calling her by the name she always had, as she approached. Tommy quickly took the box from the older woman and put it into the SUV for her. "This is Tommy Colt, a friend of mine. Could we talk to you for a moment?" She held out the pot. "I'm sorry about your plant, but I couldn't leave it in that office."

Dorothy took the pot, looked down at the skeleton of her dead plant and hugged the pot to her. For a moment she studied each of them, then nodded and led the way inside the apartment. There wasn't much left except a couch and chair and a bed in the one bedroom that had been stripped. Bella assumed someone would be picking up the larger, heavier items and taking them wherever the woman was headed.

"Please sit down," Dorothy said as she set the pot on a windowsill in the sun. "I'd offer you something to drink but…" She glanced around, her throat working.

"We don't need anything but a few minutes of your time," Bella said quickly. "What happened at the office?"

The woman's gaze was shiny with tears as she turned to her. "I was fired. In a text from the young Mr. Mattson. I tried to go back for my things, but I was met at the door by two security guards and told I couldn't enter. I asked for my plant and was told it had been thrown out."

"I'm sorry," Bella said, touching the woman's shoulder. "This was Fitz's doing?"

Dorothy shrugged. "He's the one who gave me notice, but I assumed the others knew."

"My father wasn't involved," she said. "He's been pushed out as well."

She saw concern in the woman's face. "Nolan was always kind to me. I'm sorry."

"You aren't surprised that my father was forced out."

Dorothy shook her head. "I knew something was going on."

"Do you know what?" Bella asked.

"I heard things about Nolan, but I didn't believe them."

"Fitz is blackmailing my father, saying that Nolan embezzled a lot of money. He says he has proof."

"We suspect he has doctored books that show the losses coming from Nolan," Tommy said.

"There was money missing," Dorothy confirmed. "I heard Fitz arguing with his father about it. Edwin said that if it got out to clients it would destroy the business."

"If my father didn't take the money…"

The older woman met her gaze. "It was Fitz. You've seen his sports car?" Bella nodded. "It's just the tip of the iceberg." For a moment, Dorothy didn't look as if she was going to continue. "There's the country club and his lunches with so-called clients. But his big expense is his gambling and the woman he's putting up in a penthouse in Spokane."

"Do you have the woman's name and address?" Tommy asked.

Again Dorothy hesitated but only for a moment. "I wrote it all down. I was angry. Not that I thought I could do anything about it." She went to the few items she had stacked by the door, picked up her purse and opened it.

From inside, she took out what appeared to be copies of expense sheets. "These are the real ones," she said, handing them to Bella. "These are the ones he turned in to the business. I've been keeping two sets and keeping my mouth shut. He told me that if I talked, he'd say I stole from the company and have me arrested. He made me sign a nondisclosure agreement in order to get my last paycheck."

"Don't worry, I'll make sure it never comes back on you," Bella said, knowing that this wasn't enough to stop Fitz anyway. But it was a start. "Do you have any idea where he's hiding the evidence that would show my father took the money?"

Dorothy shook her head. "I'm sorry. Clearly he didn't trust me." Her voice broke. "But..." She hesitated, then Bella saw the woman make up her mind. "One time I walked into his office and startled him. He quickly pulled a thumb drive from his laptop and palmed it until I left. I think that is probably what you're looking for."

Bella looked around the almost empty apartment. "Where will you go?"

"To Florida. My sister's until I can find another job."

"Send me your address. I'll let you know how it all ends." If it ended the way she hoped, she would get Dorothy a decent severance package from the partnership or die trying.

"I hope Fitz gets what's coming to him," Dorothy said.

"So do we," Bella agreed. Her cell phone rang. She checked. "Speak of the devil," she said. "I have to answer this." She stepped outside. Behind her, she heard Tommy asking if he could help Dorothy load anything else.

"Hello."

"Where are you?" Fitz asked. When she didn't answer, he said, "I'm making wedding plans. I need to know what your favorite flowers are."

Tommy joined her. Having overheard, he nodded and mouthed, "Tell him baby white roses."

She frowned since things were never going to go this far. Nor were those her favorite flowers and Tommy knew that. "Baby white roses."

"Excellent. That was going to be my choice," Fitz said, sounding relieved that she wasn't fighting him.

"Lonesome Florist," Tommy mouthed. His friend owned it, but she couldn't see why that would make a difference.

"I like the ones they have at Lonesome Florist," she said. "Since you're asking."

Fitz chuckled. "Got it. Oh, and you have a dress fitting scheduled tomorrow at two."

Bella looked at Tommy and had to bite down on her lip for a moment. "How thoughtful. You didn't trust me to select my own wedding dress?"

"I think you'll find that I have excellent taste," Fitz said with his usual arrogance. "I might surprise you." She shook her head but said nothing. "I'll leave the information about your fitting on the entry table in the hallway since you're spending so little time here."

"Is that all?" she asked.

"I heard you went to see your father," Fitz said. "I hope he's doing well."

"I'm sure you do," she said sarcastically. "Goodbye." She disconnected.

"He thinks your father is why you're not being so difficult," Tommy said. "So let him think that."

"Let him think I'm giving in to him?" she demanded as she pocketed her phone and shook her head. "He'd be more suspicious if I played nice, trust me. What was that about the flowers and the shop?"

"Just covering our bets. The owner is a friend. If it gets down to the wire, I could get you a message hidden in baby white roses."

Her pulse rate soared at the thought of it going that far. "Now what?"

"It seems like it wouldn't be that hard to prove that Fitz lives beyond his means and that he's the one who's been embezzling the money," Tommy said. "Have you thought any more about asking him for evidence?"

Bella shook her head. "Don't forget he's already framed my father for drug possession. But I might ask him before the fitting tomorrow to show me the proof of my father's embezzlement."

"At least Nolan's safe where he is now. I think we should check out Fitz's woman in Spokane. It will take all day to go there and come back. Sounds like you're busy tomorrow."

She hated it, but nodded. "I think I'd better go to the fitting. I can only push him so far without it hurting my father."

Chapter 14

Bella was relieved to see Fitz's car gone when she returned to the ranch. Several of the guards though could be seen on the property. She ignored them and hurried inside.

Roberto had made her a special dinner, but she didn't do it justice. She kept thinking about Tommy and their first kiss and smiling stupidly. She'd known it was inevitable and that once they stepped across that line there would be no going back. The kiss had been just as wonderful and magical as she knew it would be.

Sitting on the deck of the fire tower had been the perfect spot to finally kiss. The summer night, the closeness she and Tommy had always shared, the chemistry that had always been there all added to that moment. But now she felt herself aching to be back in his arms. She wanted more. But also she knew how careful they had to be. If Fitz found out…

She heard his car engine. A few minutes later he walked in carrying his briefcase and frowning. She wondered what he did all day. It hadn't crossed her mind until that moment that maybe things weren't going so well for him—and that it might not have anything to do with her. She thought about what Dorothy had told her. Was it possible her father wasn't the only one who was broke? If Fitz was hurting for money, then he needed what he could get for the ranch. Which meant he had to get her to the altar post haste.

The thought gave her little comfort as he came into the dining room. Roberto must have heard him. "Can I get you some dinner?" he asked Fitz, who shook his head and waved him away.

The cook quickly slipped back into the kitchen, letting the swinging door close behind him. She wondered if Roberto stood on the other side listening. Not if he was smart.

"Did you already eat?" she asked pointedly.

He met her gaze, still standing over the table holding his briefcase. "No, I'm just not hungry, but I see you've had your fill."

Food shaming? It made her smile. "And I enjoyed every bite."

That wasn't what he'd wanted to hear. "Some of us have to work. How is your business doing without you?"

"Who says it's without me?" she said, even though she hadn't given it much thought since her father's call. Fortunately, she'd hired good help and they were keeping things going without her.

"I wonder what you do all day," he said, narrowing his eyes at her.

"I wonder what you do all day," she said, narrowing her eyes at him.

He shook his head. "I'm not up to sparring with you tonight." He turned his back on her and started to walk away.

"I want to see proof that my father was embezzling money from the partnership," she said before he could escape.

He stopped but didn't turn around. "Why now?"

"I was remiss in not asking sooner."

"You wouldn't be able to understand it all. But an auditor would, especially one from the IRS." His threat hung in the air.

"I'm a lot smarter than you think. I run my own business," she reminded him. "I'm going to need to see it or the engagement is off."

He turned then. The look in his eye made her shudder inside. She realized she could have chosen the wrong time to make any demands.

She watched him fighting to keep his temper in check, refusing to drag her gaze away first or move a muscle.

"Tomorrow. After your wedding dress fitting," he said, his voice hoarse with emotion. "I'm too tired tonight." With that, he turned and stalked off, his spine rigid with anger.

She watched him storm up the stairs and disappear before she let out the breath she'd been holding.

Tommy knocked on the penthouse door. He'd brought a box of chocolates and a bouquet of flowers. He'd thought he'd have trouble getting past the security guard at the desk.

"Mr. Mattson was very specific. I am to take these to her door and make sure she gets them," he told the desk guard who started to argue. "He wants me to make sure she is alone," Tommy whispered. "If I don't call back soon…"

"Fine, but be quick. I'll call up to let her know you're coming."

Tommy stopped him with a look.

"Fine. Just go up. She's in number two. The passcode is 409." He waved him away as if to say that both the woman upstairs and Fitz were a pain in his behind. Tommy didn't doubt it.

The elevator let him out on the top floor. He walked down the hall to number two and knocked, wondering what kind of reception he would get. He couldn't wait to see what kind of woman Fitz would actually pay money to keep.

He made a mental bet with himself. The door opened. He lost the bet. Worse, for a moment, he was speechless. "Margo Collins?"

"Yes?" The resemblance to Bella was shocking. Long dark hair. Green eyes. On closer inspection, he could see that she looked nothing like her beyond the obvious. Bella's features were softer and she was a little shorter and curvier.

"I have a delivery," he managed to say around his shock.

"From Fitz?" Margo asked and frowned. "He never gives me flowers but especially not chocolates. He says they'll make me fat."

"I guess he changed his mind," Tommy said, seeing that he'd messed up already.

"Well, it's okay with me," she said with a giggle as she outstretched her arms for her gifts.

"Mr. Mattson also wanted me to pick up something for him while I'm here."

She studied him for a moment as if noticing him for the first time, then shrugged and said, "Come in."

He followed her inside the apartment. Everything was white from the walls to the ceiling to the carpet on the floor and the furnishings. There were large windows that looked out on the hillside and the city.

Margo headed for the kitchen with her presents. In the living room, the television was on a reality show. The place was so clean and neat, Tommy couldn't believe anyone actually lived here.

He noticed her rummaging around in the bouquet and realized that she was looking for a card from Fitz. "Mr. Mattson said he didn't need a card because you already know how he feels about you." Her face lit up. "I need a folder he thinks he left here."

"In here?" she asked and turned toward what appeared to be an office.

Margo busied herself, humming as she put her flowers into a vase and opened the box of chocolates. "Oh, Fitzy, you really are going to make me fat. You never give me candy. Are you being a bad boy?" She chuckled as she popped a chocolate into her mouth.

In the small office, Tommy quickly checked the desk. None of the drawers were locked. Nothing in them hardly. Nothing of interest, either.

He looked up. Margo was standing in the doorway holding her box of chocolates. "You must be a new one," she said. "Didn't find what you were looking for?"

He shook his head. "He said there were some papers…"

"I bet he put them in his briefcase and forgot he took them," she said with a chuckle. "That thing is practically attached to his arm lately, but I guess I don't have to tell you that. Kind of like that thumb drive around his neck. I asked him what was so important. He said it holds the key to his heart." She smiled and licked her lips. The scent of milk chocolate wafted toward him. "You won't tell him I said that. He says I need to say less and think more." She shrugged. "He's right." She looked sad for a moment, then considered her next piece of chocolate from the box and brightened.

"Don't worry, I won't mention it if you don't mention that I didn't find what he sent me for. Like you said, the papers are probably in his briefcase and he forgot. I don't want to tell him that he messed up."

She nodded knowingly. "Smart. Our secret."

"Maybe the flowers and chocolates should be, too. I have to confess. They were my idea. I thought it would be rude to just show up without something." He gave her his best sheepish look.

She looked guiltily down at the box in her hand. She'd already made a good dent in the contents. He watched her debating what to do.

"Probably best not to mention the chocolates especially," she said.

He nodded and smiled. She seemed nice enough, though naive. "Our secret. Want me to bring anything else if he sends me back?"

She nodded with a laugh. "Surprise me. And stop by anytime." As he started to leave, she added, "If he does remember why he sent you here, could you remind him about the rent? The landlord called again." She made a face. "When Fitz gets busy, he forgets stuff. But it's been a few months now."

Tommy nodded, feeling sorry for the woman. It appeared Fitz was phasing her out as he got closer to getting what he really wanted. Tommy wondered how to tell Bella what he'd found out. It gave him a chill as he recalled how much Margo had looked like her—at least at first glance and when she smiled.

The memory sent a sharp blade of fear through him. Apparently Fitz wanted more than revenge for what he saw as her ignoring him all these years. He wanted Bella.

Chapter 15

The next morning, Fitz was already gone by the time Bella came downstairs. She'd lain awake wondering how Tommy's trip to Spokane had gone. She didn't dare get her phone from where it was hidden in her car to call him. She'd pushed Fitz about as far as she thought she should for one day so hadn't left the ranch the rest of the evening.

Roberto had made her another delicious breakfast. She ate it quickly and, grabbing the note Fitz had left her with instructions to her dress fitting, she left. Once out of sight of the ranch and the guards, she called Tommy.

They met at a spot on the river north of town. As she parked in the pines and followed the sound of the water to the river, she thought about all the times she and Tommy had come here. They used to love where the stream pooled in the rocks to make a deep swimming hole.

Tommy sat on one of the rocks near the pool. She hopped from rock to rock to drop down beside him. The rock under her felt warm in the sun. She closed her eyes and leaned her head back to enjoy the rays for a few moments, before opening her eyes and looking over at him.

The news wasn't good. It showed in his handsome face. Those Colt brothers, she thought as she smiled to herself. They were a handsome bunch. "What don't you want to tell me?" she finally asked as she found a small piece of rock and threw it into the pool. She watched it sink until it was out of sight before she looked over at him again.

He hadn't shaved, his designer stubble making her want to kiss him. She couldn't help herself. She reached out, cupped that strong jaw and drew him to her. The kiss was sweet—at first, almost tentative. She touched the tip of her tongue to his and felt him shiver before drawing back.

"You keep doing that and you know where this is headed," he said, his voice rough with emotion.

"Would that be so bad?" she whispered.

He brushed his fingertips lightly over her cheek. She closed her eyes as his callused thumb caressed her lower lip. She wanted him with every fiber of her being. Her body tingled at his touch. She wanted to lie in the nearby grass naked in his arms.

Opening her eyes, she met his gaze. His desire mirrored her own, but there was also regret there.

"Bella." She heard the pain in that one word. "All this isn't dangerous enough for you?"

She felt the impact of his words. Not for her, for her father. If Fitz knew, he would hurt her father. She leaned back, needing to put a little distance between them. Her pulse thrummed. Only moments ago, she was ready to suggest they go into the woods. This had been building between them for years and she wanted it more than her next breath.

Closing her eyes against the desire that burned inside her, she let the sun again warm her face. "You haven't told me about Spokane." She realized that whatever he'd found out yesterday, it hadn't just made him more cautious. It had made him scared. For her father? Or for her?

"So what's she like?" she asked without opening her eyes. The sun felt so good, the smell of the river and the pines so crisp and familiar, she could almost pretend that none of this was happening. Just another summer day in Montana, her and Tommy on the river.

Tommy was quiet for a moment. "Margo Collins is like you."

She looked over at him.

"She looks so much like you that when you first see her it's startling," he said. "But then you see the differences, until she smiles. She has your hair, your eyes, your smile. Or damned close. As close as Fitz could find."

Bella let out a ragged breath. A sliver of disgust at the perversity of it followed on the next breath by fear that worked its way under her skin to her veins before roaring through her. The woman more than resembled her? She wasn't sure what she'd been expecting. Just some woman Fitz was keeping, but she should have known it was more than that. He'd kept this woman secret. He didn't want anyone to know. Maybe especially Bella. "Did she tell you anything we could use?"

He shook his head. "She isn't involved in any way

in his business from what I can tell. She's just…an ornament. Until he gets the real thing."

Tommy walked Bella to her car. "Call me later." He could tell that she was as shaken as he was by what he'd discovered. Now at least she understood. They both did. A man who just wanted to destroy didn't go to all this trouble. Fitz wanted Bella. The woman Tommy loved.

But for how long? Fitz had no idea what he was wishing for. A woman like Bella would never be dominated by a man or anyone. But it seemed Fitz wanted to try— and would do anything for the chance.

"I told Fitz I wanted proof of my father's crime. He was in a really weird mood last night and said he'd show me after my dress fitting today."

"How weird?" he asked.

"Like he'd had a bad day at the office. I don't think it was because of anything we did unless…" She met his gaze. "You don't think the girlfriend called him and told him about you stopping by?"

Tommy shook his head. "I don't think so. Maybe all this isn't going together as well as he'd hoped. I'll see what I can find out. I think I might have located the former accountant. I'm meeting with him later. If he shows up. He sounds scared."

She nodded, but he could see that she was distracted. He wanted to hold her, to kiss her and get back that moment by the river. But it was gone and any intimacy seemed like a very bad idea until they got her and her father out of this mess. Fitz was too dangerous. And not just to Nolan. Tommy worried what the man might do to Bella—the two of them basically alone in that house with Fitz believing he could do anything he wanted.

"I'll call you later," she promised. "Tommy?" He had started to walk away but turned back. "Be careful."

He smiled. "You, too."

"Yes, I wouldn't want to get stuck with a pin at my dress fitting." With that she started the SUV and drove away. He watched her go before heading to his own rig. He was anxious to talk to the partnership's former accountant. As he reached his pickup, he heard a vehicle engine start up in the distance and realized they might not have been alone.

The bridal shop was in Missoula so Bella had way too much time to think about everything that Tommy had told her on the drive. She felt as if Fitz had a life-sized doll of her hidden in Spokane. It gave her the creeps. Worse, it seemed Tommy was right. Fitz wanted the real thing—her.

He'd said this marriage was in name only, but she suspected he would never let her go once he got her legally bound to him. He wanted her, the ranch, everything he felt he'd been cheated out of in life. So basically, he had no idea what he wanted to fill the cavernous yearning hole in him.

She found the bridal shop, parked and climbed out of her SUV. As she did, she saw a black pickup pull in a couple of vehicles behind her. She recognized the man behind the wheel and felt her heart drop. It was one of the guards Fitz had hired.

Heart in her throat, she realized he could have followed her from the ranch this morning to the river. He would know that she met Tommy there. She felt herself flush, remembering the kiss and the embrace. Only a fool wouldn't have realized how intimate it had been.

She was thankful that they hadn't taken it further on the sunny shore under the pines. Fitz was dangerously close to following through with his threats. For her sake and her father's, she needed to be sure that he didn't snap.

Taking a few breaths, she tried to assure herself that if she had been followed, it had only been from Lonesome to Missoula. She watched him get out of his pickup. He didn't look in her direction as he walked into a boot shop, letting the door close behind him.

Was it possible she hadn't been followed at all? It could be the man's day off. He could have just happened to be in the area. She wished she could believe that as she entered the bridal shop. The bell over the door tinkled and a young woman appeared.

"Bella Worthington?"

All she could do was nod, her mouth was so dry.

"Why don't you come back? I have your dress ready. I'm Crystal."

Her legs felt like jelly as she walked toward the back. Before she stepped through a curtained doorway, she glanced back. She didn't see the guard from the pickup. She pushed through the curtain and tried to still her raging heart.

Tommy was right. They had to be more careful. Which meant they couldn't chance being together. The thought hurt her physically. She ached to lie in his arms, to feel his body against her own, to feel safe and loved and fulfilled.

"Step in here," Crystal said. "You can hang your clothes there while I get your dress. Did you bring shoes?" Bella hadn't. "It's all right. Your fiancé said you probably wouldn't. He thought of everything." The young woman turned and walked away. Fitz had thought of everything. Wasn't that her greatest fear?

She had a sudden urge to call Tommy on the burner phone and warn him to be careful. If she was right and the guard had followed them to the river, then he might have already given that information to Fitz.

But the burner phone was in the car. She reached for her purse, thinking it wouldn't make a difference now if she called Tommy on her cell. Not if Fitz already knew that she and Tommy had been meeting secretly. Had the guard seen them kissing? Had he taken photos from a distance?

Fear for Tommy's safety had her fumbling in her purse when Crystal returned holding the wedding dress. Bella froze. Not because of the dress. But because of the man standing behind Crystal.

"Fitz?" Her voice sounded too high to her ears. "What are you doing here?" Her mind was working. Whirling. She grasped the only thing she could think of. "It's bad luck to see the bride in her dress before the wedding."

"Don't worry," he said, his expression souring at her response to seeing him. Crystal had noticed and was trying not to show it. "I was just dropping off your heels that go with the dress."

Bella swallowed. "Thank you. That's very thoughtful. You know how stressful this is for me."

His frown softened. "I know. But now you can relax. Crystal, I think my fiancée is going to need that glass of champagne we talked about before she tries on her dress."

Crystal snapped right to it, hanging the dress on a hook in the large plush dressing room and scurrying out.

Fitz stepped in. "I was thinking about this time when we were kids. I sprained my ankle and you got a bag of frozen peas for me to put on it. Which proves you can be nice to me."

She lowered her voice so Crystal didn't hear. "My father is the one who made me be nice to you when we were kids. Yes, the same one you're trying to put in prison."

"Not if you marry me."

She gave him a side eye. "That would require trusting you."

He seemed surprised. "What would it take? Actually…" He held up his hand to stop her from answering. "People have been wondering why we don't go out together. So I was thinking…dinner tonight at the steakhouse? Don't say no."

She started to tell him that it would take more than a dinner at the steakhouse, but he didn't give her a chance. No doubt he already knew what she was going to say.

"Please don't tell me you're too busy to have dinner with your fiancé." His smile never reached his eyes. "You have been awfully busy lately. Maybe if you had your friends to the ranch instead of meeting them elsewhere…at least until the wedding…" She heard what he was telling her loud and clear. He knew about her and Tommy. Did he know it had gone beyond just friendship? Did he also suspect that she'd hired Colt Investigations to help her? She figured he would find that more amazing than worrisome. He didn't think much of her intellect or Tommy's, she was sure.

"I appreciate your concern," she said, hoping he didn't hear the break in her voice."

"Of course I'm concerned," he said, looking as if

he thought he had everything under control. "Soon we will be husband and wife. Then I'm going to take care of you." It sounded like the threat it was.

Crystal reappeared with her glass of champagne. Bella took it with trembling fingers as Fitz excused himself to take a call. She couldn't hear what was being said. Her heart was pounding too loudly in her ears. Tommy was in trouble. She could feel it.

"Great," Fitz said after finishing a quick call. "A romantic dinner tonight at the steakhouse. It's just what we both need." He stepped close again, leaning toward her. She jerked her head to the side and his kiss brushed her cheek. "I'll see you later," he said as his cell phone began to ring again.

"You are so lucky to have such an attentive fiancé," Crystal said as Fitz disappeared from view.

Bella saw the questioning look on the young woman's face. Downing the champagne, she handed back the empty glass, making Crystal's eyes widen. "You have no idea."

She could hear Fitz's voice on the phone. It sounded as if he were pleading with someone. The sound faded as the bell over the front door tinkled and he left. "I need to make a quick call," she told Crystal and dug out her phone.

"I'll get your veil," the young woman said and left with the empty champagne glass.

Bella called Tommy's cell, but it went straight to voice mail. The back of the shop was quiet. She was pretty sure that Fitz had left, but she never knew for sure, did she.

"He knows," she said into Tommy's voice mail. "Be careful, please." She disconnected as Crystal returned.

"Ready?" the young woman asked.

Bella nodded. She wondered how many nervous brides came through here and how many of them were having second thoughts. She doubted there were many like her, trying on a wedding dress she'd never seen before in heels she hadn't purchased with only one thought in mind: killing her fiancé rather than going through with the wedding.

Fitz left the dress shop congratulating himself on not losing his temper with Bella. When he'd gotten the call from Ronan earlier today, it had confirmed what he'd feared. Bella had been meeting Tommy Colt—just as she had when they were kids. Only Ronan had seen the two locked in an embrace that he'd described as "hot."

His first instinct was to throw her father to the wolves and then go after her. But he'd reminded himself that he had the upper hand only with the threat of sending her father to prison. If he hoped to get her to the altar, then he had to leave Nolan alone.

As for Bella herself… He'd wanted to grab her by the throat, and shove her against the wall in the bridal shop and… He shook his head. Fortunately, he'd kept his temper. She would be his soon enough. In the meantime, he had to deal with everything else going on.

He needed money. A few investments that didn't pay off like he'd hoped, the expense of this wedding and all that entailed and some bad luck. The past few times he'd gotten into a high-stakes game, he'd lost. Worse, he had some loans coming due—not to mention all the payments for his expensive lifestyle.

As he was driving out of Missoula, he saw a Realtor sign and swung into the parking lot. It was a little premature, looking into selling Bella's ranch. But once they were married, he had plans that didn't include keeping the place. He had a general idea of what all that land along the river might be worth. Add the house, stables and barn, it should more than take care of his problems.

Fitz told himself that everything was going to work out and when it did, he would have Bella. But first he had to make sure that Tommy Colt didn't go near her again. He pulled out his phone and made the call to Ronan, who was still tailing the Colt PI.

By the time he came out of the Realtor's office, he was humming "Wedding March." Things were looking up.

The bar where Tommy was meeting the accountant was small and dark and on the wrong side of the tracks in Butte. Because of the hour, there were only a few patrons inside at a table and a couple at the bar. The only person by himself was a man sitting at the far end of the bar away from the couple.

Tommy took a stool next to him. "Bill McMillan?"

The fiftysomething man was dressed in a suit, his tie loosened at his neck. He smelled of men's cologne and sweat, his dark hair flecked with gray and slicked down with something shiny.

"I'm sorry I said I'd talk to you," the man said.

The bartender wandered down. Tommy ordered a beer and looked to Bill. He sighed and nodded as if resigned to getting drunk. He already had two empty drink glasses in front of him.

Tommy waited until their drinks came. He took a sip of his beer before he spoke. Next to him Bill took a gulp of his drink. He started to pull out a pack of cigarettes before apparently remembering that he couldn't smoke in a bar in Montana anymore. Swearing, he gripped his glass with both hands and stared into the dark amber contents.

"Why do you think Fitz fired you?" Tommy asked after a moment.

Bill glanced over at him. "For obvious reasons." He lowered his voice although no one was paying them any attention. "He was robbing the company blind, and I was tired of covering for him."

Tommy took a wild guess. "He wouldn't cut you in."

The accountant looked offended and for a moment, he feared Bill would get up and walk out. "I was going out on a limb for this jackass. It was the least he could do to make it more worth my while."

"How'd you hide it from his partners?" Tommy asked and took another drink of his beer without looking at the man.

"I set up a shell company for him. I'd write checks for fictitious expenses. I'd cash the checks and he'd take the money."

"Is there any way to prove he was involved?"

Bill leaned an elbow on the bar to look at him. "That's the really stupid thing on my part. I made it where he could walk away clean. It would look like I was taking the money because his delicate little hands never touched a pen."

"Wouldn't all of this show up on bank records or corporate business filings with the state?" Tommy asked.

"They could. Why do you think I left without a fight? He has me right where he wants me. He wouldn't give me a recommendation. I'm having hell finding another job. He could send me to prison. I'm the one who was writing checks and cashing them," Bill said.

"What about his bank records?"

The man shook his head. "Fitz wasn't putting the money in the bank. There was no paper trail back to him—only me."

"So you cooked the books, hiding the money that Fitz was stealing from the partnership until he fired you and got a new accountant," Tommy said, trying to understand how this all worked. "Is the new accountant involved?"

"Hell, no. Right before he fired me, he shut down the operation by killing off the shell company, making it look as if he sold the businesses at a loss. The problem is, now there is no extra money coming in. The only money he has is from the partnership with his old man and Nolan Worthington. I'd say with his gambling problem and his flashy lifestyle, he's in need of a cash infusion."

Tommy thought about the marriage to Bella. He had no idea what she might be worth. Her business was too new to be making much. But the ranch was in her name. Was that what Fitz was after besides Bella?

Bill drained his drink and slammed down his glass. The bartender headed in their direction. "One more for the road."

The bartender hesitated.

"I can give him a ride," Tommy said. As soon as the bartender left to make that drink, he asked, "Isn't there a record somewhere that proves there was a shell company but no real businesses?"

"Sure, if you knew what you were looking for." Bill shook his head. "That's how these guys get away with it. They kept their hands clean and let someone else take the blame. Fitz didn't set up the shell company. He had one of the partners do it."

Nolan? Or his father? Tommy couldn't help his surprise. "Wait, you're saying one of the partners was in on it with him?" Bill shrugged. The bartender returned with his drink and looked at him pointedly. "I'm giving him a ride." He turned to Bill the moment the bartender was out of earshot. "Which partner?"

Bill took a gulp of the drink. His eyes were half-closed now. He seemed to be having trouble staying on the stool. He loosened his tie some more and shook his head. "Nolan, but he didn't know what he was signing. He'd made a couple of bad investments and was running scared. He signed whatever I put in front of him."

Downing his drink, Bill half fell off his stool.

"Come on," Tommy said. "I'll drive you home."

"I didn't drive," Bill slurred. "I walked. I live just down the alley. I can find my way home blind drunk, trust me."

"Well, I'll see you home anyway," Tommy said as the man staggered toward the back door. Throwing some money on the bar, he hurried after him.

Pushing open the door, he stepped out to see that Bill was already partway down the alley. Tommy had just started after him when he heard an engine rev and tires squeal. He looked down the alley to his right and saw a dark-colored vehicle headed directly for him.

Chapter 16

Bella still hadn't heard from Tommy by the time her fitting was over. She headed back to the ranch, half hoping Fitz wouldn't be there. But of course he was there waiting for her, sitting outside in the shade of the porch.

"How did it go?" he asked as she climbed the steps.

"Fine." She headed for the door.

"You didn't say anything about the dress."

She stopped, her hand on the doorknob. "It's a nice dress."

He laughed. "That's the best you can do?"

Bella turned to look at him. "What do you expect, Fitz? You know I don't want to marry you and that none of this would be happening if you weren't blackmailing my father."

"I wish it hadn't come to this, either," he said. "But you've never given me a chance."

She sighed. "I don't feel that way about you. It's simple chemistry. I can't control it." She saw his expression harden and reminded herself that they weren't capable of having an honest conversation without him getting angry.

"But there's chemistry between you and that saddle tramp Tommy Colt?" he snapped. He seemed to instantly regret his words as he hurriedly got to his feet and moved toward her. "Bella, I'm sorry. Let's just go to dinner and not discuss anything but the weather. Montana in the summer. We can agree on how wonderful it is, can't we?"

She realized that she feared this conciliatory Fitz more than the angry one. It made her worry all the more about Tommy. She couldn't wait to get to her room and try his cell again. It was dangerous using her regular cell phone to call him. But maybe it made no difference—if as she suspected Fitz already knew about the two of them.

"I'll go change for dinner," she said and entered the house, leaving him on the porch. She hurried up the stairs to her room, locking the door behind her. In the bathroom she turned on the shower in case someone was listening outside her door. She made the call, but like before, Tommy's cell went straight to voice mail.

Tommy yelled for Bill to watch out and threw himself against the bar's back door he'd only closed moments before.

The vehicle blew past him, hitting several garbage cans lined up along the edge of the building. Tommy ducked as one of the cans careened into him, knocking the air out of him. Out of the corner of his eye, he saw the front of the vehicle strike Bill, tossing him into the air. As the vehicle sped away, Bill's body landed in a stack of cardboard boxes piled behind a business. The accountant crumpled to the ground and didn't move.

Hand shaking, Tommy pulled out his phone as he ran toward Bill and punched in 911. Crouching next to the man, he checked for a pulse, shocked that Bill was still alive as the 911 operator answered.

He'd stayed with Bill until the ambulance arrived along with the first cop. Tommy had turned off his phone to talk to the police about the hit-and-run. He was still shaken. "It happened too fast. No, I didn't get a license number or see the driver. All I can tell you was that it was a black SUV."

Another cop arrived at the scene and pulled him aside. This one was older with buzzed gray hair and pale intense eyes. "You say the driver swerved toward you first, then ran down Mr. McMillan?"

"It appeared that way, yes. Look, like I said, it happened so fast. I was getting ready to go after Bill to make sure he got home. The SUV must have been parked down the alley waiting. I hadn't noticed it until I heard the roar of the engine and the sound of the tires squealing."

"Is there anyone who might want to kill you?" He could feel the cop's gaze intent on him.

"Not that I know of," Tommy told him. Fitz hated him and had proved how low he would stoop to get what he wanted. But murder?

"I recognize your name. Rodeo cowboy, right?"

"Was," Tommy said. "I recently joined my brother at Colt Investigations."

The cop's expression changed. "So this could be about some case you're working on."

Tommy hesitated, not sure what to say. "I really doubt it."

"Let me be the judge of that," the cop said. "Who's your client?"

"That's confidential."

The officer stared at him. "Seriously? Someone tries to kill you and you prefer not to tell me who you're working for?"

"Like I said, I doubt it's connected."

With a disgusted sound, the cop put his notebook and pen away. "Have it your way."

"How is Bill?" Tommy asked.

"Last I heard he has a broken hip but was in stable condition. You said he was extremely intoxicated?" Tommy nodded. "Being inebriated probably saved his life."

The cop got a call on his radio. All Tommy heard was "stolen black SUV." When the cop finished he looked at him and shook his head. "Could have been some teen joyriders. Guess we'll know more when we find the vehicle."

With that the cop walked back to his patrol car and Tommy turned on his phone and saw that Bella had called numerous times. He quickly dialed her number as he headed for the hospital.

Bella and Fitz were about to be seated at the steak-house when her cell phone buzzed in her purse. She started to reach for it when Fitz's hand clamped over hers.

"Not tonight," he said, his hand tightening on hers.

"Just let me turn it off." He glared at her for a few moments before his grip loosened.

She quickly dug out the phone. Just as she'd hoped, the call had been from Tommy. She turned off her phone seeing that he'd left a message she would check later as they were escorted to their table.

The moment she saw where they would be seated, Bella knew this was Fitz's doing. It was in a back corner, secluded. A candle flickered on the table and a bottle of champagne chilled in a bucket of ice next to two glasses.

Fitz pulled out her chair for her before going around to his. She could tell that he was determined to be pleasant—as hard as it seemed for him sometimes.

"Are we celebrating something?" she asked, relieved that she'd heard from Tommy—otherwise she would have worried given how in high spirits Fitz seemed tonight.

"Our first real date," he said and gave her a look that dared her to argue otherwise. He poured her a glass and handed it to her before pouring one for himself and offering a toast. "To the future. May it be happy for us both."

She wasn't sure how that would be possible, but she clinked her glass against his and took a sip. The bubbles tickled her tongue. She tried to relax, telling herself that Tommy was fine. He had gone to talk to the accountant. Maybe it had taken longer than he'd thought it would, but if he'd found out something they could use…

"You look so beautiful," Fitz said.

"Thank you." She picked up her menu. She wasn't hungry, but she was determined to get through this so-called date.

"I know you're not much of a steak eater," she heard him say. "But they have seafood. I know you like lobster. Please, this is my treat."

She lowered her menu. "Is everything all right?"

"Why would you ask that?" he inquired, frowning.

"It's just that you're being so…"

"Nice?" He let out a chuckle. "Did you really not realize how I felt about you all these years?"

She shook her head and dropped her voice even though there was enough noise in the busy restaurant that she doubted anyone could hear. "I thought this wasn't going to be a real marriage. That you were just doing this to destroy me *and* my father."

Fitz reddened and dropped his gaze. "I was angry when I said those things. I wanted to hurt you because you've hurt me." He raised his eyes to hers again. She saw him swallow before he spoke. "That wasn't what I really wanted. I've been in love with you for years."

After what Tommy had found out in Spokane it didn't come as a complete surprise. "You just have an odd way of going about asking me out."

He took a sip of his champagne before settling his gaze on her again. "You would have laughed in my face, but let's not get into that now. I want us to have a pleasant dinner. Is that possible?" Bella nodded, not up to one of their usual battles, either. "Have the lobster. I'm having a shrimp cocktail before a steak entrée. Join me. I know how much you like shrimp."

The waiter appeared and she nodded as Fitz ordered for them. Anyone watching might have thought that they were really engaged and having a nice quiet dinner before their upcoming wedding.

Bella tried to relax, but not even the champagne helped. This whole thing was a farce and worse, she sensed there was something Fitz wasn't telling her. He was in too good a mood. She felt as if she was waiting for the other shoe to drop and when it did, she knew it was going to be bad.

The rest of the evening was uneventful enough as they both steered away from anything resembling the truth.

It wasn't until they were leaving the restaurant that two men came out of the shadowy darkness of the parking lot and accosted Fitz.

"Here," he said to her, shoving his keys at her. "Go on to the car and let me handle this." She took the keys but didn't move. The men were large and burly and clearly angry. "Go!" Fitz snapped and gave her a push.

She stumbled toward the car. When she looked back, Fitz was arguing with the men. One of them shoved him back into the side of the building. Clearly they were threatening him. She couldn't hear exactly what was being said, but she'd picked up enough of it to know it had to do with money and gambling.

At the car, she opened the door and climbed in. Fitz appeared a few minutes later. He looked shaken. "What was that about?"

"Nothing," he snapped. "Drop it, okay? Just a misunderstanding. Everything is fine."

Bella really had her doubts about that. However, she could tell by the change in Fitz's mood that unless she wanted trouble from him tonight, she needed to let it go. But she couldn't help but wonder if Fitz was in financial trouble. If he owed those two men from the parking lot, then he had more than money problems.

Maybe this wedding wasn't just all about her after all. She had a bad feeling that her ranch had even more to do with it.

Chapter 17

Bella woke with a start. For a moment, she didn't know what had yanked her out of her deep, mentally exhausted sleep. Her cell phone rang. She blinked, still fighting the coma-like state she'd been in only moments ago, as she reached for it and realized it was early morning. She'd tried to call Tommy last night but with no success. His message on her phone had been short: *I'm fine. Will call later when I can.*

She checked the screen and saw that the call was coming from Lonesome River Investments, her father's office. "Hello?" She sat up, thinking it couldn't be her father. He was still in rehab. Or was he? "Hello?" She could hear someone breathing on the line. "Dad?"

"It's Edwin," said the male voice. Fitz's father. The man sounded drunk.

"Are you all right?" she asked and heard him chuckle

as she leaned against the headboard. This felt like the extension of the dream she'd been having. She wasn't sure any of it was real. "Edwin?" She heard him clear his voice.

His words were slurred when he finally spoke. "I… I thought about what you said." She held her breath. "You're right. Fitz won't stop. Even when he was little we noticed something was… That he was a challenge." He sounded as if he was struggling for his next breath. "But he's my son." He broke down for a moment.

"I'm so sorry. I know how hard this must be for you."

The man seemed to pull himself together. "You can't marry him."

"I don't plan to. Give me something to stop him."

For a moment she thought he'd disconnected. "He has a thumb drive on a chain around his neck. He did that after he caught me checking his deposit box at the bank."

She realized that she'd seen Fitz toying with the gold chain around his neck and thought it must be a new piece of jewelry he wasn't used to yet. Since he often wore a suit or at least a sport jacket, she hadn't thought he was wearing anything but a chain. Fitz had always gone for flashy gold accessories from his expensive watch to his diamond pinkie ring.

"What kind of thumb drive?" she asked.

"Silver, thin, one of those new ones," Edwin said.

"Thank you for telling me about this," she said.

Silence, then, "I had to tell him that you came by and tried to get me to help you."

"I know."

"I—I…" She heard a noise in the background like a door opening. "I have to—" The last thing she heard was Edwin say, "What are you doing here?" before the phone went dead.

Bella quickly disconnected. Someone had walked in on Edwin. Had they overheard what he'd been saying? Her cell phone rang. Edwin? She didn't think so. She listened to it ring, hugging herself against the shudder that moved through her body. All her instincts told her not to answer the call because it wasn't Edwin calling from his number. It was whoever had walked in on him wanting to know who he'd called.

Now wide-awake, she leaned back against the headboard and looked across the room, her eyes unseeing. Was it true about the thumb drive? Even if it was, how was she going to get it from around Fitz's neck? Very carefully. Unless that had been Fitz who'd caught his father calling her. If he'd overheard what Edwin had told her, then he'd be waiting for her to try to steal the thumb drive hanging around his neck.

When Bill McMillan opened his eyes the next morning, Tommy was sitting in a chair beside the man's bed. "Hey," Tommy said.

He couldn't help feeling responsible for what had happened to the man. Apparently getting drunk at the bar and walking back to his apartment was a nightly thing. But Tommy kept thinking about how paranoid Bill had been about meeting him, afraid that Fitz would find him. Had he been followed? Had Fitz not just found his former accountant—but Tommy as well?

Last night when he reached the hospital, he'd finally checked his phone and saw the message from Bella. *Fitz knows. Be careful.*

Bill tried to smile. "Was I hit by a bus?"

"Pretty close. An SUV."

The man's gaze was unfocused for a moment, as if he was trying to remember. "An accident?" Tommy shook his head and Bill swore. "I have insurance."

Tommy thought he was talking about the hospital bill for a moment. Bill grimaced in pain as he said, "We had a deal. He broke it. Screw him. Get my insurance. It's hidden in my apartment under the floorboard in the bedroom. Get the bastard." Bill closed his eyes. "My apartment keys were in my jacket pocket. The hospital probably has them."

A nurse came in. "Mr. McMillan?" she said as she neared the bed. Bill's eyes opened. "A police officer is here who wants to ask you a few questions. Feel up to it?" Bill nodded.

Tommy rose. "I'll be going now, but I'll check back later."

Bill met his gaze and gave a small nod. "Thanks for taking care of things for me. My cat," he said, turning to the nurse. "He needs the key to my apartment so he can feed my cat."

The nurse nodded. "Your belongings are at the nurse's station." She turned to Tommy. "Just follow me. You'll have to sign the keys out," she told him as he followed the nurse down the hall.

"No problem." He called Bella and told her what had happened and where he was headed.

"Give me the address," she said. "I'll meet you there.

Bella was still upset. The message Tommy had left on her phone last night just said he was fine and would talk to her today. This morning he'd filled her in on the accident. She knew he wasn't telling her everything.

She'd been worried about him yesterday—and apparently with good reason.

He was waiting for her when she drove up. As she got out and glanced around, she couldn't help being surprised that the accountant lived just off this alley. She vaguely remembered seeing Bill McMillan at her father's office. As far as she knew, he'd made a good living but since being fired by Fitz, he seemed to have fallen on hard times.

Seeing her surprise, Tommy said, "He's been hiding out. I fear I led Fitz right to him and that's why he was almost killed. The police think it was an accident. Stolen SUV. Kids on a joyride."

"But you know better. This is a really narrow alley," she said, looking down it before turning to him again. She thought of Ronan and Milo. Fitz couldn't have been behind the wheel because he was at dinner with her. Was she his alibi? She felt sick to her stomach remembering him professing his undying love last night at the restaurant. She had wondered at his good mood. Now she thought she understood.

"It wasn't only the accountant Fitz was trying to kill," she said, but knew Tommy wasn't going to tell her what had really happened.

"This way," he said, no doubt thinking he was protecting her. As they walked he filled her in what Bill had told him. "He said he got fired. From what I gathered, he'd wanted more money on the deal. He did tell me that your father was so distracted that he signed anything Bill put in front of him."

Bella shook her head. "My father was always so trusting when it came to Edwin and Fitz. His first mistake. Add in his girlfriend Caroline… He really had no idea what was going on right under his nose." She was hesitant to tell him about Edwin's call and her dinner with Fitz. With luck they would find what they needed in Bill's apartment and put an end to this.

Tommy opened a heavy metal door with graffiti splashed across it and they stepped into a small landing at the bottom of a steep set of dark stairs. "It's number four," he said and started up, her close behind.

Their footsteps echoed as they climbed. She could smell a variety of unpleasant scents as they passed several apartment doors. Behind them were the sounds of cooking, televisions turned up too loud and raised voices.

At number four, Tommy pulled out a key, but before he could use it, the door swung inward. Someone had already been here, she thought as she saw the ransacked apartment. Her heart fell. Whatever insurance Bill McMillan had hidden here had to be gone.

Tommy let out a low curse. "Wait here." He entered the residence, wading through the destruction toward what appeared to be the bedroom. The bed now leaned against the wall exposing the wooden floor. Several of the planks had been removed.

She watched him look into the gaping hole in the floor and then turn back to her in defeat, shaking his head. Fitz won again. That was all she could think about as they made their way back down the stairs to their vehicles.

They found a coffee shop and sat in a back corner. Bella cupped her mug in her hands, wishing she could chase away the cold that had settled inside her as she told Tommy first about dinner with Fitz and then the two thugs who'd been waiting for him in the parking lot.

"It sounded like he owed them money," she said.

Tommy shook his head. "I'm not surprised. Bill said that Fitz has been living beyond his means for some time. Once Bill did away with the shell company and that free money, he'd wondered what Fitz had been doing for income to support his lifestyle and gambling habit."

"We may know soon," she said and told him about the call from Edwin this morning.

"A thumb drive?" he said when she'd finished. "Bella, if it's around his neck—"

"I know. But I have to try," she said quickly.

He shook his head. "You can't be serious. If he catches you—"

"How can it be any worse than what is happening right now?" she demanded. "He would just gloat that he'd won again." She feared that he would do a whole lot more, but she wasn't about to share that with Tommy.

"I don't like it," he said.

She took a drink of her coffee and felt the heat rush through her. "I don't like it either, but time is running out. I have to try to get the thumb drive. If Edwin is telling the truth—"

"Exactly. You sure Fitz didn't put him up to this?"

Bella wasn't sure of anything except the impending wedding looming on the close horizon—and what Fitz might do to her father before this was over. What hung between her and Tommy was the realization that Fitz had gone beyond just threatening people. He or one of the men he'd hired had tried to kill the accountant and she was pretty sure the driver had also tried to kill Tommy. Ronan? Miles? Either were capable, she thought.

"You know what scares me?" she asked, feeling the tightness in her chest as she realized that she'd under-estimated Fitz. "Fitz is much more desperate than I thought. I should have realized it. He's buying drugs to frame my father, throwing this elaborate wedding, he's been stealing money from the partnership, he's black-mailing me and his father, and now attempted murder?" She looked up into Tommy's handsome face. "Now I suspect he not only knows about us, but that he had someone try to kill you last night. I can't see you any-more. I'm firing you."

As she started to rise to leave, Tommy reached for her arm. "No," he said, easing her back into her chair. "Not happening. You aren't doing this alone." He knew Bella. She wouldn't give up. She would do this alone if she had to. But he wasn't going to let that happen—even as much as he wished he could talk her out of doing anything dangerous.

"You're right. He's become more desperate." He met her gaze. "I know he wants you, but there has to be more. You're just part of the plan. I need to ask you something. How much money do you have?"

She blinked. "On me right now?"

"No," he said with a shake of his head. "What are you worth?"

"You think Fitz wants my money." She laughed. "I think you're right. I know he wants the ranch."

He twined his fingers in her hand. "I'm in this with you whether you fire me or not." He thought about Margo and the unpaid rent. Maybe Fitz could no lon-ger afford her. Or no longer needed her. Either way, Fitz was getting more desperate, which meant he was getting more dangerous.

"So what's your plan to get the thumb drive?" he asked, knowing that she would try no matter what he said. He saw at once from her expression that she hadn't had a plan. "You're going to need some strong sedatives. I'll get them for you. What does this thumb drive look like?"

"Silver, thin," she said, her voice breaking as her eyes welled with tears. "Thank you. I'll need one like it to replace the one I take."

He nodded. "I'll get it," he said, his voice also filled with emotion. He couldn't bear the thought that he might get this woman killed. "We do this together. Just like when we were kids."

She nodded and wiped at her tears. "Please be—"

"Careful? Have you forgotten that as soon as my license comes back I'm going to be a private investigator? *Trouble* is my middle name now."

"That isn't funny."

"But it's true," he said, squeezing her hand. She was shaking and he knew that she was scared. For him.

He had to bite his tongue not to tell her how much he loved her. But damned if he would do it in some coffee shop. When this was over...

"I'll bring the sedatives and the thumb drive," he said, trying to hide how terrified he was of what Fitz would do if he caught her. "Can you meet me later at that old pine where we used to ride our horses?" She nodded. "You're sure you can get away?"

"He's still letting me ride my horse," she said through gritted teeth. It more than grated on her that he had moved in and thought he could tell her what to do. Unfortunately, he could. For now. "Later this afternoon before sundown?"

"I'll be there. I'll come by horseback."

The Colt property was large but because it wasn't on the river, it wasn't worth as much as the Worthington ranch. Still, Tommy loved the land his great-grandfather had bought but never built on. All of them had spent so little time in Lonesome that building a house had remained a pipe dream.

Until James came home and fell in love with Lorelei. The house was coming along nicely. One of the first things James had done was fence off some pasture and build a stable and corral for their horses. Tommy had been keeping his horse and tack out here since he'd returned home.

After saddling his horse, he rode up over the mountain to drop down toward the river. The large pine he and Bella used to climb when they were kids was in the far corner of the Worthington ranch far from any roads—right next door to Colt land. It was very private since there were no roads into it—another reason it had been one his and Bella's favorite places to hang out as kids. While their parents knew about the tree house, they didn't know about the other spots they went to. No one found them here because no one came this far to look for them.

He spotted Bella's horse tied up some distance from the tree and reined in. As he swung out of the saddle, he saw her waiting for him under the mighty limbs of the old pine. She'd spread out a horse blanket and now sat with her back against the tree trunk. The waning sun shone on her face as he tied up his horse and walked toward her.

She looked so beautiful it choked him up. He realized he couldn't wait any longer to tell her how he felt. He'd held it in for too long. Her gaze tracked him, the expression on her face intrigued—and expectant. He chuckled to himself. Bella was too sharp not to know how he felt—or why he'd wanted to meet here. Had she, like him, been waiting for this day?

Chapter 18

Bella studied the good-looking, dark-haired cowboy headed her way and felt her heart bump in her chest. His expression stole her breath. His long legs, clad in denim, quickly covered the distance between them.

She pushed to her feet, feeling the air tingle around her like dry lightning. Tommy didn't speak, just took her shoulders in his large hands and pulled her into a kiss. She felt the electricity popping around her, felt the spark as his lips touched her. It sent a jolt through her, straight to her middle, as he backed her up against the smooth tree trunk and she wrapped her arms around his waist and brought him closer.

He made a sound deep in his throat as one hand dropped to her breast. She groaned against his mouth as he slipped his hand inside her shirt and under the cup of her bra to fondle her now granite-hard nipple.

He caught the tip between his thumb and finger and gently rolled it back and forth.

She arched against him, a groan coming from her lips. Only then did he pull back from the kiss to look into her eyes. She saw the desire burning there as hot as his callused fingers still teasing her aching nipple.

"Tell me to stop," he said, his voice hoarse with obvious emotion.

She shook her head. "I've wanted this for way too long."

The words appeared to be his undoing. He swept her into his arms and gently laid her on the blanket she'd spread out for them. For a moment, he merely stared down into her face. She smiled up at him, and then taking his face in her hands pulled him down for a kiss.

After that, Bella vaguely remembered the flurry of clothing flying into piles on the blanket before they rolled around, both naked as jaybirds. She'd known that their lovemaking would be both wild and playful—just as they had always been. She wasn't disappointed.

She'd never wanted anything more than she wanted Tommy as she began to feel an urgency. She desperately wanted him inside her. He bent to lathe each hard nipple with his tongue before trailing kisses across her flat stomach to her center. She moaned against his incredible mouth as he lifted her higher and higher until she thought she would burst. Until she felt a release that left her weak and shaking.

She drew him up to her, still desperately needing to feel his body on hers, in hers. The weight of him, the look in his eyes, the warm summer evening's breeze caressing their naked bodies. Hadn't she always known that if she and Tommy ever got past just being friends, this is where it would happen?

He started to speak, but she pressed a finger to his lips and shook her head. If he told her that he loved her right now, she feared she wouldn't be able to hold back the tears. She hadn't let herself admit how afraid she was that they couldn't stop Fitz.

She guided him into her and began to move slowly, her gaze locked with his. Their movements grew stronger, faster, harder. She arched against him, filled with a desire that only he could quench. When the release came it was powerful. Pleasure washed through her as she rose to meet him again and again, before they both collapsed together, breathing hard.

"I knew it would be like that," she said as she looked into his pale blue eyes.

"Bella—" She slipped from his arms. "Come on." Reaching back, she took his hand and pulled him up to run toward the river where it pooled among the rocks. The sun was all but hidden behind the mountain and yet the evening was summertime warm as they ran into the water, laughing. Droplets rose in the summer air and seemed to hang there.

Bella filed it all away in a special place in her heart, memorizing the scents, the light, the feel of the water and Tommy for fear this was all they may get when the dust settled.

Later Tommy would remember the water droplets caught in her lashes. Her laughter carrying across the water. She hadn't let him tell her how much he loved her. But she knew. He'd seen that moment of fear in her eyes and felt it heart deep. They had no future unless Fitz could be stopped.

It was the only thing on his mind as he rode his horse back to his brother's place. He and Bella had air-dried off in the evening warmth before dressing and riding off in different directions.

He'd given her the sedatives and thumb drive. "Call me when you can," was all he'd said. There was no reason to warn her to be careful. Or to try to change her mind about what she planned to do. The wedding was approaching too quickly.

"Don't come to the ranch," she warned him as she swung up into the saddle. "The place is crawling with the men he hired."

"How will you get me the thumb drive?"

"We'll meet tomorrow morning. Ten o'clock. At the fire tower."

"And if you don't make it?" he asked.

"I'll find a way to call you." She'd known that wasn't what he was asking, but he let it go. "Just don't try to come to the ranch. I'll get the thumb drive and find a way to get it to you."

He thought of their lovemaking and ached to feel her body nestled against his. He recalled the pale light on her skin and trailing a finger through the river water that pooled on her flat stomach before they made love a second time.

What terrified him was the way they'd parted as if they might never see each other again.

"Your bouquet," he'd said before she could ride away. "If things go wrong, there will be something in the roses from me."

Her eyes had widened but then she'd nodded. Neither one of them wanted this to go that far. But in case it did… "Thank you. I'll see you tomorrow."

Chapter 19

Bella fingered the small packet of crushed sedatives in her pocket for a moment before she took her seat at the dining room table across from Fitz.

She felt flushed from being with Tommy Colt and feared it showed on her face. If Fitz had known where she'd been and what she'd done... But if he'd noticed a change in her, he didn't show it.

"To marriage," Fitz said, lifting his full wineglass. She hesitated to raise her own glass that he'd already filled. She didn't want to drink tonight. Later, she would need to be completely sober, completely in touch with her every movement if she hoped to succeed, because there was no way she wasn't going through with this.

"To truth and justice," she said and raised her glass, holding his gaze.

He laughed. "Whatever." He took a long drink. He

seemed to be in a good mood...for some reason. Which concerned her.

She pretended to take a sip and put down her glass. Roberto brought out their meals. She ate distractedly. Fitz ate with gusto, as if he hadn't eaten all day. He probably hadn't. She watched him out of the corner of her eye.

All she could think was that she needed a distraction so she could get the powder into his wineglass, but he seemed settled in, his gaze on her when he wasn't shoveling food into his mouth. Did he know what she planned to do? Had Edwin confessed that he'd told her about the thumb drive?

Fitz's cell phone rang, making her start and him swear. She had to relax. If he noticed how tense she was—

"I have to take this," he said and, dropping his napkin onto his empty plate, excused himself to head for the den. "What?" he demanded into the phone before he closed the door behind him.

She had no idea how long she had. Maybe only a few seconds. Quickly, she pulled the packet with the pulverized sedatives from her pocket. It took way too long to get the packet open, her fingers refusing to cooperate. She could hear Fitz still on the phone, but he was trying to keep the call short. He could open that door any moment and catch her. She feared she wouldn't get another chance tonight.

The bag finally opened. She poured the contents into his wineglass. Some of the white powder stuck to the side. She hurriedly poured some of her wine into his glass and swirled it around, spilling a little on the tablecloth.

She heard the door open and Fitz's raised voice.

"We're in the middle of dinner," he said into the phone, the door opened a crack. "We can talk about this to-morrow."

All she could do was cover the spot with his plate, moving it though from where he had it set perfectly in front of him. Would he notice? He might. She moved the plate back to where it had been. Or at least close.

As he came out of the den, she reached for the wine bottle to refill her glass. Then she began to pour more wine into his glass, spilling just a little on the already stained tablecloth.

Fitz grabbed the wine bottle from her hand. "Clumsy. That's not like you." His heated gaze burned her as he walked around the table. Picking up his cloth napkin, he covered the spilled spot on the tablecloth and called for Roberto to bring him another napkin and take their empty plates.

She could feel his eyes on her, suspicious. The two spots on the tablecloth. He would see it. He would know. She looked up at him. He looked disgruntled with her. Would he demand the tablecloth be changed just to show that he was still in charge?

He took a deep breath, let it out and finally sat down. As he did, he straightened the salt and pepper shakers. She hadn't realized that she'd knocked over the salt in her hurry to cover up her crime.

She picked up her wine and pretended to take a drink. Had she gotten away with it? Not until he drank his wine.

Roberto whisked away their plates, promising to return with a surprise dessert. She saw Fitz open his mouth as if to say he didn't want dessert.

"I do, please," she said quickly, cutting him off. Then

she looked at Fitz and said, "I've been thinking." She lowered her eyelashes.

"Oh?" From under her lashes, she saw him pick up his wineglass and take a drink as he watched her.

"Maybe we could make a deal."

He chuckled. "You really aren't in a dealing position."

She met his gaze, ran her finger along the rim of her wineglass and wet her lips. She had his attention. More than that, she saw something in his eyes that surprised her. Yes, he wanted to punish her, destroy her, but he also wanted her as well as her ranch. His look was lustful. Maybe she had more to bargain with than he wanted to admit.

She took a sip of her wine and this time swallowed it. *Easy, girl. If this works, you need to be dead sober.* She continued to hold her wineglass. She'd heard somewhere that diners often mirrored their dinner companions. Reach for bread, they were apt to as well. Same with drinking?

Bella realized there must be some truth to it because Fitz took a healthy drink of his wine. She needed him to finish it, though. He was a big man. But there'd been enough sedatives in the packet to put down a farm animal. If he finished his wineglass, he should start feeling the effects fairly soon.

But not too soon, she hoped.

"So?" he asked. "What is this…deal you want to make?"

She could see that he was interested, and it had gotten his mind off the spilled wine on the tablecloth. "I feel like we should call a truce."

He grinned. "A truce? What do you have in mind?"

She took another sip of her wine. She could feel the heat of it rush to her chest. But she had to get him to drink all of his. He had put his wine down but now picked it up again and nearly drained the glass.

She noticed with a jolt that there was white powder in the bottom of his glass. "It's going to take more wine," she said with a little laugh and reached for the bottle, knocking it over. There wasn't much left to spill but enough to cause him to leap to his feet as the bottle banged into his glass, spilling the last of the contents onto the already soiled tablecloth and running like a river straight for him.

He swore and jumped back just as she'd hoped. He didn't want to get red wine on his linen trousers.

She leaped up as well and grabbed his glass and spilled hers as well. "Roberto," she called. "We need help." She giggled as she felt Fitz's hard suspicious gaze on her again. "We're going to need another bottle of wine," she said, laughing as Roberto came into the room.

"I believe you've had enough," Fitz said. "Clean this up." He stepped back from the huge red stain on the white tablecloth as if it were blood.

Squeamish a little? She swayed and pretended to have trouble focusing. "I think we should discontinue this conversation for the moment. I might have to lie down or throw up," Bella said and grabbed the edge of the table for support. Had he noticed that her wineglass was less empty than his?

She told herself to be careful. Fitz watched everything. If he thought that she wasn't as tipsy as she was… Or worse, that she'd put something in his wine…

Roberto appeared and quickly took the dishes and the stained tablecloth. He saw that they were both standing and neither of them had sat back down. "No dessert?" he asked, sounding disappointed. "I made something special—"

She cut him off before he could say what. "Save me some please, but I really have to…" She didn't finish, just exited quickly, hurrying up the stairs to her room where she locked the door behind her.

Her back against the door, she stood listening until she heard Fitz's footfalls. Then she made gagging sounds until the footfalls quickly faded back down the hallway in the direction of the guest hallway.

Going to the intercom, she called down to the kitchen. "Roberto, I could really use some hot black coffee."

"And maybe dessert?" He lowered his voice and smiled. "I made tres leches."

She couldn't help but smile. "Why not?"

A few moments later there was a tap at her door. She couldn't be sure that Fitz hadn't waylaid Roberto and she would find him standing outside her door holding the tray, waiting to be let into her room.

She grabbed a towel, wrapped it around her head and splashed water on her face. As she was leaving the bathroom, she remembered to flush the toilet.

Unlocking the door, she opened it a crack. To her relief, Roberto was holding the tray. She stepped back to let him enter.

"Thank you," she said. "I don't feel so well."

"There are some over-the-counter pain relievers on the tray as well," he said and smiled as he quickly left.

She locked the door and reached for the coffee. If the sedative worked, then Fitz should be feeling the effects right now. She glanced at the time. She'd give it another fifteen minutes.

Chapter 20

Tommy had taken his suspicions about Fitz's gambling debt to his brother James. It hadn't taken long before they had a completely different picture of Edwin Fitzgerald Mattson the Third. "He's in trouble. His lifestyle seems to have caught up with him."

"The car is leased," James said. "He's behind in his apartment rent and his credit cards are maxed out. Have you seen the wedding invitations?" He shook his head. "Cash-only gifts as the couple will be moving overseas."

Tommy swore and snatched the invitation out of his brother's hand. Did Bella know about this? He didn't think so. But since she wasn't planning to go through with the wedding, maybe she wasn't worried about it.

"So he does plan to sell everything, including the

ranch," Tommy said. "Even taking all of this into consideration, it still seems like Fitz is too desperate."

James nodded. "I saw the police report on the hit-and-run. I have a friend in the police department. You didn't mention that the bastard tried to kill you first."

"If it was Fitz's doing. Did your cop friend also tell you that the SUV was stolen and that they suspect it was an accident?"

"Yeah, like either of us believe that. Still, you're right. Fitz wouldn't know how to steal a vehicle unless the keys were in the ignition."

"There's more going on here," Tommy said. "From what Bella told me, he's gotten involved with the wrong people." James nodded. "I think this might have started with him wanting Bella, but that he now needs her money. The ranch is in her name. With the way things are selling in Montana right now…"

"That place is worth a small fortune, being on the river with the main house, bunkhouse, stable, new barn and all that land," James said.

"She has a couple of trust funds and some other money as well," Tommy told him.

"If Fitz is as desperate as it seems, he'll be even more dangerous," James said.

"That's what has me terrified, because of what Bella has planned." He couldn't sit still. How could he let her go through with this? How could he stop her?

"It's Bella," his brother said at seeing how anxious he was. "I'd put my money on her any day of the week to come out a winner."

Tommy smiled at his older brother. "I can't help but be scared. I don't know what Fitz will do next. He's already proven how dangerous he is."

* * *

Bella pocketed the empty thumb drive Tommy had given her to replace Fitz's. If she didn't switch them, then he would know too quickly that his was gone. She needed time to find out what was on the drive before he realized what she'd done.

That was of course if she could pull this off. She checked the time. Now or never. Taking a deep breath, she unlocked her bedroom door, peered out.

The hallway was empty. This time of night most of the security guards were either at the bunkhouse or outside on the grounds. Not that one of them couldn't appear at any time in the hallway since she knew that they also made sure the house was secure.

She let her bedroom door close softly behind her before starting down the hallway in her stocking feet. The house seemed unusually quiet tonight. The moon would be up soon. But right now, it was dark outside, even with a zillion stars glittering over the tops of the trees. Shadows hunkered in the depths of the pines. Not a breeze stirred the boughs.

At the guest room wing she stopped to listen. She heard nothing but the pounding of her own pulse, as if the house were holding its breath.

Making her way down the short hallway, she stopped a few feet from his door and listened before she pulled out her passkey. As quietly as possible, she stepped to the door and slipped the passkey into the lock.

Breath held, she listened as she turned the key. It made a faint tick of a sound. She waited and then turned the knob and slowly eased open the door, terrified to think that Fitz could be lying in wait and about to ambush her.

The room was filled with pitch-black darkness. The drapes were partially closed. Faint starlight cut through the gap to cast a dagger-like sheen on the carpet. The room held a chest of drawers and a king-size bed with a club chair and two end tables. The door to the bathroom stood open, its interior also dark.

Over the thunder of her heart, she heard it. The sound of heavy rhythmic snoring came from the direction of the bed. She tried to breathe for a moment. She was shaking. If she hoped to get the thumb drive, she had to calm down.

Stepping in on her tiptoes, she let the door close quietly behind her and moved toward the bed and the snoring man sprawled there. With each step, she expected him to bolt upright. Surprise! Maybe the sedatives hadn't been powerful enough. Or maybe he hadn't drank enough. She tried to remember how much white sediment had been in the bottom of the wineglass.

She neared the bed, ready at any point to turn and run. It wasn't until she was next to the bed that she saw Fitz had lain down with all his clothes on. The way he was sprawled, it appeared he'd barely made it before passing out. She wondered how fast the sedative had hit him and whether he'd realized what was happening before he hit the bed.

Bella told herself that she couldn't worry about that right now. Once she had the thumb drive, once she got it to Tommy, then it wouldn't matter what Fitz suspected let alone what he knew.

But because she didn't know how long it would take or even how she was going to get the drive to him, she had to replace the drive with the empty one.

Edging closer she listened to his snores. He lay on

his back, one arm thrown over his head, the other lying across his rising and falling chest.

The moon rose up over the mountains, over the tops of the pines, the bright light fingering through boughs to shine through the space behind the partially opened drapes. That dagger of faint light was now a river of gold that splashed across the room.

The light glinted off the chain around Fitz's neck.

Tommy paced the floor, unable to sleep. He should have talked Bella out of this. That thought made him laugh. Once Bella made up her mind... Still, he had to know what was happening out at the ranch.

His cell phone rang, making him jump. Bella? He snatched up the phone. "Hello?"

"Tommy, it's James."

His heart jumped into this throat. He couldn't speak, couldn't breathe. He gripped the phone, terrified of what his brother would say next. "Edwin senior is dead."

It took a moment before the unexpected news registered. "What?"

"I just got the call here at the office from my friend with the Missoula police," James said. "Apparently it was suicide. They think he's been dead since sometime yesterday."

Tommy didn't know what to say. He recalled Bella telling him about Edwin's call to her. She'd said someone had come in. She'd feared it was Fitz and that he might have heard what his father had told her. "Does Bella know?" he asked. "What about Fitz?"

"I have no idea if he's gotten the call yet. Can't imagine why anyone would call Bella."

But they would try to reach Fitz. Tonight. And given what Bella might be doing at this very moment…

"Bella's in trouble," he told his brother and explained about her plan.

James swore. "That's a bonehead idea if I ever heard one, but if anyone can pull it off it is Bella."

"If you're just trying to make me feel better—"

"I'm not. You know her. I'm sure you tried to stop her without any luck, right?"

"Right."

"What's the worst that can happen?" James said. "He wakes up and catches her. He isn't going to kill her. He can't."

"I hope you're right." But Tommy knew that if Fitz caught her trying to steal the thumb drive, he would make her life even more miserable and God only knew what he'd do to her father.

Bella edged closer to the bed. Her chest hurt from holding her breath. She let it out in a soft sigh as she kept her gaze on the bed and the man lying on it. Fitz hadn't moved. He continued to snore loudly. She assured herself that he couldn't hear her.

But once she touched him…

Her plan was simple. She would gently lift the chain at his neck. Except as she reached down, he let out a sharp snore and stirred. She froze. There was nothing else she could do. What would she do if he caught her? A half dozen lies flitted through her brain, all of them so lame they were laughable.

After a few moments Fitz fell back into more rhythmic snores again. She shook out her hand, her fingers tingling as if asleep. Then she reached down and with slow, careful movements, pinched the thick gold chain between her fingers. Slowly, she began to lift it.

As she did, she could see the shape of the thin thumb drive moving beneath his shirt as it headed for the V opening at this throat. Her mind started to play tricks on her, telling her that he was faking it, that he'd been expecting her, that once the thumb drive was visible his eyes would flash open and he'd grab her by the throat.

Her hand trembled and she had to stop for a moment. *Almost there, don't give up now.* She felt an urgency and yet she still pulled the chain slowly until she'd eased the thumb drive out from the shirt opening. It lay against his bare throat for a moment. She drew it over onto his shirt and let out the breath she'd been holding.

Now it was just a matter of unhooking the golden chain from around his neck. Hanging onto the thumb drive, she pulled on the chain until the clasp was reachable.

But in order to unhook the clasp, she had to lean forward over him closer than she'd ever wanted to be. She could smell his cologne and their long-ago-consumed dinner on his breath and tried not to gag. Her fingers shook with nerves. She tried not to look at his face as she worked at the clasp and yet she was still expecting his eyes to flash open, his hand to grab hold of her wrist. She was still expecting to be caught.

The chain came unhooked so quickly that she dropped one end of it. She hurriedly slipped off the thumb drive and pulled the new empty one from her pocket—and switched them. Now all she had to do was reconnect the clasp.

The whole process felt like it had taken too long and yet she knew it had only been a few minutes. Would Fitz be suspicious when he woke up to find his chain pulled out? She thought about trying to stick the thumb drive back under his shirt and was still considering it when his cell phone, right beside the bed, rang.

The sound was so loud in the room that she jumped and dropped the chain as she lurched back. Her gaze shot to his face. He'd stopped snoring. His eyelids fluttered.

Move! But her feet felt nailed to the floor.

The cell phone rang again. She took a step backward, then another and another, all the time watching his face as he attempted to drag himself up from the drugged sleep. She was to the door when she heard the phone stop ringing. She could only see the end of the bed from here.

Had he answered it? Her heart was pounding so hard she couldn't be sure. She eased open the door and stepped into the hall, pulling it gently closed behind her.

In those few seconds, she'd expected him to yank open the door and grab her. Inside his room, his phone began to ring again. Her heart banging like cymbals against her ribs, she turned and took off down the hall. At the end, she finally had the courage to look back— fearful that if she turned she'd find Fitz right behind her.

The hallway was empty, but she could hear someone coming up the stairs. She hurried down to her room, unlocked the door with trembling fingers and stepped inside. It wasn't until she had the door locked behind her and stood, trying to catch her breath, that she heard banging.

Someone was pounding on Fitz's door. In the distance, she could hear another cell phone ringing. She hurried to hers where she'd thankfully left it next to her bed. But as she picked it up to call Tommy, she heard a noise outside her bedroom door and then a knock.

"Bella?"

She recognized the voice. Ronan. The other guards called her Miss Worthington. He knocked again. She waited realizing she was supposed to be asleep. "Yes, what is it?" she called, hoping she sounded as if she'd just woken up.

"There's been an accident," Ronan called through the door. "Open up."

She reached for her robe, pulling it around her and hiding her clothes under it. "What kind of accident?" She could hear him waiting. She looked around the room clutching her cell phone. The thumb drive was in her jeans pocket under the robe.

At the door, she eased it open a crack. "What is it?" She sounded as impatient as she felt. She could hear Fitz's phone still ringing. Something had happened, that much was obvious.

"It's Edwin Mattson. He's dead. Suicide," Ronan said. His dark eyes bored into her.

She pulled the collar of her robe tighter. "Does Fitz know?" she asked.

"I thought you would want to know. Your fiancé is going to need you." There was censure in his words, in the look in his eyes.

Bella felt sick to her stomach. What did Ronan know? But when she met his gaze, she realized he was probably the one who'd followed her and Tommy to the river. He knew. So Fitz knew as well—just as she'd feared. "I need to get dressed." She slammed the door and quickly locked it an instant before he raised his hand to stop her.

She leaned against the door. Just minutes before she'd been home free. She had the thumb drive. She'd done it. Now this? Edwin? Suicide. A feeling of doom washed over her, making it even more difficult to breathe. She'd heard someone interrupt her call with Edwin. Had it been suicide?

This might change everything, she realized. What if she couldn't meet Tommy at ten at the fire tower? She held her cell phone to her chest remembering their lovemaking at the old pine tree. As badly as she needed to hear his voice, she realized she couldn't chance calling him. She could hear more footfalls in the hallway. Ronan could be standing out there listening.

No, she'd just find a way to meet Tommy at the fire tower and give him the thumb drive. In the meantime, it sounded as if the guards had managed to awaken Fitz. She needed to change clothes and go downstairs. The best thing she could do, she told herself, was to act as normally as possible. It wouldn't be hard to appear shocked about Edwin's death. It would be much harder to accept that he'd committed suicide—and hide her true fear that Fitz was behind it.

She closed her eyes, thinking of the man who'd tried to help her and her father. But mostly thinking of Edwin's call and the sound of someone interrupting them—someone he'd feared. His own son?

Dropping her cell phone into her purse, she hurried to her laptop and inserted the thumb drive. She might not have much time, but she needed to know that this wasn't another of Fitz's tricks and that there really was something on this drive.

She could hear the sound of footfalls in the house,

the commotion mostly in the guest hallway. Had he realized by now that he'd been knocked out?

There was only one file on the thumb drive. She clicked on it just an instant before there was loud knocking at her door again. Data. Lots of data, everything she needed, she hoped. Edwin had told her the truth. Hurriedly, she ejected the thumb drive and pocketed it in her jeans.

"I'm getting dressed," she called through the door—not about to open it again. She didn't trust Ronan. That was the problem with mad dogs. Sometimes they even turned on their owners.

But this time the voice on the other side came from one of the other guards. "Mr. Mattson would like you to join him downstairs."

She glanced at the time. It would be daylight soon. What could Fitz want with her? "I'm getting dressed. Please tell him that I'll be down shortly."

She waited until she heard the man move away from the door before she hurried to change. Exhaustion pulled at her. It had been a nerve-racking night. She considered what to do with the thumb drive and decided keeping it on her was best. Her burner phone was in the car. She'd call Tommy on the way to the fire tower.

Dressed in a clean pair of jeans and a blouse, she pocketed the thumb drive, pulled on a jacket and went downstairs, taking her purse with her. As soon as she could, she'd go to Tommy.

Fitz was so adamant about them looking like a loving engaged couple, he would probably want her to go with him to talk to the police and make arrangements for his father's body to be taken to the funeral home.

But with Fitz she never knew what to expect. He

could still be somewhat out of it because of the sedatives. She figured one look at him would tell her whether or not he knew what she'd been up to.

Chapter 21

Fitz tried to think. His head felt filled with cotton. "Coffee," he demanded once Roberto had been awakened and sent to the kitchen. "Keep it coming." The police had called with the news. They would want to see him. But they couldn't see him in this condition.

He caught a glimpse of himself in a mirror in the dining room and recoiled. He couldn't meet with anyone looking like… He narrowed his gaze at his reflection. He hadn't consumed that much alcohol at dinner. No, the way he was feeling wasn't from the wine.

At the sound of footfalls, he turned to see his lovely future bride coming down the stairs. Every time he saw her, he was stunned at how perfect she was. She'd always been like this, even as a girl. So self-assured, so adorable, so capable of just about anything.

The reminder sent a stab of worry through him. He

touched the chain at his neck. When he'd awakened fully clothed as if from the sleep of the dead, the chain and thumb drive had been outside his shirt. He'd hurriedly stuffed it back in as he'd gone to the door to find the guards standing in the hallway looking worried. Apparently they had been banging at his door for some time.

"Sir, your phone is ringing and the police are on the landline downstairs," one of his men had said, eyeing him strangely.

Fitz had had to fight to make sense of what the guard was saying. He'd turned back to his bed, shocked to see that he hadn't been under the covers. He hadn't even removed his clothing from last night. That was when he'd realized that his phone was ringing. He'd stumbled to the end table and grabbed up his phone. His father was dead. Suspected suicide?

He'd felt as if he'd missed more than a phone call. He'd lost hours of time and didn't have any idea how it had happened.

"I'm sorry to hear about your father," Bella said as she joined him.

He looked into her green eyes. It was like looking into a bottomless sea that beckoned him before the lids dropped, shutting him out. "Thank you," he said, his tongue feeling too large for his mouth. He turned and yelled into the kitchen. "Where is my damned coffee?"

"Let me go see," Bella said and started past him.

He grabbed her arm and shook his head. "Stay here with me." His voice broke, surprising him. He sounded like a man who'd just lost his father. He was taking this much worse than he'd expected. He and Edwin senior had been at odds for so long now…

She didn't argue. "Would you like me to go with you to talk to the police?"

The offer touched him and made him suspicious at the same time. She looked guilty of something. He would eventually find out, he told himself. Right now just keeping his eyes open was hard enough. Thinking hurt. "Thank you," he said, knowing he had no intention of taking her up on her offer. He'd go alone. Bella had spoken to his father recently. He couldn't trust that she wouldn't say something that might cast suspicion on him.

Roberto hurried out of the kitchen with the coffee. Also on the tray along with the cups and spoons were what appeared to be small cakes and a bowl of strawberries.

"I thought you might like something while I make your breakfast," Roberto said.

Fitz was touched by the man's thoughtfulness, until he realized that the gesture wasn't for him. The cook was beaming at Bella. He waved Roberto away and pulled out Bella's chair. "It seems you have a not-so-secret admirer," he said as he shoved her chair hard into the table.

She let out an *ooft* that made him feel better as he moved to his chair and sat down. Bella had recovered quickly. She busied herself pouring him a cup of coffee. Yes, she definitely felt guilty about something, he thought. He couldn't wait to find out what. Something more than Tommy Colt?

Just the thought of her with that cowboy made him grit his teeth. His head ached with a dull constant throb. He couldn't make sense of why he felt so…sluggish.

Ronan came into the room and motioned that he

needed to speak with him. Fitz shot a look at Bella. Did she suddenly look pale? He believed she did. What now? he thought as he rose and excused himself to go speak privately with the man.

Bella sipped her coffee and tried not to act interested in whatever Ronan was telling his boss. She couldn't hear what was being said, but she saw, out of the corner of her eye, Fitz turning around to look at her.

When he came back to the table, he apologized for the interruption and sat down. He seemed even more uncoordinated than usual, as if his balance was off from the sedatives. She saw him frowning as if trying to understand what was going on.

Whatever Ronan had told him had him upset. She could feel waves of anger coming off Fitz like electrical currents. She braced herself, knowing that whatever the guard had told him, it wasn't good. She thought about her lovemaking with Tommy yesterday evening. She'd been so sure that she hadn't been followed.

Helping herself to some strawberries and one of the small cakes, she offered to dish up a plate for Fitz. He growled under his breath and shook his head, hardly taking his eyes off her. The waiting was starting to get to her. Fitz sat rigid, staring a hole into her.

"I'm sure you're upset now that the wedding will have to be postponed," Bella said as she lifted her coffee cup to her lips.

Fitz roared, slamming his hand down on the table. Dishes and silverware rattled. His coffee slopped over onto the tablecloth, making him let out yet another oath.

He threw his napkin down on the stain as he appeared to fight for control. Was this about what Ronan had told him? Maybe his father's death had hit him harder than it had first appeared. Maybe he hadn't killed Edwin. Maybe it had been suicide after all and now it was interfering with Fitz's plans. Whatever the reason, his mood was worse than anything she'd seen before.

"Roberto," he called. "Please bring me another napkin." The cook responded at once and then quickly went back to making their breakfast plates. She watched Fitz carefully wipe coffee from the side and bottom of his cup before just as carefully folding the napkin and putting it aside.

One of his guards came into the room, stopping at the end of the table. Her heart dropped as she saw what he held in his hands—her laptop computer. The man set it down and left.

She shot a look at Fitz. He had been watching for her reaction and was now smiling. Picking up his cup, he took a sip of coffee and then another. She knew that the sedatives were probably partially to blame for the man's mood—but not all of it. His face was now composed but she could see fury just beneath the surface. It wasn't just his father's death that had him so upset.

Bella tried to remain calm but as she took another sip of her coffee she had to hold the cup with both hands to hide her trembling. Had he plugged in the thumb drive around his neck and found it empty? If so, he would know that she'd switched them. In which case, he would also know that she'd drugged him last night, which would explain why he wasn't thinking clearly.

She knew he was waiting for her to ask about her laptop so she didn't. Roberto brought out their breakfasts and she dug in, even though she had to choke it down. She could feel Fitz's gaze on her as she ate and pretended that everything was fine. She could feel her pulse just below her skin thumping. How much did he know? And what would he do now?

What she'd found on the thumb drive was more than bank and business records. There had been bank account numbers and passcodes for three foreign banks. She hadn't had time to find out how much money might be in each, but she suspected the money might be more of an issue with him than her destroying his hold over her.

"We are not postponing the wedding," he said calmly. He held out his hand. She looked from it to his face, uncertain what he might want from her. "Give me your keys."

Bella instantly bristled. "I will not."

"I'm afraid you now have no choice. Your…behavior with Tommy Colt will no longer be permitted. You are *my* fiancée. As such you will no longer sneak off to have sex with another man." She started to speak but he talked over her. "You will not be allowed to leave this house until the wedding this Saturday. If that cowboy comes around, he will be shot."

"You can't hold me here," she said with more conviction than she felt and saw in his expression that he could and would keep her here. She was now his prisoner. She thought about the burner phone hidden in her car and the thumb drive in her pocket. Tommy would be waiting for her at the fire tower at ten.

"Give me your cell phone and your keys. I already have your laptop and I've had the landline disabled. I don't want to have one of my men frisk you any more than I want to have them tear your room apart, but I will."

She reached into her purse, took out her keys and her phone and set them on the table, her mind racing. She had to get the thumb drive to Tommy. She had to at least call him. It would be just like him to come to the ranch if he didn't hear from her.

"What about your father?" she asked as Fitz reached across the table and scooped up her phone and keys. She'd actually thought that he'd been close to Edwin. But then again, Fitz had been blackmailing him—just as he had her father and her. Wasn't that why Edwin killed himself? If Fitz hadn't murdered him, she reminded herself. Edwin had turned on his son. If Fitz had been the person she'd heard in the background on the phone…

"His last wish was to be cremated," Fitz said. "Given that he killed himself, I think a quiet family-only memorial after we get back from our honeymoon would be best."

She met his gaze. "But we aren't coming back from our honeymoon."

He had the good grace to redden at being caught in one of his lies. "Why would you say that?"

"Because you've already made arrangements to sell the ranch while we're gone," she said.

"We won't need it any longer," he said, defensively.

"As your wife, I'd be glad if I had a say in what happens to my family ranch," she said, refusing to cow down to this man. She would never be his wife.

Fitz laughed. "You have no say in anything. Haven't you realized that by now? I have both you and your father exactly where I want the two of you. We will be married Saturday and if you do anything to embarrass me, both of you will regret it to your dying day. Am I making myself clear?"

She swallowed. Fitz had her laptop, her phone and her keys. Unless she could get the thumb drive to Tommy, then Fitz would win. She couldn't clear her father—and the wedding was only two days away.

Chapter 22

Tommy had been waiting for word from Bella. He'd gone to the fire tower and waited an hour before returning to the office where he now paced. "She should have called by now." He hated to think what Fitz might have done if he'd caught her attempting to take the thumb drive last night. The not knowing was killing him.

"She probably couldn't get away because of Edwin's suicide," James told him. Tommy knew that could be the case. Or it could be something much worse. If Bella had the thumb drive, she would do whatever it took to get it to him.

When his cell phone rang, he jumped and quickly pulled it out, praying it was Bella. It wasn't. It was FBI agent Ian calling from back East.

"Our face recognition program identified Caroline Lansing," Ian said. "Her real name is Caroline Brooks.

She's a con woman and wanted in numerous states for fleecing rich older men. But with the information you gave us, we might be able to pick her up before she does it again."

"What about retrieving his money?"

"Sorry, he'd have to wait in line. I'm sure the money is long gone. But I doubt she was working alone. We have a lead on her. I'll let you know once we have her in custody."

"I suspect she didn't find this mark by accident," Tommy said. "If so, it would help the case I'm working on. The man's name is Edwin Fitzgerald the Third, better known as Fitz."

"You're thinking she might want to make a deal. I'll let you know."

He disconnected, feeling even more anxious. If there were a connection between Caroline and Fitz, she might implicate Fitz for a lighter sentence. Tommy held on to that hope.

Right now, he was more worried about Bella. He didn't dare call her cell. He'd already tried the burner without any luck. He didn't dare keep calling it. His only hope was that with Edwin senior dead, Fitz would delay the wedding.

Fitz was as good as his word when it came to locking her up inside the ranch house. She wasn't allowed to leave. A guard had been posted at each door—including her bedroom.

"Ronan and Miles give me the creeps," she'd told Fitz. "I don't want to see either of them outside my room. You do realize that neither of them can be trusted, don't you?"

He'd laughed at that. "Talk about the pot calling the kettle black."

She'd held her ground and had been relieved when she hadn't seen either of them around. But she'd known they were still on the ranch and that if she tried to escape, they would be the most dangerous to come across.

There was no escaping though and Fitz knew it.

"What am I supposed to do over the next two days?" she'd demanded. "Stay in my room?"

"That's a very good idea," he'd agreed. "That way I'll know you're safe."

She scoffed at that. "I won't be safe until you're out of my life and my father's."

Fitz looked hurt. "I'd hoped we were past that by now. I've asked you to marry me."

"You've blackmailed me, moved into my ranch, threatened me with armed guards and now you're holding me prisoner," she said. "Let's not pretend that you're the victim here."

"Neither are you," he snapped. "You want out?" He picked up his phone. "I'll call the auditor who will call the FBI. They've been looking for enough evidence to put your father away. When they arrest Nolan, they'll find the drugs." Fitz shrugged. "You've always had a choice, Bella. Your father was a fool. If you hate me so much, then let your father get the justice he deserves and you can walk away."

He knew she couldn't throw her father to the wolves, no matter what foolish mistakes he'd made. Fitz knew that she'd never had a choice. She had the thumb drive but unless she could get it to the authorities...

No, she'd realized that there was only one way out.

"I want to check on my flowers," she said the morning before the wedding.

"Is that really necessary?"

She stared at him. "Do I really not get any say in the wedding?"

He studied her for a moment, then relented. She could tell that he was hopeful she was accepting their upcoming nuptials. He started to pass her his phone, but then thought better of it. Getting up from the table, he went into the den and, after a few minutes, came back with her phone.

Bella knew he wouldn't let her leave the room to call the florist and was grateful when he got a call that at least took him away from the table. He didn't go far.

She hurriedly made the call. Susie Harper was a friend of hers and Bella was relieved when she answered. "It's Bella. I wanted to check on the bouquet."

Susie was silent for a moment. "The one that was ordered for you?" Before Bella could clarify, her friend said, "Tommy told me what you needed. With his help, it is ready to his specifications. Unless you want to change—"

"No," she said quickly. He must be planning to have a note inside the bouquet for her. She could tell that her friend desperately wanted to ask what was going on. "Thank you so much for doing that for me. I'll come by soon and we'll go to lunch and have a long talk."

"I hope so," Susie said, worry in her voice.

"You're a lifesaver," Bella said and hung up as Fitz cut his call short and returned to the table.

"Did you get what you wanted?" he asked.

She handed back the phone before he snatched it from her. "At least I'll have the bouquet I want."

"But not the groom," he said and cursed under his breath before saying he would be going out. "Do I have to warn you not to try to leave?"

She said nothing, just glared at him, wondering what she would find in the bouquet tomorrow.

Fitz couldn't wait for the wedding. Soon he would have everything he wanted. As it turned out, his father had done him a favor by taking his life. The man must have realized that if Bella agreed to be married to his son, someone still had to take the fall for the legal and financial problems with the partnership. If Fitz kept his promise and didn't give the Feds the books that made Nolan guilty, then he had to make it appear that Edwin senior was behind everything. His father must have come to that same conclusion.

With Edwin senior dead, it would be easier to let Nolan off the hook—unless Bella did anything to stop the wedding, Fitz thought.

But you aren't married yet, he reminded himself as he looked across the table at his fiancée later that evening. The past couple of days had been hell. If looks could kill, he'd be a molten pile of ash on the floor. She hated him.

Still he held out hope that if he kept his promise, she might come to love him. It wasn't like she had a choice. Once they were married, if she didn't come around, then he would punish her in ways she couldn't yet imagine.

That wasn't really what he wanted, though. He was in love with her—in his own way. The thought made him angry since he knew she was in love with Tommy Colt. He'd ached for this woman for years. Now, he told himself, he would have her any way he had to take her.

Just the thought of their wedding night made him shift in his chair to hide his desire for her.

In another twenty-four hours, she would be his.

"There is something I've wanted to tell you," he said. He'd hoped to tell her this when they got married, but thought maybe if she knew it might soften her feelings toward him enough that tomorrow would go smoothly.

Bella looked up at him. It was the first time he'd let her come downstairs to dine with him. Instead, he'd been sending up her meals to her room. He'd hoped being locked in her bedroom would bring her to heel. He should have known better.

But this evening, she'd looked surprised when he'd tapped on her door and invited her down to the dining room. At first, he'd seen that she'd been about to decline out of stubbornness. Clearly she'd been going a little crazy in her room for all this time.

"I wanted to talk to you about something," he'd told her, giving her a way to accept gracefully. Grudgingly she'd agreed to have their last dinner together before the wedding tomorrow at ten in the morning. He'd opted for a morning wedding because he couldn't bear waiting all day. This way they would have a brunch reception and slip away to start the honeymoon.

Roberto, of course, had made her something special for this last supper before the wedding. Bella had been polite with Roberto, thanking him and even sharing just enough small talk to have Fitz gritting his teeth. She could be so sweet to other people. To Fitz himself, she snarled like an angry dog. But he assured himself that if he had to, he'd beat that out of her.

Now she stopped eating to stare at him as if waiting patiently for whatever he had to tell her.

He took a breath, let it out slowly and smiled as he cleared his throat and said, "I fell in love with you the first time I saw you." No reaction. "Seriously, Bella, I love you." She started to speak, but he stopped her, afraid of what she might say to ruin this moment before he could finish. "I hate the way I've gone about this." He saw disbelief in her expression. "I would have loved to have simply asked you out, but I knew…" He let out a self-deprecating laugh. "With our history from childhood that you wouldn't have gone out with me."

Bella was glad she hadn't spoken in the middle of his touching speech. She saw Fitz's vulnerability unmasked in his face, in the nervous way he kneaded at his cloth napkin, in the way his eyes shone. She warned herself to step very carefully.

"I'm sorry too that this happened the way it did," she said. She couldn't very well say that she was glad he'd finally shared his feelings. She wanted to tell him all the reasons she couldn't stand the sight of him. But that too wouldn't help right now.

"I had no idea that you felt like this," Bella said, thinking of his awful threats as to what he planned to do to her once they were married. Fitz had always struck out in anger from the time he was a boy.

She knew whatever she said next could bring out that anger in him and make things worse. But she wasn't sure how to make things better without lying to him and agreeing to marry him.

"I have to wonder…" She met his gaze. She felt her heart begin to pound. Careful. "Is this how you envisioned it going?"

"I'd hoped that if we spent time together maybe…"

"It's hard to force something like this," she said.

"But in time…" He still looked as if he really believed that she would come to love him once they were married.

"What if our feelings don't change?" she asked quietly.

He tossed his blond hair back and she saw the change in his expression. "You mean what if *your* feelings don't change."

"It would only cause us both pain."

When Fitz smiled, she saw the bully he'd been as a boy and was now as a man. "I can promise it will be more painful for you."

Bella sighed and picked up her fork. Roberto had made her a special meal and she was bound and determined to do it justice. Also it was the first time she'd been out of her room.

She could feel Fitz's angry gaze on her and wondered how long it would be before he threw one of his tantrums. Fortunately, his phone rang. He let it ring three times before he shoved back his chair and stormed into the den to take the call. All she heard was him say, "I told you not to call me, Margo," before he slammed the door.

Bella looked toward the exits. Armed guards blocked both. She concentrated on her food. Tomorrow was the wedding. She'd found no way to get Tommy the thumb drive. She just hoped that whatever Tommy had put in her rose bouquet would save her.

Roberto came back to the table to see if she needed anything.

"Everything is wonderful, thank you," she said and dropped her voice. "Have you heard of anyone trying to get onto the ranch?" She saw the answer at once in his eyes. Her heart dropped and tears flooded her eyes. "Is he all right?"

The cook nodded. "I believe there was an altercation. Several of the guards needed to be patched up." He smiled then. "But when the sheriff came, the...intruder was escorted from the property."

Fitz came out of the den.

"Roberto was wondering if you needed anything else," Bella said, seeing that he suspected the two of them had been talking. The intruder would have been Tommy. She was so thankful that he was all right.

"I'm no longer hungry," Fitz snapped. "If you're finished, you should go back to your room. You need your rest. You're getting married tomorrow. I can have Ronan escort you." The threat had the exact effect he knew it would.

"I can see myself to my room." She rose and put down her napkin. "Roberto, thank you again for a lovely dinner," she called to the kitchen. With that she headed for the stairs.

Fitz followed her as far as the landing. He stood waiting as she entered her bedroom. A few moments later, she heard footfalls and then a key turned in the lock. She wanted to scream. Or at the very least cry.

But she did neither. She walked to the window and stared out at the ranch she loved, vowing she would do whatever it took tomorrow but she would never marry Fitz.

Tommy's one attempt to get onto the ranch and see Bella had been thwarted quickly. He'd known there would be guards. What he hadn't expected was to be accosted by two obvious thugs. He'd held his own in the fight even against two of them, but he was smart enough not to go back to the ranch alone.

As the wedding day had quickly approached, he'd become more concerned for Bella's safety.

"Fitz won't hurt her," James kept telling him. "He's planned this elaborate wedding and invited most of the county. If you're right and he's in love with her…he won't hurt her."

Tommy mostly agreed with James. "But we're talking Bella. She won't go through with it."

"How can she stop it?"

"That's what bothers me. I have no idea what she has planned," he said. "Fitz knows her, too. He'll be expecting her to do something. We have to stop the wedding before she does."

James sighed and nodded slowly. "You do realize that Fitz will also be expecting you to do something." He held up his hand before Tommy could argue. "I've already called Davey and Willie. They're coming in tonight. What we need is a plan."

Tommy nodded. "Whatever we do will be dangerous."

"I warned our brothers," James said. "This might surprise you, but they didn't hesitate even when I told them what we were up against."

The Colt brothers, Tommy thought as a lump formed in his throat. He'd always been able to depend on his brothers. But he'd never needed them as much as he did right now.

His cell phone rang. It was his friend with the FBI. "Tell me you have good news," Tommy said into the phone. Right now, he'd take all he could get.

"We have Caroline. She is willing to give evidence against Edwin Fitzgerald Mattson the Third, or Fitz as you both call him," Ian said. "Apparently the two had crossed paths when she'd tried to latch on to his father. Fitz told her about Nolan and gave her inside information that helped her take all of his money."

"So you're going to arrest Fitz?" Tommy couldn't contain his excitement. "Right away?"

"Probably not until Monday."

"That will be too late," he told Ian. "Is there any way you can get some agents here tomorrow? Fitz is blackmailing Nolan's daughter into marrying him in the morning."

"I can try, but I wouldn't count on it. Have you talked to the local sheriff?"

"If Fitz had found out, he'd plant drugs on Nolan as part of the frame and blackmail. Bella was trying to get the evidence. But I've been unable to get near her the past couple of days. I'm really worried about her."

Ian sighed. "Let me see what I can do."

Chapter 23

The wedding day broke clear and sunny. Fitz had one of the guards bring her the wedding dress and shoes.

"Your attendants will be arriving soon," the guard said. "Mr. Mattson suggested that one of them help you get ready."

She thought about his controlling behavior and was surprised he hadn't tried to see her before the wedding. Instead he wanted to send someone up to make sure she got ready?

"No, I can manage," she told him. Fitz had chosen her attendants, women she knew but wasn't close to. Again optics. The women were ones who would look good in the wedding photos. "Tell Mr. Mattson that I'm fine."

She'd awakened with a start this morning, heart hammering. Getting up, she'd checked to make sure she still had the thumb drive. Her fear was that Fitz would check his and realize that they'd been switched. It wouldn't take much for him to find it in her room, no matter how well she hid it. That was why she kept it on her except when she was sleeping.

Fitz had kept her from seeing Tommy before the wedding. But she wanted to make sure the thumb drive got into the right hands depending on how things went in the next hour.

She'd showered, put on her makeup and fixed her hair, gathering it up into a do on top of her head. She had to look the part. Fitz still had time to call the cops on her father. Timing was everything, she told herself, wondering how she was going to be able to stop him. Was he planning on giving her the thumb drive around his neck before the ceremony?

Or would he break his promise and still turn in her father?

At the knock on the door, Bella stepped to it. "Yes?"

"Your bouquet has arrived," a male voice informed her.

She opened the door a crack and the guard handed her the tiny white rose bouquet. She took it and closed the door. Her heart pounded. Tommy knew her, knew she would be desperate. He had put something in the bouquet, she told herself. She'd heard something in her friend's voice who owned the floral shop.

Carefully parting the roses, Bella saw something glint silver at the center hidden deep in the roses. But it was the note, the paper rolled up into a thin tube tucked in among the petals, that she pulled out and quickly read.

"This is only a last resort," the note read. "I love you, Tommy."

Heart in her throat, tears in her eyes, she reached into the bouquet and pulled out the deadly-looking slim blade. She swallowed, nodding to herself. Tommy knew her, he loved her. He knew how desperate she was or she would have been in contact with him. He'd given her a sense of power, last resort or not. She carefully slipped the blade back in between the tiny white roses.

A knock at the door. She took one last look at herself in the full-length mirror. The perfect bride about to head down the aisle to the wrong man. She dabbed at her tears, willing herself that there would be no more. She couldn't think of Tommy, not now, because just as he knew her, she knew him. He would do everything in his power to stop this wedding. She had to be strong. She had to survive this—one way or another.

Another knock. This time it was Ronan's voice she heard just outside. He would be getting impatient to walk her over to the barn where all the wedding guests were waiting. She looked down at the bouquet in her hand knowing that when the time came, she couldn't hesitate.

She checked to make sure the thumb drive was still tucked securely under her garter. Over the past few days she would have done anything to get the drive to Tommy, but Fitz had made sure that she had no way to get away—or get a message to the man she loved.

Bella still didn't know if Fitz was aware that she'd switched the thumb drives. She told herself he'd been so busy with the wedding arrangements that he probably hadn't given it a thought.

Had he known he would have torn up her room looking for it. Or maybe he would have realized she could have hidden it anywhere in the house and that he might never be able to find it.

It didn't matter now. It was too late for either of them to do anything about it. She took a breath, knowing she couldn't put this off any longer. Fitz would be worried that she might pull something before the ceremony. She'd seen all the extra guards he'd hired outside the barn. They were for Tommy Colt. Fitz was so sure he'd thought of everything and that nothing could stop this wedding.

Bella opened the door. Ronan looked upset that she was taking so long. She stepped out, moving past him, ignoring him. But she could feel him behind her. His eyes burned into her back where the fabric of her wedding dress left her bare. The man frightened her under normal circumstances and these circumstances were far from normal.

They went downstairs and walked the short distance to the barn where the wedding was being held. Vehicles were parked everywhere. She let her gaze sweep over them, taking in all the guards. Fitz had outdone himself and she suspected there would be even more on the way into the ranch—all to make sure that Tommy Colt couldn't get onto the property.

Her chest hurt at the thought of Tommy making another attempt to rescue her because if he did, she feared it would get him killed. She knew that Ronan and his friend Miles would have been ordered by Fitz to shoot to kill.

"Can't have any...trespassers on our wedding day," Fitz had said more than once over the past few days. "I'd hate to have any bloodshed. Ronan and Miles have promised to keep it at a minimum—unless necessary." The threat had been clear.

Bella thought of the blade in her bouquet. How ironic. *There would be bloodshed.*

As she and Ronan neared the barn, she heard the music and voices and spotted her attendants. They were all beautiful, slim and dressed in matching peach-colored gowns. Fitz had chosen well. Had there been photos of this wedding, they would have been quite gorgeous.

She gave the women a mere nod of her head as she stepped into the entry. The women had to be wondering why they'd been invited let alone why they weren't allowed to help the bride get ready for her big day.

Ronan moved past her to where her father was pacing nervously. He turned, looking both surprised and relieved to see her. He was dressed in a tux and looked quite handsome, she thought. He looked better than he had since she'd returned home, but he didn't meet her gaze as he came to stand next to her.

Bella stared straight ahead as she took his arm and waited as her attendants began the procession down the carpeted aisle between the seats that filled the barn to overflowing. A huge tent had been erected at the back of the house where Fitz had said the reception would be held.

He'd seemed disappointed that she hadn't wanted to see everything he'd arranged. She'd known she would never be going into the tent for the reception even before she'd seen the blade hidden in her bouquet.

"I'd rather be surprised," she'd told him. They hadn't spoken since dinner last night when Fitz had poured out his heart. She wondered if he really believed that he loved her or if it was just his excuse for what he was doing. Knowing that he was desperate for money, she figured that was more likely his true motivation.

But soon he thought he would have the ranch. With his father's death, he would have another third of the partnership. Or one hundred percent if he reneged on the deal and sent her father to prison.

He would however never have her, Bella told herself, knowing what she would do. Tommy had to have known how desperate she felt. That was why he'd seen to it that she had a way out.

Now as the attendants took their places, the aisle opening up, she saw Fitz standing next to his best man and a group of handsome tuxedoed attendants. She met his gaze. The look in those blue eyes was one of appreciation as he took her in.

But there was also relief on his face. He'd been worried that Ronan would have to drag her to the altar. That would have definitely messed up his optics.

But that was the problem, wasn't it? He knew her. He had to know that she didn't trust him to destroy any evidence that would send her father to prison. Just as he had to know that she wasn't going through with this wedding no matter what he did.

Did he really think this barn full of people would stop her? The man was a fool. He'd lied, cheated and bullied his way to this point. It wasn't going to get him what he wanted. He didn't know the first thing about love.

But Bella did. Just the thought of Tommy made her stumble a little. Her father placed his free hand on hers. She could feel him looking at her. She didn't have to see his face to know there was fear there. He didn't want to go to prison. They both knew it would be a death sentence.

But had she looked at him, she knew there would also be regret in his eyes. This wasn't what he'd wanted for his daughter. It wasn't what he'd wanted for himself. He'd lost so much, his business, his money, his only daughter. No matter how this ended, he would be a broken man.

There was nothing she could do about that, she told herself. She had to think about her own survival—and keeping her father out of prison. The thumb drive under her garter would do that—once she was arrested.

Bella tried not to think about taking Fitz's life. She despised him but not enough to kill him under any other circumstances. He'd asked for this, but that still wouldn't make it easy.

He was still staring at her. She met his gaze and suddenly he looked nervous. She almost wished he had his usual smirk on his face. It would make things much easier.

As she reached him, her maid of honor started to reach for her bouquet. She shook her head and sniffed the roses as she joined Fitz. The music stopped. There was the racket of everyone sitting down. The preacher cleared his voice. She could feel Fitz's gaze on her face as she held the bouquet close, as if she couldn't part with it.

Would he insist she hand it to her maid of honor? Would he take it from her? She couldn't allow that. Glancing up, she saw his expression and knew that the time had come.

She pretended to touch the soft petals of the baby roses. Her fingers brushed over the cool steel of the knife. She looked up at Fitz and sunk her fingers into the roses.

* * *

Fitz couldn't help being nervous as he watched his soon-to-be bride fooling with her beautiful bouquet as if she were as nervous as he was. That gave him hope that she'd accepted the marriage. Accepted him.

It had taken her so long to appear that he'd worried that she'd somehow tricked Ronan and escaped. She wouldn't have gotten far—not with all the guards he had on the property—but it would have spoiled their wedding day. That was the last thing he wanted.

While he was waiting, he'd looked over the crowd. Anyone who was anybody was here today. He felt a sense of pride that they'd all come. But that little nagging voice in his head reminded him that they had come for Bella, not for him. Everyone loved Bella, he thought and tried not to grind his teeth.

He'd been worried about Nolan showing up, but the man looked like the quintessential father of the bride in his tux. He must realize that his life was now in his soon-to-be son-in-law's hands. Fitz hadn't decided if he would let Nolan off the hook or not. That was up to Bella.

He'd met her gaze as she'd headed down the aisle toward him. He'd tried to sense what she was thinking. Her face looked serene, too serene, and that bothered him. Did she look like a woman who knew she'd been bested and wasn't going to make trouble? He could only hope, but he knew that until the pastor declared them husband and wife, he was going to be holding his breath.

When her maid of honor reached for her bouquet, Bella ignored her. Instead, she sniffed the tiny white roses before looking up at him. He'd seen something in her gaze that had threatened to loosen his bowels.

A shudder had moved through him as they'd locked eyes. His breath had caught in his throat and for an instant he'd felt…afraid. He swallowed now as he watched her fiddle with her bouquet. He tried to tell himself that she was merely nervous, something he'd never seen in her before.

He swallowed and was about to take the bouquet from her so they could get this over with when he heard a thunderous roar.

The guests heard it, too, he saw as he glanced toward the door. What in the world? He'd barely gathered his bearings when he recognized the sound. Horses. Dozens of them.

Bella would never forget the look of panic and surprise on Fitz's face as the door to the barn burst open and Tommy came riding in on a horse. The horse thundered down the aisle through the barn between the seats, coming to a rearing stop before the altar. The moment Tommy reached for her, she swung up onto the back of the horse.

The barn broke out in pandemonium as the two of them rode toward the exit door—which was now blocked by Ronan. She saw the gun in his hand and the look on his face. She could hear Fitz screaming for Ronan to shoot to kill.

She pulled the knife from the bouquet and leaned off to one side of the horse, drawing Ronan's attention. He hadn't seen the knife until she slammed it into him. Ronan's expression registered surprise as he dropped the gun and fell back. He got off one shot, but the bullet missed its mark, the report of the gunshot lost in the roar of horses and panicked screaming guests.

As she and Tommy Colt rode out of the barn, she tossed her bouquet over her shoulder. She didn't look back. The ranch yard was full of horses and riders. She recognized townspeople, neighbors, friends—who hadn't been invited to the wedding—all on horseback.

Some carried baseball bats. Others lengths of pipe. Most of the guards had backed down from what she could see. But Davy and Willie Colt were off their horses and involved in a fistfight with two of the guards.

The sound of sirens filled the air. Bella saw the sheriff and several more patrol cars roaring up the road. But Tommy didn't slow his horse as he headed into the woods at a gallop. She held on, wrapping her arms around his waist.

She looked back only once. Fitz stood in the barn doorway watching her ride away. The front of his tux was dark with what appeared to be blood. Had Fitz been hit by Ronan's stray bullet? Before she turned away, she saw him fall backward and disappear from view.

They hadn't ridden far when Tommy reined in and helped her off the horse. He swung down beside her and took her in his arms. She leaned into him and for the first time in forever let herself breathe freely.

"You're all right now," Tommy said as he loosened her hair and let it drop to her shoulders. His fingers wound into her locks as he drew her to him. She finally felt tears of relief flood her eyes as she looked into his handsome face. Of course, he'd come to her rescue. Hadn't she known in her heart that he would do whatever he had to. As she had done what she had to. Together, they were one hell of a team.

"I got the thumb drive," she whispered as she turned her face up to him.

"I never doubted it," Tommy said, grinning at her as he dropped his mouth to hers for a kiss that quickly deepened.

At the sound of someone approaching, they drew apart and turned.

"You remember Ian?" Tommy asked. "He's with the FBI."

She nodded, then lifted the skirt of her dress and slipped the thumb drive from under her garter. "I think everything you need is on it," she said, holding it out to the agent. "I hope this will help put him away." If he wasn't dead already. "At least, I hope it will clear my father."

Ian nodded as he pocketed the thumb drive. "They'll want a statement from you, probably at the Billings office."

"I'd be happy to give one," she said, surprised to hear her voice break. She'd come so close to taking Fitz's life. As it was, she'd stabbed a man. Ronan could be dead for all she knew.

Tommy put his arm around her and pulled her close. "Fitz?"

Ian nodded. "I heard he was shot. He's being taken to the hospital."

"One of his own guards I think shot him," Bella said, her legs feeling suddenly weak. She leaned into Tommy's strong body, loving the feel of his arm around her.

Everything had happened so fast. It now felt like a dream. She feared she would wake up only to find herself standing at the altar with Fitz, her fingers searching for the knife in her bouquet.

"Are you going to be all right?" the FBI agent asked.

She nodded as she looked up at Tommy's handsome,

familiar face. For so long she'd feared that she might never see him again. Or that Fitz and his guards would kill him. She smiled at the loving look in his eyes and felt her heart float up. "I'm going to be fine."

Chapter 24

The next few days were a blur of cops, FBI and visits to the hospital where her father was recovering from a heart attack.

"I'm sure the stress played a major role," the doctor told her. "But he's recovering nicely. In fact, he's determined to get out of here as soon as possible."

Bella had been surprised by how quickly he'd recovered. When she entered his room later that week, she found him sitting up in bed. The change in him was nothing short of astounding. It was as if he was his old self again.

He smiled when he saw her. "Did the doctor say when I can get out of here?"

"He's keeping you a little longer." She studied her father and shook her head. He'd been so beat down before the wedding. Now though he looked ready to pick up the pieces of his life and move on as if nothing had happened. She wished she could put the past behind her that quickly.

"You and that Colt boy were brilliant," Nolan said. "I really thought you were going to marry Fitz." He shook his head. "I should have known better." He should have, she thought as he reached for her hand and squeezed it. "You saved your old man. Strange the way things turn out. Edwin…" He let go of her hand and looked away for a moment. "The police think he really did commit suicide."

Bella had been told the same thing. Edwin was facing prison for his part in framing her father. But also he had to know that Fitz might let him take the fall for all of it. She wondered what it must have been like for him to realize that he couldn't trust his own son, and worse, that he held some responsibility for creating this monster.

"The company is mine now," her father said after a moment before he turned to look at her again. "With Edwin and Fitz gone…"

So he was no longer broke. "What will you do?"

"Rebuild it," he said without hesitation. "I did it once, I can do it again." He sounded excited about the prospect.

She wondered how much the bad publicity would hurt the business, but she figured her father wasn't worried. He liked a challenge. She told herself that he was smarter now, at least she hoped so.

"You know they caught Caroline."

He nodded and avoided her gaze. "I loved her." He shrugged. "I hadn't realized how lonely I was for female companionship. Maybe I'll find myself a nice woman.

Or not," he said with a laugh. "But you don't have to worry about me anymore."

She hoped not. If Nolan did find a woman, Bella would have Tommy do a background check, she told herself.

Her father grew quiet and for a moment he looked his age. "I'm so sorry I put you in that horrible position I did."

"It's over," she told him, putting her hand on his shoulder. He covered her hand with his own for a moment. "But you're going to have to stop calling Tommy 'that Colt boy,'" she said, smiling. "After all, he's going to be your son-in-law."

Her father smiled, no surprise in his expression. "He's perfect for you."

She laughed. "Yes, he is."

Chapter 25

Fitz opened his eyes. For a moment, he couldn't remember where he was or what had happened. A hospital. A nurse came running, followed by a doctor.

It all came back to him as he started to move, only to realize there was a handcuff attached to his left wrist and the bed frame. He closed his eyes. He could hear voices around him, but he preferred the darkness of oblivion.

He'd come so close to getting what he wanted. Bella. Just the sound of her name in his head made him wince in pain. His breathing was already shallow. His chest ached with each attempt to draw in oxygen.

He suddenly felt for the chain and thumb drive around his neck. Gone! All of his gold jewelry. He realized the doctor would have removed it once he reached the hospital. Did that mean the cops already had it?

He closed his eyes, wishing that he'd died.

At a sound, he opened his eyes to find a man standing over him. His first guess? FBI.

"I'm FBI agent Ian Brooks," the man said. "I have a few questions."

Fitz shook his head. "I have nothing to say."

"We have your thumb drive and a statement from Bella Worthington," the agent said.

"You have no right to take my thumb drive," Fitz said. "That's my private property and should be locked up downstairs with my other personal items."

"The thumb drive on the gold chain, is that what you're referring to? No, that one's blank. I'm talking about the one Bella Worthington removed from the chain you kept around your neck."

Fitz felt his insides go liquid. "That's not possible." He thought of Bella. She would have had to— Like a flash of lightning, it hit him. "I have nothing to say to you," he said to the FBI agent. "I want my lawyer. Get out of my room. Now!"

"We'll talk soon," the agent said and left.

With a curse, Fitz knew how Bella had done it. She'd drugged him. That explained why he couldn't seem to wake up with the guards pounding at his door and the phone ringing to tell him that his father was dead.

He slammed his fists into the bed he lay in. The bitch. She'd taken the thumb drive. When had she gotten it to the FBI? He couldn't believe this. He'd kill her once he got out of here.

If he got out of here.

He closed his eyes, fighting panic. He would get out of here. Bella thought she was so much smarter than him. He'd show her.

At a noise right next to his bed, his eyes flew open. He'd expected to find the FBI agent back. But instead it was a pretty young nurse.

With a shock, he saw that she had green eyes. Her hair was blond, but he could imagine her as a brunette. She looked more like Bella than Margo. She was the right age though and her body wasn't bad. He smiled at her.

"I see you're feeling better," she said.

He was feeling better. Seeing this woman, he told himself it was a sign. This wasn't over. He would beat the rap against him. He would have what he deserved. "What's your name?" he asked.

"Roberta, but everyone calls me Bobbi."

"Bobbi." He whispered her name. "I like that." He rattled the handcuff on his wrist. "This isn't comfortable. It shouldn't be on there anyway. I didn't do anything wrong." He chuckled. "They got the wrong man. But once I'm out of here, I'll clear it all up." He'd hire a good lawyer. Or the best he could afford. So much of what the cops had against him was hearsay, his word against Bella's and her crooked father's. Even what was on the thumb drive he could explain away as Nolan trying to frame him.

"In the meantime," he said to the Bella-like nurse, "if you could take off the handcuff—just so I can get some feeling back in my wrist…"

"I'm sorry, but it has to stay on except when you go for your MRI," she said, looking sympathetic. "I heard you were shot at your wedding?"

He nodded. "A terrible mistake. I can't wait to get out of this bed so I can clear it up. I was framed by a woman I thought I loved."

"I'm sorry," she said. "Now that you're better, I'm sure you can straighten it out."

"Oh, I will." He looked from her to the handcuff and then to the door. "What's the MRI for?" he asked.

"I'll let the doctor explain it to you," she said. "But don't worry."

He wasn't worried. Bella was the one who should be worried. Once he got out of here… He smiled at Bobbi and noticed she wasn't wearing a wedding ring. Not that it would have mattered. He would have her one way or another.

There was a noise out in the hallway. "I think they're ready for you," the pretty nurse said. "I'll have the officer come in now."

"Have you ever wanted to be brunette?" he asked.

She gave him a funny look but laughed. "Haven't you heard that blondes have more fun?"

Fitz chuckled. "Wait until you're a brunette and with me." Not that even this woman could satisfy his need for Bella. He would have them both. Only this time, he wasn't going to be so nice to Bella. He'd make her pay for this.

Bella looked up at the sound of a vehicle. She'd spent a few days at Tommy's cabin by the river, not wanting to go back to the ranch yet. She told herself that the bad memories of Fitz would eventually fade. Tommy and his brothers had cleared all signs of Fitz from the ranch house, he'd told her, but she was happy being with Tommy out at the cabin. It was nice on the river. It was nice feeling safe and happy. She never wanted it to end.

But she had a business to run, and she'd decided to move the operation to the ranch. She had plenty of room there. And she couldn't hide out forever. Fortunately, when she'd walked in the front door, all the good memories of the place she loved came back in a rush.

Fitz was gone and forgotten. At least for a while. She'd heard that he was recovering from his gunshot but that when he'd collapsed from the wound at the barn that day, he'd hit his head. The doctor thought there might be some internal bleeding. She felt only glad that he was out of her life and tried not to worry what would happen if he were ever released from prison.

There was enough on the thumb drive to convict him of numerous felonies. Add to that kidnapping and blackmail and all that it entailed, and he shouldn't see freedom for a long time. He would hire the best lawyer he could. He would lie. She tried not to let that make her nervous.

Now she glanced out to see Tommy drive up in his pickup. She felt a smile immediately pull at her lips. Just the sight of him made her happy. She opened the door, then froze as she saw his expression. "What is it?"

He led her over to one of the porch chairs and they sat. "It's Fitz. He was being taken to get an MRI when he apparently tried to get away from the officer guarding him. He fell and hit his head."

"Is he…"

"He died. Hemorrhaged. Nothing they could do."

She stared at Tommy for a moment before he pulled her into his arms and held her. Fitz was gone. She hated the relief she felt and reminded herself that she'd been pushed to the point that she'd wanted to kill him and might have if Tommy hadn't shown up when he did.

Fitz had been misguided and power hungry, but it seemed wrong to be so thankful that a childhood acquaintance was gone. She told herself that maybe now he was finally at peace. Because otherwise, she'd known that he wasn't finished with her. He would have come after her again. Only the next time, she might not have been able to get away.

She shuddered and Tommy held her closer.

"You're all right now," he said. "We're all right." She nodded against his chest. "It's all rainbows and sunshine from here on out."

Bella laughed and looked up at him. "Rainbows and sunshine," she said and kissed him. As long as they were together, it definitely would be.

Tommy was surprised to find all three of his brothers waiting for him at the new office a few days later. "What's going on?" he asked, sensing trouble.

"It's official," James announced and held up Tommy's framed PI license. "I thought I'd let you put it on the wall." Some of the posters and photos of the cowboys in their family were now on the walls of the ground-floor office.

Tommy took the framed license and spotted the hook next to his brother's PI license. "You left a lot of room on that wall," he commented.

"For Davey's and Willie's PI licenses," James said, and his brothers laughed.

"Who said we were quitting the rodeo?" Willie said.

Davey was quiet. When Tommy had told him that Carla Richmond down at the bank had asked about him, he'd seen how his brother had brightened. "That all she said?" Tommy had suggested that maybe Davy should stop by the bank and see her sometime. Davy had said that maybe he would. He was smiling when he said it.

"Even if I gave up the circuit, I'm not becoming a private eye," Willie said, shaking his head. "It's too dangerous. I got shot at and thrown in jail for the night before James bailed me out and all I was doing was helping you steal a bride." They all laughed.

"I guess time will tell," James said and motioned to the front of the building. "Tommy, you should check out our new sign."

He stepped out the front door and looked up. Colt Brothers Investigations. He couldn't help the sudden bump of his heart or the lump that rose to his throat. He was doing this.

Smiling, he stepped back inside. James had pulled out the blackberry brandy and the paper cups. They lifted their cups and the room suddenly grew very quiet. Tommy knew what they all were thinking about even before James made the toast.

"To Dad." His voice broke. "We haven't forgotten." They all nodded.

"We will find out the truth," Tommy said, and they all drained their cups.

Chapter 26

Bella wanted to pinch herself. She couldn't believe she was standing in front of a full-length mirror again wearing a wedding dress. This one was of her own choosing though and so were the shoes on her feet and that smile on her face was real, she thought as she winked at her reflection.

She glanced over at the woman next to her. Lorelei was also wearing a wedding dress. They grinned at each other. It had been James's idea that they have a double wedding on the Fourth of July.

"I would love that," Lori had said. "This could be fun, unless you haven't completely gotten over your last wedding."

Bella had laughed. In the time that had gone by, she'd put Fitz and what had happened behind her. The FBI had cleared her father and he was rebuilding the business and doing better than even she had hoped.

"We could get married at the ranch," Bella had offered. "Maybe an outside wedding by the river." She hadn't been anxious to have another one in the barn and she'd realized that the Colt men didn't care where they got married—as long as they did.

She smiled to herself now, remembering the day Tommy had saved her. "Marry me," he'd said as he'd dropped to one knee after Ian had left them in woods. "I love you and I should have done this a long time ago. Come on, Bella, it isn't like you aren't already dressed for it."

They'd both laughed. She'd taken his hands and pulled him to his feet. "Remember when we were really little and we would pretend to get married?"

"I didn't think you'd remember that," he'd said.

"I remember everything the two of us did growing up," she'd said, smiling. "You promised me an outdoor wedding by the river."

He'd laughed. "A promise is a promise."

"I will marry you this summer if you still want to get married. Who knows, you might decide being a PI isn't for you and go back to the rodeo. It was your first love," she'd teased.

"You're my true first love and always have been," he'd said. "I will marry you this summer by the river. In the meantime, can I put a ring on it?"

Bella had looked down at the huge diamond on her hand. She'd slipped it off without a second thought and hurled it into the pines. Tommy had shaken his head in surprise. "Some kids will be searching for treasure like we did at that age, and they'll find it in the dried pine needles," she'd said laughing. "Can you imagine it?" She'd seen that he could. "I just hope it brings them happiness."

He'd pulled her into his arms for another kiss. Then he'd opened the small velvet box he'd taken from his pocket. She hadn't needed him to get on one knee again. He'd taken the small diamond ring from the box, and she'd held out her hand. It had fit perfectly. She'd smiled down at it on her hand and then up at Tommy. "It's exactly what I wanted."

"Ready?" Whitney asked from the doorway, bringing her out of her reverie. It would be a small wedding, just family and a few friends. There would be a campfire afterward. There would be beer and hot dogs over the fire, Colt family style even though Roberto had offered to cater their weddings.

She and Tommy would be moving into the ranch after they were married and she hoped Roberto would stay on as she rehired staff both for her business and the ranch.

"I've never been more ready," Bella said now.

Whitney got tears in her eyes. "I'm going to cry. After everything you've been through to finally find the man of your dreams?" She wiped her eyes and handed Bella her bouquet. This time it was daisies, reminding her of spring and new beginnings.

Tommy and James were waiting for them at the river along with the pastor who would be performing the ceremonies. Both men were dressed in Western attire, including their best boots and Stetsons.

"Colt men," Lori whispered. "Aren't they handsome."

"Especially Willie," Whitney said, making them both laugh.

But Bella had to admit, seeing the four brothers together like this, it took her breath away.

She looked at Tommy. He had a huge smile on his face that made her laugh. She knew that they'd been heading toward this moment since they first met all those years ago. She was marrying her best friend, her lover, her future. She couldn't wait to become his wife and join his family.

"We are going to make some adorable children," she said as she and Lori walked toward the altar they'd built by the river and Tommy waiting for her.

Lori giggled. "We've already started," she whispered.

Bella grinned over at her. "Congratulations. I suspect we won't be far behind," she said as she turned to meet Tommy's gaze. She was finally coming home to the one place she'd always belonged with the cowboy who'd stolen her heart at the age of four.

* * * * *

SECRET WEAPON SPOUSE

This book is for fellow writer Marty Levine,
who was in my thoughts all the time I was in Miami.
Thanks for adding a ray of sunshine
to those otherwise drab days.

Chapter 1

Trouble. Samantha Peters knew it the moment she saw the bride-to-be. Caroline Graham looked upset but trying hard not to show it as she stepped into Samantha's office, followed by a man who was clearly not her fiancé.

"Thank you for making time to see me today," Caroline said, then seemed to remember she wasn't alone. "This is my brother, Alex."

Samantha came around her desk to shake his hand. He was tall, broad in the shoulders with light brown hair—almost blond—and intense eyes that at first she thought were blue but on closer inspection found they changed color with the light. Right now they were more green and flecked with gold.

As her hand disappeared into his large one, she found his touch dry and warm, his grip strong, self-assured.

But Samantha wouldn't have expected anything less from one of Caroline Graham's brothers.

Alex, she recalled from her research, was the fireman. In her business, Samantha made a point of knowing as much as she could about her client's family.

As she shook Alex Graham's hand she told herself he could just as easily have been the brother who ran the Graham financial empire instead of the black sheep of the family. He looked completely at home in the expensive pin-striped gray suit that fit him perfectly.

Her eyes locked with his for just an instant. He seemed distracted, his sister Caroline nervous. Samantha couldn't help but wonder why Caroline had called, insisting she had to see her—let alone why she'd brought her brother with her today instead of her fiancé.

"Please sit down," Samantha said as he released her hand. She pushed her tortoiseshell-rimmed glasses up and braced herself for the worst.

She'd been in this business long enough not to jump to conclusions let alone panic. Cool under pressure. That was Samantha Peters. Some said ice water ran through her veins. They had no idea. But if there was one asset she brought to her job as a wedding planner, it was unruffled composure. The same went for her other job—the one that took place in the hidden soundproof room upstairs over the shop.

At Weddings Your Way, Samantha was the detail person. She was the one who saw that each client's wedding came off without even the tiniest snag. It was one of the reasons she was paid the big bucks.

"Is there a problem?" Samantha asked when Caroline and Alex had taken their chairs. Normally, she would have pulled up a chair, as well, making the meeting more informal, more personal.

Today, Samantha chose to sit behind her desk. That alone should have told her something.

The thing about brides was that they often panicked for all kinds of reasons: family arguments that required a change of setting at both the wedding and reception; the loss or gain of too much weight before their final dress fitting; bridesmaids who got pregnant, broke their legs, cut their hair or dyed it a hideous color before the wedding. The list went on and on.

It was Samantha's job to pacify all parties and solve those problems if possible before the big day. She wasn't too worried even though the Graham-Wellington wedding would be one of the largest affairs Weddings Your Way would handle this year and that was saying a lot given their clientele. Also Samantha had been working on this wedding for more than six months and still had six months to go since Caroline wanted a Christmas wedding and it was only June.

"How can I help you?" she asked looking up from her desk at the bride-to-be. Caroline Graham was tall and willowy, blond and beautiful with a grace born of good genes and unlimited money.

"There might be a problem," Caroline said, fiddling with her engagement ring. Another bad sign.

Alex shifted in the plush chair provided for clients, his gaze lingering on his sister, a frown furrowing his brow.

Samantha could feel the tension in the air, a high-pitched electric inaudible buzz. He looked at Samantha as if he didn't have any more of a clue than she did.

She felt an unexpected jolt as he continued to probe her gaze for…for what? She had no idea.

She'd already pulled out the Graham-Wellington file and gone over the details after Caroline's call. But she opened it now and picked up her pen, concentrating on the checklist form in front of her to regain her balance. She had a gift when it came to hysterical brides and grooms with cold feet. She would have taken either right now. There was something about Alex Graham that she found unnerving and clearly Caroline was upset. Her instincts told her this was much more serious than wedding jitters.

"Are there some changes you would like to make?" Samantha asked looking again at the bride-to-be.

"Just one," Caroline said quietly, seeming almost embarrassed. "We'd like to move the wedding up by three months."

To her credit, Samantha didn't even blink. She told herself nothing a bride requested could surprise her at this point in her career. "Three months?"

Caroline explained that her fiancé's father wasn't in good health. They feared that if they waited he might miss the wedding. "It can't be helped under the circumstances."

Samantha flipped to her calendar. The Graham-Wellington wedding was set for the first week in December. For more than six months the date had been set, the plans made, arrangements being prepared. The kind of wedding required for the daughter of one of the wealthiest men in Florida took time. Starting from almost scratch and pulling off something of that magnitude in less than three months was impossible.

"I know it's not much time," Caroline said apologetically.

Samantha glanced at Alex. He was staring at his sister as if this was the first he'd heard of this change. Samantha shifted her gaze to Caroline, saw the set of her jaw and didn't bother to ask if this was something the bride-to-be was sure she wanted to do. Clearly it was.

"All right," Samantha said and flipped through her book. "Do you have a date in mind?"

"The first Friday in September."

September. There went the winter-white dress, the ice-blue bridesmaids dresses, as well. "Were you thinking fall colors then?" she asked calmly.

"I suppose so," Caroline said.

Samantha noted that Caroline's fingers were digging into the fine fabric of her purse now on her lap. She'd never seen the woman nervous before.

The bridesmaids had all been fitted for the dresses that were being made by an impossible-to-get Miami designer. Impossible to get, unless you were Samantha Peters and had the full power of Weddings Your Way behind her.

Maybe they could keep the original wedding dress since there was no way to get another designer original made in three months, not with the designers booked solid. Not even Samantha could pull that off.

But blue was all wrong for a fall wedding this year. That meant new dresses for the twelve bridesmaids. Each would have to be refitted for original designs. Even if Caroline might have agreed to off-the-rack bridesmaid dresses, Samantha doubted C. B. Graham would.

"A fall wedding will be much warmer," Samantha

said cheerfully. Fortunately, the wedding was to be held at the Graham estate. So a change of venue wouldn't be required. But that was only the tip of the iceberg. She pulled out a stack of new forms. "What flowers do you have in mind?" Arctic white roses were all wrong for September.

Caroline sighed. "I suppose this changes everything, doesn't it?"

For the type of wedding C. B. Graham had insisted his only daughter have? Yes, this changed everything.

As they began the arduous task again, Samantha made suggestions keeping with what was socially required of a Graham heir. She didn't bother to tell Caroline that the wedding would cost ten times as much—not to mention any money already spent on the first wedding plans was lost. Money, of course, wasn't the issue. Samantha was going to have to call in some favors to pull this one off.

Caroline looked close to tears as she made her selections for a second time. Samantha did her best to make it as painless as possible since Caroline was clearly upset.

Her brother shifted uncomfortably in his chair and said nothing, but Samantha was very aware of him.

She caught him studying his sister from time to time and couldn't help but wonder why Caroline had brought him with her today. For support? He seemed to be as confused by all this as Samantha herself. And where was Preston Wellington III, Caroline's fiancé?

But what worried Samantha was that Caroline's heart didn't seem to be in the choices she was making this time. The bride-to-be seemed more relieved than anything else when the basics has been decided and Samantha walked the two of them to the front door of

Weddings Your Way. Caroline looked a little pale and unsteady on her feet as Alex opened the door for her.

"Are you all right?" Samantha heard him say. She didn't catch Caroline's reply as the door closed, but she watched the two of them from the large glass doors as they started down the long flower-and-palm-lined walk to the street. Samantha couldn't shake the feeling that Caroline was anything but all right.

Alex Graham was thinking the same thing as he and his sister stepped out into the Miami heat, Caroline in the lead.

She's in some kind of trouble.

The thought came out of nowhere and had no real basis. Sure it was unusual that Caroline had changed her wedding date, maybe especially this late. But things happened.

No, what was really odd and unnerving was the fact that she'd called him out of the blue and asked him to meet her at the wedding planner's today. For years he'd been on the outs with his family, Caroline included.

Caroline was the baby girl of his blue-blooded family. It didn't help that their mother had died shortly after she was born. Or that C. B. Graham had tried to make up for it by giving Caroline any and everything she wanted.

Caroline, or the little princess as Alex called her, had been spoiled and difficult. For years he'd avoided her as well as his father and brother, telling himself it was no big loss.

In truth, his family avoided him probably more than the other way around. He'd been the black sheep ever since he refused to attend an Ivy League college—and then had the audacity to become a fireman.

His father, C.B., was an overachiever who swore that the bottom line was always money. Fortunately for C.B., his firstborn, Brian, had followed in his footsteps attending the old man's alma mater and going into the family investments business.

C.B. had almost disowned Alex when he'd gone to a state college and then become a Miami fireman. Needless to say, they still didn't get along. In fact, his father had nothing but contempt for Alex's choices and did little to hide it.

"Caroline?" Alex called after his sister as she walked ahead of him. The afternoon sun hung over the brightly painted buildings along the street, the day uncomfortably hot and humid. It was only June. He hated to think what August would be like. Palm fronds rustled in the hot breeze off Biscayne Bay. Somewhere in the distance came the screech of tires, the blare of a horn. Had she not heard him?

"Caroline?" She'd said little since he'd met her here and he wasn't going to let her get away until they talked. Really talked, something his family avoided at all costs.

She'd stopped and seemed to be leaning against a wrought-iron bench as if she felt ill.

Alex caught up to his sister and saw that she was flushed and appeared close to tears. He took her arm. "Hey, are you all right? You don't look so good. What's going on?"

He couldn't shake the feeling that his sister asked him here today to confide something in him—and changed her mind.

"I told you, I'm fine," she snapped, pulling free. "I

just need to get to the car and sit down for a minute. The heat." She blew out a breath and fanned herself, stepping away to head for her car and driver waiting at the curb. "I'll call you later," she said over her shoulder, her pace increasing as if she couldn't wait to get away from him. "Thank you for meeting me here."

Alex swore under his breath, wondering what he'd done. Nothing. They hadn't even spoken two words from the time he'd met her in the Weddings Your Way lobby. It wasn't him this time, he told himself. She was upset about something else. Being forced to change the date of the wedding?

He saw her look around as if she'd been expecting someone. Her fiancé?

Where was he anyway? Why hadn't he met Caroline here? Alex had the feeling she'd been expecting him. Maybe that's what had her upset—the fact that he hadn't showed.

Alex had yet to meet his sister's soon-to-be husband but he already disliked him based simply on the man's name: Preston Wellington III. He, no doubt, was a clone of their brother, Brian, which meant that once Caroline married him she would be spending most of her life never seeing him. Just as they had hardly ever seen their father. He was always too busy making more money to spend any time with them. Alex couldn't bear to think what his sister's life would be like. He'd wanted more for her.

He sighed and started after her, hoping he could change her mind about leaving. Maybe they could go somewhere, have a cool drink, talk.

Out of the corner of his eye, he noticed a white limo pull up to the curb behind his sister's car. He slowed, thinking it was probably the missing Preston Wellington III.

The driver got out to open the rear door. An attractive dark-haired young woman stepped out onto the curb. Caroline had stopped as if she also thought the limo contained someone she knew.

And then everything happened too fast. At first Alex heard rather than saw the commotion that ensued. He turned as a black limo pulled up behind the white one. Two men leaped from the rear doors. They grabbed the woman who'd just exited the limo in front of them. Her driver tried to fight them off but was knocked to the ground as they dragged the woman to the open doors of the black limo.

Alex charged across the lawn toward the two men who'd shoved the woman into the backseat of the waiting black limo and jumped in after her. The limo engine roared, then to Alex's horror, the large black car jumped the curb as if aiming directly for the woman's limo driver who was still on the ground.

The driver managed to roll out of the way as the limo shot toward Alex. He yelled to Caroline as he dived aside, hitting the ground and rolling, coming up in time to see that the speeding car had turned and was aimed directly at his sister.

Caroline seemed frozen to the spot. He let out a howl of anguish as he heard the limo hit her, her body flying off to the side.

The dark limo had no rear license plate and the windows were too tinted to see inside as it crashed between two cars at the curb and sped off down the street. Everything had happened so fast, he didn't even get a good look at the two men who'd taken the woman.

"Caroline. Oh God, Caroline." Alex was on his feet, running to where she was slumped on the grass. He dropped to the ground next to his sister and felt for a pulse with one hand as he fumbled out his cell phone and dialed 911 with the other. "Oh, Caroline," he whispered as he brushed her hair back from her beautiful face.

He felt a hand on his shoulder but it wasn't until later that he recalled the feel of the woman's touch, let alone remembered her name. Samantha Peters.

Inside the speeding black limo, the man in the back made the call. "We've got the girl," he said when the phone was picked up at the other end.

There was no reply. Just a soft click. In the backseat Sonya Botero's eyes fluttered.

"Give her more of the drug," the man ordered. "I don't want her waking up."

He leaned back and closed his eyes. The job hadn't come off as clean as he'd planned. Unfortunately, he'd left loose ends, he thought glancing back.

Craig Johnson sat on the grass in front of Weddings Your Way and watched the black limo disappear down the street, tires squealing and engine roaring.

The limo driver-bodyguard was too shocked to move. The blow to his head had left him dazed but not so dazed that he didn't realize what had just happened.

The men had taken the woman he'd been hired to protect and there would be hell to pay.

But what was utmost in his mind was one startling realization: the men had tried to *kill* him. If he hadn't rolled out of the way when he had...

Suddenly he couldn't catch his breath at just the thought of how close it had been. He gasped, the weight of the knowledge like a weight on his chest.

He was glad that no one was paying any attention to him now. They'd all crowded around a woman on the ground a dozen yards from him and he realized that unlike him, she'd been hit by the car.

He felt light-headed, his stomach weak and queasy. That could be him over there on the ground.

He tried to get up but his legs wouldn't hold him. Sitting back down heavily on the ground, he watched people rushing around, calling for help. More people were running over. He heard voices above him asking if he was all right. Did he need an ambulance?

He was shaking so hard he couldn't answer. He closed his eyes and lay back on the ground, lucky to be alive. But for how long?

Chapter 2

Samantha Peters pushed her tortoiseshell-rimmed glasses up as she sat at her usual spot at the table in the soundproof room on the second floor of Weddings Your Way, watching the monitors on the wall.

The police had left hours ago. Now the only illumination came from the security lights that bathed the long palm-lined entry into the shop.

Weddings Your Way had been in an uproar all afternoon and evening. No one could believe that Sonya Botero had been abducted right out front and client Caroline Graham had been injured in the hit-and-run that followed.

"We are prepared for a ransom demand," Rachel Brennan was saying now to the elite group of undercover agents positioned around the table. "Everything is in place. Since the abduction took place here, the kidnappers might contact us first. If it *is* a kidnapping."

Samantha found herself only half listening as she watched the monitors that provided surveillance. She focused on the two that covered the front of the building.

"I've heard from Sonya's father as well as her fiancé," Rachel was saying. "Both are flying in tomorrow. Both will demand answers. Let's do our best to have some for them."

The air conditioner hummed in the large room devoid of windows. One end was a wall of computers and electronics. This was the command center, the heart of the true operation with Weddings Your Way being the front. Not that each agent didn't perform wedding-related duties, living and working in the community while working undercover as part of the Miami Confidential team.

Rachel Brennan, tall, ebony-haired with sparkling blue eyes, in her early forties, was head of the elite group.

"I've looked at the surveillance tapes," Rachel said. "The men knew about the cameras. They were careful to keep their heads down, faces in shadow. It was all very well planned and executed. We can't rule out that Sonya's abduction is connected with the recent assassination attempt on her fiancé."

"So are we assuming this is politically motivated?" Sophie Brooks asked. Sophie, tall, willowy with long blond hair, had been sketching on a pad in front of her and now looked up. Along with being an agent, she was also Weddings Your Way's invitation designer.

"It *has* to be connected to politics," Julia Garcia said in a quiet voice at the end of the table. Julia was friends with Sonya when they were young and now worked as a seamstress for the wedding shop along with being an agent. "When you're about to marry a politician from Ladera who has been making war on drug dealers throughout South America, you can't help but be a target."

The room fell silent for a long moment. Samantha continued to watch the monitors, the tragic events of the day weighing heavily on her. She knew what she was waiting for. Her instincts told her it wouldn't be long now.

"Any word on the condition of Caroline Graham?" Isabelle Rush asked. The agent was small with shoulder-length strawberry blond hair and light brown eyes. She'd been handpicked for the Miami Confidential team as an expert in criminology.

"Still unconscious," Samantha said without looking from the monitors. "The doctors aren't sure she's going to make it."

"Is it possible she was a target, as well?" Isabelle asked.

Samantha recalled how the car had careened up onto the curb, just missing the limo driver and Alex Graham but hitting Caroline. "I don't see how. Caroline didn't even have an appointment. I had to fit her in at the last minute so no one could have known she was coming here."

"Maybe," Rachel said and turned to Clare Myers, who was sitting at one of the computers. "Let's not take any chances. Find out everything you can on both. Did Sonya and Caroline know each other? I want to know if there is even the remotest connection between them."

"I'm on it," Clare said tapping at the keys. The small pixie-ish blond woman had a sharp mind and worked for the IRS investigating corporations trying to rip off the government before she was enlisted by Miami Confidential to work as the accountant for the wedding shop as well as use her expertise on digging up anything on anyone via the computer.

"What about Botero's limo driver?" Rachel asked, checking her notes. "Craig Johnson?"

"He was admitted to the hospital complaining of headaches," Isabelle said. "The police questioned him after he was admitted. Johnson said he didn't remember anything after being struck on the head by one of the men."

"Could be lying," Julia said. "But it also could have happened so fast he really didn't get a good look at his attacker."

Isabelle shook her head. "I think one of us should go by and see how he's doing, see what our take on Mr. Johnson is. After all, he was hired as Sonya's bodyguard as well as her driver."

"I'll pay him a visit," Samantha said. "I want to go to the hospital and check on Caroline Graham anyway."

Rachel nodded her approval. "I'm sure the police questioned Caroline's brother. Alex, right?"

Samantha nodded and looked to Isabelle.

"He told police he only got a glimpse of the men," Isabelle said. "The car had no plates on the back and tinted windows."

"Check limo rentals," Rachel said. "It's a long shot."

"I saw the car," Samantha said and felt everyone look toward her again. "I saw some of the incident from the window after I walked Caroline and Alex to the door. You're right. It happened so fast there wasn't anything anyone could have done. I got a good look at the limo, though. It was an older model. Definitely not a rental. You might want to check used car lots."

Rachel gave her a smile. "Good idea." She looked toward Clare who said, "I'm already on it."

Samantha saw movement on the monitors. Just as she'd been expecting, a dark figure started to bang on the door, then saw the receptionist Samantha had asked to stay late. He shoved his way through the front door and into the reception area.

Samantha stood. "Excuse me, but Alex Graham is here. I need to take care of this."

As a former agent and profiler for the FBI, Samantha was the go-to person. Not only did she make sure every wedding went off without a hitch, as an agent she assisted in investigations by noticing the little things about people and cases.

As she rose to leave, everyone's attention turned to the monitor, the same one that had recorded Alex Graham's entrance earlier today. Only now Alex was dressed in jeans, a Miami Fire Department T-shirt that stretched across his broad shoulders and running shoes. His light brown hair curled at the nape of his suntanned neck and looked as if he'd just come from a hasty shower.

"At this point, I don't think it would be wise to assume that Caroline Graham was just an innocent victim," Rachel said. "Find out everything you can about her. And her brother," she said frowning at the monitor screen. "It might not be a coincidence that the two of them just happened to be here at the same time Sonya Botero was abducted."

Samantha nodded and slipped out. She'd known Alex Graham would be back. And she knew even before she'd seen him storm in what he would want.

As she descended the stairs, she caught the scent

of him before he saw her. Some kind of masculine-smelling shampoo. Fresh from a quick shower, just as she'd suspected. She noted that his hazel eyes were red rimmed and he looked as if he'd been to hell and back. As she neared him, she felt anguish coming off him as well as a raw angry energy. She braced herself.

Alex Graham looked up as she came down the stairs to meet him. His eyes locked with hers and she thought she glimpsed relief. "I wasn't sure you'd still be here."

"Mr. Graham, why don't we step into my office?" Samantha said in her all-business voice.

He gave a sharp nod and stalked ahead of her into her office. She closed the door behind them and took her place behind the desk.

"How is your sister?" she asked, although she'd called the hospital not long before.

"Still unconscious," he said his voice hoarse.

To think that he'd sat in that same chair with his sister beside him only hours before. Except then he'd been ill at ease, nervous.

Now Alex Graham was grieving and angry. "What the hell happened here today?" he demanded.

"You know as much as I do," Samantha said quietly as she adjusted her glasses.

"I highly doubt that. Who was that woman in the limo?"

"One of our clients," Samantha said. "I'm afraid I can't tell you her name because the police have instructed us not to."

A muscle in his jaw bunched. He was furious and looking for someone to blame for his sister's accident, but also looking for answers. Samantha wished she had some for him.

"I'm already getting the same runaround from the police, I don't need it from you," he said, his voice rising. "I want to know why my sister was run down outside your business."

She nodded and spoke in the same soothing tone she used with jittery brides-to-be. "We want to know the same thing, Mr. Graham."

"Alex. Mr. Graham is my father." He raked his fingers through his already tousled hair. "My sister may not make it." His voice broke. "I can't reach her fiancé. You know a hell of a lot more than I do. Are you going to help me or not?"

She felt a shiver as she glimpsed the raw pain in his gaze. This man was angry and hurting but he was no fool. He wasn't going to be put off by sympathy and reassuring words. Maybe the hit-and-run had just been an unfortunate accident. But what if for some reason Caroline Graham *had* been a target?

"I'm going to help you."

Alex Graham leaned back in the chair, all his anger spent. He needed to calm down, to sleep, to eat, but more importantly he needed answers. "Thank you."

She nodded and he found himself settling down a little. She had that kind of effect on people, he thought, remembering how she was with Caroline earlier that day.

He studied her, trying to put his finger on what it was about her that bothered him. She was rail-thin, with huge brown eyes and straight brown hair that fell almost to her shoulders. She peered at him through tortoiseshell glasses. A quiet, unassuming woman, the kind who blended in with the wallpaper.

At least that's what she wanted him to believe.

Where had that thought come from? He met her steady gaze and felt both sympathy and compassion and true concern. And yet as he looked into her eyes, he had the distinct impression that there was more to her, something she didn't want him to see.

"How can I help you?" she asked.

He took a breath. "Let me be honest with you, Miss Peters. It is Miss, right?" Was there a slight flush under the cool porcelain of her skin? "I have never met Caroline's fiancé and quite frankly, I don't even know how to reach him."

"I have a number for him," she said taking a fabric-covered book from her desk drawer. From where he sat, he could see that the contents of the drawer were as neat as the writing in the book.

He watched her turn right to the page.

"Preston Wellington III," she said picking up a pen and printing the number on a Post-it in the same concise handwriting. She tore off the note and handed it to him, closing the book and crossing her arms over it.

He stared at the number for a moment, then at her. "You already tried to call him, didn't you?"

"Yes."

"And you weren't able to reach him."

"I'm afraid not."

He nodded, suspecting he wasn't going to get much help here, either. "And this is the only number you have for him, right?"

"Yes."

"I've tried it, as well, with the same results." He sighed. "Have you met him?"

She nodded. "He always came with Caroline for her appointments."

"Except today?" he asked, sounding surprised.

"Yes."

"And your impression of him?" He saw her hesitate. "I realize I'm putting you on the spot here, but I need to know what I'm up against. I'm worried sick about my sister. Don't you think it was more than odd that the only day her fiancé didn't come with her she changed her wedding plans and then was struck down out front?" He saw something in her eyes that confirmed she, too, thought it odd. "Now no one seems to be able to reach him…. I need to know your impression of him."

She nodded slowly. "I liked him. He seemed very nice, very attentive to your sister. I felt the two of them were very much in love, they seemed to be… soul mates."

He heard the small catch in her throat, not sure what surprised him more—her obvious emotional reaction to witnessing what she'd thought was true love or that his sister and this Wellington III might really share something real.

Was it possible he was wrong about the guy? "Would you mind trying the number again for me?" Maybe they would get lucky.

"Certainly." She picked up the phone and dialed the number from memory, then handed him the phone.

With each ring, his uneasiness grew. He got Preston's voice mail again but didn't leave another message. He handed the phone back to her. "He hasn't returned any of my calls or contacted the hospital. Don't you think that's odd?"

She didn't comment.

He raked a hand through his hair in frustration. What was he doing here? What had made him think this wedding planner could help him? Maybe she really didn't know any more than he did.

But she had met Preston Wellington III, she'd thought the man was in love with Caroline. Then again, maybe she thought all her clients were in love. Maybe the woman was a hopeless romantic.

He looked into her brown eyes, eyes the color of Cognac. But behind all that rich warmth was something steely. This woman was no hopeless romantic. There was intelligence there and something else—a wariness that made him wonder if she knew a whole lot more that she wasn't telling him.

"I found another number for Wellington in Caroline's purse and called it," he said, watching for her reaction. "It was his office supposedly. I was told he was out of the country and couldn't be reached. Apparently they don't know when he'll be back." He saw surprise and something else register in her expression: doubt. Finally.

He felt relieved, needing someone else to confirm that his fears might be justified. He recalled the feel of her hand on his shoulder earlier today when he'd been kneeling over his sister's body.

"Thanks, Miss... Could I possibly call you something besides, Miss Peters?"

She seemed to hesitate. "Samantha."

"Thank you." One barrier down, he thought studying her. He couldn't shake the feeling that she was hiding something from him. If it had anything to do with his sister's hit-and-run, he would find out what it was. One way or another. "Samantha, if you're serious about helping me, then you will come with me now."

* * *

"Come with you?" Samantha hadn't been able to hide her surprise. He'd caught her off guard. She'd known he would come back tonight. He was the kind of man who would demand answers and not give up until he got them.

But she worked behind the scenes at Weddings Your Way as an agent. And that's the way she liked it.

"Go where?" she asked.

"I have the keys to my sister's condo and I found what I believe is her new address," he said, sounding almost embarrassed. Obviously he hadn't known where his sister now lived.

He sighed and leaned forward, elbows on his knees as he scrubbed his hands over his face. "I can't go over there by myself."

Samantha swallowed, hearing again the raw pain in his voice, and had she been closer she would have placed a hand on his arm and tried to reassure him. But this wasn't some groom having second thoughts. This was a man whose sister was lying unconscious in a hospital room, possibly dying, a man who was more than a little suspicious not only of Weddings Your Way and why his sister's accident had happened out front—but of Samantha Peters as well.

Samantha had shielded herself from this kind of pain, this kind of intimacy. It was why, after completing her training with the FBI she'd taken the job Rachel had offered her. Samantha wanted to work behind the scene. She didn't want to get close to the victims—let alone the killers.

"I know what I'm asking is an imposition," Alex

said not looking at her. "But I can't face it alone. I think Preston has been living with her," he continued before she could say anything. "There might be some clue as to where he is at Caroline's place. Or a number or address that would give me an idea how to reach his family. Something."

"Caroline's friends don't know?" The moment she asked, she realized how foolish the question had been.

He raised his head and met her gaze. "Frankly, I don't know any of her friends. Before yesterday, I hadn't seen Caroline in months."

"And the rest of your family couldn't help?"

His smile held no humor. "My father thinks my concern is premature. He insists that he has left a message for Preston and expects to hear from him soon. He's convinced there is no problem."

"Maybe that's the case."

But clearly Alex didn't believe it. Samantha had to admit she was starting to have doubts, as well. It had been hours since the accident. Preston should have checked his messages and called by now.

"You think something has happened to him?" she asked. She'd feared Sonya's abduction was much bigger in scope than any of them suspected.

"That's just it, I don't know what to think," Alex said. "You saw my sister earlier today. She seem upset to you?" He nodded as if he already knew the answer.

"Something was wrong," he continued. "And I haven't the slightest idea what it was. All I know is that my sister asked me to meet her here today. So where was her fiancé? My sister is fighting for her life and needs him and yet no one can reach him. Don't tell me that doesn't make you wonder. I have to find this Preston Wellington III and satisfy myself that this guy is on the up-and-up." He rose to his feet.

She had no choice but to go with him even though every instinct told her to watch herself closely. She'd seen the way Alex had been studying her. He was suspicious. Which was only natural under the circumstances.

But she had reason to be suspicious of him as well. All she had was his word that Caroline had told him to meet her here today.

Even if Alex Graham was telling the truth, he unnerved her, threw her off balance and made her feel exposed. And that made him dangerous. She would have to be very careful around him.

She pushed out of her chair and reached for her purse, remembering that her gun wasn't in it. "Just give me a minute."

Chapter 3

Samantha was seldom surprised by a man. But Alex, she realized, could turn out to be the exception. He led her to an older model pickup parked at the curb. That didn't surprise her as much as the music that came on when he started the truck.

Country western. He grinned and turned it down. "I'm a big Willie Nelson fan," he said almost apologetically.

There was something so refreshing about Alex—and at the same time, she didn't dare relax around him. Her instincts told her he was trying to get her to lower her guard around him. And she had to wonder why.

The cab of the pickup felt too confined, too intimate. And she was too acutely aware of the man behind the wheel.

Alex, though, seemed relaxed as if relieved to have

her with him. Because he thought she was doing this out of the kindness of her heart? Or like her, did he have his own agenda?

She hadn't been paying much attention to where he was driving. He had large hands and he held the wheel like a man who enjoyed driving and drove well.

It wasn't until he pulled to the curb and let out an oath that she looked around.

He had stopped in front of an old five-story building on the edge of an area of the city that had gone to seed long ago. "This can't be right," he said handing the address to Samantha.

"It's the address you have written here," she said, equally surprised. The neighborhood had a deserted feel to it and had for blocks. "It looks like some sort of renewal project."

"My sister can't possibly live here."

A set of headlights flashed behind them, followed by the single whoop of a siren and the flash of blue from a light bar. Samantha looked in her rearview mirror as a patrol car pulled up behind them. Not a cop car but a private security company.

"I'll handle this," Alex said and climbed out to walk back as a uniformed man exited the patrol car.

"Wait—" But her words were lost as the door closed. She picked up her purse from the floorboard, slipping her hand in to close her fingers around the grip of the gun she'd brought as she watched the two in the side mirror.

She waited, reading their body language, one hand on the gun, the other on the door handle. She didn't like the looks of the neighborhood and she knew some of the types who filled security cop openings. This one was late middle age, Hispanic and looked harmless enough.

She saw the security guard point in the direction of the building with the address Alex had found for Caroline.

A moment later, Alex started toward her. The guard climbed back into his patrol car, but didn't leave.

She released her hold on the gun and put her purse back down as Alex opened his door and leaned in.

"You're right about this being a renewal project," he said. "It seems my sister owns it and is its first resident. She lives on the top floor of this building."

He looked as skeptical as Samantha felt. Why would Caroline Graham live here when she could afford to live anywhere? There had to be a mistake.

Alex shut the car door and came around to open hers. As she got out, she looked back at the security guard still sitting in his car behind them. She could see his face under the streetlight and she knew he could see hers, as well.

She gave him a small smile and a nod. The guard would remember her if she needed to come back here.

Alex used one of the keys on the ring he said he'd found in his sister's purse at the hospital and braved the elevator although it appeared to be new and in good condition. It hummed up to the fifth floor and opened.

"What the hell?" Alex said beside her.

Samantha was equally surprised to find the hallway under construction. The location was questionable although she suspected it would have a great view of the Atlantic and was on the edge of an area that was obviously seeing some positive changes. But this place didn't appear to be finished.

"I don't believe this." Alex shook his head and didn't step out of the elevator for a moment as if only more convinced he had the wrong place. "Caroline can't be *living* here."

Apparently she was. At least according to the address Alex had found. And what the security guard had told him.

"Seems to be undergoing a renovation," Samantha said following him as he finally stepped off the elevator into the unfinished hallway.

He shot her a disbelieving look. "The Caroline I know—or knew anyway—wouldn't be caught dead living under these kinds of conditions." He realized what he'd said and grimaced. "It's just that she's always demanded the best that money could buy and had enough money that she never had to compromise."

"I'm sure there is an explanation," Samantha said as she watched Alex try several keys before the knob turned and the door swung open.

From what she could see, most of the condo was walled off behind large sheets of plastic with work being done behind them. "Maybe she saw it as a good investment. Investing does run in your family, right?"

Alex shot her a smile. "If you're trying to make me feel better, it's working."

She pushed aside a corner of the plastic into what was the living room and adjoining kitchen. There was new Sheetrock on the walls and new tile on the counters and backsplash in the kitchen. But the cupboards were still missing and there was Sheetrock dust everywhere.

In fact, Samantha could see tracks in the thick white dust on the floor. Alex might be feeling better about all this, but she wasn't.

Something was wrong here. She just didn't know what yet.

She followed Alex as he pushed aside another plastic area and opened a door on the right. The master suite and bath—and obviously the first rooms completed because it appeared someone had been living in there. There was carpet on the floor, the rooms were furnished and several items of discarded clothing lay across the foot of the crumpled sheets and duvet on the large unmade bed.

Samantha spotted two champagne glasses and an empty bottle on one of the nightstands. She itched to collect both for prints but couldn't in front of Alex without making him suspicious. Wedding planners usually didn't run fingerprints as a sideline.

She would have to come back for them.

Alex had hoped he'd find something in his sister's condo that would convince him he had nothing to worry about when it came to his sister's fiancé. But coming here had done just the opposite.

What the hell was going on with Caroline?

"Well, this was a mistake," he said and noticed the way Samantha moved to the closet but was careful not to touch anything as if this was a crime scene.

Is that what she suspected? he wondered with a jolt. That Caroline's hit-and-run wasn't an accident?

She seemed to scan the clothing inside as if looking for something in particular.

"I'm telling you my sister can't be staying here," he said. "Look, when I asked my father, he said that she was in the process of moving and had most of her stuff stored at the house."

"Isn't this her clothing?"

He glanced into the closet. While the walk-in closet wasn't overflowing with clothing so it couldn't be Caroline's—at least not yet—there were enough items to make it clear that someone had been staying here.

That's when he noticed a purse on the top shelf with an odd-print scarf tied to the strap.

"That's hers," he said. "I saw her with it one day uptown." He didn't mention that he'd ducked in a store to avoid talking to her. It had to be hers. He remembered the unusual scarf.

"I smell her perfume on some of the clothing," Samantha said from inside the closet. "I also recognize one of the dresses she wore at an appointment I had with her."

Her movements were slow, purposeful. He found himself watching her rather than looking for evidence of Preston Wellington III in the condo.

At first glance, Samantha Peters wasn't the type of woman a man would even notice. Hell, he wouldn't have given her a second glance under other circumstances. It was the way she dressed, he realized with a jolt.

Not that he knew anything about women's clothing, but even he could see that the suit she wore was too large for her slim, small frame, the cut all wrong. She wore it like armor, as if protecting herself, he thought with surprise.

And her hair. It was colored too dark for her pale skin and cut shoulder length, long enough that it often covered part of her face.

And those tortoiseshell glasses. The frames took away from the gold in her brown eyes.

He frowned, wondering why she dressed like that.

The woman was too savvy for it to be anything but a calculated choice. Almost as if she was hiding from something, he thought, even more intrigued.

He realized she was looking intently at one of the men's shirts hanging in the closet. "What is it?"

She let go of the sleeve. "Nothing."

Like hell. As she came out, he slipped past her to reach for the shirt, wondering what she wasn't telling him. Was she trying to protect him? Why else wouldn't she tell him?

One glance at the shirt and he saw it was old, looked more like it might belong to one of the construction workers. "Her fiancé left behind only his old clothes, nothing he would bother to come back for. Is that it?"

She turned from where she had stopped midway into the room. "None of this proves anything."

"You still want to believe this guy really loves my sister and isn't just using her, don't you? I admire your optimism," he said as he joined her in the middle of the large room. "I guess optimism is something you have to have in your line of work given the divorce rate, but I've got to tell you, I don't like any of this." He glanced around the room. "What the hell is Caroline doing here? You've seen her more than I have the last six months. Doesn't this strike you as odd?"

Samantha seemed to hesitate. "A little. Maybe."

He looked at her and shook his head, unable not to smile. He actually did admire her for holding out hope that Preston Wellington III was a good guy with good intentions.

"Earlier today I had the feeling that Caroline wanted to tell me something and that's why she asked me to meet her at your office."

"You had no idea what it was?" she asked.

He shook his head. "But I can think of only one reason my sister would be living like this. She's broke. What if her fiancé has taken all of her money and skipped out on her and that's what she was going to tell me today?"

Samantha frowned. "But why go to the trouble of moving the wedding up three months if that's the case?"

"Hell, I don't know. Maybe she thought she could save the relationship by getting him to the altar sooner."

"Wouldn't she just elope if that were the case?"

He laughed at that. "My father would cut her off without a cent of her inheritance if she did. No, she has to go through with the big wedding. It's required of the only daughter of C. B. Graham and she knows that."

"They were celebrating *something*," Samantha said as she nodded toward an empty champagne bottle and two glasses on a nightstand beside the bed.

He'd been so upset over everything he hadn't even noticed them until now. What would Caroline and Preston have had to celebrate? "He was probably just saying goodbye and she didn't know it," Alex said as he moved closer, noticing the lipstick on the rim of one glass and feeling a horrible sinking feeling as he imagined maybe one of his sister's last happy moments.

That's when he saw it.

He let out a curse.

"Nonalcoholic champagne?" Turning, he stalked into the bathroom where he found what he was looking for in the small wastebasket beside the commode.

"Holy hell, Caroline's *pregnant*," he said as he came out of the bathroom and saw Samantha Peters's expression.

She didn't look the least bit surprised and he realized she'd already figured it out and was way ahead of him.

Hell, he had the feeling she was way ahead of him on a lot of things.

Samantha saw all the color suddenly drain from Alex's face.

He grabbed for his cell phone, panic in his expression. "*No!* The accident today." He hurriedly tapped in a set of numbers. "Oh, no."

Samantha went into the unfinished living room while he called the hospital. She stepped through a break in the plastic and opened one of the windows, needing fresh air as she said a short prayer for Caroline's baby.

She caught movement from the dark shadows of a building across the street. Someone had been standing there looking up at Caroline's building. The security guard? She couldn't be sure. But why wouldn't he just wait in his car on the street? Unless he needed to relieve himself and couldn't leave the area until his shift was over.

Behind her she heard the rustle of plastic and said another silent prayer before turning. Alex pulled aside the plastic and stepped through into the dimly lit unfinished room.

She held her breath, afraid.

The confirmation of a pregnancy explained a lot—the change in the wedding plans, the way Caroline had looked yesterday, pale and shaky in Samantha's office—and, unfortunately, possibly the missing fiancé.

"I just talked to the doctor. The baby's okay," he said, breathless and scared but looking relieved."

Samantha released the breath she'd been holding and

smiled at him, surprised by the tears that misted her eyes. "I'm so glad."

He nodded and pushed aside the plastic again so they could step back into the bedroom out of the construction area. She watched him move to the middle of the room, his back to her, as if he didn't know where to go or what to do next. She knew the feeling.

After a moment, he faced her again and she saw that he was angry. "You *knew* she was pregnant."

"I suspected," she admitted. "She wouldn't be the first bride to move her wedding up because of a pregnancy."

His expression softened. "Sorry. I just feel like everyone is keeping things from me, you know?"

She knew.

He raked his hand through his hair, making him look all that much more vulnerable—and irresistible.

The stab of desire took her by surprise. Her first in a long, long time. She smothered it the way she would have a flickering candle. But unlike a candle flame, this still burned, a slow smoldering burn inside her that never let her quite forget.

"I have to admit, when she moved the wedding up three months, I *did* wonder," he said and lowered himself onto the edge of the bed, then seemed to think better of it and shot back up. "Come on, let's get out of here."

She glanced back at the champagne glasses and bottle. She would come back. It would be fairly easy given that there was no security system installed in the condo yet and she'd made a point of letting the security guard see her—not that she planned to get caught when she returned.

Looking up, she felt a jolt as she saw that Alex Graham was watching her, frowning slightly—almost as if he could see beneath her oversize suits, the glasses, the dyed hair to the woman she tried so hard to hide.

Chapter 4

Alex seemed lost in thought as they left the condo—
making her even more convinced he was on to her.

As she slid behind the wheel of the pickup, he looked
over at her, his eyes narrowing. His expression changed
so quickly, he caught her off guard. "I'm starved. I know
you haven't had dinner because I've been dragging you
all over Miami." He smiled, bathing her in soft warmth.

Food was the last thing she'd have expected he would
want right now. She looked away for a moment, trying
to come up with a good excuse and regain her balance.

"I know this great little Mexican food place," he was
saying, his enthusiasm growing. "Lupita makes a chile
verde that is to die for. Fresh homemade tortillas. And
the best margaritas in Southern Florida. Tell me you
like Mexican food," he said starting the engine.

She didn't have the heart to tell him that she avoided

spicy food. It didn't go with her wedding planner persona. But his enthusiasm was contagious. "Who doesn't like Mexican food?" she said, smiling as she turned back to him.

He gave her one of his heart-stopping smiles. "You should do that more often," he said, suddenly serious again.

"What?" She hadn't realized she'd done anything.

"Smile. It looks good on you."

She ducked her head, embarrassed by the way she felt when Alex Graham looked at her like that. It was as if he could see behind the facade. That he could see *her*. The real her. And if that was true, then she was in big trouble.

As he drove toward the café, she looked out her side window, trying to get her feet back under her. Alex Graham was like a whirlwind. He caught you up, taking you places you never expected to go, promising the wildest ride of your life. But she knew that eventually he'd let her down. Men always did. And the drop back to reality this time would be a killer.

Something caught her eye in her side mirror. She'd seen that car earlier when they'd left Weddings Your Way. One of the headlights had a different bulb in it giving the car the appearance of winking.

The car was staying back, changing lanes, even disappearing for short periods of time. Whoever was driving knew what he was doing.

As Alex pulled into the dark parking lot next to the café, Samantha saw the nondescript tan car drive past. She only got a glimpse of the man behind the wheel, his face in shadow.

"You all right?" Alex asked.

"Sorry, just daydreaming," she said with a shrug.

He nodded, but she could tell that he'd seen her reaction when she'd realized they were being followed. He didn't seem to miss much but he let it go as he insisted on opening her door as if they were on a date.

The café was small and quiet no doubt because it was late and a weekday night. Samantha excused herself to freshen up. In the empty ladies' room, she used her cell phone to call Rachel.

In as few words as possible, Samantha filled her in.

Rachel let out a low whistle when Samantha finished. "You're sure Preston was the man who shared the champagne with Caroline in her condo?"

"No. But I smelled his aftershave. He'd been in the condo recently. That doesn't mean there isn't another man."

"What's bothering you?" Rachel asked. "I hear it in your voice."

Rachel knew her too well. Samantha glanced at her watch. She had to get back to Alex before he began to worry—and wonder. "The men's clothing in the closet. It's all wrong." She explained that the shirts were an inferior brand, constructed of cheap fabric and worn at the cuffs. "They weren't shirts a man like the one I met with Caroline would wear."

"So there could be another man," Rachel said.

A man at the opposite end of the financial spectrum. "There is the possibility that Preston Wellington III found out about the other man," Samantha told her boss.

"Which you think could mean Caroline's hit-and run was no accident," Rachel said.

"It does make me wonder since Alex Graham and I

seemed to have picked up a tail. I can't help but wonder what someone is afraid we're going to find out."

Victor Constantine was used to taking orders. He wasn't even that particular who was doing the ordering but he had to admit, he didn't like his latest job any more than he liked the arrogant voice on the other end of the line.

He had two simple rules. He never knew who he was working for. He didn't care. And his jobs came in by word of mouth, which meant he only did jobs for clients who'd been referred through other clients. The kind of people who had the kind of money required for his unique services.

It made his life easier that way. He received a call, waited for the money to appear electronically in a numbered account and then he did the job.

The more dangerous the job, the more money went into his account. Victor had an ironclad reputation for getting the job done, no matter how dirty. It had made him a rich man, a man on the verge of retiring at a very young age.

That's why he was having trouble taking orders from his latest "client." The guy was an arrogant bastard, Victor thought as he dialed the number he'd been given.

The man didn't even say hello. "Where the hell are you? I told you to let me know what was going on."

Victor was hot, tired and hungry and he didn't like being talked to like this. "Why do you think I'm calling?" he snapped, silently reminding himself how much he was getting paid. His fees tended to triple when he didn't like the job—or the client.

Victor glanced up the street. "After the hospital, he

drove to Weddings Your Way, picked up a woman and drove to a seedy part of town." He gave the client the address and heard the man let out an oath under his breath.

"The woman is still with him?"

Victor described her. "They're in some dive of a Mexican café across the street eating dinner."

"He took her out to *eat?*"

Yeah, exactly what Victor should have been doing right now instead of sitting down the street in the dark. "Apparently so. I'd like to have some dinner myself."

"I don't pay you to eat."

"You don't pay me enough to miss meals, either."

Silence. "I'm sorry you missed your supper. But with what I pay you, I'm sure you can order in later."

Victor smiled to himself. The man had no idea.

"Call me when they leave the restaurant and stay with them. Don't let them out of your sight." The line went dead.

Victor stared down at the phone for a moment, then thought, what the hell. He called information, got the number of the Mexican café and ordered himself the nightly special: a plate of seafood enchiladas, beans and rice.

"Do you want that delivered?" the female voice on the other end of the line inquired.

Victor smiled. "As a matter of fact I'm parked just down the street. There is a big tip in it if you get it out to me in a hurry."

As Samantha returned to the café, she glanced at the other tables. A few people had come in. But none were singles. None, she surmised, was the person who'd been following them.

Alex looked up as if sensing her return, never taking his eyes off her from the time she started toward the table until she sat down.

It didn't just surprise her that he could unnerve her the way he did. It scared her. The wall she'd thrown up and her cool reserve, coupled with the way she dressed and acted, kept most men at a distance. But then Alex Graham wasn't most men. That point was starting to hit home.

"Thank you," he said when she was seated again. "You've been great tonight. I can't tell you how much I appreciate you going with me to the condo. I really don't think I could have done that alone. You've been amazing."

She felt embarrassed by the compliment. "I'm just glad I could help." *Help, indeed,* she thought with a stab of guilt at just the thought of returning to the condo for the champagne bottle and glasses. Who was helping whom?

"So tell me. How did you become a wedding planner?"

She picked up a corn chip and gave him her standard reply. "You wouldn't believe it if I told you."

"Try me."

She looked at him and saw that he seemed to genuinely be interested. Maybe too interested? Talking about that part of her job seemed safe enough. As if being here in this dark intimate café with Alex was safe.

"Well, there's not much to tell," she said, going with the abbreviated version. "I met Rachel and she offered me the job. I had no experience but I guess she saw what a detail person I am..."

"You had no experience as a wedding planner? You

don't strike me as one of those women who always dreamed of her own wedding day," he said.

She'd been playing with the chip but now set it down on her napkin. She could feel the heat of his gaze and felt her throat go dry. "No. I always thought I'd elope." Her smile felt like plastic left out too long in the sun. "But I can understand why some couples want a large wedding. For most people it's the biggest event they will ever..." He'd made her remember how she'd once pictured her own wedding.

"Endure?" he suggested when she didn't go on.

She could only nod.

"Frankly? It sounds awful," he said as if he'd seen her discomfort. "Months of planning and hassle for a few minutes before a preacher. Months and months of planning."

She took a drink of the beer the waiter put in front of her, thankful to him for saving her from a strained silence. "It *does* take a lot of planning because basically you're putting on a theatrical production not that much different from a Broadway play."

"Interesting perspective and appropriate since a wedding has so little to do with a marriage, don't you think?"

She smiled. "The wedding is fantasy, that's for sure. Some more than others. Look at some of the popular wedding themes. Antony and Cleopatra, Romeo and Juliet, Lancelot and Guinevere and then there are Royalty and Fairyland weddings, weddings In the Clouds, On the Rooftop, By the Sea..."

He laughed. "I had no idea." He shook his head, seeming to be enjoying himself. "No wonder I've never gotten married." He turned serious. "I don't mean to make light of what you do, but it really is a lot of smoke and mirrors, isn't it."

If he only knew. Both of her jobs were a lot of both. She began to relax. "We joke that we're in show business. But if you put on a great show everyone is happy and that's what it's all about."

They snacked on the chips and salsa for a few moments, a comfortable silence falling between them.

"Three months isn't enough for the type of show my father wants, is it," he said after a while.

"Not really," she admitted. "I'm going to have to pull a few rabbits out of my hat but don't worry, I won't let your sister down."

He smiled almost ruefully. "I'm sure you won't but it might not be a problem. There might not be a wedding because there might not be a groom." He held up his hands as if in surrender. "I know. You're convinced this fiancé of hers is in love with her and wouldn't desert her—especially pregnant. I hope you're right."

So did she, but it was getting tougher to keep making excuses for Preston Wellington III.

Alex couldn't remember a meal he'd enjoyed more. While Caroline was never far from his thoughts, he stopped obsessing over her missing fiancé. He liked the idea of being an uncle. It wasn't like Caroline would be alone or penniless. He would see to that.

Even though he wasn't sure he should, he liked Samantha Peters. She'd drawn him out, asking about his job as a fireman. She'd seemed genuinely interested and had laughed at his stories from the firehouse. He'd steered clear of the anguish that often came with his job.

As they finished their meal, he asked, "The woman who was abducted. Have they found her?"

Samantha shook her head. "There's been no word."

He was shocked to hear it and even more shocked to realize he hadn't given the other woman a thought. He'd been too involved with his sister's hit-and-run.

"I'm sorry," he said. "You think she was kidnapped?"

"I don't know."

"But no ransom demand has been made yet?" he asked, still convinced that there had to be a connection between his sister and the driver of that car.

"Not that I've heard."

"Thank you again," he said. Just looking at her made him feel better.

"It's been my pleasure—" She broke off, seemingly a little flustered. It wasn't like her and he found himself smiling at her again. "I enjoyed dinner," she amended.

"Me, too." His gaze locked with hers, her brown eyes seeming to shimmer. He wanted to reach across the table and remove her glasses, brush her hair back from her face and—

Her cell phone rang. He watched her glance at the caller ID and saw her expression change.

"I'm sorry," she said. "I need to take this."

He nodded, the moment lost as she got up and stepped away from the table. He didn't know if he should feel disappointment. Or relief. He had been about to make a fool of himself.

"Peters," Samantha said into the phone, hoping this was going to be good news.

"Samantha, it's Rachel. I just wanted to let you know that you were right about the black limo. Looks like it was stolen off a car lot in Fort Lauderdale. Matches the description."

"Has the car been found?" Samantha asked, glad she had gotten something right since there was a good chance that she'd been wrong about Caroline's fiancé.

"Not yet," Rachel said. "How are things at your end?"

Interesting. "Fine," she said glancing back toward the table and Alex. "I'm still going by the hospital tonight. I thought I'd drop in on Craig Johnson. I know it's late, but maybe he's remembered something. I'll visit Caroline tomorrow, instead."

"Good idea."

She rang off and walked back to the table.

Alex was just putting his cell phone away. He'd paid their dinner bill and looked anxious.

"I should get to the hospital. Would you mind if we stopped on the way back?" he asked, rising.

She'd hoped to go to the hospital alone but maybe she could make this work and save herself a trip since she would have to go back to the condo as it was. "Of course not. Is everything all right?"

He nodded, his expression grim. "No change."

Samantha felt the weight of his disappointment and her own. She'd been on such a roller coaster of emotions. Now, she felt too warm from the spicy food and the entertaining company. Mostly, she'd felt too content just before the phone call from Rachel.

And that was dangerous. She needed to get back to work behind the scenes, back to what made her feel safe and that was far away from Alex Graham.

At the hospital, they rode together up the elevator to Caroline's floor. "I'll wait here for you," she said as he started down the hall. She noticed that a guard had been posted outside Caroline's door. "Is that your doing?" she asked, surprised.

"I hired guards 24-7 to keep an eye on her. I'm still not convinced the hit-and-run was an accident. And until I am…"

"Can't hurt having the guard here, especially if it makes you feel better."

"*You* make me feel better," he said touching her hand and seeming not to notice when she flinched at his surprise touch. "I won't be long."

"Take your time. Really."

She headed down the hall toward the nurses' station, slowing as Alex nodded to the private guard and entered his sister's room. Before the door closed, Samantha caught a glimpse of Caroline lying in the bed surrounded by equipment. It was so sad to see this beautiful, young woman bandaged and broken, let alone to think about the baby she was carrying.

In her line of work, Samantha dealt with bad guys all the time—just not up close and personal. For the first time, she was on the front lines and she'd never wanted to see justice done more than she did right now. She would do anything to find the person behind Sonya Botero's abduction, behind Caroline Graham's hit-and-run—even if it turned out that she'd been wrong about Preston Wellington III and he was involved.

She walked down to the nurses' station on the pretense of inquiring about Caroline Graham's condition. As she spoke with the nurse, Samantha noted Craig Johnson's room number. It was just up the hall from Caroline's room.

Alex was still in with his sister as Samantha passed

the guard. She waited until he was busy reading a magazine in his chair outside Caroline's door before Samantha headed for the chauffeur-bodyguard's room.

She recalled what she'd witnessed earlier from the front window of Weddings Your Way. The driver of the car carrying the men who'd abducted Sonya Botero had appeared to purposely try to run down Johnson before striking Caroline Graham. Had there been more than one target?

She hesitated at the door to Johnson's room. According to the Miami Confidential team, he was complaining of headaches and claiming he couldn't recall anything about the incident.

Talking to him would no doubt prove to be a waste of time and possibly make Johnson suspicious, but maybe he had remembered something by now. Something that would help.

She pushed the door to his room partially open and stopped at the sound of his raised voice. He was speaking to someone, his tone strained.

She froze as he moved into her field of vision and she saw that he was on the phone, pacing back and forth in front of the window, his back to her. Cautiously he lifted a corner of the blind and peered out to the street.

"I'm telling you they tried to run me down," Johnson said. "I was almost killed. What if they try again?"

So much for him not remembering anything about the incident, she thought, and wondered if he might be right about being in danger. But why kill him? There were other witnesses at the scene.

Thinking of the killers hitting Johnson here at the hospital, she heard movement behind her and whirled around, all her FBI self-defense training coming back in a rush.

* * *

Alex hardly recognized the woman who spun on him, her hands going up in a self-defense move. He jerked back in nothing short of shock. Even Samantha's expression wasn't one he'd seen before. She looked ready to kick his butt. More than that, she looked scared as if she'd been expecting someone to harm her.

"You all right?" he asked, glancing toward the hospital door she'd just let close. He'd caught her eavesdropping. Had she overheard something that frightened her?

"Sorry," she said instantly, seeming embarrassed. "You startled me."

"I guess."

"I was just checking to see how Mr. Johnson was doing."

Mr. Johnson, from what Alex had overheard, was the driver of the limo, the man who was attacked and his client abducted.

"He seems to be on the phone," Samantha said, with a nonchalance that she didn't quite pull off.

Alex had noticed Johnson on the phone when he'd come up behind her.

"How is Caroline?" Apparently she'd expected him to spend more time with his sister.

"The same," he said, wondering again about Samantha. Just about the time he thought he might be figuring her out, she threw him another curve.

Suddenly, he felt exhausted as if the day's events had finally caught up with him. "I should get you back," he said. "It's late. I didn't mean to take up so much of your time."

"Really, it hasn't been a problem. Dinner was wonderful, but I'll take a cab back," she said quickly as if she wanted to get away from him. "After the day you've had, you must be anxious to get home. Like you said, it's late, and you look drained. No reason to go out of your way."

How did she know that her office wasn't on his way home? "It's too late for you to go back to your office tonight anyway," he said, suddenly wondering where she lived and why she was trying to get rid of him. "Let me take you home. I'd be happy to give you a ride to work in the morning. Just tell me what time to be there."

She started to argue but he stopped her.

"I won't hear of you taking a cab. Not after you were kind enough to spend the evening with me. I really didn't want to be alone. So you must let me take you home."

"I have to go back to the office tonight before I can go home."

Why wasn't he surprised? "Well, then I'm taking you."

She nodded as if she'd accepted that he wasn't going to take no for an answer. But he could see that she would have much preferred taking a cab. Why was that? Earlier they'd been so close. But now she seemed uncomfortable in his presence and had been ever since he'd caught her listening in at the chauffeur's hospital room door. Or was it after he'd caught her in her self-defense mode and seen her expression?

Either way, he'd heard enough to know that this Mr. Johnson was scared—and that the man thought the driver of the black limo had purposely tried to kill him and might try again.

And all this just when Alex had almost convinced

himself there was nothing going on, that Caroline's accident had been just that—an accident.

As they reached the outer door, he took Samantha's elbow and felt her jump at his touch—her reaction even more pronounced than it had been the other time.

Who was Samantha Peters—a woman who seemed to do everything possible not to be noticed?

Whatever her motivation, he told himself he had every right—and possibly every reason—to find out more about this woman his sister had been working with over the past six months.

Chapter 5

Victor Constantine had the worst case of heartburn he'd ever had in his life. He knew better than to eat spicy food. He parked down the street and watched as the woman got out of the man's pickup.

She had great legs, he noticed as she bent back into the truck to say something. Nice posterior, too. But that suit she wore was all wrong for her. The woman didn't have a clue how to accentuate her assets.

Victor had taken some classes the one and only time he was in the joint. He thought he would have made a pretty good designer. He had the eye. Maybe he would try to get back into that when he retired—which wouldn't be long and he would still be plenty young enough to make something of himself as a designer.

The chick shut the door and headed for the building again with the sign out front that read: Weddings Your Way.

Was she a wedding planner? That was interesting.

He sighed wishing he could call it a night as he un-
snapped his cell phone and hit redial. "He just dropped
the woman off at Weddings Your Way. You want me to
follow him? Or her?"

"Her. Find out where she lives. While you're there,
see what kind of security system she has at her house.
Check the place out. You might be going in." Click.

Victor wasn't happy about breaking into the woman's house at some time in the future. While it meant he
could charge the client even more, it also meant that this
job wasn't going to be over as quickly as he'd hoped.
His heartburn was killing him and now he would have
to sit and wait.

He watched the man walk her to the door. Quite the
gentleman. But what was she doing going back to an
office this time of the night?

Rubbing his chest, Victor glanced down the street
hoping to see a place he could buy some antacids, but
the area was too hoity-toity to have a gas station or
a convenience store. To add insult to injury, the car
smelled like refried beans.

He thought again about bagging this job. The only
thing that stopped him was the money. He had a pretty
good idea where all this was headed given what a bastard he was working for. The end pay would be primo.
It would be his last job. End on a good note.

Maybe he would become a designer. Or hell, a wedding planner. He would be great at either.

As Samantha closed the front door of Weddings Your
Way behind her, she waited until Alex drove away be-

fore she headed straight upstairs to the secret room on the second floor.

"I had a feeling you'd still be here working," she said as she stepped in and closed the sealed door behind her.

Clare Myers turned from her computer. "You and I should really get lives, you know that," she said, grinning.

Samantha smiled as she pulled out a chair next to Clare. The only way to eliminate Caroline Graham's fiancé as a suspect was to find him and she hoped Clare would be able to help. "I need to find out everything I can about Preston Wellington III."

"You still haven't been able to contact him?" Clare asked, sounding surprised.

"No. And I'm starting to worry." She gave Clare all the information she had on the missing fiancé—which she realized wasn't much.

"How is Caroline Graham doing?"

"She might not make it and she's pregnant."

"Oh, no," Clare said. "I'll see what I can do to find him for you. I planned to do a preliminary search earlier but I got sidetracked doing some checking on the Sonya Botero and Juan DeLeon side of the investigation."

"Still nothing on that end?"

Clare shook her head. "They say in the case of a kidnapping that the first twenty-four hours are critical."

That explained what Clare was still doing here.

Clare's words stuck in her mind as Samantha headed down the stairs toward her office. She hoped to have something on her end of the case by then, as well. Unfortunately, she was starting to wonder if Alex's concerns might be justified.

As she reached the ground floor, she heard the phone in her office ringing.

She thought about letting the machine pick it up. If it was Rachel, she would use Samantha's cell. Other than Clare, no one knew she was here and from the ring she could tell it wasn't an inside-the-office line.

Surely whoever was calling wouldn't expect her to be in her office. Not at this hour.

Unless it was Alex.

Maybe he'd thought of something he'd forgotten to tell her. Because he was the only one who knew she was here.

Or was he?

She thought about the tail and with a chill, picked up the phone, automatically touching her keypad to be sure the shop's security system was up and working tonight. She hadn't noticed the tail after they'd left the hospital but that didn't mean anything. She'd been distracted after being caught outside Craig Johnson's room.

"Hello?" she said into the phone.

At first she heard nothing, then the sound of breathing. Great, an obscene phone call. Just to prove this day couldn't get any worse.

She started to hang up when an obviously disguised voice said, "You're making a mistake. Stop butting into Caroline Graham's life or you'll regret it." There was a click. The caller was gone.

A chill wound around her neck like a garrote.

Samantha hit star 69 but the number was blocked. The phone rang and rang. No answer.

She hung up, confused and even more afraid for Caroline. Samantha would have sworn that Sonya Botero's abduction had nothing to do with Caroline Graham.

Maybe it still didn't. But something was definitely going on with Caroline. Beginning—and possibly ending—with her missing fiancé.

One thing kept bothering Samantha. The men's clothing in Caroline Graham's closet. They hadn't just been old. They'd been cheap. Not the kind of shirts a rich man wore even when he was doing manual labor.

But the Preston Wellington III that Samantha had met at Weddings Your Way dressed like a rich man, acted like a rich man, to all appearances *was* a rich man on the same financial playing field as Caroline Graham. He wouldn't be doing manual labor. He would hire it done.

So that left the big question: Whose shirts were those in Caroline's closet?

Someone had followed them after they'd left the condo. She had to assume the caller knew she'd been to the condo tonight. Knew she and Alex were digging into Caroline's life—and Preston Wellington III's.

That meant there must be something to find.

More and more Samantha thought Alex had been smart to put a private guard outside his sister's hospital room. Caroline might be in serious danger. And Preston Wellington III could be the person she had to fear most.

Samantha had no choice—especially after that threatening phone call.

She would have to go back to Caroline's condo tonight and get the champagne bottle and glasses. It was time to find out what was going on.

She considered who the caller might have been. The list of suspects was fairly short at this point. It came down to who had something to hide.

Right now that seemed to be Preston Wellington III since no one had heard from him.

Samantha didn't even want to think what that meant. She'd liked the man. What did that say for her instincts? Nothing good.

One way or the other, she had to answer some nagging questions about him and what had happened to Caroline. There'd been no word on Sonya Botero and the clock was ticking.

But first Samantha had to make sure she wasn't followed this time. She checked her gun. Fully loaded with an extra clip in the bottom of her bag.

She added two large evidence bags and a pair of latex gloves to her oversize shoulder bag, then leaving the light on in her office, she went into her private restroom and changed her clothing, stripping out of the business suit and dressing in black running gear.

She pulled her hair up and under a black hat and checked herself in the mirror, pleased. Then she left by the back way.

The humid Florida air hit her as she stepped from the air-conditioned building into the well-lit staff parking area under Weddings Your Way. Sliding into her small black sports car convertible, she turned the key.

The car was the only hint of the woman Samantha kept hidden from most people. The one crack in her armor. Her one little secret vice since she drove a midsize white sedan except on those rare occasions that called for cloak-and-dagger, speed or letting the real her out under the cover of darkness.

The engine roared to life with a throaty rumble that made her smile. *Catch me if you can.*

She blasted out of the parking garage and onto the

street. A set of headlights flashed on behind her. She could imagine the driver half asleep, bored, caught off guard since her office light was still on. And in this car, he couldn't be sure he was even following the right person.

Samantha smiled to herself and gunned the engine, rocketing around a corner, then another. Losing her tail had been almost too easy. But she still zigzagged her way to Caroline's condo enjoying the feel of the night air.

"What the hell do you mean *you lost her?*"

Victor swallowed back the bile rising in his throat. After he'd lost her, he'd stopped at a drugstore and bought himself some antacids but they were taking their sweet time working.

"I can't even be sure it was her," he said, hating the apologetic tone of his voice. He was a professional. How had he let a snip of a wedding planner trick him like that? The light was still on in her office when the little black sports car had come flying out of the back of the place. "She switched cars on me." She'd had a head start and was driving like a bat out of hell. Driving nothing like he had expected her to do.

"So maybe she's still at her office?"

He swore under his breath. "I don't think so. I think that was her. Given the way she dresses, it was unlikely but still…"

A curse on the other end of the line. "Never mind. I'll take care of it. Go home. I'll call you when I need you." The line went dead.

The antacids were starting to work. Victor Constantine began to breathe a little easier.

But he didn't go home. Instead, he circled back to Weddings Your Way. He had a hunch. And he wasn't going to be able to sleep until his heartburn got better anyway. She'd fooled him once. But she wouldn't again.

The same guard was on duty as when Samantha had been to the renewal project with Alex. She spotted him from a safe distance but avoided detection by parking some distance away and keeping to the darkness as she worked her way to Caroline's condo.

There were no lights on in any of the buildings. Apparently it was true that Caroline's was the only one occupied.

It definitely made things easier. Samantha let herself in. The lock for the front door took a little longer than she had planned. Seemed her skills were a little rusty.

She took the stairs to the penthouse condo using her penlight to open the condo door, then she turned off the light and listened to make sure she was alone.

Cautiously, she swung the door open and stepped in. The condo was pitch-black, no light coming in back here from the street. She heard nothing and smelled the same scents as before. If Preston Wellington III had come back here, he hadn't been wearing his usual aftershave or cologne.

She moved by memory through the dark condo to the plastic curtain, aware that the windows facing the streets had no coverings. Any light could be seen from down below.

Slipping past the plastic, she found the doorknob to the bedroom, turned it and stepped in, closing the door behind her before she snapped on her penlight. In this room, there were thick drapes that covered the windows and let in no light and, so she hoped, let *out* no light.

Everything appeared to be just as it had before. She was reasonably certain that no one had been here. The champagne glasses were in the same place, the bed still unmade, the sheets rumpled, a few articles of clothing flung across the end.

As she moved to the bedside table, she pulled on the latex gloves and carefully collected the champagne bottle, placing it into one of the evidence bags then into her purse. She did the same with the glasses.

As she turned, she studied the room again trying to understand what might be going on with Caroline Graham. Samantha's first guess was a lover. This could be a lovers' hideaway that Preston hadn't known about. Until recently. He'd definitely been here. Unless the lover wore the same aftershave.

Was it possible that Caroline was financing the entire building project for her lover? That might be enough to set off Preston Wellington III. But enough that he would hire someone to try to kill her in a hit-and-run?

Samantha made a mental note to have Clare run financial reports on both Caroline and Preston. But given the shirts in the closet, Samantha suspected there was another man besides the one she'd met with Caroline. And that raised the question of whose baby she was carrying.

Another possible motive for Preston Wellington III to commit murder.

Samantha felt a wave of disappointment. She'd believed that she'd been in the wedding planning business long enough that she could spot the couples who were truly in love and had a chance of making their marriage work. She would have bet all of her money on Caroline and Preston. They seemed that much in love.

She glanced at the rumpled sheets of the bed and to her chagrin thought not of the wedding couple—but of Alex. With a curse, she shut off the penlight and moved to the bedroom door. She knew only too well where those kinds of thoughts would get her.

She had just started to open the door when she heard a warning sound on the other side. Before she could react, though, the door flew open, slamming into her and driving her back. As she fell next to the bed, her shoulder bag smacking the floor next to her, she heard one of the expensive glasses shatter.

She groped for her bag—and her gun—as a dark figure filled the bedroom doorway. She couldn't see his face. In the dim light coming in from the street through the plastic behind him, he was nothing more than a blurred silhouette.

But from his stance, she could tell he held a gun in one hand and he was trying to find her in the dark bedroom, no doubt afraid to turn on the light for fear that she would see him—and possibly get off the first shot.

Her hand found her bag. Carefully, she slid her hand in until her fingers closed on the gun's grip.

Alex Graham couldn't sleep. In the kitchen, he took a beer from the fridge and wandered through the house, feeling lost and unsettled.

He had way too much on his mind. Caroline. Preston Wellington III. Samantha Peters.

He remembered her face in the warm lights of the café, the soft cadence of her voice, her engaging smile. He found himself smiling at just the thought of her.

His smile faded at the memory of her expression when she'd turned away from the chauffeur's hospital room door. She'd been on the offense, ready to strike out, expecting someone else behind her.

Why would a wedding planner instantly think she had to defend herself? Especially in a hospital with a guard right down the hall?

And it didn't seem like her style, eavesdropping like that. Nor had she been happy when he'd caught her at it.

He frowned and realized how little he'd learned about her after spending hours with her this evening. When he thought about it, he recalled how she'd side-stepped any personal questions, turning the conversation back to ask about him.

Maybe it was just part of her training as a wedding planner. Like self-defense?

He shook his head. Nothing odd about a single woman knowing self-defense. That wasn't what was bothering him. He couldn't put his finger on it but at every turn he felt there was a hell of a lot more going on with Samantha Peters than she wanted him to know. Than maybe she wanted *anyone* to know.

He took a sip of his beer and spied his sister's purse lying on the table by the door where he'd dropped it earlier. The hospital had insisted he take it home with him.

He'd only made a cursory search of the purse looking for keys, Preston's phone number, his sister's home address.

Now he wished he hadn't seen where she'd been staying. All it had done was leave him more upset and worried. What was going on with her? When he'd called his father, he hadn't mentioned what he'd found out. But when he'd asked about where Caroline was living, his father had said she was staying with a friend while some new place of hers was being renovated. Basically it didn't sound like C.B. knew any more than Alex did.

And where was Preston Wellington III?

Not knowing anything was driving him crazy.

He retrieved his sister's purse and took it to the couch where he sat down, and after a moment's hesitation, dumped the contents out on the coffee table.

He had no idea what he was looking for as he rummaged through the assortment of makeup and vitamins and lotions in between taking drinks of his beer. The bag was like a small drugstore. Did his beautiful sister really need all this beauty stuff?

He picked up her wallet, opened it and found a dozen different credit cards, her driver's license, a few snapshots. One of a good-looking man who he assumed was Preston. Another of Alex himself. It was an outdated family photograph when he and Caroline and Brian were kids.

Guilt stabbed through him. He'd made no effort to get along with his family for years. Hell, he'd had a chip on his shoulder as big as a California redwood.

Maybe that's why Caroline had called him today and wanted him to meet her at the wedding planner's. Because she was hoping to bring the family back together before her wedding. Maybe that's all there had been to it. And her hit-and-run had been just an accident.

He had to admit he liked the idea of being close to his sister again. No chance of him being close to his brother, Brian. Or even their father. He was barely civil with them and he didn't feel as though it was all his fault. But he could try for Caroline's sake, he promised himself. He would do anything—if she would just get better.

He opened her checkbook and was surprised to see how low her balance was.

And then he saw why. He would have expected her most recent checks to be to Miami's most expensive clothing stores. Instead they were for plumbing and lighting fixtures, drywall contractors and material, lumber.

He sat up, spilling his beer. What the hell? She was footing the bill for all the renovations to the condo? Where was this fiancé of hers? And why wasn't he paying for the repairs?

Then Alex saw something that stopped his heart cold. Check after check to the same company: Wellington Enterprises, a company no doubt owned by his sister's missing fiancé.

Samantha could tell that the man in the doorway hadn't seen where she'd fallen. He was listening, trying to find her in the dark room.

She told herself he might be the security guard. But she hoped a security guard would have more sense than to silhouette himself in a doorway. And the security guard would have said something by now.

Whoever this man was, she could hear him breathing hard. He was either scared or winded. Or both. He was swinging the gun back and forth in a short arc, his hands shaking, indicating he had little experience with a firearm. But even an inexperienced gunman could kill her at this close range.

It was a chance she wasn't willing to take.

She didn't dare move. Nor take a breath. She knew she didn't have time to draw her gun from her bag before he would hear the sound and fire. Her only hope was to draw his attention to another part of the room.

She inched her hand free under the bed, remembering the clothing that had been tossed across the end of it. She was betting on what she would find and was rewarded when her fingers closed around a high-heeled shoe, just as she'd suspected.

Moving in slow motion, she drew it from under the bed, careful not to make a sound. She couldn't hold her breath much longer. With luck, he wouldn't see her movements—just hear the shoe drop.

She had to be ready. Once she threw the shoe she would have to move quickly.

She needed to breathe, to move from her awkward position on the floor. She counted to three and launched the high heel through the open bathroom doorway.

The gunman swung in that direction and fired off two quick shots, the sound of breaking glass raining down on the tile floor. The huge mirror over the sink had shattered, making more noise than the shots especially since the gun he carried seemed to have a silencer on it.

Under the cover of the racket, Samantha scrambled up, staying in a low crouch and swung her gun toward the door.

She'd been trained to kill when necessary. Not that she'd ever had to kill anyone. She didn't want tonight to be the first. Especially if the man with the gun was Caroline Graham's fiancé.

But the doorway was empty.

She blinked. He couldn't have had time to come into the room. He must have stepped to a side of the door. That meant he was waiting for her to make her next move.

Listening, she waited, afraid he had somehow slipped into the room. That he might even be hiding in the closet. Or on the other side of the bed.

Then she heard the rattle of plastic.

He was making a run for it!

She rushed to the doorway, dodged to one side, and took a quick look around the edge of the doorjamb in case it was a trick.

She heard the thunder of footfalls and took off after him. As she pushed through the plastic and turned the corner toward the door, something solid struck her in the face just below her left eye and dropped her to her knees.

She blinked back stars and blackness as she grabbed the wall to keep from passing out. She could hear the sound of heavy footfalls, the sound of him retreating down the stairs, getting away.

She tried to get to her feet, but the blackness closed in and she had to sit down in the Sheetrock dust and lean her head back against the wall.

It wasn't until she turned on her penlight that she saw what he'd thrown at her. A foot-long piece of two-by-four lumber.

No chance of any prints on the board. She waited until the dizziness and darkness stopped, then she returned to the bedroom to retrieve her shoulder bag.

Victor Constantine felt a hundred times better. The antacids had done their job. He'd opened the car window while waiting down the street from Weddings Your Way and the refried beans smell was almost gone.

But that wasn't why he felt so good.

He'd had a hunch that the wedding planner would return to her office. And she had.

He'd been taken off guard when she'd switched cars the first time. But now she returned, with the top down on the sleek black sports car convertible, her hat gone and her hair blowing in the wind. He wondered where she'd been and what she'd been up to.

He'd waited, figuring she would switch cars again. And she had, driving a white sedan—just as he'd been told she drove.

Following her at a safe distance now, he couldn't help but wonder why he'd been hired to follow her and the man he knew only as Alex, although he'd found out that Alex drove a pickup, worked as a fireman and that his last name was Graham. He'd never wondered about why he was hired by his clients. It was dangerous.

But this time, he found himself considering what his client was so afraid these two were going to find out. A fireman and a wedding planner. Hell, how dangerous could they be?

Several things about the two did make him wonder. One, the car switching and how fast the wedding planner drove. And that she went home alone. What was wrong with this Alex guy that he'd let that happen?

Victor looked up and realized he didn't see her car. He sped up. No way had she seen him tailing her. No way. Traffic was light. If she could have turned, he would have seen her. But somehow she'd given him the slip. Again.

She must have suspected someone might follow her. But how had she known how to lose him like that?

Who the hell was this woman?

Victor Constantine planned to find out.

* * *

Samantha thought she would never be able to get to sleep. Her mind raced with the day's events, her thoughts always circling back to Alex Graham.

She took a hot bath and climbed naked between the cool sheets, her head aching from where she'd been struck by the board at the condo. Her body also aching for a man's touch. Not any man's touch. Alex Graham's. She squeezed her eyes shut, praying for sleep. Praying for Sonya and Caroline.

The next thing she knew she was awakened by the phone. "Hello?"

For some reason she thought it would be Alex. Probably because he'd been on her mind again right before she'd fallen asleep.

"I woke you. Sorry," Clare said. "But I knew you'd want this right away."

Samantha sat up. Clare couldn't have already heard from the lab with a match on the fingerprints from the champagne bottle or glasses. It hadn't been that long ago that Samantha had dropped them off.

She turned on the lamp and glanced at the clock beside her bed. "What are you doing still working at this hour of the night?"

"Couldn't sleep."

Samantha knew that feeling. Normally.

"It's about Preston Wellington III."

She felt her heart leap in her throat. Something had happened to him. Isn't that what she'd been afraid of?

"According to every record available in the U.S., no one by that name exists," Clare said.

"*What?*" She sat up straighter, trying to make sense of what Clare was saying.

"No record of a birth, social security card, employment, library card, school attendance, graduation, marriage or death. Nada," Clare said. "There was no Preston Wellington III. Until a year ago."

Samantha groaned. "You're sure?"

Clare chuckled. "He must have made some impression."

"It wasn't just him. They were one of the few couples who made me think, 'Wow, they truly love each other. These two might really make it.' He seemed so head-over-heels for her. How could I be so wrong?"

"She's rich? And he's one hell of an actor?" Clare suggested. "You know what amazes me? That someone with Caroline Graham's money wouldn't be suspicious of every man she met. I'd run a check on the man before I even dated him—let alone agreed to marry him. I guess the old adage is true: Love is blind."

"She must not have wanted to know," Samantha said, thinking about the shirts in the closet at the condo. Love was indeed blind—and stupid, she thought. "Well, if Preston Wellington III is just some name he's taken, then who is he?"

"Your guess is as good as mine. I see your note here about sending some fingerprints to be analyzed? If his prints are on file, I guess we'll know soon enough."

If his prints were on file. Samantha had a bad feeling they would be and not because of some employment requirement. She wouldn't be surprised now to learn that the man had a record. After all, Caroline's fiancé had already proven himself a liar. Chances were good he would have had a run-in with the law.

In fact, chances were even better that Samantha had run into him tonight at the condo.

Chapter 6

The next morning on her way into Weddings Your Way, Samantha passed Juan DeLeon leaving. Sonya Botero's fiancé was tall, dark and incredibly good-looking but today he appeared shattered, like a man who feared he'd lost everything. The expression on his handsome face broke her heart.

To find someone you wanted to spend the rest of your life with and to lose them— The thought broke off abruptly as she recalled the single time she'd felt that way. And how incredibly wrong she had been.

It wasn't long after that that Rachel had approached her about working with the Miami Confidential team. She'd been ecstatic. Until she heard what their cover was.

"Weddings?"

"Is that a problem?" Rachel had asked her, sounding surprised by her reaction.

"No," Samantha had quickly covered, cursing silently to herself. *Weddings?*

It was hard sometimes seeing how happy the brides were. Like Caroline Graham.

And Sonya Botero.

It had been almost twenty-four hours and still there was no ransom demand, no word at all. Where was Sonya? Who had taken her?

Samantha was reminded of last night and the man who'd tried to kill her in Caroline's condo. She quickly went to her ultra neat desk and pulled out her appointment book.

If Preston Wellington III had been after Caroline Graham's money and that plan was soured by her pregnancy, maybe he saw a way to still get the fortune he was after.

She leafed through her appointment book, already knowing what she was going to find. Sonya Botero's appointment had been right after Caroline Graham's.

That meant that Caroline's fiancé would have seen Sonya. Had he found out who she was? More to the point, had he found out *what* she was worth?

Samantha shuddered at the thought, shocked by what that could mean. Was it possible that Sonya Botero's alleged kidnapping was nothing more than a smoke screen for the true crime—the murder of Caroline Graham.

Samantha went into the small kitchen adjacent to her office and made herself a cup of tea, feeling chilled and needing the calm that hot tea always brought her. Taking the cup to her office window, she looked out over Biscayne Bay. The water shimmered in the sunlight.

Several sailboats leaned in the breeze, canvases bright white against the blue horizon.

"Samantha?"

She turned to find Rachel standing in the doorway of her office.

"I was waiting for your report," her boss said.

"I was just going to check in," Samantha said quickly.

Rachel closed the door and moved deeper into the office, stopping short when she saw the cut and dark bruise that even makeup couldn't hide on Samantha's cheek.

Without further hesitation, Rachel slid into a chair, motioning for Samantha to do the same. "What happened?"

Samantha touched the injury and winced. "Some of my skills in the field are a little rusty, but I got what I went for." She told Rachel what had happened. "I'm just waiting to hear from the lab."

Fortunately the champagne glass that had broken when she'd fallen was the one with the lipstick on it and the pieces were large enough that the lab would probably still be able to lift a print or two from it.

"Caroline Graham hasn't regained consciousness?" Rachel asked.

Samantha shook her head. "Luckily, the baby is all right. At least so far."

"And the fiancé?"

She shrugged. "He's still missing. And on top of that he's not Preston Wellington III. No person by that name existed until a year ago—about the time Caroline met him."

Rachel looked surprised. "I saw him come in with Caroline. I didn't suspect a thing."

"Neither did I. I really believed he was in love with her. That they were in love with each other. And this morning, I did some checking. Caroline and Sonya had some appointments after each other. Preston or whoever he is would have seen Sonya, might even have learned who she was." She realized what she was saying. The man was looking even more like a suspect in Sonya Botero's abduction as well as Caroline's hit-and-run.

Rachel didn't look pleased to hear the news. "Did you talk to Craig Johnson last night at the hospital?"

She told Rachel about her visit to the hospital and what she'd overheard in Craig Johnson's hospital room. "He sounded scared. I have a feeling the reason he is complaining of a headache and memory loss is so he can stay in the hospital where he feels safer." She went on to tell her boss about the threatening phone call she'd received.

Rachel took in the information. "Do you think Caroline should have some protection on her at the hospital?"

"Alex hired a private guard to stay outside his sister's room just down the hall."

"Alex?" She gave Samantha a questioning look.

Samantha felt her face flush and realized the way she'd said his name had cued her boss. "He insists I call him by his first name."

"Of course he would." Rachel smiled, studying her. "I've never seen you flustered like this before, though. Are you sure you're all right?"

"It's Alex. Mr. Graham. He…" She shook her head. "He's rather intense and he doesn't miss much. I have to watch myself around him all the time."

Rachel frowned. "I've seen you turn hysterical bridezillas into purring pussycats, deal with drunk wedding guests and irate fiancés, but if you think you can't handle Alex Graham…"

"No, I can handle him," Samantha said with more confidence than she felt. She was a trained professional. Surely she could handle one handsome fireman. One very handsome, charming, intelligent fireman. "If I tried to hand him off to someone else on the team now, it would only make him more suspicious. He's suspicious enough that we're hiding something from him."

"Under the circumstances, I suppose we can't blame him," Rachel said.

"Any news on Sonya Botero?" Samantha asked, not wanting to discuss Alex Graham further.

"No. No ransom demand. Nothing."

"I saw Juan DeLeon as I was coming in," Samantha said. "He looked devastated."

"He is. He's inconsolable, blaming himself for Sonya's presumed kidnapping," Rachel said. "He assumes, as we do, that it's politically driven, but he hasn't been able to find out who's behind it and neither have we."

Samantha nodded. "I suppose the wedding will be postponed."

"No. He insists we continue with the wedding preparations vowing that there will be a wedding in August," Rachel said. "He refuses to believe he might have lost her. That's why you have to stay on this end of the investigation. If Caroline Graham's fiancé lied about who he was, who knows what else he might be hiding."

Samantha nodded absently and realized she'd been thinking about Alex again and hadn't heard what Rachel had just said. "Sorry?"

Rachel cleared her throat. "I was saying I want you to continue working on this end of the investigation.

Clare hasn't been able to come up with any connection between Sonya and Caroline other than what you have about them possibly crossing paths here. But let's not take any chances especially given what we know about the fiancé. The fact that he's missing worries me."

Me, too, Samantha thought.

"The rest of the team will be working on the theory that Sonya's abduction is political and connected to the assassination attempt on Juan DeLeon and the unrest in his country." Rachel rose to leave. "Be careful," she said her gaze going again to Samantha's bruised cheek. "Keep your eye on Alex Graham. He could be more dangerous than you think."

Samantha already suspected just how dangerous Alex could be—at least to her. That's why he had her running scared.

"I'll write up my report and then make sure everything is ready for the Holcom-Anders wedding," Samantha said, mentally shifting gears back to her other job.

Rachel had stopped in the doorway. "Are you sure you don't want me to put someone else on this?"

Samantha wasn't completely sure if she meant the wedding, or Alex Graham. "I have it covered."

Rachel seemed to study her again as if trying to make up her mind about something.

"The next time Alex Graham sees me I hope to be working on the Holcom-Anders wedding," Samantha said. "I think the best thing that could happen is for him to see me doing my job as a wedding planner."

Rachel nodded. "Yes, I think you're right about that. Watch your back. In this business, you never know who you can trust." She could just as easily have been talking about the wedding planning business as their sideline.

But Samantha was more worried right now about when she would see Alex Graham again—and how to break the bad news about Preston Wellington III. Alex was no fool. He wasn't going to believe this kind of information just fell into a wedding planner's lap.

The last thing she wanted was to make him more suspicious of Weddings Your Way—or worse, of her.

"Keep me informed," Rachel said as she saw someone come in through the front door of Weddings Your Way.

Samantha nodded distractedly, knowing that Alex wasn't going to give up on finding Preston Wellington III, either.

"Sonya's father Carlos Botero," Rachel said quietly and straightened her immaculate suit as if bracing herself for the worst.

"What is going on?" Carlos Botero demanded as Rachel went to meet him.

Samantha couldn't hear the soft words that Rachel spoke to him as she led the older man to her office.

"I've already lost one daughter," Samantha heard Botero say. "I can't lose another." Rachel closed her office door.

Not far away, a man made a call he'd been dreading. "We haven't been able to get to DeLeon."

"You fool. First you botch his assassination attempt and now you mess up this, as well?"

"I got his woman."

A disapproving sound was made on the other end of the line. "You messed that up, as well, and you know it."

He ground his teeth. "DeLeon is too well guarded."

"Figure it out. But in the meantime, make sure you

finish up the other job you were given. No mistakes this time. Clean up the mess you've made of this." The phone slammed down.

He sat for a moment, then clicked off his cell phone.

Samantha sensed Alex standing in her office doorway. Her gaze came up to meet his. For a moment neither spoke. She wouldn't have heard him over the hammer of her blood anyway.

He stepped in, closing the door behind him as he cleared his throat. "Sorry to bother you. I hate to ask but I was hoping you could help me with something. What happened?" he asked in alarm as he spotted her bruised, skinned cheek.

"Just clumsy," Samantha said. "I can't even remember what I bumped into."

She'd been expecting him but still her heart had started pounding when she'd looked up and seen him standing there. The man had that kind of effect on her. What had she been thinking telling Rachel she could handle this?

"Help you?" she managed to ask.

"I need to go see my father. I'd appreciate if you'd go with me. It might make it easier."

"I don't understand."

"You will when you meet my father. We don't get along." There was pain in his tone. "Truthfully? C.B. will be forced to be cordial with his daughter's wedding planner there. Otherwise, hell, it could turn into a knock-down-drag-out fight."

"I'm sure he isn't that bad," she said, smiling.

"Oh, I think you might be surprised." His smile lit up the office.

She looked down at the work on her desk just to give her a chance to regain her equilibrium. This was crazy. But this man of all men had awakened feelings in her she thought long buried. It was the last thing she needed. Or wanted. Especially under the circumstances.

"If you think your father will be more forthcoming with me there," she said, "then I'd be happy to help."

He chuckled at that, his gaze heating as he looked at her. "My father has always had an appreciation for beautiful women."

She started to object since she was far from beautiful. She worked at being unexceptional. "You *must* be desperate. You're resorting to flattery."

"Just the truth," he said softly.

His eyes seemed deeper, richer and more vibrant tonight. But it was his gaze that started a slow simmer inside her. It had been so long since she'd felt anything. She fought the heat that shot through her veins and sent her pulse pounding in her ears. It scared her, feeling like this.

But at least Alex Graham had no clue as to who she really was. As long as he never got a glimpse of the woman she kept hidden, she was safe. She drew in a shaky breath and let it out slowly.

It was getting harder and harder to fight the feelings Alex Graham stirred in her. For that reason alone, she should have taken off running in the opposite direction.

Alex wanted to believe Samantha's story about how she'd gotten the bruise on her cheek. Unfortunately, he just couldn't imagine her being clumsy. Nor could he shake the feeling that there was a lot more she wasn't telling him.

Not that it was any of his business.

He felt guilty. He'd coerced her into helping him. Dragging her first to Caroline's condo last night and now to the Graham lion's den. He knew what visits there were like. Hell. So why had he thought bringing her along would help?

Because there was something about her. Samantha tended to smooth troubled waters. She'd worked her magic on him and he'd seen the way she handled Caroline yesterday in her office.

But he knew his real reason. He still hadn't been able to shake the feeling that she knew more about what was going on than she was letting on. She'd at least spent time with Caroline—and Preston Wellington III—over the last six months. Maybe more time than anyone in his family.

He was also curious how she would fare with his father. C. B. Graham tended to overpower everyone he came in contact with. Would C.B. rattle Samantha? Alex was anxious to see. If he had to put his money on anyone it would be Samantha. She seemed impervious to the kind of browbeating his father was so good at. Hell, the woman had to deal with brides all day. Alex couldn't even imagine.

His father did like pretty young women. And as much as Samantha tried to hide her beauty, Alex didn't think his father would miss it any more than he had.

Alex pulled up to the gate and cursed under his breath as the attendant stepped out of his stone booth and gave Alex's pickup then Alex the once-over before hitting the button that opened the gate into the huge estate.

Samantha had said little on the drive and Alex hadn't

felt like trying to draw her out. He had too much on his mind. The last thing he wanted to do was to see his father.

"You grew up here?" Samantha asked now.

He glanced over at her. "You sound surprised."

"It's just that you seem so down-to-earth," she said, then seemed embarrassed as if she'd spoken without thinking, something he'd learned she seldom did.

He laughed. "I'm going to take that as a compliment."

He was sure in her business she'd seen her share of the rich and pretentious, but as he looked at the grounds and the huge mansion looming out of the palms, he saw it through her eyes.

"It takes ostentatious to a new level, don't you think?" he said. "I left here the first chance I got and haven't looked back."

"It's really magnificent."

"I suppose. I always felt like I couldn't breathe here. I guess it's the burden that comes with being a Graham. The price was too high."

He glanced over at her wondering about *her* background. It was impossible to explain to someone who didn't come from the kind of money the Graham family had what it was like. Most people thought if they had money their problems would be over.

After a winding lane of towering palms and flower-choked beds, Alex pulled around the circular drive and swore at the sight of his brother's sleek, red sports car parked out front.

"Great," he said, cutting the pickup's engine. "You're going to get to meet my brother. Brian is always a real treat," he said sarcastically as he opened his door and hurried around to open hers.

She stepped out and he watched her take it all in, the massive white gleaming Spanish-style mansion, the English garden, the Olympic-size swimming pool and huge rock waterfalls, the six-car garage, the man-made lake, the guest cottages that were larger than most people's houses.

"I've only seen photographs of where the wedding was to be held," she said, sounding like a wedding planner again. "We hadn't gotten to the on-site preparations yet. I knew there was plenty of room but this is a phenomenal space for a wedding the size of your sister's."

How could the woman still think Caroline was getting married, let alone here. He couldn't imagine getting married here. If it didn't put a curse on the marriage he didn't know what would.

He took Samantha's elbow and walked her to the front door, smiling to himself as he felt her pulse jump at his touch.

Samantha tried to find that cool calm she'd become famous for as she surreptitiously studied the man next to her. He rang the doorbell and waited. From inside the house came a few bars of a Mozart classic.

She felt jittery, even a little light-headed with her heart beating too quickly. She promised herself that when she returned to the office she would ask Rachel to put someone else on this case. She couldn't handle being around Alex Graham. Not for another second.

Alex fidgeted, clearly nervous and getting upset as he pressed the doorbell, holding it down this time. He'd been quiet driving here except for a brief thumbnail sketch of his family: father C.B., overbearing; Brian equally pretentious and overbearing and Caroline— That was where his expression softened. "Spoiled rotten." He'd smiled. "But you couldn't help but love her."

"Herbert," Alex said as the butler opened the door. Alex didn't wait for an invitation, just pushed past the uniformed stiff-necked man, drawing her with him as he ushered her into a foyer that was as big as the house she'd grown up in.

Herbert called after them, his voice echoing through the marbled entryway. "Was Mr. Graham expecting you?"

Alex gave a humorless laugh. "Not hardly," he said over his shoulder.

With Samantha in tow, he headed down the long tiled hallway. All she caught was a blur of crystal chandeliers and rich rare wood paneling.

At a large solid wood door, Alex stopped, took a breath and threw the door open exposing an opulent den and making the two men inside turn in surprise.

Both men wore suits, the younger man in an expensively cut navy pinstripe, the elder in a dark gray with a faint red thread running through the fabric. In this setting, they looked like a magazine ad for today's top executive and his dream office. The room around them was all glistening wood, supple dark leather and knee-deep carpet.

Their surprised gazes went from her to Alex and back again. Neither looked happy to see him.

She felt Alex stiffen next to her, his hand searching out hers. He squeezed it gently. "Welcome to the lion's den," he said under his breath, then stepped into the room, drawing her with him.

Chapter 7

"Alex?" his father said, sounding as if he hadn't seen him in months and hardly recognized him. He hadn't.

Alex had gotten a glimpse of his father and Brian talking with Caroline's doctor at the hospital. He had hardly spoken to his father when he'd called yesterday to tell him about Caroline's accident.

Neither his father nor his brother had made an attempt to talk to him since and Alex hadn't bothered, either. He could only assume that his father blamed him for Caroline's accident. It would be just like C.B.

"Is this about Caroline? Is she—" His father's voice broke.

Alex shook his head. "She's still unconscious."

His father's look said, "Then why are you here?"

"I've been trying to contact her fiancé," Alex said. "Have you heard from him?"

C. B. Graham shook his head. "Pres spends quite a lot of time out of the country." Pres? "He's a busy man."

Yes, as C.B. had been when Alex was growing up.

What C.B. didn't say, but Alex heard: Unlike you, Alex, who only works part of the week as a fireman.

Alex felt that old frustration and resentment rising in him. Already his father had bonded with Preston Wellington III, practically a complete stranger, but C.B. made no effort to understand his youngest son.

Brian, Alex realized, was staring at Samantha.

"This is Samantha Peters. She's a wedding planner with Weddings Your Way. Caroline's been working with her."

"You're from the place where Caroline was struck down," Brian said with interest as if contemplating a lawsuit. He shifted his gaze to Alex. "What were you doing there with her anyway? I didn't even think the two of you had spoken in years."

"This must be very difficult for you all," Samantha broke in, stepping forward to shake each man's hand.

Alex watched in amazement as his father seemed to melt at her touch, at her softly spoken soothing words. What was it about this woman?

Brian, though, was his usual cold self. He seemed suspicious and angry. Nothing new there.

"Of course you're worried about Caroline, but she's in good hands," Samantha was saying. "All we can do now is find her fiancé. I know how devoted he is to her and he'd want to be here with her now."

C.B was practically falling all over himself saying, "Yes, of course. He's a fine young man. This is such a tragedy with the wedding not that far off."

Did either his father or brother know that Caroline

had moved the wedding up three months? Did they know she was pregnant?

"We've tried several numbers in an attempt to reach Mr. Wellington," Samantha was saying. "Any information you can give us would be appreciated."

"What exactly is your involvement, Miss... Peters, was it?" Brian asked.

"Since I've been working with Caroline and Preston, I thought I might be of some help," she said.

"That is very kind of you," C.B. said. He was like putty in her hands. Alex felt a little jealous.

"Pres owns a couple of companies," C.B. said. "Would you like the names?"

"If you don't mind, that would be very helpful," she said.

Alex gritted his teeth. Yesterday he'd asked his father for other ways to reach Preston and got the runaround. C.B. had insisted on handling everything himself, as usual.

C.B. went to his desk, flipped open a folder lying right on top. Apparently, he'd been trying again to reach *Pres*. "One is a company called Wellington Enterprises."

The same name as the one Caroline had written all the checks to.

"The other is—" C.B. dug through the folder "—Maple Ridge Unlimited."

"Are those companies in Miami?" Samantha was asking.

"Both out of New York," C.B. said with obvious pride. "Pres is quite the young man. Smart and ambitious."

Alex groaned inwardly. Even Brian looked a little

green around the gills. Their father admired ambition almost as much as he did money.

As C.B. closed the folder on his desk, Alex had a very bad feeling. "Let me guess, you invested money in Pres's companies."

C.B. shot him a hard look. "You wouldn't presume to advise me on how to invest my money, would you, Alex?"

"What would a fireman know about such things," Alex quipped.

Exactly, his father's look said before the older man moved closer to Samantha and said something Alex didn't catch.

Alex glanced at his brother.

Brian had wandered over to their father's desk and had lifted the corner of the folder from which C.B. had gotten the names of Preston's companies just moments before. Brian appeared to be scanning the information inside the folder.

"Brian, you're awfully quiet tonight," Alex said.

His brother started, letting the folder fall shut as he stepped away from the desk. "I don't speak when I have nothing to say."

Alex groaned at his brother's arrogance. "Oh, I suspect you have plenty to say—behind my back."

"So why did Caroline take you with her yesterday?" Brian asked.

Alex wished he knew. "I guess she wanted one of her brothers with her and I was available."

Brian smirked at that. "One of the benefits of having what amounts to little more than a part-time job. What I don't understand is why you've taken it on yourself to find Preston. I thought Dad told you he had already left a message. What are you trying to prove anyway?"

Alex started to step toward his brother but felt Samantha's cool touch on his arm.

"Thank you for your help," she said in that calming tone of hers. "I know how much Preston would appreciate our efforts to locate him. He will want to be at Caroline's side."

Yeah right, Alex thought as he let her steer him toward the door. He was still fuming when they climbed into his pickup, but he didn't say anything until they were out the gate and he could no longer see the grounds in his rearview mirror.

"That went well," Alex said with a laugh, his large hands gripping the wheel. "Now you see why I give my family a wide berth. But you were great with my father." His gaze met hers and locked for an instant. "You really are amazing." He turned back to his driving but she could still feel the heat of that gaze warming her to her toes.

"You know something good might come out of this," he was saying. "This might be just the humbling experience my father and brother need. I have a feeling that my father probably invested a bundle with his future son-in-law *Pres*. And Brian, too." He glanced over at her. "And they're both going to lose it all."

"How can you be so sure of that?"

Alex shook his head. "I hope to hell I'm wrong about *Pres*, but I have a bad feeling we won't be seeing him again."

Samantha considered telling him what she'd found out about Preston Wellington III. But she needed the fingerprints from the champagne bottle and glasses first. She needed to know exactly what they were dealing with before she hit him with the bad news.

And Alex was in enough of a temper as it was. In the mood he was in, he would return to his father's house and slap them with the news that Preston Wellington III didn't even exist. At least not until a year ago.

She didn't want that happening. It would only open a bigger can of worms. A man like C. B. Graham would demand to know how she'd come by such information. She couldn't chance blowing her cover. It would be hard enough to convince Alex.

Alex dropped her off at her office saying he had to go by the firehouse. He was taking some time off.

After he left, Samantha went upstairs to be briefed on the other members parts of the Sonya Botero case.

Unfortunately, there was little news. Julia, who'd been friends with Sonya, had been working to see if there was a connection between any of the people they knew, friends, relatives, acquaintances.

Sophie was working on the Craig Johnson part of the investigation. Isabelle was getting ready to go to Ladera. Nicole was using her background as a private investigator for wealthy clients to follow up on some leads. The rest of the team was beating the bushes as well, making contacts with informants, leaving no stone unturned.

After the briefing, Samantha spent the day finalizing last-minute details for the Holcum-Anders wedding. While not one of the shop's largest or most extravagant, the wedding had been in the planning stages for almost a year now and would culminate in the ceremony tomorrow.

Everything was set but still she went over the details again. Her mind had been wandering all day and wandering in an annoying and worrisome direction: Alex Graham.

Her phone rang, making her jump. For just an instant, she thought it would be Alex and was disappointed when she saw it was an inner-office line.

"I've got more bad news for you," Clare said without preamble. "A woman's body was found this morning in the Miami River. Rachel asked me to let you know. I guess she's gone down there to make the identification if it turns out to be Sonya. She's hoping to spare both Juan and Carlos. Might not even be Sonya, although the description sounds close."

Samantha felt sick. "It can't be her. Why take her only to kill her? They didn't even make a ransom demand."

"Sometimes it isn't about money, you know that."

Hadn't she suspected that if Preston, or whoever he was, was behind this that he'd taken Sonya just to hide his true crime—his attempt on Caroline's life. "Let me know as soon as you hear?"

"I will. And as for Preston Wellington III..."

Samantha braced herself for the worst.

"During the last year he's made a bunch of investments. Looks like he might be overextended. Big-time."

Just as Alex had suspected. "Check something for me?" She hated to even voice her latest fear. "Did he by any chance take out an insurance policy on his future bride?"

Alex made a dozen more attempts to reach his sister's fiancé, then did something drastic. He called his brother.

"I'm sorry but Mr. Graham is in a meeting," the third secretary he spoke to told him.

"I don't want to speak with Mr. Graham, I want to speak with Brian. Which secretary are you?" Alex asked.

"I'm his private secretary," the woman said.

"What man needs three secretaries? Look, tell Brian his brother is on the line and if he doesn't take my call I will come down there. It's urgent."

"One moment, please."

It wasn't a minute later that Brian came on. "What the hell are you doing threatening my staff?"

"*Three* secretaries?"

"Did you want something? I'm busy."

Alex raked a hand through his hair and sighed. "I still haven't been able to reach Caroline's fiancé."

"That's why you got me out of an important meeting?" He swore. "I told you Dad was handling this."

"Don't you think the man should know that his fiancée is in the hospital, possibly even..." He veered away from even the thought. "I know Dad invested some money with him. He wouldn't have done that without checking with you first." Silence. "Dammit, Brian, if you have some way to reach the man, I want it. And if you don't, I want to know why the hell not."

His brother sighed deeply. "I have the same numbers you do."

"Dad did invest with him, didn't he?"

"I have to get back to my meeting."

"How about addresses then? These businesses *Pres* sold the two of you on, they have addresses, right?"

For a moment, he thought his brother would just hang up on him. Or at the very least refuse to give them to him. "I'll have one of my secretaries find them for you and call you back," Brian said.

"I'll hold." But while he waited Alex realized Brian wouldn't give him the addresses unless Brian had already tried finding Preston through them—and couldn't.

Another dead end.

It surprised Samantha that she hadn't heard from Alex again. Had something happened? She called the hospital but Caroline was still unconscious.

Maybe Alex had located Preston. He might already know more than she did about his sister's fiancé.

Samantha got up and went to her office window to look out on the bay and was surprised it was dark outside. The shop had been closed all day because of what had happened but the team had still been working—getting ready for the Holcom-Anders wedding tomorrow and trying to find out what had happened to Sonya Botero.

Now, though, the place had taken on an eerie emptiness as she straightened her desk and picked up her purse to leave. She had done everything she could for the wedding tomorrow. She couldn't just sit here but she didn't want to go home, either. She was too anxious waiting to hear about the body that had been found in the river, to hear about Caroline's condition, to hear more news about Preston Wellington III—or whoever he was.

She headed for the door, not completely sure where she was going to go. She had Clare looking into Preston's two companies.

There was no one at the desk. The place looked deserted. She hadn't realized how late it was. She couldn't even be sure there was anyone left upstairs.

For the first time since working here, she felt vulnerable as she walked to her car parked on the side of the building.

Her car, like her and her cover, made a point of not standing out—white, midsize with few bells and whistles. It perfectly fit the Samantha Peters she'd become.

But part of her wanted to take the black sports car and that was the part of her she was worried about as she got into the white sedan and checked the gun in her purse. Now, maybe more than ever, she needed to go unnoticed. Both by whoever had been following her and Alex. But mostly by Alex.

She couldn't shake the feeling she was being watched as she reached into the secret compartment where she kept extra ammunition. She slipped another clip for her gun into her purse along with a small can of pepper spray. She really was feeling paranoid. But better to be safe than sorry. She started the car and pulled out.

This part of town was always busy but she saw no one paying any attention to her. At least not that she could see. But that didn't mean anything.

As she pulled away from the shop, she watched to see if she was followed. She didn't see a tail but she couldn't shake the feeling that someone had taken even more interest in her after last night—an interest that now was deadly.

She almost hoped she would pick up the tail as she drove around aimlessly for a good fifteen minutes before heading for the hospital. Whoever had tailed her and Alex last night had to be tied to Sonya Botero's abduction or Caroline Graham's hit-and-run. Or both, if they were connected. If she could catch whoever had been following her and Alex at least the team might get some answers.

But she saw no one following her. Unfortunately, at this hour of the day, there were too many cars, making it easy for the tail to go unnoticed.

After parking in the visitors section at the hospital, she tried Preston Wellington III's phone number again. No answer. As futile as she feared it was, she left another message.

Inside the empty elevator, she pushed the button for Caroline Graham's floor and leaned back against the wall, her thoughts scattered in a hundred different directions. She had to tell Alex what she'd learned about Preston Wellington III. She knew he would be even more suspicious of how she'd come by the information and that worried her.

But her biggest concern at this point was Caroline. If her fiancé had tried to kill her—

The elevator door opened and she stepped off on Caroline's floor. The nurses' station was empty.

The guard outside Caroline's room was busy reading a book. He didn't even look up. Samantha stuck her head into Caroline's room. She was sleeping.

The hallway was so quiet she heard the faint creak of a door opening as she neared Craig Johnson's room.

A doctor in surgical garb had come out of the stairwell. He didn't even look in her direction as he stepped into Craig Johnson's room.

Samantha stood for a moment, trying to pinpoint what was bothering her about the doctor. Why was he dressed in surgical garb and wandering around the hospital? And why had he gone into Johnson's room? John-son didn't need a surgeon.

Had Craig Johnson been right to fear for his life?

Chapter 8

As the surgeon disappeared into Craig Johnson's room, Samantha quickened her step, all the time telling herself she was mistaken. She wasn't thinking clearly. Why else had she let her guard down with Alex Graham?

At the door to Johnson's room, she hesitated, then throwing caution to the wind, she burst in.

She heard a clatter and saw at once why. Someone had wedged one of the chairs under the knob. But the chair hadn't held on the slick floor. It skittered across the linoleum to crash into the wall.

Past it, she saw the doctor. He was struggling to hold the patient down, one arm locked around Johnson's throat, the other clutching a hypodermic needle. Johnson was bucking on the bed, his face already turning blue, the hypodermic needle dripping a clear liquid.

At the sight of Samantha, Johnson's eyes bulged. He opened his mouth but no sound came out.

The doctor had spun around at the sound of the chair clattering to the floor. Samantha had her hand in her bag, but instead of her fingers closing around the gun, she felt the small can of pepper spray.

She brought it out, but the man moved too quickly. He released Johnson and launched himself at her, the hypodermic needle raised in the air.

She brought up the can of pepper spray, her finger fumbling for the button, as he grabbed for her. The spray caught him in the face. He let out of a howl of pain, now groping blindly for her.

She stepped out of his reach to grab up the over-turned chair, swinging it at him with one hand. It caught him in the knees. He stumbled and almost fell, catching himself awkwardly as he tripped and banged into the wall.

He let out an oath and wiped frantically at his eyes with the sleeve of the surgical gown. His face was beet-red, his eyes running with tears, but his gaze found her.

Her hand was shaking as she groped in her bag, this time coming up with the gun. She leveled it at him, ready to fire.

He reached down and before she could fire, hurled the chair at her. She ducked but it caught her in the shoulder and knocked her back. She hit the floor hard, coming down on her butt, the gun still in her hand, though.

Not that it mattered.

The imposter doctor was gone. The door closing behind him.

She struggled to get up, her limbs like water, her

shoulder aching. This was the second time she'd been hit in two days. She felt out of her league, in pain and frustrated.

Hurrying to the door, she looked out. The hallway was empty. The man was gone.

Turning she looked to the bed and Craig Johnson. He appeared scared as hell but alive.

"Are you all right?" she asked, realizing he hadn't hit the call button for a nurse. Nor had he picked up the phone and called the police while she'd been trying to save his life or jumped in to help her. She felt a wave of anger wash through her as she moved to the bed.

Johnson was sitting up in the bed, rubbing his throat, color coming back into his face as he sucked in deep breaths.

She stepped to the call button, but he grabbed her hand before she could push it.

"I'm all right," he said hoarsely.

"That man tried to kill you."

Johnson gave her a look that said he knew that better than she did.

"Why would he want you dead?" she demanded.

"How should I know?"

"Because it has something to do with Sonya Botero's abduction."

Johnson shook his head. "It is a private matter."

"We need to call the police."

"No. It is my business alone."

She didn't believe him. "If this has something to do with Sonya Botero's abduction—"

"It is gambling debts. What do you care anyway?" He was eyeing her with suspicion. "You are that wedding planner and yet you carry pepper spray and a gun?"

"Any woman who's smart and lives and works in Miami does," she shot back.

"Stay out of my business, wedding planner."

"I just saved your life. I would think you would be more grateful."

"It isn't the first time someone has tried to kill me for the money I owe. Nor will it be the last time."

"Sounds like a motive for kidnapping someone like Sonya Botero," Samantha said.

His eyes narrowed. "You don't want to get involved in this."

"I got involved when I saved your life."

"Your mistake," Johnson said and closed his eyes. "Now get out of my room and if you call the police I will deny everything."

"Yes," she said tamping down the urge to shoot him herself. "You are very good at denying everything."

He didn't open his eyes. Nor did he respond. She checked to make sure she had her gun and her pepper spray. Her eyes were burning from what little she'd sprayed as she left the room, letting the door close behind her.

Out in the hall, she took deep breaths of air and let her watering eyes clear. Then carefully she opened the door to Johnson's room a crack and listened.

Just as she'd suspected, he was on the phone.

"The bastards tried to kill me again!" he said, his whisper shrill. "Do something." He slammed down the phone.

Samantha eased the door closed and walked down to the elevator. She was still a little wobbly on her feet, still shaken, her eyes still burning. Changing her mind, she headed for the outdoor terrace at the end of the hallway.

It wasn't until she'd dialed Rachel's cell that she noticed she had a message from her. Rachel answered on the first ring as if she'd been expecting a call.

"The body in the river? Was it Sonya?" Samantha asked quietly.

"No."

Samantha leaned against the garden wall, relief and the aftereffects of her latest encounter with a killer, making her weak. She thought about the dead woman. Some other family and friends would be grieving tonight.

"Are you all right?" Rachel asked. "You sound funny."

"I'm at the hospital. Someone just tried to kill Sonya's chauffer. I didn't get a good look at the man. All I know is that he was Hispanic, medium height and weight, no visible scars or tattoos. He was wearing a surgical mask, posing as a doctor. Johnson refused to let me call the police. He says it has to do with gambling debts."

"So he needed money," Rachel said. "I'll have the team see if he's telling the truth. Are you sure you're all right?"

"A few new bruises, nothing serious." Her shoulder ached. All she wanted to do was go home to her hot tub, pour herself some wine and soak. "He placed another call after I saved his life and he kicked me out of his room without even a thank-you."

Rachel let out a long breath. "We got the number Johnson called before. It's a pay phone in Ladera. He has family ties there so it proves nothing. We'll see where he called this time and keep an eye on him. I thought there was a guard down the hall in front of Caroline Graham's door?"

"He was reading and not paying any attention," Samantha said. "No reason he would. The guy looked like a doctor in all that surgical garb and he didn't try to go into Caroline's room. Johnson's running scared, but even so, he isn't talking."

"And Caroline Graham?" Rachel asked.

"Still unconscious. I'm going to go home now."

"Good idea. By the way, nice work." Rachel hung up.

Samantha stuffed her phone back in her purse and headed for the elevator, glad to see it was empty. She hit the lobby button, closed her eyes and leaned back against the cool surface of the wall.

All she wanted was to be out of this hospital and in her car headed home. She really wished she'd brought the sports car now. She could make it home much faster.

The elevator doors started to close.

Her eyes flew open as she heard someone slam the elevator doors open again.

Chapter 9

Alex was startled to see Samantha. Almost as startled as she was. He saw her hand go to her purse and for an instant he thought she was going for a gun.

He half laughed at how crazy that thought was. A wedding planner with a gun?

But was that any crazier than some of the more personal thoughts he'd been having about her?

"Well, hello." He couldn't believe how happy he was to see her.

She, however, didn't look all that happy to see him. She looked…guilty of something. He'd already suspected that Samantha was hiding something from him. Now he was almost positive of it.

He decided what he needed to do was keep an eye on her. He smiled at the thought. It really was no hardship. The woman was easy to look at. And she already intrigued him. And any excuse would do to get closer to her.

"Were you visiting someone in the hospital?" he asked, watching color flood back into her face as he held the elevator door so it didn't close. She released the death grip she had on her purse and straightened.

He realized he'd caught her at a rare moment. Had this prim and proper woman actually been leaning against the back of the elevator resting and he'd startled her?

He recalled the other time he'd startled her and wondered again what had happened to her that made her fearful. A man, he thought with some clarity. That might explain the way she dressed. This woman didn't want to attract attention.

Her hair swung back from her face and he saw the bruise and cut he'd seen earlier when he'd come by her office and talked her into going with him to his father's. She'd said she banged into something being clumsy. Even at the time he couldn't imagine her ever being clumsy.

He suspected there was another story—one much more interesting that she wasn't telling him. Nothing new there.

"I was worried about your sister," she said and stepped toward the door as if to escape. "I just came up to see how she was doing."

"Really?" His heart beat a little faster. "Then you know she's conscious." He could tell by her expression she hadn't heard. Had he caught her in a lie? Possibly not her first. He suspected she'd been down the hall visiting the chauffeur again. More eavesdropping?

"She was sleeping so I didn't know she'd regained

consciousness. That's wonderful news." He could hear Samantha's obvious relief that Caroline was alive and getting better. While he didn't understand this woman, something told him that whatever she might be up to, she was one of the good guys. At least he hoped to hell that was true because he felt something for her. Something he hadn't felt in a long time for a woman.

But then he had a track record for falling in love with the wrong woman. Usually one he couldn't trust, he reminded himself.

"Did you get to talk to Caroline?" she asked.

"The doctor let me see her for a few moments. She's pretty out of it still."

"So you didn't ask about Preston."

He shook his head as he let the elevator doors go and stepped in. She'd already pushed the ground floor button. "No reason to hit her with any of that the moment she wakes up, right?"

Samantha nodded and smiled. "I'm sure once she's able she'll clear this all up."

Right. "Any word on that other woman?" he asked.

She shook her head.

The elevator doors opened on the ground floor. He told himself that he couldn't let her get away—maybe even more so because she looked as if that's exactly what she wanted to do.

"I still can't believe it but the doctor says Caroline and the baby are going to be fine. Don't you think this calls for a celebration?"

Instantly, she started to decline.

"Just one drink. Please. I can't tell you how relieved I am, but then I suspect I don't have to."

"No, you don't." He could see that she was weakening.

"Just one drink to celebrate this good news."

"All right." She seemed different. It took him a moment to put his finger on what it was. She was always in control. Except tonight. Tonight there was a vulnerability to her. He felt a pull toward her like the force of gravity. He wanted to take her in his arms and hold her, protect her, comfort her.

"Still no word from Preston?" she asked giving him the impression she was just trying to make conversation since he would have told her if he'd heard anything.

He shook his head. "I think Preston probably used Caroline to get to my father. I'm not sure how much money C.B. gave Preston but I have a bad feeling it was considerable." He told her that his brother, Brian, had provided him with the addresses of Preston's supposed businesses. They had proved worthless, just as Alex had suspected.

Samantha Peters looked sick. "I can't imagine what this will do to Caroline."

"I still think he's behind what happened to her. So, one way or another, I'll find him and get to the truth."

That was what Samantha was afraid of—that Alex was the kind of man that settled for nothing less than the truth.

It was one reason she felt so jumpy. That and almost being killed earlier upstairs in Craig Johnson's room. That and the intimacy of being in this elevator alone with Alex. That and the fact that she was lying to this man. Not lying exactly, but definitely not being honest with him.

And what made it all the worse was that he didn't realize how dangerous the situation had become. She had to warn him, had to tell him everything she knew. It was the only reason she'd agreed to have a drink with him. At least that's what she told herself. She would tell him everything. Well, enough that he would stop his investigation of Preston Wellington III or whoever the man was. She couldn't live with herself if anything happened to Alex.

As they stepped off on the ground floor, Alex reached over and touched her hand.

She felt a jolt of warmth and did her best not to react.

"I'll get my truck. Wait here." He didn't give her a chance to argue. She watched him walk away, no wasted effort, his body lean and strong, the man himself self-confident. She felt a pull so strong that she couldn't look away and chastised herself for wanting to watch Alex for those few moments longer before he disappeared into the darkness of the parking lot.

He had struck a chord in her and she didn't know what she was going to do about it. She'd tried fighting her feelings for all the good it had done. She felt excited and scared and had to remind herself that Alex Graham didn't know who she was. And when he did—

He drove up in his pickup and smiled at her as she stepped out into the humid night air. She could feel him watching her. Looking for something? Or just looking? She feared either way that ultimately he would be disappointed.

For the second time, Alex sensed there was something she wanted to say but had stopped herself as she climbed into the truck.

"Something on your mind?" he asked as he drove.

She touched her upper lip with her tongue. "I need to tell you something."

"Okay," he said slowly. "You're going to kill me but first… I'm starved and I'm willing to bet you haven't had a thing to eat all day. I know this place that serves the best marinara sauce you've ever tasted. It's not far from here and we can have the celebratory drink."

"You're always feeding me," she said, sounding a little embarrassed.

"I like to eat and I hate to eat alone." He didn't add that he liked to see her eat. Or that she looked better since he'd started feeding her. "Great, then," he said and reached over to squeeze her hand as he drove toward the restaurant. He felt her start, tension jumping just under her skin.

He picked up a small buzz of electricity himself when he touched her, but his was attraction. He feared that hers was something entirely different.

Victor Constantine made the call the minute he saw them come out of the hospital. Alex Graham and the wedding planner, Samantha Peters, crossed to the parking lot and got into Graham's pickup. He'd broken his number-one rule. He'd found out who he was following.

"They just left the hospital." Probably to visit Alex's sister, Caroline Graham. He'd made a point of finding that out, too. Just as he had found out who the woman was with Alex Graham. Caroline Graham had regained consciousness. He wondered if his client knew that. Or cared.

Victor couldn't help but wonder what his client's stake was in all this. It was a first time for him, wondering. Worth doing some investigating on his own. He was looking forward to breaking into Samantha Peters's house once he got her address. Her, he was very curious about.

It should have worried him more that he'd broken his own rules. But he told himself this was his last job. Why not indulge his curiosity?

"Follow them. Maybe we'll get lucky tonight and find out where the woman lives. That is, if you don't lose her again."

Victor said nothing. There was nothing he could say. His client didn't even know that he'd lost her not once but twice.

Tonight he would be more careful. Tonight, he would be ready for her. But even as he thought it, he wasn't sure that would help.

The Italian café was small and intimate and just perfect for a romantic evening—or a place to talk to Samantha Peters and find out what she was hiding.

But at the same time, he knew that once she told him it was going to change things. He wasn't sure he was ready for that.

"Romano," Alex said cheerfully as he greeted the owner.

The large Italian clasped his hand warmly. "Alex, so nice to see you and who do you have here?" He released Alex's hand to take both of Samantha's in his. He said in Italian, "She looks like you've been starving her. But not to worry. I will fatten her up."

"Fattening up is the last thing I need," Samantha answered in perfect Italian.

Alex stared at her in surprise. Samantha Peters was just full of surprises, wasn't she?

Romano laughed heartily, warming to her even more. "I have just the thing for you. I'll have my chef make it special." He let go of her hands and touched his lips with his fingertips in a kiss.

"You speak Italian," Alex said.

"As do you," she said in Italian.

He smiled over at her. "A nice quiet booth in the back?" he said to Romano, although never taking his eyes off Samantha. The woman never ceased to amaze him.

The café owner led them back through the narrow room, past red-and-white-checked tablecloths, glowing candles and tall wooden booths draped with brightly colored curtains.

Samantha slid into the booth and looked around, seeming uncomfortable, as if she felt out of place. As he sat down across from her, he wondered if she was sorry she'd revealed a little more of herself by acknowledging that she understood Italian.

Candlelight flickered warmly over her face and with a stab of desire, he realized that she'd never looked more beautiful than she did tonight.

She must have felt his eyes on her. She brushed a lock of brown hair from behind her ear and let it fall so it hid part of her face again.

She picked up her menu. "All I really need is a salad...."

Alex laughed. "Trust me you are not getting out of here that easy. Romano would not allow it."

"Really, Alex—"

"What are you afraid of?" he asked, leaning across the table toward her.

A wary look leaped to her eyes.

"It's only food," he said smiling at her. "One of many fun indulgences I have a feeling you've been missing out on." Her cheeks flamed. Was she actually *blushing?* "I'm sorry, I didn't mean to embarrass you."

He leaned back as a young Italian waiter put down a basket of warm, savory-smelling bread, a small bowl of whipped fresh creamery butter and a bottle of wine and two glasses. "Compliments of the house," the waiter said with a bow.

"I'm not even going to pretend I know anything about wine," Alex said to Samantha and laughed, hoping to relieve some of her tension. She looked ready to spring out of the booth and run. "I can only assume it's a very good year, given that Romano is obviously trying to impress you."

The waiter uncorked the wine—Alex waved away the offer to smell the cork—and poured them both a glass and left.

Alex raised his glass in a toast and realized he didn't want to talk about Caroline, her fiancé, anything that might spoil this moment. And just maybe there was an even better way to find out about this woman. "Tonight let's just enjoy ourselves. I really want to forget about *everything* and just enjoy your fascinating company. Whatever it is you want to talk to me about, I'm sure it can wait. Indulge me this one night?"

Indulging Alex Graham? That's the last thing she wanted to do, she thought as she reluctantly touched her wineglass to his. She'd seen his appetite for food.

Was keenly aware of his appetite for life. As a fireman, she knew the man enjoyed taking chances, living on the edge—the exact opposite of Samantha Peters.

Being this near him she couldn't just feel his enormous energy, it seemed to infuse her with the desire to not only indulge him, but herself.

She took a sip of her wine, her hand shaking, and tried to concentrate on something else. The music. An Italian love song. Alex was looking at her with that intensity that warned her he saw beneath the surface. He saw what she had been so successful at keeping a secret for years.

He got to his feet and reached for her hand. "Dance with me."

Before she could decline, he had drawn her up and into his arms, whirling her expertly onto the small dance floor she hadn't noticed before. She saw Romano smiling at them from the shadows and suspected he'd intentionally played the song. He gave her a wink.

She tried to relax. Being in Alex's arms was heaven. And hell.

"You dance very well," he said, holding her close as they moved to the sensuous beat of the music.

She was intensely aware of the places his body touched hers. The smell of his light aftershave and distinct male scent filled her senses, making her dizzy in a way the wine never would have.

She felt both relief and disappointment when the song ended and he led her back to the table, releasing her hand as he slid into the booth across from her.

The food arrived in a flurry of dishes and aromas. Alex was like a kid in a candy store and she felt herself being swept up by his enthusiasm.

He began to explain each of Romano's specialties as he spooned them onto her plate. She listened, enjoying the sound of his voice as much as the smell of the food.

He waited for her to taste each one.

She indulged him—and herself. Obediently, she tried a bite of each one, giving the appropriate responses all of which met with a smile from Alex. "This is *wonderful*," she said with a wave of her hand.

He laughed as he refilled her wineglass.

They ate and drank, laughing and joking. The meal, the music, the warmth of the café and each other totally relaxed her.

Just for tonight, she told herself, watching Alex savor each bite, each sip of wine, each laugh they shared, she would let herself enjoy this. Enjoy Alex. Just for this magical, wonderful tonight.

Alex was smiling at something Samantha had said when he saw from the corner of his eye someone approaching their booth.

He glanced up and saw the last person he wanted to see. "Brian?" He'd never seen him here before.

"Looks like the two of you have been enjoying yourselves." Brian picked up one of the two empty wine bottles on the table.

Alex hadn't realized they'd drunk that much. Nor had he realized how late it was. They'd been here for hours. He'd been having too much fun to notice.

"We were just leaving," Alex said to his brother, amazed how quickly the tone of their dinner had changed when wet-blanket Brian appeared.

"You've both had too much to drink for either of you to drive," Brian said.

Alex started to argue that he didn't need Brian telling him what to do.

"I insist," Brian said, a little less abrasively. "Please, let my driver take you both home. Can you let me do this one small thing for you? I am your brother." Brian seemed to have had a little to drink himself and appeared sincere. Alex figured Brian was just trying to impress Samantha. And it seemed to be working.

"It's a gracious offer," Samantha, the peacekeeper, said and looked to Alex as if she thought Brian was trying to be kind.

"Be gracious for once," Brian said quietly.

Alex didn't want to make a scene and truthfully, he had drunk a lot of wine and so had Samantha. He'd planned to call a cab for them, but why not take Brian's limo and driver and let Brian take a cab.

"Sure," Alex said with a smile. "Whatever the lady wants."

Samantha gave him a thankful smile. The woman actually thought she could make peace in the Graham family? Her optimism was one of the things Alex found so delightful about her.

Alex watched Brian pick up their bill. "I'll get this," Brian said and smiled at Samantha. Yep, his brother was just trying to impress her. "Good night." Brian turned and walked back to a booth down the aisle. Alex couldn't see who he was sitting with.

The limo driver leaped out to open their doors the moment they came out of the restaurant. Alex realized that Brian had called the driver, no doubt with instructions.

Alex tried to be gracious even though he found a

limo and driver too pretentious, not to mention the inside of Brian's limo.

"Pretty impressive," Alex said as he sank down next to Samantha on the deep warm leather seat. He had a wayward thought. Why was Brian going out of his way to impress Samantha? Did he think Alex and Samantha were an item and wanted to steal Samantha away?

He felt a stab of jealousy. And more than a little concern. Could Samantha be taken in by Brian's success, his lifestyle, his money?

Alex glanced over at her as the limo driver asked for Samantha's address. She gave it and the driver put up the thick glass between him and the back.

Samantha was gazing around the inside of the most expensive limo that money could buy. She *was* impressed, Alex thought.

He couldn't help himself. "You do realize that my brother has an ulterior motive."

She cut her eyes to him and seemed disappointed that he was looking a gift horse in the mouth.

"Trust me, my brother is up to something," Alex persisted.

"Maybe he really was just being nice," she suggested.

Alex laughed and shook his head. "Brian doesn't do things just to be nice. You can bet there's something in it for him."

But what Brian didn't know was that Alex was willing to fight for this woman. He might not have all the things that his brother did, including a prestigious job and a cool limo, but Alex did have something to offer this woman.

He put his arm around her. She turned to regard him. He'd expected surprise. Or at least the usual wariness.

Instead it was almost as if she wanted this as much as he did. Almost as if she'd been expecting his kiss.

Victor couldn't believe his luck. There was no way he was going to lose this fancy-pants limo, not in a million years. And unless he missed his guess the driver was going to lead him right to Samantha Peters's house.

This was finally working out. He thought about calling his client and telling him the good news.

But even as he thought it, he knew he wasn't going to tell his client. Another broken rule of his. Withholding information from a client.

Victor felt a rush of expectation. He'd been following this woman all over Miami. Finally he would get a look at her house. Not to mention, she would be home.

He felt a tightness in his belly. Normally, he didn't desire women. But this one… This one was different. And he did like to take his passion by force on occasion.

Yes, he would break every rule tonight.

This would definitely be his last job.

He would end it with Samantha Peters.

Chapter 10

The kiss was everything Samantha knew it would be. His mouth was warm and soft at first, tentative then insistent.

She'd wanted it, wanted him, wanted to feel his lips on hers. He was strong, his chest rock hard, and yet there was a tenderness about the way he held her, the way he kissed her.

At first.

Then he drew her closer until her breasts were crushed against his chest, her nipples as hard as pebbles and aching.

Desire raced along her nerve endings, heating her blood, quickening her pulse. She felt need rush to her center. Her breath came faster.

He deepened the kiss, the tip of his tongue brushing over hers. She felt a quiver of excitement as he shifted in the seat so his hand could cup her breast. His fingers brushed over the turgid nipple and she quaked at his touch, a soft moan escaping her lips.

They were completely alone. Nothing could stop them from making love.

Samantha knew *she* should stop him. Stop herself. Nothing good could come of this. It was wrong in every way, given that he was part of a case she was working on. And she was lying to him about who she really was. Not to mention that he would end up hurting her. That was a given, wasn't it?

But she wanted him as she'd never wanted any man. She told herself that if she could have him just for tonight it would be enough—no matter what the future held. She lied to herself because right now she couldn't have stopped him if her life had depended on it.

He pulled her skirt up until he could reach under it. She felt his hand between her legs. He cupped her there through her panties and she pushed against him, needing him inside her.

His cell phone rang. He ignored it as he began to open the button of her suit jacket, his fingers working hurriedly as if, like her, he couldn't wait to bare her breasts to his touch, to his lips, to his tongue.

The cell phone rang again.

She groaned and arched against him as his left hand cupped her breast and the other finished unbuttoning first her suit jacket, then her silk blouse down to the lacy black bra she wore.

She heard his intake of air as he saw the bra, saw the smooth white curve of her abundant cleavage, the nipples pressing against the sheer black fabric. His nimble fingers unhooked the front latch freeing her breasts.

He let out a groan as he dropped his head down to suckle at one, then the other.

He was working her skirt up, his hand snaking under her panties when the phone rang again.

With a curse he drew back and reached for it as if to turn it off. His glance fell on the caller ID and he swore again, his gaze coming to hers.

"It says caller unknown, could be the hospital. I have to take this," he said.

She nodded when what she really wanted to do was scream. But the call might be about Caroline. Of course he had to take it.

She pulled down her skirt and drew her blouse over her breasts even though Alex had turned away from her, the side windows were tinted and there was only darkness outside, and she couldn't see the driver through the privacy screen.

She placed a hand on Alex's broad back, not wanting to break the connection between them and closed her eyes, the ache painful. She could still feel his mouth on her breasts. She was wet with need for this man. It had been so long and no man had ever made her feel like this.

She felt him tense under her hand and opened her eyes, knowing it was bad news. Slowly she removed her hand from his back and began to button up her blouse, then her jacket.

For a few moments, Alex thought he hadn't heard the caller correctly. The voice on the other end of the line was disguised. It threw Alex for a moment.

He'd assumed that the call was from the hospital and

had taken it expecting it to be a doctor. Or maybe Preston calling about Caroline.

Instead it had been the strange-sounding voice. The words even stranger.

"Thought you'd like to know that your girlfriend broke into your sister's condo last night. Now why would a wedding planner do that?"

"What?" he'd asked, sitting up straighter. He no longer felt Samantha's hand on his back.

"Why don't you ask your girlfriend if you don't believe me. Ask her how she got that bruise on her cheek."

The line went dead.

Alex sat holding the phone, the caller's words finally starting to register. His girlfriend? Samantha? He glanced back at her. She'd dressed again.

"Bad news?" she asked, looking scared. "Is Caroline all right?"

He nodded. "It was just…just a crank call." Or was it? He tried to imagine Samantha in her business suit breaking into anyone's condo let alone Caroline's in that not-so-fine part of town.

Anyway, she couldn't have gotten past the guard.

Or maybe she could, he thought as he recalled her defensive reaction when he'd come up behind her at the hospital.

So she had some self-defense training. But that didn't make her a woman who committed B and Es.

For a moment he thought about asking her. But what would he say? "Break into any condos lately?"

That was just plain crazy.

What possible reason would she have to go back to the condo, let alone break in? None.

He sat back, disappointed because the moment was

lost. The driver tapped on the security screen. Alex hit the button, the separator coming down.

"We've reached your guest's residence," the driver said.

Alex looked out at the beach house. Nice location. This hadn't come cheap. He wondered what wedding planners made and hated that he was even more suspicious of a woman he would have made love to if it hadn't been for the call.

Something had changed. Samantha could see it in his eyes. If Caroline was all right, then what had the call been about? Whatever it was, Alex didn't seem to want to tell her.

The interruption had definitely sobered them both up. The driver opened her door.

"I'll be right back," Alex said as he slid out and walked her to her front door. Apparently he wasn't coming in.

She felt as if she'd been saved—and hated every moment of it. "Thank you for tonight."

He smiled at that. "It didn't go the way I had hoped."

"Maybe some other time," she said brazenly.

"Maybe," he said with a nod as he leaned toward her. It was a goodbye kiss and it took every ounce of her strength not to put her arms around him and pull him down for a real kiss.

But by then he had turned and was walking back to the limo.

She opened her front door and stepped inside, not having the strength to watch him walk away. Who had the call been from? Whoever it was had changed things instantly. Another woman?

The thought almost floored her. Of course a man like Alex Graham would have a lover. How foolish of her not to realize that.

Suddenly she felt the ache in her shoulder, the fatigue of the last two days, and yet she knew sleep would never come. Not tonight. Not after what had almost happened.

She walked through the house, not bothering to turn on a light and went straight to the garage. The motorcycle was a crotch-rocket, the fastest, sleekest one that money could buy. She didn't even bother changing her clothes as she lifted her skirt and swung a leg over the leather seat and snugged down her helmet.

The moment she heard the limo drive away, she hit the garage door opener and the door began to rise. She didn't wait for it to reach the top before she shot out, signaling the door to close automatically as she took the first corner and sped toward her office.

She passed the limo going eighty-five. Even if Alex had looked over, he wouldn't have recognized her, she told herself. His mind would be on the woman who'd called him. If indeed it had been a woman. He was probably on his way to her house.

Samantha pushed the bike up to a hundred, trying just as hard to push Alex Graham from her mind. Tonight should have taught her something. Not to make the same mistakes she had in the past with men.

Alex couldn't get the call out of his mind. He knew he wouldn't be able to sleep. Was it possible that the caller had been Preston?

Maybe Preston was just trying to get him over to Caroline's condo again tonight. Could it be a trap of some sort?

That made even less sense than Samantha going back over to the condo last night and breaking in.

The driver had put the window up between them. Alex touched the intercom button. "Drop me back at the restaurant so I can pick up my truck."

The driver nodded. "Whatever you say, sir."

Alex realized, a little belatedly, that the driver would be reporting to Brian. Alex wasn't sure what bothered him more, that the driver would know hanky-panky was going on in the back during the ride—or that Alex hadn't even tried to spend the night with Samantha.

That, he realized, was the least of his worries, though. If the caller was right about Samantha going back to the condo last night...

It would be just his luck to start falling for another woman he couldn't trust.

Victor could not believe his luck. His bad luck, that is. He'd followed the limo straight to Samantha Peters's door, staying back enough not to be conspicuous.

Everything had been going his way. Alex Graham had kissed her at the door and left. The guy had to be a loser. Even from a distance, Victor could see that the woman was ripe and ready.

Victor couldn't wait for Graham and the limo to leave. Breaking into the place would be child's play for him. He was debating whether to wait until she was asleep or to surprise her now when the garage door opened and a motorcycle came shooting out.

It was her. There was no mistake about it. She was still wearing that awful oversize suit but it was hiked up her slim bare thighs as she zoomed past.

Victor had thought he couldn't want this woman more. He was wrong.

He hurriedly swung his car around and started after her, angry with her that she'd disappointed him more than she could ever know tonight.

But he hadn't gone far when he realized there was no way he was going to catch her. Instead, he fell behind the limo. It was little consolation, but at least he would see where Alex Graham was headed.

Alex Graham stopped to tell the security guard he needed to get something from his sister's condo again.

"How's she doing if you don't mind me asking?" the guard asked.

"Better. She's conscious."

"Oh, I'm glad to hear that. She's a real nice woman. And her fiancé, too. He never fails to ask about my wife and kids."

Alex thanked the man, surprised by his concern and what he'd said about Caroline's fiancé.

"Have you seen Mr. Wellington around lately?"

The guard shook his head. "He has a lot of irons in the fire so he comes and goes a lot." There was respect and admiration in the man's voice. Alex nodded, thinking Preston certainly fooled a lot of people.

"One more thing," Alex said. "Has anyone else been around the condo since I saw you last night?"

"Not that I know of." The guard looked worried. "Is there a problem?"

"No," Alex said quickly to reassure him. The guard obviously took his job seriously and clearly didn't want to let Preston or Caroline down.

Alex dug out a card with his number on it. "If you see Preston before I do, would you give me a call?"

The guard took the card. "Of course. Tell your sister she's in my prayers."

"I'll do that."

Alex couldn't get the man off his mind as he headed for Caroline's building. His footfalls echoed as he entered. He noticed no sign of a break-in. Taking the elevator, he rode up to Caroline's rooftop condo.

The empty building had an eerie feel to it as he stepped off on her floor. He shone the flashlight he'd brought on the door to her condo but could see no signs that the door had been forced open. For all he knew someone could be waiting inside for him.

If his caller had been telling the truth, how had Samantha gotten in? The caller's story seemed even more outlandish and he wondered what the hell he was doing here this late at night on an obvious wild-goose chase.

He inserted the key and hesitated, hefting the weighty flashlight, as he slowly opened the door. It was dark inside the condo but a little light from the streetlamps outside bled through the plastic.

He turned on the light. Nothing looked any different than it had earlier.

That was until he stepped deeper into the room. A piece of two-by-four lay in the middle of the hallway. He frowned, sure it hadn't been there earlier.

Stepping over it, he started toward the wall of plastic and stopped. Part of the plastic was torn from where it had originally been tacked along the ceiling to keep the dust out of the bedroom.

He stared at the floor. He couldn't swear to it, but there appeared to be more tracks in the Sheetrock dust.

Taking a step back, he picked up the two-by-four and shifted the flashlight to his left hand as he thought about the call he'd received. The caller had known that he and Samantha had been here last night. How? Had they been followed?

Cautiously, he slipped through the opening in the plastic and saw that the bedroom door stood open. He'd made a point of closing it the last time he and Samantha had been here. He gripped the board and flashlight and stepped toward the bedroom.

At first glance, everything looked the same as he remembered it. But then he'd been so upset about his discovery that his sister was pregnant, he wouldn't swear to anything. Just the thought of her celebrating it in this room...

His gaze went to the nightstand beside the bed. The champagne bottle and glasses were gone. His heart began to beat a little faster. He glanced toward the bathroom, expecting to see his reflection in the large mirror just as he had earlier.

Instead, he saw only fragments of himself—and what was left of the mirror.

"What the hell?" He reached for the bathroom light. He'd lived in Miami long enough to recognize a bullet in a wall. There were two in this one, most of the mirror shards on the floor.

He looked around for blood, thankful he didn't see any. What had happened here last night? And why hadn't the guard seen—or heard something?

Because the guard patrolled the entire complex. No doubt whoever had been here had known about the guard and made a point of avoiding him.

Samantha knew about the guard, Alex reminded himself. So did Preston Wellington III.

Alex swore and snapped open his cell phone, but as he started to punch in 911, he stopped. The caller had said the wedding planner had been here.

Someone sure as hell had.

If he called the police he'd have to tell them what little he knew—which was next to nothing. The police were already investigating the abduction of that other woman—and Caroline's hit-and-run.

If he told the police about the call he'd received, they'd question Samantha and probably get nothing. Either way, they wouldn't tell him what they'd learned— just as they hadn't about Caroline's hit-and-run.

No, he thought, putting his cell phone away and thinking about the interlude in the back of the limo tonight. He wanted a shot at Samantha Peters first. If she was involved in this, he would damn well find out.

When Samantha reached the office, she wasn't surprised to find Clare working late again, along with several other agents.

"I was just going to call you," Clare said. She didn't look happy. More bad news.

Well, that was the way the night seemed to be going.

"I just got the fingerprint analysis results from the champagne bottle and one of the glasses you sent in last night tagged Urgent," Clare said.

Samantha held her breath. The fact that Clare had gotten results this quickly meant that Preston Wellington III's fingerprints were on file. It was looking more and more as if Alex was right—and she was dead wrong about the man. What a surprise.

"The prints belong to a man named Presley Wells," Clare said with a lift of one eyebrow. "Preston Wellington III. Presley Wells. You think?"

Samantha groaned. She felt sick. Alex had been right. The names were too similar for there to be any mistake.

Still she held out hope, telling herself he could have changed his name for all kinds of reasons. And his prints could be on file because of a job—not because he had a police record. "He have a record?"

"More than a few problems as a juvenile, but only one arrest as an adult," Clare said. "A burglary. Served some time in Tennessee."

"Tennessee?" Samantha echoed, growing sicker at this news. Alex had been right to worry.

"Tennessee. That's where he was born," Clare said. "I thought you might want an address for his next of kin. His mother is still alive and living outside the town where he was born."

Samantha took down the information. She couldn't keep this from Alex. She was tempted to call him, interrupt whatever he had going on tonight, with the bad news.

But she feared she would hear a woman's voice in the background and it would make her feel even worse than she did right now.

She thanked Clare and went back to her office.

She'd been wrong about another man. She was batting a thousand.

Chapter 11

The next morning in her office Samantha tried to keep her thoughts on her work, namely the Holcom-Anders wedding.

She went through her list of to-dos and even double-checked the weather channel to make sure there would be no surprises.

The Holcom-Anders wedding was being held on the beach today—one of those huge unpredictable outdoor weddings that drove wedding planners crazy.

With indoor weddings at least you could control the environment. But beach destination weddings were the big thing this year so most of the Holcom clan had flown in several days before and been up in Orlando doing the Disney thing before the wedding. The Anders part of the family had Miami connections so many of the guests would be driving down to Key Largo today.

The weatherman promised sunny skies. Satisfied there was nothing more she could do, Samantha gathered her things and went down to the parking garage to meet the rest of the team for the van ride to Key Largo.

She hadn't seen or heard from Alex since last night. She'd been disappointed when she'd returned home after working as long as she could only to find no message on her machine. She'd promised herself she wouldn't let what almost happened in the back of the limo happen again.

Instead, she would tell Alex what she knew about Preston Wellington III. She regretted not telling him last night before the limo ride. But he'd asked for one night without any bad news. And she had to admit, she'd enjoyed herself immensely.

Meanwhile she had a wedding to take care of, then she would be flying to Tennessee to find out what she could about Presley Wells.

She was her usual quiet self as she loaded into the van with the rest of the Miami Confidential team.

The talk among the group was of everything but weddings—and undercover work. Samantha leaned against a side window and listened, enjoying the fact that today they were all women and could chat about the craziest things.

Fortunately, the road to Key Largo was open, the traffic not too bad. Samantha breathed a sigh of relief when they arrived and saw that all of the details she'd so meticulously been working on with the rest of the team seemed to be in place.

This was a part of her job that she loved. Often it rivaled the other part of her job. But surprisingly, she had become a pretty good wedding planner.

The beach and leased hall for the reception were beehives of activity. Samantha checked in with Nicole O'Shea, Weddings Your Way's photographer; Jeff Walsh, the shop's music coordinator; and finally Ethan Whitehawk, the team's all-around handyman. The three had ridden down together earlier. Ethan had been involved in building an arch on the beach where the actual wedding would take place.

"The arch is beautiful," she told him. "I've heard nothing but raves."

As was his nature, Ethan only smiled as he made some minor changes to the outdoor bandstand.

Samantha left him and saw that Isabelle, the shop's spokeswoman, was talking to the mother of the bride as if trying to reassure her. Samantha started over but Isabelle motioned that everything was fine.

Normally, this many agents didn't attend the weddings. Most of them worked behind the scenes before the big day and weren't needed.

But this was the first wedding since Sonya Botero had been abducted. Rachel had worried that what had happened wasn't an isolated incident. That instead, another bride-to-be from Weddings Your Way might be in danger, so the whole team had come.

Samantha opened her notebook and began to check off items to be attended to. Alex Graham was hardly in her thoughts as she did what she did so well: tended to details.

The team disappeared during the wedding, all breathing a collective sigh of relief that there had been no problems. The weather had held, all the guests had arrived and the ring bearer hadn't lost the rings. All small miracles.

And maybe a larger miracle. The bride-to-be had made it through her vows without any problems—including another abduction or hit-and-run.

Samantha had already made sure the reception hall was ready, fully decorated, the wedding cake in its place with the small plastic bride and groom snugly on top.

She started to retreat as the guests filed in. Behind them she caught a glimpse of the turquoise water and sunlight. She had only a moment to appreciate it before someone stepped into her line of vision.

"I wondered if you would be here," the man said.

He'd taken her by surprise. "Mr. Graham."

"Brian," he said, seeing her moment's hesitation. "Obviously I didn't make as big an impression on you as my brother."

There was an edge to his tone.

"I didn't realize we were on a first-name basis," she said.

"Even after I lent you my limo last night? I was surprised to see the two of you on what certainly appeared to be a date."

She ignored the last part. "Thank you for the use of your car. That was very generous of you," she said, hoping to get away from him as quickly as possible. Clearly he was curious about her relationship with Alex.

Brian resembled his brother only slightly. Unlike Alex, Brian didn't look particularly fit. He was pale skinned as if the only light he spent much time under was fluorescent. His hair was a darker blond, his eyes brown but without any of the gold flecks that warmed Alex's.

The little time that she'd spent around Alex's brother

and father had been sufficient to convince her Alex's problems with them weren't all his fault.

"You really *are* a wedding planner," Brian said, seeming to find amusement in that.

"Did you doubt it?" she asked.

He didn't answer, just studied her openly. She felt his gaze light on her bruised cheek but he said nothing about that. "I heard you do all the big weddings," he said instead.

So he'd been checking up on her.

"There must be money in it." He made it sound as if that would be the only reason someone would resort to her kind of work.

She wondered what he'd have to say if he knew about her other job. She smiled as patronizingly as she could, not about to answer such a crass question.

"So did you find my sister's fiancé?"

"Not yet."

"I'm sure my brother won't stop until he does," Brian Graham said. "I guess he doesn't have anything better to do."

Odd the way he didn't refer to his siblings by their names, not to mention his condescending tone.

"I'm sure when Alex finds Preston, he'll be glad your brother went to the trouble. After all, we're talking about Preston's future wife," she said, not at all sure of that anymore, given the man's name wasn't even Preston.

"Has it dawned on you yet that maybe Pres doesn't want to be found?" Brian asked.

As a matter of fact… Out of the corner of her eye she spotted one of the caterers looking around frantically.

"If you'll excuse me, I need to attend to a few more details," she said.

"The perils of being a wedding planner," he said glibly as she left him.

But she felt his gaze on her, and later, when she finished calming down the caterer, she was surprised to see that Brian Graham was still standing where she'd left him, apparently watching her.

She turned away, hoping to avoid any more conversation with him, and almost collided with the black sheep of the Graham family.

"*Alex*," she cried, hating how breathless she sounded.

It surprised—and upset—her how pleased she was to see him.

That was until she caught his expression.

"Miss Peters," he said.

So they were back to that?

"I didn't know you were going to be here," she said.

He raised a brow. "Actually, I didn't, either."

There was something very different about him today. She saw it in his eyes. He seemed wary of her. Yesterday, she'd caught him watching her closely as if trying to see beneath her skin, today his gaze probed even deeper, definitely looking for something.

She felt a sliver of worry burrow under her skin. What had changed? Something more than even the phone call in the limo last night.

"How is Caroline?" she asked, afraid that was the cause.

He scrubbed a hand over his face. "They took her into surgery for her broken leg this morning but she is improving all the time." His gaze came back to hers and she saw the suspicion in his eyes.

It gave her a strange sense of loss that affected her more than she wanted to admit. He didn't trust her anymore and she felt sick at the thought.

Without his trust she couldn't do her job.

But she knew that wasn't what made her sick to her stomach. She liked Alex Graham. Was attracted to him. More than that, she had to admit. He was the first man in a long time with whom she'd actually let her guard down. She could have fallen in love with him. Had already started.

The thought shocked her and at the same time, admitting it made her feel a little more steady on her feet. It was one of the reasons he unnerved her.

"Anything wrong?" he asked.

She blinked at him. "Why would you ask that?"

"Because you're frowning at me," he said, his eyes intent on her face. He reached over before she could draw back and brushed his fingers over the bruise on her cheek. "How did you say you did that again?"

He seemed to be waiting for her to explain the bruise and anything else she had to hide. She gulped, not sure what he wanted from her. Worse, what she might confess. "Like I said, I can't even remember. I bumped into something obviously."

He seemed disappointed in her. "Obviously."

A strained silence fell between them. He raked a hand through his hair, his gaze on her. "Can we get out of here?"

She hated to think what would happen if she went off some place alone with him the way she was feeling right now. Fortunately, she didn't get a chance to answer.

Brian came up behind his brother. "So where is Preston?" he demanded, clearly enjoying that he'd interrupted their conversation. Samantha smelled booze on his breath. "You have found him, haven't you?"

Alex didn't look the least bit happy to see his brother. "What do you care?"

"She's my sister, too. But for some reason you seem to need to play the hero. So where is he?" Brian's eyebrows shot up. He smiled obnoxiously. "What? The great Alex Graham, brave fireman and all-around good-guy blue-collar worker, couldn't find him, either?"

Alex visibly tensed. "Back off, Brian. Today is not the day to cross me."

"Oh? Having a bad day?" Brian glanced at Samantha. "Things not going quite like you'd hoped?" He laughed. "Stick to what you know, Alex. Let me handle cleaning up the mess Caroline made."

"So you and Dad did invest with him," Alex said. "I hope you and the old man lose your shirts. I'd love to see this guy take you for everything."

Brian's face turned a mottled dark red. "Don't you think I know you're just waiting for me to fail? But don't hold your breath, little brother. I will come out on top. No matter what."

"I'm sure you will," Alex said. "But I'm not worried about you. Or Dad. Caroline is in love with this guy. If he really did hook up with her just to get to you and the old man, it's going to break her heart."

Brian scoffed. "Caroline will get over him. With her money, she can always find another man. Dad, however, stands to lose considerably. If I were you, I'd worry about your inheritance."

Samantha could see that Alex was doing everything in his power to restrain himself. "It's always about the money with you, isn't it? Have you ever been in love? Or lost someone who meant something to you?"

Brian's eyes sparked with fury. "Oh, none of us could have loved and lost with such feeling as you, Alex."

"I don't want to argue with you."

Brian hadn't seemed to hear him. "You have no idea what it takes to run an empire, the responsibility, the pressure. I don't have the luxury of whiling away my time falling in and out of love."

"No, your idea of love is the twenty minutes you pay for a woman's company."

Brian looked as if he might take a swing at his brother. When he spoke, his words seemed to vibrate with his fury. "You know nothing about my life or how hard it is to be the one in the family who everyone depends on. You turned down the job. You couldn't handle it even if you hadn't. So stay the hell out of it." With that, he stormed away.

"What an arrogant ass," Alex said through gritted teeth.

Samantha touched his arm. He was trembling.

He looked over at her. "Please, let's get out of here." He didn't wait for an answer, just took her hand and drew her out the door.

"Alex, I—"

"I need to talk to you." There was a command in his tone. But also a plea.

She couldn't have denied him anything right then. "All right. Just let me tell someone I'm leaving."

He seemed to relax a little. "I know a place we can go. It's cool and dark. I don't know about you, but I could use a drink." He steered her toward his pickup.

The last thing she wanted was a cool, dark, intimate

place to go with him, let alone a drink. Isn't that the way it had started last night?

He didn't drive far before he pulled into a small beach bar overlooking the water. As he shut off the engine, she heard music drifting on the warm afternoon breeze. The air smelled of sand and surf with the faint scent of burgers and fries and beer.

Once inside, he headed straight for the crowded bar. She hesitated by the door, half-afraid of what he wanted to talk to her about. Maybe it was just her guilty conscience, but she felt an icy chill skitter up her spine.

Then she glanced behind her and spotted a car parked just down the street. She couldn't be sure, but it looked like the one that had been following them before. It was hard to see if there was anyone behind the wheel because of the glare off the windshield. Had they been followed? Again?

She stepped back out of the bar and walked toward the car, turning down a short alley and circling around in order to come up behind it. The car looked like a rental. There was no one behind the wheel and on closer inspection she could see that the car was locked.

She glanced around but didn't see anyone who looked suspicious. Maybe the driver had gone into one of the businesses and was watching her.

She made a quick call to Clare to run the plates. "I think you're going to get a rental car agency. Find out who rented the car and let me know ASAP."

As she headed back inside the bar, she told herself she wouldn't be surprised if the car was rented by Presley Wells. It wouldn't be the first time she'd been dead wrong about a man. Or the last, she thought as she saw the expression on Alex's face.

He stood by the door to the beach with a drink in each hand, a frown on his face. "Let's take these outside."

She started to lie and tell him she'd been trying to find the ladies' room. But she was tired of lying to him and determined to end it here today.

He didn't say another word as he put down the drinks at one of the empty tables and pulled up a chair. He seemed to be waiting for her to say something.

She picked up the margarita he'd ordered her and touched her tongue to the salt, avoiding his gaze as she looked out over the water and thought about how to tell him the bad news.

Alex had planned to ask Samantha outright as soon as he saw her if she'd gone back to Caroline's condo the night after they'd been there together.

Looking at her now, though, the question seemed ludicrous. What possible motive would a wedding planner have to break into anyone's condo? It made no sense.

What did make sense was someone trying to make him distrust her. Trying to muddy the waters. He and Samantha had been working together to find Caroline's fiancé. Someone didn't like that. It told him that he and Samantha were getting close.

Even with all that wonderful rational thinking, Alex knew he was kidding himself. He'd already suspected that Samantha was hiding something from him. Now he would be watching her. And she already intrigued him.

"You look pretty today." He meant it. Even with the bruise on her cheekbone.

The compliment seemed to embarrass her. He watched her swallow and look away and a sinking feeling gripped his stomach. He still wanted to believe that the call last night had been a prank.

He raised his glass and said, "To you, thank you for all your help."

Samantha raised her plastic glass trying not to squirm. He couldn't have made her feel more guilty than if he'd toasted to honesty.

She didn't drink alcohol other than an occasional glass of wine. She liked to be in control. Always.

And, she needed all the control she could muster around Alex. The last thing she needed was alcohol and this beautiful beach on this wonderful afternoon. Her defenses were already down at just the hint of his smile.

"To happy endings," she said, wondering where that had come from, and took a sip, pleasantly surprised at how good it tasted.

She licked the salt from her lips, the alcohol in the margarita sending a shot of heat through her. She could feel Alex watching her, measuring her. The man definitely made her feel unsettled, unsure. Vulnerable. But it was the other emotions he made her feel that scared her. Especially the big one: desire.

She recalled the last time she'd felt desire—and how badly it had ended. She reminded herself that she was happy being a chameleon, blending in, going unnoticed by men.

She didn't want her life disrupted by him stirring up feelings, needs. She felt oddly exposed as if for all her care at hiding behind her glasses, her clothes, her front at Weddings Your Way, he could see through her.

It was the way he looked at her. There were moments when she was positive he could see right through her veneer to her deepest, darkest of all secrets. Not only that she was an agent but that her real guise was pretending to be a wallflower so she didn't attract men like Alex Graham.

Was it possible Alex already knew that while she was cool and collected on the outside, she was a mess below the surface whenever she was around him? That it was a battle to keep anything from him?

Her heart beat a little faster at the thought that he knew her and that was one of the reasons she felt so drawn to him.

He started to say something but stopped as a waiter slid a basket and a dish with what looked like jalapeño peppers onto the table.

"Wait until you taste this." He stabbed one of the pepper slices with his fork, uncovered the warm bread, took a piece and shoved the pepper into it before he holding to her lips, his gaze meeting hers.

There was nothing she could do but open her lips, all of her senses on alert at the intimacy of him feeding her.

Hesitantly she took a bite. The bread was warm and wonderful, the pepper both hot and sweet. She'd never tasted anything like it.

"I knew you'd like it." He sounded a little sad, the pad of his thumb deliciously rough as he dabbed at the corner of her mouth when some of the pepper juice escaped. She felt the sudden intense heat of the pepper.

But it was nothing compared to what the look in his eyes did to her. Heat skittered over her skin, firing her senses and sending a shaft of desire straight to the heart of her.

"Well?" he asked.

She took a drink and had to swallow twice before she trusted herself to speak. "Wonderful."

He smiled that beguiling smile of his. "That was just the beginning. There are more surprises in store."

She was almost positive he wasn't referring to food now.

He didn't want to ask her if she'd gone back to the condo last night. But he knew he couldn't put it off any longer.

He wiped his mouth on his napkin then took a drink of his margarita. Funny, but he hated to disappoint her. He knew how much she was hoping that Preston would turn out to be one of the good guys.

Putting down his glass, he said, "I'm afraid it's just as I feared. Caroline is broke. I have connections at the bank. She's gone through most of her inheritance. From what I can tell she's completely financing the condo development along with her own condo renovation. The checks are being run through Preston Wellington III's construction company." He could see that Samantha wasn't any happier to hear this than he had been.

She took a sip of her drink, lashes hiding her eyes, and said nothing, giving him the impression that, as bad as this news was, it hadn't exactly come as a surprise.

"You still want to believe in him, don't you?" he said.

"For Caroline's sake and the baby's? Yes, I do."

He sighed, unable to wait any longer. "I went to Caroline's condo last night after I got a call that someone had broken into it."

Something flashed in her eyes—or had he just imagined it?

"The champagne glasses and bottle were gone and the bathroom was shot up," he said. "There were two bullets in the wall where the bathroom mirror used to be." His gaze locked with hers.

He hadn't realized how much he was hoping she would say she didn't know anything about it. For the life of him, he couldn't think of a good reason she would break in to steal an empty champagne bottle and two dirty glasses.

Unless she was covering for somebody.

And he hoped to hell that wasn't the case, since he was falling for her.

She opened her mouth and said the last thing he wanted to hear. "I was the one who broke into the condo and took them."

Chapter 12

Alex let out a curse and rose, almost knocking over their drinks as he reached for her hand. "Come on."

He headed down the nearly deserted beach, practically dragging her. The sun hung low on the horizon, a ball of golden fire that cast the afternoon in dramatic light.

They hadn't gone far when she stopped to pull off her sensible heels. He let go of her hand and watched her slip off one shoe, then the other, her toes digging into the warm sand. Her toenails were painted a bright red. For some reason it made him smile—even as angry as he was.

He turned away from her and walked farther down the beach until he reached a small cove surrounded by water, rocks and trees. The place was secluded and they were completely alone.

She hadn't caught up to him yet. He watched her walk through the white sand, the turquoise water behind her, and couldn't help but remember the feel of her in the back of the limo last night. Looking at her, he would never guess that there were amazing curves beneath that boxy suit jacket. Or that the woman looking at him right now could be as passionate as the one he'd kissed last night.

He walked slowly back to her, never taking his eyes from her face. When he reached her, he cupped her cheek, thumbed away a tear, then rubbed the pad of his thumb over her full lips remembering how his mouth had felt on them, remembering the taste of her as he dragged her into his arms.

Her eyes widened, her lips parting. He heard her sharp intake of breath, felt the slight tremble in her body, as his mouth dropped to hers.

The moment their lips touched electricity arced between them setting off a storm in him. He felt a flash of desire as sharp and intense as a bolt of lightning. It set off a fire that rushed through his veins.

He grabbed the back of her suit jacket, fisting the material in his hands as he dragged her tighter against him until he could feel her wonderful body even through the fabric.

She quaked in his arms as his tongue explored her lips, her mouth, as if he could break through her cool reserve and unlock her secrets.

She wasn't so cool right now. Her mouth was hot and tasted of citrus and salt. He wanted nothing more than to go on kissing her forever.

He heard a chorus of giggles behind him and reluctantly withdrew his mouth to glance back and see a gaggle of young children all tittering, small hands over their mouths, eyes wide as platters. Behind them, several women who appeared to be day care providers gave him a disapproving look.

Alex could only smile as he opened his fists, released the wadded-up fabric of Samantha's jacket and stepped back, but kept his arm around her. He could feel her still trembling, one of her arms around his waist, a piece of his shirt in her fist as though, if he let her go, her legs might not hold her up.

The interruption gave him time to come to his senses and he knew he should have been thankful for that. But he wasn't. His heart was beating wildly and desire still burned in every cell.

Who was he kidding? He wanted this woman even knowing what he did about her.

As Alex stepped away from her, Samantha sank down to the sand, not worrying about her expensive suit.

She was shaking, her head spinning, her body devoid of the strength to remain standing.

He looked down at her, a combination of anger and desire shining bright in his gaze. "Who are you?" he asked in a hoarse whisper. "Just when I think I know you..." Pain registered in his expression, a sharp anguish that squeezed her heart as if he held it in his fist.

He sank to his knees in front of her and took her shoulders again in his large hands.

All she could do was look up into his handsome face. The kiss had been so unexpected. He'd been angry at her, demanding answers. Why kiss her?

"Talk to me," he commanded. "Dammit, Samantha.

Why would you break into Caroline's condo to steal an empty champagne bottle and two glasses?"

She tried to get to her feet, forcing him to rock back, giving her space but losing the smile, a hard wary edge to his expression.

She felt a little more in control again with distance between them although she was still shaking inside, her heartbeat slower but more painful. "I'm sorry I didn't tell you right away."

"Sure," he said, getting to his feet and turning his back to her, the Gulf of Mexico blue-green and endless.

Her eyes burned with tears as she stood and brushed sand from her suit. She wanted to step toward him, to place her hand on his back, to have him take her in his arms. She wanted him to make love to her.

The truth shocked her. She barely knew the man and yet she felt as if she knew him better than herself. Worse, he didn't know her.

Or maybe he did, she thought as she noted the angry set of his shoulders. She remembered the look on his face when she'd turned to see him back at the wedding reception.

She took a deep breath, smothering the urge to touch him and instead brushed again at the sand on her skirt, buying herself a little more time. Where was her famous cool now? And what was she going to do about these feelings?

"Alex…"

He glanced back at her. The look in his eyes hurt more than if he'd struck her. He didn't say a word. He didn't have to. She couldn't have denied him anything at that moment.

"Alex, I went back to Caroline's the other night. I took the champagne bottle and the glasses."

"Why would you do that?"

She was sick of lying but there were some things she couldn't tell him. She had to protect the anonymity of the team. She couldn't let what she was feeling for him cloud her judgment. Or worse, endanger their lives or those of the people involved in this case.

And yet she knew if she let him go on believing she'd betrayed his trust, she would never forgive herself. Alex Graham mattered. More than she ever dreamed a man could matter again. Every instinct told her not to trust her feelings. Not to trust another man. That it would end badly. That this time it would kill her.

"I took the bottle and glasses for fingerprints."

"What would a wedding planner need with fingerprints?"

Leave it to Alex to get straight to the heart of it.

"I have a friend who works at the lab." True enough.

"Why didn't you just tell me you wanted to take the champagne bottle and glasses when we were there together?" he asked. "I would have let you."

She swallowed. "I didn't know you well enough then." Which was laughable. She'd only known him a couple of days. And yet she believed she knew him now?

"I didn't want to upset you since I had no idea what I would find out."

He was shaking his head, his smile devoid of any humor. "Upset me? A call in the middle of the night telling me my sister's wedding planner is breaking into the condo upsets me. Lies upset me. Finding my sister's condo shot up upsets me." He reached out and brushed his fingertips lightly across her cheek.

She felt a stab of heat shoot straight to her center.

"Seeing that bruise on your cheek upsets me." He drew back his fingers. "What happened at the condo?"

"Someone showed up. He had a key—and a gun. I didn't get a look at his face."

Alex just stared at her. "You're telling me someone tried to kill you?"

She swallowed, holding his gaze, seeing the play of emotions cross his face and desperately wanting to tell him anything he wanted to know. "I managed to get away. Alex…" She started to reach for him, but he drew back.

"Who *are* you?" he asked again. His gaze cut to her core. "And what the hell is going on?"

Samantha's cell phone rang. She flinched as if pained by the sound, reached into her bag and looked at the caller ID. "I'm sorry. I have to take this."

Alex let out a frustrated laugh. "Saved by the bell," he said, turning to walk a few yards up the beach, half-afraid of what he would do if he didn't put space between them.

He couldn't believe what an idiot he'd been. He didn't know what surprised him more—that she was admitting to breaking in to Caroline's condo or that she had a friend who could run fingerprints on champagne bottles and glasses.

At least she had told him the truth about being at the condo, although he wasn't fool enough to believe that's all there was to it.

Instead of demanding answers, he'd kissed her and

only managed to make things worse. This wasn't about him. Or even about her, he reminded himself. It was about finding his sister's fiancé, finding out just how much trouble Caroline was in. And making sure she was okay.

He'd gotten sidetracked with this woman. He turned to look back at her. She was listening intently to whoever was on the other end of the line. The woman had more secrets than the CIA. Every instinct told him to give her a wide berth. The last thing he needed was another deceitful woman and he'd had his share.

He walked farther up the beach away from her, trying to get his head on straight. She'd broken into his sister's condo to get fingerprints. Amazing. And he thought the last woman who lied to him was bad. Hell, all she'd done was try to marry him for his money.

"Sorry, I had to take that," she said behind him.

He braced himself before he turned. She'd taken off her suit jacket. Her arms were lightly freckled, her skin much fairer than he'd realized.

She squinted up at him, one hand raised to shield her eyes. "I need to go back."

He nodded. "Wedding business, right?" He hadn't meant to sound so scornful. The sun was in her face and he saw now the sprinkling of tiny golden freckles across her nose and cheeks that she normally kept so well hidden under makeup. "What is your real hair color?"

"*What?*"

"That brown, it's not your natural hair color, is it?"

Her eyes widened a little. "I don't understand why—"

"Never mind," he said. "It doesn't matter. Like you said, you need to get back." He turned and started down the beach away from her.

"Red," she called after him.

He stopped walking but didn't turn around again.

"I'm betting it's a strawberry blonde." He heard a catch in her throat.

He turned slowly to look back at her. There were tears in her eyes.

"His name isn't Preston Wellington III," she said. "It's Presley Wells. He has a record, served time in jail for burglary. He took out a large insurance policy on your sister, five million dollars. I'm going to his hometown in Tennessee to see if I can find him."

"And you are...?" he whispered.

Her eyes filled and he had the feeling that it took every once of her strength to keep the tears from spilling. "A wedding planner. Among other things."

He nodded. "And who called me last night and told me you were at Caroline's condo?"

She shook her head. "It had to be the man who shot at me. I'm fairly sure no one else saw me there."

He said nothing for a moment as he shifted his gaze from her to the water. "Wouldn't you say the chances were good that the man you had your little...run-in with at the condo was this Presley Wells?"

"I can't say. He was average height and weight—like half the men in Southern Florida."

"Except half the men in Southern Florida don't have a key to Caroline's condo," he said, looking at her again. "I'm going to Tennessee with you unless you have a problem with that."

"If that's what you want."

He studied her for a long moment. "Eventually, you're going to tell me what your investment is in all this, aren't you."

Her gaze softened. "Maybe."

He shook his head again. "I must be crazy." But at least this way he could keep an eye on her—for more reasons than he wanted to list. He just had to be careful and not get too close, although he had a bad feeling it was too late for that.

Samantha watched Alex on his cell phone as he made arrangements for a chartered flight to Tennessee this afternoon.

He didn't trust her. But who could blame him?

She hated this. But there was no way around it. She had a job to do. It didn't matter what Alex Graham thought of her. All that mattered was getting to the bottom of Sonya Botero's abduction. And while Samantha didn't want to believe Presley Wells was behind it any more than she believed he was behind Caroline's hit-and-run accident, she knew she had to go to Tennessee and find out the truth.

"So where do we fly into?" Alex asked.

Samantha told him the town Clare had given her. "Knoxville would be the closest airport. We'll have to drive down into the Smoky Mountains south of there."

Alex hesitated, then said into the phone, "I'll need a four-wheel-drive rig waiting for us at the airport. That's right. Just as soon as we can fly out."

Two hours later, Samantha was sitting across from Alex in a soft leather seat, the rest of the small jet empty except for the pilot. She hated to think what this was costing Alex, but apparently he could afford it.

Samantha closed her eyes as the plane took off, recalling her hurried phone conversation with Rachel before takeoff. The Holcom-Anders wedding had gone off without any trouble. No more Weddings Your Way clients abducted or injured. But also no ransom demand on Sonya Botero yet.

"I'm on my way to Tennessee," Samantha told her. "Alex is chartering a plane."

"You told him then?" Rachel asked.

"I couldn't keep this from him."

"Have you blown your cover?"

"No."

"But you've considered telling him you're an agent." It wasn't a question. "I would think long and hard about doing that. You could be jeopardizing the team—let alone your own life. I don't think I have to remind you that in this business you have to be very careful who you trust."

"No, you don't have to remind me," Samantha said.

"Let me know as soon as possible what you find out in Tennessee." Samantha had heard the warning in her boss's voice and the disappointment. Samantha's cover had been blown only once before while in the FBI but she was sure Rachel knew about it. That time it had cost her dearly but she feared this time it could cost her her life.

"So who was he?" Alex asked.

Her eyes came open with a start. "*What?*"

"The man who let you down, who was he?"

She stared at him. Alex had to be a mind reader. "I don't know what—" She stopped. His gaze held so much compassion. She looked away. "What would make you think—"

"You don't have to tell me if you'd rather not," he said and turned to look out the window. Wisps of clouds blew past against a backdrop of blue. She caught a glimpse of the Gulf as the plane banked and headed for Tennessee.

"I met him after college," she said, her voice barely a whisper. Alex said nothing. He didn't look at her and for that she was grateful. "It was the first time I'd been serious about anyone. Even at the time, it seemed too good to be true. It was. He'd been playing me to get to my roommate—his real target."

He looked at her then, his gaze filled with empathy. "I'm sorry."

She nodded, deciding to tell him all of it. "The thing was, my roommate didn't want him. His obsession led to him kidnapping and killing her. He's on death row now."

Alex's eyes widened in shock. "My God."

She didn't tell him that she and her roommate were both FBI agents working undercover or that her cover was blown and her career almost lost before the man was captured.

"He totally fooled me," she said. "What does that say about me?"

He shook his head. "That you're trusting. His kind are pathological liars with no feelings other than basic survival instincts. It's like they were born with something missing inside them. They're so good at lying, no one can see through them." He fell silent. "I'm afraid this Presley Wells might be one of them, that's how he fooled my sister." He looked over at her. "You do realize that all men aren't like that, right?"

"It's just hard to trust your instincts after something like that," she said quietly. "I've always felt I should have seen what was going on. If I had, I might have been able to save Meredith."

He reached over and took her hand. "You certainly aren't the first woman to be taken in by a man. At least you weren't pregnant with his baby."

"My instincts told me that Preston… Presley was a good man," she said with a lift of her brow. "If I'm wrong about him, too…"

"Then you could be wrong about *me*?"

Heat warmed her cheeks. She looked away. "It's not quite the same thing."

"No," he said. "It's not, because I'm not like either of those men."

Silently she said the words she couldn't bring herself to voice. How time will tell.

Victor Constantine watched the plane until it disappeared into the clouds before he made the call. "They just left in a chartered plane for Knoxville, Tennessee." He held the phone away at the sound of loud swearing.

"I want them stopped. Whatever you have to do."

Victor frowned. "How would I stop them? Shoot down the plane?"

"Not *now,* you fool. Catch the next flight to Knoxville, Tennessee. Take care of them out there. The roads where they're headed are narrow mountain lanes. It should be easy for you to make sure they never make it back here."

"Do you realize what you're asking me to do?" Victor said mentally adding up the cost for two murders.

"I'm not *asking* you. I'm telling you. I want them taken care of."

"Then we'd better discuss my fee." He tossed out a number, having no desire to go to Tennessee. And even less desire to kill Samantha Peters. He'd missed catching her at home last night and clearly tonight was out, but maybe when she returned…

"I'll pay you double your fee. Just make sure that neither of them returns to Miami." The phone went dead.

His client had just raised the stakes. Only a fool would turn down that kind of money.

He waited, not surprised when his cell phone rang. "Yeah?"

"I've chartered you a jet. You're still at the airport, right?"

"Right."

"Take down this address in Tennessee. The area is isolated, nothing but squirrels, mountains and timber."

"You want it to look like an accident?"

"That would be nice but not necessary. I just want them both dead."

Chapter 13

They hadn't talked the rest of the short flight. Samantha had dozed. Or possibly pretended to. It gave Alex a chance to just look at her. He had so many questions. At least one of the big ones had been answered.

He knew the first time he'd touched her that she was more than a little gun-shy when it came to the opposite sex. He knew the look, the feelings, the reactions. He'd been burned himself and hadn't even dated in months. It took a while to trust again and he wasn't to that stage yet himself.

But he couldn't imagine going through what she had. It proved how strong she was.

He wondered if that was why she'd changed her hair, tried to hide her body beneath the oversize suits. She came off as an ice princess when there was molten lava burning inside her. Their kisses had proven that.

She was scared of those feelings. So was he. And with good reason. She knew who he was. He couldn't say the same of her. More than a wedding planner. But how much more?

Once they landed, Samantha gave him directions and they left Knoxville and quickly found themselves in the Smoky Mountains.

As they left the city and the roads became steeper and narrower, he caught her several times watching her side mirror. With a jolt, he realized why. "You think we've been followed?"

"It wouldn't be the first time," she said. "Someone's been following us since the day Caroline was injured in the hit-and-run."

He gritted his teeth. "And you didn't bother to mention it?" How did she know about these things anyway?

She seemed to let that go without comment.

"Isn't it pretty obvious who would be following us?" he asked. "Let's see. Who lied about who he was? Who doesn't seem to want to be found?"

"It could be someone who's hoping we'll find Presley for them," she said.

He saw her expression. "Like my brother or my father?" He let out a curse. He hadn't thought of that.

The road was now only a single lane as it climbed up a series of switchbacks. "You sure we're on the right road?"

She was staring back at the road behind them. "It shouldn't be much farther according to the directions we got back at the station."

"Don't get me wrong, I wouldn't put it past either my brother or my father to hire someone to follow us. But you can't think they hired the guy who almost killed you the night in the condo."

"I don't think he came there to kill me. Maybe scare me. But then I surprised him," she said.

He glanced over at her, recalling what had happened at the hospital when he'd sneaked up behind her. "I'm sure you did." He had to shift into four-wheel drive to make the next switchback up the mountain. "Or maybe he was there for the same thing you were. Maybe he'd realized he'd left something incriminating in the condo and had gone back to retrieve it. I'm putting my money on Presley Wells. Unless you know something else I don't."

"I don't know any more than you do now."

He shot her a look, wanting to believe her. Up ahead, the road flattened out a little and he spotted an old rusted mailbox with WELLS printed in crude letters on the side. "Looks like we found it."

As Samantha caught a glimpse of the house set back in the woods, she felt her stomach knot. The house had once been white but was now in desperate need of paint. Wash flapped on the clothesline out back and trash burned in a fifty-five-gallon barrel off to the side, the smoke rising slowly to fill the air with a rank smell.

Alex brought the rental SUV to a stop in the rutted yard sending a half-dozen chickens scurrying across the bare dusty ground. Several old dogs slept in the shade, not even stirring as flies swarmed around them. Through the tall weeds along the side of the house she could make out the remains of aging vehicles rusting in the sun.

"You all right?" Alex asked as he parked next to a battered old pickup.

She could only stare at the house. She knew this kind of poverty, this kind of despair. She'd lived it in Iowa, where she'd grown up, and had run like hell from it the first chance she got.

"Samantha?"

She nodded, not trusting her voice, as she caught movement behind the faded curtains. Faded like her mother after having so many children and being caught in a cycle of hopelessness.

"You don't have to come with me if you don't want to," Alex said, obviously seeing her hesitation to get out of the car.

She could feel his gaze on her, that same curious searching look he'd been giving her for several days now. How much could he see? Could he see her fear at the possibility of witnessing her earlier life in this family's faces? Did he have any idea what a coward she was when it came to her past?

She'd been running all her life, she thought as she opened her car door in answer and got out. A rusted sprinkler spat out a trickle of water in a tight circle near the porch on what might have once been a lawn but was now a mud hole. The sun was an oppressive ball of heat directly overhead. It beat down on her as she walked toward the rotting porch steps, Alex by her side.

The porch sat at a slant, the boards weathered and rotted. The smell from the trash hit her again and Samantha was struck with the image of her mother, her body thin and stooped, wearing a worn old housedress and slippers, taking out the trash to be burned.

The woman who opened the door could have been Samantha's mother. She wore a worn-thin homemade housedress, her graying hair limp and hanging around her narrow weary face.

"Yes?" she asked, squinting into the bright day as she eyed first Alex, then Samantha.

"Mrs. Wells?" Alex asked.

"Yes?" She looked at them suspiciously as if they were bill collectors.

Alex seemed at a loss as to what to say to the woman and glanced at Samantha. "I know your son Presley," she said.

The woman raised a brow, her narrowed eyes filled with even more suspicion. "He done something?"

"No, it's nothing like that," Samantha assured her. "His fiancé has been in an accident and we're just trying to find him to let him know." Her voice sounded shaky but not half as unsteady as she felt.

The woman looked more than skeptical and Samantha realized it was the kind of story that bill collectors used to come up with when they were trying to track down her daddy.

"I'm Samantha Peters," she said, holding out her hand to the woman.

Mrs. Wells ignored it.

"I'm planning Caroline and Presley's wedding and this is her brother Alex Graham," Samantha continued, dropping her trembling hand to her side again, feeling the dampness. She wiped her palm on her skirt trying to find that cool she'd once been so famous for. It had deserted her.

The woman frowned. "Caroline? That the woman he goin' to marry?"

"Could we step inside?" Alex asked, swatting at the flies swarming around them.

With obvious reluctance the woman stepped back. "But I ain't got no idea where he is."

Samantha stepped into the living room. Even the smells took her back to her childhood. The house was unbearably hot and dank. Everything looked as worn-out as Presley's mother.

"He don't come here no more," she said, wiping her hands on her dress. "Ya'll want to sit down. I got some sweet tea—"

Samantha glanced toward the sagging couch and felt Alex's gaze on her. "Are you all right?" he whispered.

She felt light-headed but nodded. "Fine."

"Thank you, but we can't stay," he said to Mrs. Wells.

"Did Presley tell you anything about Caroline?" Samantha asked.

She shrugged. It seemed to take all her energy. "He mighta said somethin' in his last letter."

"Do you remember the letter's postmark? Where it was mailed from?" he asked.

"Miami. He lives down there," she said. "You sure he ain't in trouble with the law again?"

"Why would you ask that?" Alex said.

The woman made a face. "His letters. There's money in 'em." She looked up at Samantha. "Says he's an... investor. Don't know what that is but it don't sound legal."

Samantha saw Alex hide a grin.

"Investing can be legal," Samantha said.

The woman didn't look as if she believed that.

Samantha pulled one of her business cards from her purse. "If you hear from Presley would you let me know?"

Mrs. Wells took the card in her rough hands. Through the window Samantha could see the old-fashioned wringer washing machine out back. She remembered her mother bent over one.

"You should buy yourself an electric washing machine with some of the money Presley sends you," she said.

Mrs. Wells narrowed her eyes. "The one I got works good enough."

Samantha said nothing as four children, ages from about ten through sixteen, came running in through the back door. They all looked a little like the man who'd been with Caroline the first time the two had come in to talk about their wedding.

"How many children do you have?" Samantha asked, her voice cracking, and quickly softened the question by adding, "I come from a large family myself."

"Twelve, only six left at home."

Samantha nodded. Her own mother had her first child at fourteen and spent the next thirty years having babies. She could feel Alex's eyes on her, feel his surprise at hearing about her large family.

"Your husband gone?" Samantha asked, knowing he probably was, since there were no diapers on the clothesline.

"Died some years back."

A silence fell over the house.

"I always wished I'd grown up in a large family," Alex said into that silence.

Samantha looked away, not wanting him to see her contemptuous expression. He had no idea what it was like. But then he'd never been dirt-poor. Samantha had. So had Presley.

He is no different from you.

She cringed at the thought. It was true, though. Like

Samantha, Presley had escaped what her father used to call the snake pit. But did anyone ever really escape the scars of their childhoods?

She thought about Presley sending money home in his letters but realized even crooks often still cared about their mothers.

"Thank you for your time," Samantha said. "We can see ourselves out."

Mrs. Wells said nothing as Alex opened the screen door and they stepped out on the porch.

As they crossed the porch, Samantha saw a face staring out at her from the trees and froze.

The girl stood watching them. She couldn't have been more than twelve. Her feet were bare, her dress too small and scrubbed as threadbare as the white sheets hanging on the clothesline, her hair straight as a stick hanging in dirty hanks on each side of her narrow face.

But it was the eyes that grabbed Samantha. She recognized that look because she had been that girl.

Maybe still was that girl inside.

As Samantha started down the stairs she was unable to take her eyes off the girl. That's why she didn't even realize she'd missed a step until she went sprawling forward. She saw Alex reach for her but he was two steps behind and she was falling too fast. She tried to catch herself, but her hand landed in the muddy yard and she fell to her knees.

Alex was there at once, helping her up. "Are you all right?"

All she could do was nod. Her hands were muddy and her clothing soiled. She looked at the spot where she'd seen the girl. She was gone. If she'd ever been there to begin with.

Tears burned Samantha's eyes.

"You *are* hurt."

Samantha shook her head harder, the tears impossible to stem. She'd thought she'd dealt with her past. She'd thought she'd escaped that life, that girl she'd been. But all the pain came gushing out, hot tears scalding her cheeks.

She pulled free of Alex and stumbled toward the rental car, trying to brush the mud from her hands and forearms, the dirt from her clothing. She heard Alex behind her. He handed her one of the raglike towels that had been hanging on the clothesline and opened the car door for her.

She wiped what she could from her with the towel, returned it to the clothesline even though it was now soiled and stumbled into the car seat, knowing how foolish she must look to him. It wasn't until he joined her in the car that she finally got the sobs to stop.

Alex started the engine and drove away from the house without a word.

Samantha didn't look back. Couldn't. She was afraid she would see the girl watching them, longing to go with them.

"I'm sorry."

He looked over at her, aghast. "What do you have to be sorry about?"

"For…for falling apart on you like that." She took a ragged breath. "I… I…"

"You don't have to explain," he said, glancing at her again as he drove.

Alex was mentally kicking himself for bringing her to Tennessee, to this place. He'd seen her reaction back there before she fell, before she broke down. Damn. He wanted to stop the car and pull her into his arms. But he feared that would be the worst thing he could do right now.

"That was me."

She'd spoken so softly he wasn't sure he'd heard her correctly.

"You?"

"That was my childhood back there," she said.

She couldn't be serious. But then he looked over at her and finally understood. "You're the Presley in your family, aren't you?"

She nodded and turned her face away.

"I shouldn't have brought you here. I'm sorry."

She shook her head. "I thought I'd gotten over my childhood, the poverty, the bleakness of that life, but seeing Mrs. Wells and her children…" She brushed a hand over her cheek, her eyes red and shiny from her tears.

Alex said nothing as he drove and tried to imagine what it would be like growing up back at that house.

She watched the trees rush past, feeling foolish. She'd worked so hard to hide who she was from Alex and to break down like that…

Alex reached across, took her hand and squeezed it. "You must think I'm a real jackass complaining about my family."

Her throat hurt from trying not to cry again. "I've never thought you were a jackass."

He smiled then, those wonderful eyes of his brightening as he glanced at her. "You're just letting me off easy and we both know it." His gaze caressed her face. "You are one remarkable woman, you know that?"

She felt anything but remarkable right now.

He turned back to his driving and she watched the thick dark leaves of the trees brush over the SUV and thought about Presley Wells. Where was he? She couldn't shake the feeling that his mother was right and that not only was Presley in trouble, but so was Caroline.

"I don't want to be wrong about Presley," she said.

He looked over at her. "I don't want you to be wrong, either. You never suspected where he'd come from when you met him?"

"Just like you never suspected when you met me."

He smiled sheepishly. "No. But you made something out of yourself."

"Maybe Presley did, too."

"You didn't change your name."

"No," she admitted. "But I changed everything else." And yet she was still that poor, scared little girl inside.

Samantha saw a flash as something shiny caught in the sun on the side of the mountain ahead.

The back window of the SUV exploded. An instant later, the windshield turned into a spiderweb of white.

Chapter 14

"What the—" Alex hit the brakes, at first not sure what was going on. The SUV went into a skid on the narrow road. He brought it back under control as his side window exploded.

"Keep your head down," he yelled as he hurriedly knocked out the windshield so he could see where he was going. The glass slid down the hood. He heard it crunch under the tires and cranked the wheel to make the next turn, almost too late.

Then he looked over at Samantha and saw what she had in her hand. A gun. He knew he shouldn't have been surprised. Hell, hadn't it crossed his mind that she had one in her purse back when he thought she was nothing more than a wedding planner? Nor did it seem he had to tell her someone was shooting at them.

"There!" she cried and pointed to a road that dropped

almost straight off the mountain through a thicket of trees, the branches a canopy over the top. "Take it!"

"Hang on!" He jerked the wheel. The front tires dropped over the side and he felt as if he was hanging by his seat belt as the SUV careened downward through the trees. He tried to brake but the back tires hadn't touched down yet. He swore again as he side-swiped a stand of young maples, the saplings snapping off like toothpicks.

The back tires finally hit dirt and he was able to brake and shift down. Limbs scraped the top of the roof. They were still moving way too fast. And to make matters worse, he couldn't see what lay ahead. Could easily be a cliff or a ditch or a huge tree that would stop them dead.

He fought to get the rig slowed down and finally came to a halt in the heart of the thicket. They were completely closed in by the trees. They couldn't have opened their doors on either side and the SUV was sitting at such an angle, nose down, that he was practically standing on the brake pedal.

"You aren't hit, are you?" he was finally able to ask as he looked over at her, a tremor in his voice.

"I'm fine. Are you…?" She looked frightened at the thought.

"I'm just great," he said sarcastically. He'd really had it with this woman and her secrets.

She was looking back up the mountainside, the gun clutched in both hands in a way that convinced him it wasn't her first time. "I think we're far enough down the road he won't be able to take any potshots at us anyway."

"Wanna keep defending Presley Wells?" he asked

her. "Unless there's someone else who wants to kill you for reasons you haven't told me."

"Not that I know of," she said.

"Let's try this again," he said, anger filling the hole fear had just deserted. "Who are you? What the hell is going on? And wait, how did you get that gun on the plane?"

She met his gaze, cool and calm, making him want to shake her. "Which question would you like answered first? As for what's going on, someone just tried to kill us."

"Okay, that part was pretty clear." He saw her glance back again. "You think he'll come down here and try to finish us off?"

"I think we'd better see where this road comes out since it doesn't look like turning around is an option," she said.

He didn't move, just glared at her, waiting. He wanted answers and he wasn't moving another inch until he had them. She'd put him off too long. His whole body was vibrating, adrenaline spiking his pulse as though he'd taken a wild drug.

She turned in her seat, her gaze locking with his. "I'm an agent."

He blinked. "An agent. Like—"

"Like FBI."

He pulled back in surprise. "I thought you were a wedding planner."

"I am. I'm both. I work undercover."

Yeah, right.

"You wanted the truth."

He did. But could he handle it? "You do this for a *living?*" An agent? The buddy at the crime lab, the wealth of information her "friends" came up with. He should have known. He shook his head. "I knew there was more to you, but I never guessed this. So you're after Presley Wells?"

"I'm *after* whoever abducted one of our wedding clients and ran down your sister. I'm still not sure who that is. But..." she added before he could argue, "I'm no longer convinced that your sister's fiancé is the man I thought he was."

"Well, I suppose that is something."

"Now could we get out of here?" she asked.

He studied her a moment longer. "You are definitely somethin'."

Samantha wasn't sure he meant it as a compliment. In fact, she was pretty sure he intended it as just the opposite as he put the SUV into drive and let his foot up off the brake.

The car bounced down the mountain through the trees, Alex expertly handling it. She watched him, so filled with pain it took everything she could muster not to cry.

He was all right. He hadn't been hit by the gunfire. She tried to assure herself that he was safe. That after this she would make sure he stayed that way. Some agent she was. She'd almost gotten them both killed.

"Any idea which way to go?" he asked when he reached a fork in the steep road.

She had no idea but pointed to the left, her throat too dry to speak.

He reached over and cupped her cheek with his warm palm. "You didn't get me into this, so stop looking at me like it's your fault, okay?" He let up on the clutch and the SUV lurched downward again. "Damn, this mountain is steep. But I got to hand it to you. Dropping off through here seems to have worked."

Ahead, through the trees, she saw a shallow creek where the road flattened out and another intersected it. Alex saw it, too. He drove across the shallow creek and turned on the more traveled road, looking over at her and grinning.

"What?" she had to ask.

"We're alive and, damn, but it feels good."

He made her smile, too, as he pulled her over, looping his arm around her, holding her close as he drove. When they hit the highway, he turned on the radio. He couldn't go fast, not with the missing windshield. He had to turn the radio all the way up. The wind whistled through the SUV, blowing back her hair.

She snuggled against him to the sound of country music. He was right. It felt damned good to be alive. Even better to be with Alex Graham.

At the first town, he pulled under the awning of a motel office just as it began to rain. The sky was dark, the clouds ominous. The radio announcer broke into the song to say that tornadoes had been seen and a weather alert was in effect. Just as Samantha feared, all flights had been canceled until further notice.

"I'll get us a room," he said, hopping out.

She caught sight of her reflection in the side mirror. Her hair was windblown, her face dirty and her clothing covered with dried mud. She looked as if she'd been in a pig wrestling contest and the pig had won.

He came back out with two keys and squatted next to her missing side window. He handed her the key to number nine, then seemed to see the tiny cuts on her face where the window had splintered and cut her. There were specks of dried blood mixed with dirt.

He swore. "Oh man, I didn't realize—"

"I'm fine," she said, taking his hand as he reached out to touch her cheek and kissing the palm. "I just need a bath. I'll be good as new." He didn't look convinced, but he opened her door and stepped back. "I'm next door if you need me." She had her purse, the weapon inside. She needed him, but not to protect her. At least not at the moment.

Inside the motel, she called Rachel and reported what had happened.

"You're sure you and Alex Graham are all right?"

"Yes." She fingered one of the cuts as she stared in the bathroom mirror. "There is no reason to report it to the locals. Whoever took the potshots at us is long gone." At least she hoped that was true.

"It had to be someone who knew where you were going. Either Presley Wells or a member of his family," Rachel said.

It certainly looked that way. The shooter had positioned himself on the hillside using a high-powered rifle at a spot where he knew they would be most vulnerable.

"I think it is time to pick up Presley Wells for questioning," Rachel said and seemed to wait, expecting an argument. "If he's in the States, we'll find him."

Samantha doubted that. She had a feeling Presley was in hiding. But why, if he wasn't guilty as sin? "I'll get back to Miami as soon as I can. The weather…" It was tornado season. A hurricane whose name she couldn't remember had just come ashore in the redneck Riviera. This whole part of the country was expected to be drowning in water by midnight. Already she could hear the wind howling outside. All aircraft were grounded until further notice, according to the reporter on the radio.

"There is no rush," Rachel said. "Get some rest."

Samantha hung up and turned on the water in the shower. Then she stripped down, stepped under the wonderfully hot spray, and closed her eyes and thought about what could have happened on that mountain. The tears came then, tears of fear and relief, not for herself but Alex.

She quit crying, chastising herself for her moment of weakness—not her first today. As she shampooed her hair, she tried to drown out the sound of the SUV's windows exploding, the sound of the wind just outside, the eerie sound of silence around the Wells home and the vision of a young girl standing in the trees.

Samantha lathered soap over her body as if she could wash away the memories. It hadn't been just growing up poor. It was growing up without hope. When you were that poor, when you knew nothing but hardship, you didn't know there was a way out.

She thought of her family. Like Presley, she'd run away, trying to run fast enough to escape what had felt like quicksand pulling her down.

It was hard to explain to a man like Alex Graham who had grown up in his kind of wealth.

She didn't know how long she stood under the spray, letting the water pelt her skin until she was numb. Finally she shut off the water and stood for a moment in the tub listening to the wind and rain pelting the back-side of the motel.

Presley was in trouble. That much she knew and would have bet the ranch on it. But was it of his making? It didn't matter now. The police would be on the lookout for him. What worried her was Caroline and the fear that Caroline might somehow be involved.

She dried with one of the large towels and wrapped her hair in another one turban-style, then pushed open the door, needing to let some of the steam out.

Her mind was working again, trying to fit the pieces together. It always came out the same. One big piece was missing. The centerpiece, the one that would give her all the answers. And that piece was Presley Wells.

She started to reach for her soiled clothing and realized it was gone. For one startled moment, she thought her purse and gun were also missing.

But her purse was right where she'd left it on the counter within reach. Hurriedly, she checked. Her gun was still there. Still loaded. But her clothing was gone.

She peered into the bedroom and spotted a large shopping bag. Wrapping the towel more securely around her, she padded into the bedroom.

There was no one in the room but for the first time she noticed the adjoining room door. She'd bet the adjoining room was Number Eight—Alex's room.

Upending the bag, she dumped the clothing on the bed and gingerly picked up a pair of panties, surprised that he'd gotten the right size. He'd underestimated a little on the bra, but the top and skirt would fit perfectly. Too perfectly. How had he known?

The fabric was cut to slide over her curves. Even before she took the clothing back into the bathroom and put each item on, she knew there was no more hiding from him. She'd told him she was an agent, something she'd failed to tell Rachel, she realized.

She'd been so tired and dirty... No, she knew she'd

purposely left that part out. She'd deal with it once she got back to Miami.

She looked at herself in the mirror, dragged the towel from her hair and tossed it aside. Finger-combing her hair, she watched it curl.

Alex had guessed that muddy brown wasn't her natural color. But wouldn't he be surprised to find out that she had naturally curly hair that she usually spent hours brushing straight each morning? She could see some of the red highlights in her hair. She'd had to skip her appointment to have the color covered this week because of what had happened at Weddings Your Way.

She stared at herself in the mirror, seeing her old self and wanting to flee from it. But at the same time, wanting to embrace it for the first time in years. This was all Alex's fault, she thought. He'd done this to her.

Behind her, there was a soft tap at the door. Anxiously, she raked her fingers through her hair again. But it was useless. Her hair was going to do what it wanted and that was curl.

Another tap.

She took a breath that sounded a lot like a sob.

Alex Graham was about to see the real her.

Her feet felt like lead weights, her legs rubber, as she walked to the door. With trembling fingers, she turned the knob, bracing herself for his reaction.

He let out a sharp breath, eyes widening. "Wow."

She felt self-conscious, just as she had as a young girl when her breasts had budded out early. She'd always been thin and having breasts had made her stand out. She'd hated the attention from the boys and did everything she could to hide her curves even back then. Now, though, she had no choice but to reveal her true self.

* * *

Alex couldn't believe it. Finally, he felt as if he was seeing the real Samantha Peters. "You look *fantastic*," he said. Tears welled in those big brown eyes of hers but she smiled, then worried at her lower lip with her teeth.

Without makeup, there was that adorable trail of tiny golden freckles that arched across the top of her high cheekbones over her perfect nose to the other cheek.

"Samantha." The word caught in his throat as his eyes met hers. Heat shot through him.

He had a flash of memory. His mouth on hers. The taste of her in the back of the limo. On the beach. He knew he was lost long before she stepped to him and, standing on tiptoe, gently touched her lips to his.

He didn't move. Didn't breathe.

She pulled back just enough to look into his eyes. Desire burned in her gaze but so did uncertainty.

She kissed him again, this time parting her lips to touch the tip of her tongue to his. Desire rocketed through him, as hot and moist as her mouth on his.

His arms came around her. He dragged her to him with a sound like a curse or an oath. Or a prayer. His hands splayed across her strong back as he dragged her even closer and kissed her as if there was no tomorrow.

He knew better than to get involved with another woman with secrets. But he could no more stop kissing her than he could forget the way she'd looked when she'd opened the door.

Heat blazed through his veins. Every instinct told him to stop as he cupped her wonderful behind in his hands and pulled her tightly against him.

She let out a gasp against his mouth but her arms had found their way around his neck. She drew his lips down to hers again, her eyes sexy slits, as he lifted her and, kicking the motel room door closed, shoved her back against the wall.

He slipped her out of the skirt and slid his hand beneath the panties. She arched against him as his wet fingers took her to pleasure. Her own fingers found the buttons on his jeans and in moments he was driving into her. She cried out, her fingers twined in his hair. His mouth on one breast. He felt her release, a dam breaking. She slumped against him.

He wrapped her in his arms and carried her to the bed where he slowly made love to her again as the wind howled at the window and rain beat down in a steady torrent.

Victor Constantine made the call right after he saw the SUV careen over the side of the mountain and disappear into the trees. No one could have survived that.

He'd hoped for an explosion. Or at least to see flames. But he was convinced, even if they hadn't died at once, they would be injured too badly to ever climb back up that mountain to the road.

"That nasty little problem you had is taken care of," he said when his client answered. Victor had mixed feelings about it. He still wished he could have spent some quality time with Samantha Peters. He'd just have to find another woman like her and relieve this itch he had before he started his retirement.

"Good. Don't call again. As far as I'm concerned you and I never did business." The phone went dead.

Victor sat for a moment before he dialed his foreign bank. He couldn't put his finger on what was bothering him. Not until the bank representative took his password and told him his greatest fear had been realized. The client had wired money from an account which was then cleaned out and closed.

Another first for Victor Constantine. He'd been duped by a client. His last client.

He called the cell phone number the client had given him and wasn't surprised to get nothing. Not even a ring. No doubt the client had destroyed the phone, believing it was the only connection between them.

Victor smiled to himself, more amused than angry. Did the fool really think Victor Constantine would just let this go? Was anyone that stupid?

Apparently his former client was.

Victor couldn't wait until he found him, until he looked the man in the eyes and saw not just fear—but the realization that he was about to die a very painful death.

Chapter 15

The phone woke Samantha from the most peaceful, contented sleep she could ever remember.

"Peters," she said, after groping her cell out of her purse beside the bed and snapping it open.

She could see a sliver of gray daylight coming through the blinds. It took her a moment to remember where she was. Last night came back in a rush. Her skin warmed at the memory and she swung her legs over the side of the bed and headed for the bathroom with a glance over her shoulder at Alex.

He lay on his side, eyes closed, an indentation in the bed where she had been snuggled next to him.

A feeling of euphoria flooded her. Had she ever been this happy? She found herself smiling as she closed the bathroom door.

"Samantha, can you hear me?" It was Rachel. She sounded worried.

"Yes. Sorry. I dropped the phone." She had tucked the phone against her hip as she was looking back at Alex and now realized that Rachel had been speaking that whole time.

"Is everything all right there?" Rachel asked.

"Great." The word was out before she could catch it back. But it was the right one—just not one Rachel was used to hearing from her. "Fine. Everything is fine."

"I woke you," Rachel said.

Samantha glanced at her watch and realized it was after nine. "No, that is…" She mugged a face at the bathroom mirror, grimacing at how ridiculous she must sound. Rachel was no fool. Of course she could tell she'd awakened her.

"Is Alex there?"

"No." Samantha took a breath and let it out slowly. "He's in the next room."

"I see."

She figured Rachel did see.

"Does he know?"

Samantha didn't have to ask what she meant. "I had to tell him about me, but not about the team."

Silence, then, "You do understand that this puts your position in jeopardy?"

Samantha knew what she was asking. Was her relationship with Alex important enough to put her work on the line—as well as her life? "Yes."

"You surprise me, Samantha," Rachel said. "In the four years we've worked together has there been anyone else?"

"No. No one."

"And within a matter of days you have fallen for

this man." It wasn't a question but Samantha answered it anyway.

"Yes. But it won't affect how I complete this assignment."

Rachel chuckled softly. "That's what they all say."

Samantha had seen others come and go at Miami Confidential. Some not under the best of circumstances. At least one had gotten herself killed. Samantha knew Rachel was concerned for her welfare—and that of their clients.

"I will do my job. No matter what," Samantha said with more force than she'd intended.

She could hear the smile in Rachel's voice when she spoke, "I believe that. Clare wants to talk to you. Let me know when you fly out."

"I will."

Clare came on the line. "I did that financial you asked for on both Presley Wells and Caroline Graham."

Samantha held her breath.

"Looks like they have everything invested in an area called Sunrise Estates."

The project where Caroline's condo was located. "So everything is riding on it?"

"Everything."

Samantha glanced toward the bathroom door. "I need you to check out a couple more names," she said and turned on the shower, covering her words. "Brian Graham, C. B. Graham and—" she took a breath and let it out slowly "—Alex Graham."

"What exactly am I looking for?"

"Any irregularities, recent large investments, anything that sends up a red flag," Samantha said. Rachel didn't think she could be impartial, objective. Rachel was wrong.

"I'll get back to you."

Samantha stepped into the shower feeling guilty and yet righteous. She had a job to do. If Alex was the man she believed him to be, he would understand that. She just prayed he *was* that man and that she hadn't just jeopardized not only her career but her life for a man she couldn't trust.

Alex rolled over on his back and stared up at the ceiling. After a moment he heard the shower running and thought about joining Samantha.

Last night had been amazing. The intimacy they'd shared surprised him. He'd never felt anything like it before.

He heard the shower shut off. As he turned to watch her come out of the bathroom, one towel wrapped around her hair, the other around her slim body, he reminded himself who she was.

A federal agent masquerading as a wedding planner. He corrected that, a wedding planner masquerading as an ordinary woman.

Samantha Peters was no ordinary woman. Not by a long shot. And Alex Graham wondered if he could handle this much woman.

She stopped beside the bed and looked down at him. He wondered who'd been on the phone, but he only wondered if for a moment.

Light shimmered in her brown gaze like an expensive whiskey. He could smell the fresh scent of soap on her smooth skin. Her lips parted slightly and she knelt forward and kissed his cheek.

He closed his eyes, weak with desire for this woman. He opened them when he heard her straighten.

Slowly she took the towel from her head, dropping it on the floor. She raked a hand through her wet curly hair. She couldn't have been more beautiful, her skin glowing from the shower, her face flushed—just as it had been during their lovemaking.

And those eyes, deep and dark. His gaze locked with hers and a bolt of desire ricocheted through him, but he didn't move, barely breathed as he watched her.

Slowly, she unhooked the end of the towel wrapped around her. It dropped to the floor with barely a whisper.

She smiled at his intake of breath and was already leaning toward him as he threw back the covers and pulled her down on top of him.

The storm passed, leaving devastation in its wake. Everywhere there were downed trees and power lines. Once the hurricane farther south had come ashore it spawned high winds and tornadoes. One tornado had touched down not far from where they were staying.

As Alex drove them to the airport in the new rental car he'd procured, they passed some of the debris. Samantha found herself wishing they didn't have to go back to their real lives.

And that surprised her. Her two jobs had been everything for so long, she'd never believed anything else could fulfill her the way her work did.

But that was before she'd met Alex Graham.

He'd grown quiet, as well. For a while they'd escaped everything, but those many hours together couldn't last and they both knew it.

Eventually, they'd known they would have to return to Miami. Samantha feared that would change everything. In Tennessee in a motel with Alex, she hadn't been a wedding planner or a special agent. She'd just been a woman.

Alex had called Caroline the minute the plane landed in Miami. His sister was doing much better. He hadn't talked to her that often over the years, so when she came on the line, he didn't really know what to say to her.

"Pres called," she said. "He feels so badly that he is out of the country and unable to return but he'll be home soon."

Alex knew she was lying, but he said, "Good. That must be a relief to you. I know about the baby, Caroline." Silence. "Hell, I'm ready to go out and buy a football. Or some dolls. It doesn't matter. I can't wait to be an uncle." He heard her crying.

"That's all I've ever wanted, Alex. For us to be a family. You're going to love Pres. I planned to tell you about him the other day at Weddings Your Way...before the accident. I was just afraid you wouldn't understand. You know, about the baby and all."

"You know I'd love to talk to this fiancé of yours," Alex said. "Congratulate him and welcome him to the family. You have a number for him?"

Silence. Then, "He said the phones are terrible where he is, can't get calls in but he'll be calling me again soon and I'll tell him. He'll be glad and it won't be that long before you'll get to meet him in person."

Yeah right. "What country did you say he was in?"

More silence, then a weak laugh. "You know I didn't

even ask. Somewhere in South America, I think he said. He moves around so much, who can keep track?"

It broke his heart to hear his sister try to cover for the man. How long did she think she could keep this up?

"Okay, sis," he said. "You just take care of yourself. I'll see you real soon." He had ended the call, anxious to get back to Miami, afraid for his sister even with an added guard on her room.

He understood that she'd lied about Pres because she loved the man. He understood love, maybe now more than he ever had before, he thought, looking over at Samantha as they walked through their terminal at Miami International Airport.

"Caroline says she's heard from Pres." He raked a hand through his hair. "I can hear the love in her voice for this guy. It kills me." He saw her expression. "I know you still want to believe in this guy, but if you're wrong about him, it doesn't mean you're wrong about me."

Samantha hoped that was true as she smiled and took his hand in hers. "I still believe he loves her." She couldn't have been wrong about that.

She wanted Presley to be innocent of any wrongdoing even more now that she'd met his family. She wanted him to be like her—the one who'd escaped that life, made good, prove it could be done. She needed that reassurance.

"If what you say about your father is true, he would never have accepted Caroline marrying Presley Wells of Tennessee," she said, trying to convince herself as much as Alex that that was the reason Presley had called himself Preston Wellington III.

Alex nodded slowly. "You saw how much my father

admired him. Pres did a great selling job. I think he fooled my sister, as well."

"Maybe. Maybe not."

Alex narrowed his gaze at her. "How can you say that? She had to have fallen for his lies. Let's not forget that she's pregnant with his child and he is nowhere to be found."

"His shirts in the closet," Samantha said. "Your sister had to have seen them. I think she knows who he really is."

Alex looked stricken. "You're saying she was in on this deception?"

"I'm saying it's likely, given that Presley became Preston Wellington III about the time he met her."

"Exactly." Alex sighed. "Even if you're right, he could still be behind her hit-and-run."

She couldn't argue that.

"And how do you explain the man who's been following us. Or the attempt on our lives? Someone doesn't want us returning to Miami with what we know. Who else could it be besides Presley Wells?"

She wished she had an answer. But she knew C. B. Graham would never have accepted Presley Wells as a son-in-law if he knew about his background. Just as he would never accept Samantha Peters of Algona, Iowa, dirt-poor farm girl as a daughter-in-law.

"You all right?" Alex asked, his gaze softening with concern. He squeezed her hand gently. "Let's hope Presley is the man you thought he was. Believe me, nothing would make me happier for my sister's sake." He leaned toward her, meeting her gaze as he leaned in to kiss her. The kiss was soft and gentle. Almost a goodbye kiss.

"Let's go see my sister."

* * *

Alex was glad to see that Caroline was awake and sitting up in bed when he and Samantha entered her room. She smiled and seemed happy to see them.

"Pres just called again," she said, her hand going to her stomach, her smile broadening.

"I'm sorry I missed that," Alex said.

Caroline's smile slipped a little. "You'll meet him soon enough."

"Oh? Is he on his way back?" Alex asked.

Caroline seemed to ignore his question as she turned to Samantha. "It is so good of you to stop by."

"How are you feeling?" Samantha asked, brushing Alex's hand as she stepped past him.

He moved to the end of the bed, telling himself to let Samantha handle this. She was much better at this kind of thing. That's right. She was an agent. How did he keep forgetting that?

His gaze settled on her as she visited with his sister and he felt his body heat with a desire he wondered if he could ever quench. Even a lifetime with that woman wouldn't be enough, he suspected.

Caroline seemed relieved to have Samantha there. "The doctor told me I was unconscious for a while. I'm so glad the baby is all right." She looked up and caught him watching Samantha. She quirked an eyebrow. "Has something been going on that I don't know about?" Her expression made it clear that she couldn't imagine a more unlikely pair.

"Alex?" Caroline's gaze seemed to take in Samantha's attire that he'd purchased for her in Tennessee, an admiring glance before she met his gaze again. "You both seem…different."

"We need to talk," Alex said, moving to the other side of his sister's bed. "And not just about me and Samantha."

He saw Samantha take Caroline's hand as if to protect her, to protect Presley.

"I went by your condo," Alex said.

Caroline's eyes widened. "Why?"

"Why do you think? You were unconscious. I wanted to find your fiancé and get him to the hospital."

Caroline said nothing, but seemed to stiffen as if bracing herself for the storm.

"You know Preston is really Presley Wells, don't you?" Samantha asked before Alex could.

Surprise, then resignation registered on his sister's face before being quickly replaced by a steely determination he knew only too well.

"We went to Tennessee," Alex said. "We know everything."

Not quite, but Samantha didn't correct him.

Caroline had closed her eyes. He could see that she was squeezing Samantha's hand. "Have you told Daddy?"

"I wouldn't do that."

Her eyes came open again.

"Tell me what's going on," Alex demanded.

"If you know everything then what is there to tell?"

"Where is your fiancé?"

His sister shook her head, tears brimming in her eyes.

All the anger seemed to rush out of him. He slumped on the edge of her bed. Then, as if on impulse, he leaned into Caroline and because of her broken arm and leg, gave her an awkward hug.

Caroline let go of Samantha's hand to wrap her arms around his neck. "Trust me," she whispered. "Everything is going to be fine." They stayed like that for a long moment.

He heard Samantha step out of the room to give them some privacy. A moment later he heard the ring of her cell phone.

"Let me help you," Alex said to his sister as he pulled back from the hug.

"You already have. I'm glad you know about Presley. I tried to tell you the other day at Weddings Your Way, but I was afraid of your reaction."

"It isn't my reaction you have to worry about," he said.

"In time, Daddy will come around, you'll see." Caroline pressed his hand to her stomach. "You're going to love Presley." She smiled. "He reminds me of you."

Walking down the hall away from the two guards outside Caroline's room, Samantha took the call, glad to see it was Clare getting back to her.

"Are you sitting down?" Clare said.

"No, should I be?"

"Maybe. I did some checking on the names you gave me. I started with Alex Graham, since I knew you were in Tennessee with him and Rachel seemed to be worried about you."

Samantha held her breath.

"Financially solvent and then some. It doesn't look like he spends even the money he makes."

"What are you saying?"

"He's loaded and apparently has made some good investments. He could live much better than he does.

From what I could find out, he lives in a small beach house, old neighborhood, though not a bad one."

Samantha felt a wave of relief. No red flags. Nothing to cause her concern. Maybe Alex Graham was just what he appeared to be. She sure hoped so because she was crazy about him. And it scared her half to death.

"Of course Alex doesn't have anything compared to his father," Clare continued. "Whew! Is C. B. Graham rich."

"Any recent big investments?"

"As a matter of fact…"

Just as Samantha had been led to believe, C. B. Graham had invested quite heavily with his future son-in-law, Pres. It wasn't enough to make a dent in his overall wealth, but it was substantial enough that it wouldn't go unnoticed if C.B. lost it.

"And Brian Graham?" Samantha asked, pretty sure he had invested, as well.

"No record of him investing any money with Wells," Clare said, surprising her. Samantha had been so sure. Brian had seemed awfully eager to find Pres. But maybe it had just been concern for his father.

"Probably didn't invest because he's in trouble financially," Clare said.

"What?" She remembered the cocky way Brian had been at the Holcom-Anders wedding. "But I thought he ran the Graham empire?"

"Not all of it. That kind of wealth is never all in one pot—or all under one control," Clare said. "But Brian Graham had been given a substantial amount of it to control it appears."

"And he's lost it?"

"No, but he's made some bad investments and unless he gets a windfall, he will have lost it all," Clare said.

Brian was in trouble financially? Did C.B. know? And what did that have to do with Presley? Everything, she thought. If Brian were desperate, would he invest in one of Presley's projects secretly as a last-ditch effort to save himself? It might explain why Brian was so anxious to find Presley.

She thanked Clare and closing her phone started back down the hall toward Caroline's room. A nurse Samantha had seen before came out of Craig Johnson's room just down the hall.

Samantha slowed to talk to her, the nurse smiling as she recognized her. "I saw you coming out of Craig Johnson's room. How is he doing?" In truth, she was surprised he was still in the hospital. Shouldn't he have been released by now?

The nurse's smile instantly faded. "I'm sorry, you must not have heard. He's in a coma."

"A coma?" But Samantha had been convinced there wasn't anything wrong with him. "I don't understand."

The nurse shook her head. "It happened about an hour ago. We found him on the floor. He'd obviously hit his head when he fell. No one knows what happened. Possibly some sort of seizure from his other head injury during his attack."

Samantha had a pretty good idea she knew what had happened to Johnson. Whoever had tried to get to him before had been more successful this time.

"I saw that you were visiting Ms. Graham," the nurse said. "A lovely woman. I'm so happy for her and her fiancé. He obviously loves her so much."

Samantha came alert at the nurse's last remark. "You've seen him?"

The nurse realized her mistake at once but Samantha wasn't about to let the woman off the hook.

"It's all right. You can tell me," Samantha said. "I'll keep your confidence. He's been here?" She thought of Craig Johnson down the hall now in a coma. Was it possible Presley...

The nurse glanced around then leaned in conspiratorially. "He's been by every night."

The woman had to be mistaken. Samantha stared at her, trying to hide her surprise. "Ms. Graham's fiancé has been coming to see her every night?"

"Every night since the accident. The nights she was unconscious, I found him asleep in a chair next to her bed when I checked on her before the shift change."

"You're sure it was her fiancé?"

The nurse nodded and smiled. "Good-looking man with dark hair, pale blue eyes and a great smile."

That would be Presley. "And that's the only time he comes by to visit, at night?" Samantha asked keeping her voice down.

"Every night since she was admitted," the nurse said. "Sneaks in after visiting hours." She shrugged as if it was no big deal he was breaking the rules. "Leaves before dawn. I guess he has a job to get to. He obviously is a workingman, you know, by the way he dresses."

Presley was working *something*, that was for sure. "What about the guard at her door?" Samantha asked.

The nurse looked sheepish. "We distract him."

Samantha groaned inwardly. What if the man the nurse had described had been a killer? Quite simply, Caroline Graham would be dead.

"I take it Ms. Graham is in on this?" Samantha asked, knowing that had to be the case.

The nurse grinned. "It is kind of romantic. Just seeing the two of them together. They are so much in love."

And in cahoots. But over what? Caroline had led them to believe that Pres was out of the country and still trying to get back to her.

The question was, why had she lied? None of this made any sense. Unless the nurse was mistaken and the man who was visiting Caroline each night wasn't Presley. Had Caroline found not just one but two men who were that good-looking and obviously charming, as well?

But the nurse had mentioned Presley's pale blue eyes and they *were* incredible. A cool-water blue accented by dark lashes. And when Presley smiled, it was quite remarkable. No, the man had to be Presley.

"It's that other man that we hate to see here," the nurse said, then seemed to regret having spoken out of turn.

"What man was that?" Samantha asked, her ears perking up.

"The brother. Not the nice one who's in there with her now but the other one."

Brian. "Has he visited much?"

"A couple of times with their father. Is he really as rich as everyone says?" She saw Samantha's expression. "Sorry. A few times he came by alone. He was fine when the father was with them but the other times he upset Ms. Graham and this last time—"

"When was that?"

"An hour or two ago," the nurse said, frowning as she looked at her watch. "I think he came about the time we were trying to revive Mr. Johnson. Anyway, I heard them arguing all the way down the hall and finally had to ask him to leave."

What had Brian been arguing with his sister about? Presley Wells no doubt.

A call bell rang at the nurses' station. The nurse excused herself and hustled down the hallway.

Samantha heard Alex come out of his sister's room and turned to look at him. He looked awful and the news she had to give him wasn't going to make him feel any better.

Chapter 16

Alex raked a hand through his hair as he looked at Samantha. She looked as down as he felt. "Caroline's lying through her teeth."

Samantha nodded and motioned for him to follow her to the solarium. "Presley isn't out of the country," she said the moment they were alone. "He's been here every night, staying by your sister's bedside while she was unconscious."

Alex swore. "How—?"

"He's charmed the nurses into helping him sneak past the guards."

"We'll see about that." He started to storm past Samantha, planning to see that those nurses lost their jobs—along with the guards he'd hired.

"Wait," Samantha said, grabbing his arm. "You don't

want to do that. Think about Caroline. Obviously Presley cares about her. Why else hang around here?"

He swore and walked to the sliding doors, shoving them open to step out into the hot humid night air as he looked out at the city. What Samantha said made sense. Or did it? He stepped back into the air-conditioned room, closing the door behind him.

"Why *would* Presley hang around here, especially if I'm right and he's hoodwinked my family, stolen their money and planning to take off?"

"Exactly," Samantha said. "Maybe he did con your father and brother into investing with him. But he already has their money, right? What reason does he have to stick around but the fact that he loves your sister and can't leave her now?"

"He wants something."

"What?"

Alex shook his head. "Why sneak around the hospital at night? Why have Caroline and his office tell everyone he's not even in the country? He isn't done," Alex said as the theory began to grow. "He's waiting for something. Something he needs before he's done. Maybe one more big score."

"And how do you explain him coming to the hospital every night to be with Caroline?"

Alex looked up in surprise. "That's it. He needs whatever it is from Caroline." He glanced at his watch. "Presley comes by every night, right?"

She nodded.

"Then tonight we'll be ready for him." She started to object but he cut her off. "You have all those wonderful contacts. Can you get a video set up in my sister's room? I'm sure we can get her out of the room long enough for your contacts to set up the equipment. Given what I have on that nurse I'm willing to bet she'll help us."

Samantha had the good sense not to argue. She got on her cell phone, turning away from him, as she made the arrangements. Clearly she thought the video would prove that Presley was just a man in love.

Alex was betting it was going to prove to be a lot more than that.

Samantha got the technical team to come in and install the equipment while the nurse wheeled Caroline down the hall for what was supposed to be more X-rays.

Both Samantha and Alex stayed out of sight, wanting Caroline to believe they had left for the night. Samantha suspected that Caroline would call Presley when the coast was clear for him to return to the hospital.

She'd had the team set up a monitoring device so she and Alex would be able to not only see but hear everything that went on in Caroline's room. All they had to do was wait in the empty hospital room down the hall.

Alex was sprawled in one of the chairs next to Samantha, both of them facing the screen. Nothing had happened since the nurse had returned Caroline to her room. Samantha was beginning to think that Caroline had warned Presley not to come tonight.

Then, just past nine, Caroline checked her watch and made a call.

"Brian, I need to see you," she said, sounding more upset than she appeared on the video screen. "Yes, now. It can't wait. No, I can't talk about it on the phone. I have to see you. It's about Preston." She listened for a moment, then hung up and checked her watch before lying back in the bed and closing her eyes.

"What the hell?" Alex said.

Samantha was just as surprised as Alex by the call to Brian. "The nurse told me that Brian upset Caroline on his recent visit and they had to ask him to leave."

"Something's up," Alex said. "You saw the way she was acting."

Samantha nodded and they waited. Not twenty minutes later, Brian slipped into Caroline's room. Clearly, he had figured out a way to get past the nurse.

"So where is he?" Brian said without preamble once in Caroline's room.

She shook her head, tears filling her eyes. "I don't know. I just found out that he isn't even Preston Wellington III. His name is Presley Wells." She began to cry.

"I had no idea my sister was such a good actress," Alex said under his breath.

Brian swore as he moved to the bed and tossed his sister the box of tissues. "I already knew that. I thought you had some new information. You got me over here for this?"

"You knew?" Caroline cried. "Why didn't you tell me?"

Brian shook his head, looking more than a little upset. "I need to find this fiancé of yours. Do you understand?"

Samantha figured Caroline understood perfectly.

"Could you just hold me for a minute?" Caroline asked, still crying.

Brian looked as though he'd rather leap out the window but he awkwardly leaned over and put his arms around her.

Caroline put her arms inside his coat and pulled him

closer, drawing back a couple of times to blow her nose, until Brian seemed to have had enough.

"Look, you got the family into this mess, Caroline, you have to help me find him. If he calls you, find out where he is. You owe me."

Caroline nodded, red-eyed and still weepy. "I'll do everything I can, Brian. I'm so sorry."

"Brian's actually buying her act," Alex said, sitting up and shaking his head in wonder.

As Brian left, Caroline shut down the waterworks instantly and reached beneath her covers to pull out a small object that Samantha recognized at once.

"She's got Brian's PDA."

Alex was up out of his seat and pacing the floor. "What the hell? You can bet Presley Wells is behind this."

But Samantha was thinking about what information Brian would have on his PDA—and what Alex had said about a last big score.

Presley showed up a little after eleven. It was all Alex could do not to storm down the hall and beat the hell out of him.

Instead, Samantha stayed between him and the door just in case and he watched the monitor with her, pretty sure he knew what would happen next.

He watched Presley go to Caroline, hold her, kiss her, brush her hair back from her face, and felt uncomfortable witnessing something so personal and intimate.

Alex could feel Samantha's gaze on him. "Okay, maybe he loves her. Or maybe he's an even better actor than my sister."

He watched Presley Wells lean over Caroline as if to

give her a kiss, his heart in his throat. If the man made any kind of move to hurt her—Presley pulled back.

Caroline was smiling up at her fiancé. It broke Alex's heart to see the love in her eyes. As Presley started to leave, she pulled him back as if somehow she knew she might never see him again. Alex saw fear in her face as Presley left. Then tears.

"Son of a bitch. She knows he's not coming back. I have to see her. Keep an eye on Presley but I think we both know where he's headed."

Caroline's eyes widened with fear when she saw Alex step into her room. "What are you doing here?" she asked, hurriedly drying her tears.

"I know Presley was just here. I know you gave him Brian's PDA. Caroline, why?"

"Alex, you don't understand. It isn't what you think."

"I know we sometimes do things when we're in love..."

She shook her head. "It isn't like that. Presley found out that Brian has been skimming money out of my trust fund. He needs to get into the records to prove it."

Alex shook his head sadly. "Caroline, don't you realize what you've done? He is going to clean out every dime and take off."

"You're wrong, Alex. He's trying to protect me, our family, our baby. He loves me. You'll see tonight, after he finds the evidence, you'll see that you're wrong about him."

Alex nodded, unable to argue anymore with his sister. She loved the man and was blind to what was happening. Later, Alex would come back because Caroline was going to need him. Arguing with her now wasn't going to make that easier for her later.

"Everything is going to be all right," he said.

"Presley knows what he's doing."

Alex didn't doubt that for a moment.

"Don't go after him," Caroline cried. "You don't realize how dangerous this is. Someone has been trying to hurt Presley."

Alex stopped at the door. "Caroline, someone tried to kill me and Samantha in Tennessee."

Shock registered on her face. "It wasn't Presley."

He gave her a sympathetic look. "I'll be back." Then he pushed out of the door, trying to ignore her cries for him to stop.

When Presley left he had Brian's PDA and it didn't take much to figure out where he was headed. To the Graham building headquarters and Brian's personal offices. No doubt Caroline had given him the codes to get in.

Both guards were at their posts again. Alex promised himself he would fire them both as soon as he returned.

Samantha was waiting for him downstairs. "He took a cab. I have the number."

Alex swore, finding it hard to believe that his sister would be taken in by this man. "Obviously, he's coerced Caroline into helping him rip off the family. Even love can be a form of coercion," he added, looking at Samantha.

"I like to believe love doesn't make you do things you don't want to do," Samantha said.

He met her gaze, the depth of his feelings for her convincing him that a person in love did a lot of things he wouldn't have conceived of just days before. He knew firsthand since the last person he wanted to be in love with was an agent. Especially right now.

Samantha started to reach for her cell phone but he placed a hand on her arm to stop her.

"Let me handle this," he said. "It's my *family*. Can you give me this? I know you're an agent. I've accepted that." Her look said she didn't believe it. He wasn't sure he did, either. "I have to handle this in a way that Caroline will be hurt the least. Do you understand?"

"You know I do."

"Then no agents. Just let me go alone."

"I can't do that, Alex. Maybe Presley's only crime was falling in love with a rich woman. Maybe it's swindling your family. But one of Weddings Your Way's clients is still missing after her abduction in front of the shop. There still hasn't been a ransom demand. For all I know Presley is somehow connected to all of it. And if that's the case, I can't leave the agency out of it."

"But you can give me a little time," Alex said, knowing that he was using her feelings for him. Wasn't he just as bad as Presley? He saw the pain in her expression.

"I won't make the call *yet*," she said. "But don't try to stop me from coming with you."

"Would it do any good?"

She shook her head.

"That's what I thought."

"Let's take my car," Samantha said. "He doesn't know it." A set of car lights blinked in the lot.

The headlights Alex saw were connected to a sleek black sports car convertible, the top up. "That's yours? You had someone deliver it?" He couldn't help his surprise. But then how could he forget the body she'd been hiding under those baggy suits? Or the brain and determination of the woman she'd been hiding behind the role of wedding planner?

* * *

Samantha tossed Alex the keys. He looked surprised, then grinned at her. All she could think about now was Presley. How could she have been so wrong about him? She hadn't stopped believing in him—even when all the evidence was so weighted against him. Until tonight.

Caroline had taken her brother's PDA. Unless Samantha missed her guess, it would contain passwords to Graham accounts. Presley could clean out whatever funds Brian managed for the family. Why else get Caroline to steal it for him?

"Ready?" Alex asked as he slid behind the wheel.

"You do know how to drive something other than a truck, don't you?"

He cranked up the engine. As it roared to life, he shot her a look. "What the hell's under that hood?"

She grinned back at him. "You're about to find out."

He hit the gas and they careened out of the parking lot. "I think in this we might be able to beat Presley to the Graham building."

Samantha nodded, her thoughts on what she'd agreed to do. She should have called Rachel. She should have had the team meet them. She'd broken one of the cardinal rules of Weddings Your Way. It might cost her her job.

But as she looked over at Alex, she also knew that he needed to do this on his own. The team was standing by. All she had to do was call them and they would be there in minutes. She could give Alex a little time. And it wasn't as if she was letting him go in alone.

"There is something you should know," she said as Alex took a corner. "Brian's in financial trouble. Possibly on the verge of losing everything your father entrusted to him."

Alex didn't ask how she knew this. He seemed to remember who she was, what she was. His face clouded. "You're sure?"

She nodded. "So the only thing Presley can steal is the rest of Caroline's trust fund."

Alex seemed to concentrate on his driving without looking at her. "Do you have any idea what my father is going to do when he hears about this? How much did my father invest with Presley?"

"A lot, but," she added quickly, "not enough to jeopardize the family fortune."

"And Brian. He invested, too, right?"

"Apparently not. At least not on paper."

Alex let out a low whistle. "What about Caroline and Presley?"

She hesitated. "They both sank most everything into this condominium project near the water."

"Presley had some money?" Alex asked, sounding surprised.

"Some. Not as much as Caroline of course."

"You think Brian invested with Presley under the table knowing how risky it was. Maybe made a deal to bring our father into it to sweeten the pot. That would be like Brian. So Brian lied to C.B. about how risky the venture was. He put his head on the chopping block and now Presley is about to chop it off."

That did seem to be the case. Samantha watched Miami became a blur as Alex drove toward the Graham building. "But if Presley had it all working for him, why try to kill us?" she asked, thinking aloud.

"Because he couldn't let us return from Tennessee

and tell Brian and C.B. who he really was before he finished whatever it is he's doing tonight," Alex said.

Maybe. Samantha was still having trouble believing it. "Why tonight? Why not a month ago?"

Alex cocked his head at her, his smile heart-stopping. "I'll ask him when I see him."

She leaned back in the seat unable not to think about Caroline and Presley. No more an unlikely match than she and Alex. C.B. would do everything possible to prevent Caroline from marrying Presley even if it turned out that his only crime was lying about his background—and possibly losing Graham money in one of his schemes.

She glanced over at Alex. He was already the black sheep of the family. Imagine how C.B. would react if he knew about her and Alex. If C.B. knew about her past. It wasn't as if a person could keep something like that a secret. Hadn't Caroline and Presley known that?

"You know my whole life history," she said. "But I don't know anything about you."

"Your whole life history?" He chuckled as he was forced to stop for a light. "Not likely. You know as much about me as I do you."

She shook her head. "I told you why there was no man in my life."

The light changed. Alex seemed to concentrate harder on his driving. A muscle jumped in his jaw. "You and I have both been hiding. The last woman I trusted proved to want nothing more than my money. I guess I've always had a hard time believing a woman could love me for anything but my money." He shot her a glance. "Once they hear the Graham name…"

Samantha smiled ruefully and nodded. "The exact opposite of Presley Wells."

Alex's lips turned up at little. "At least he knows Caroline loves him for who he is. Or did."

Ahead, the Graham office building loomed up into the Miami sky.

"This car, it's the part of you that I'm just getting to know, isn't it?" Alex said, his face serious as he parked and shut off the engine.

"Yes." She felt his gaze flick over her as they both exited the car and headed for the security entrance. The question was: was Alex Graham man enough to handle that woman? At least that was the question she imagined he was asking himself.

Samantha on the other hand had been convinced a long time ago that Alex Graham was plenty man enough for both of her lives.

In the end, he would have to make that decision. Whether or not he could live with her being an agent.

Or she would be faced with her own decision. Could she live without Alex Graham?

Samantha glanced back at the street and saw a tan sedan drive slowly by. They'd been followed from the hospital. She reached into her purse, her hand closing on her gun as Alex put in a call to his father.

"I need the code to get into the Graham building," he said into his cell while Samantha watched the street. "There isn't time to explain. For once, Dad, just don't fight me. Give me the code *now*."

Alex listened, then pressed the key pad. The door opened and he ran toward the stairs, Samantha right behind him. The door thunked shut as a set of headlights swung past, reflecting in the window in the door.

"Dad, I have to go. I don't care if you call Brian. I figured you would the moment you hang up anyway," Alex said into the phone. "But when you do, ask him where his PDA is." He closed his phone and pressed his back against the wall of the stairwell next to her.

Samantha heard the outer door open and close. A moment later the elevator doors hummed open. She waited next to Alex until she heard them close and the elevator begin its ascent.

Pushing open the stairwell door, she looked up to see what floor Presley got off on. Fourth.

Behind her, she heard Alex already running up the stairs to the fourth floor.

Chapter 17

Samantha caught up to him. Alex was trying to open one of the doors. "Here, let me," she said, stepping past him and pulling out her kit.

"How could I forget you have a talent for breaking into places?" he said stepping aside.

Yes, she thought, meeting his gaze. How could he forget? She felt her heart ache. He *couldn't* forget. Any more than he could forget what she did for a living and it wasn't the wedding planning part that she feared he couldn't live with.

"Shh," Alex said. "He's coming this way."

She got the door open. "In here." But when she turned, Alex was gone. Damn him. Where had he gone? She could hear footfalls. Presley was headed in her direction. Quickly, she ducked into the room and looked for a place to hide.

If she was right about why he'd had Caroline take Brian's PDA, then Presley would head for the computer. She ducked behind one of the large overstuffed leather chairs off to one side of the desk and waited.

The door creaked open. Footfalls headed for the desk. She heard the squeak of the office chair as someone sat down. Cautiously, she peeked out. From where she hid, she could see the backside of a man's head but there was no mistaking who it was. Presley Wells aka Preston Wellington III.

Samantha wondered where Alex had gone. She just hoped he stayed put. She needed to get Presley with the evidence, otherwise all they had on him was trespassing. From what Clare had been able to find out, the money Presley had taken from C. B. Graham was for a legitimate investment.

She waited, her heart in her throat as she watched Presley search Brian's PDA until he found what he was looking for, then turned to the computer to key in the passwords.

Somewhere in the building she heard a door slam. Presley heard it, too. He began to work faster and in a few moments she heard a pleased sound come from him, then pages began to come out of the laser printer.

Presley stood and went to the printer, his back to her. She drew the gun from her purse but didn't rise. Not yet. Just a few more moments and he would have the evidence on him. The printer stopped. She saw him pick up the sheets of paper, fold them and start to put them in his breast pocket. Samantha made her move.

Victor Constantine loved the element of surprise. But wasn't wild about being surprised.

Unfortunately, upon his return from Tennessee, he'd

gone straight from the airport to the hospital only to find Alex Graham's pickup parked in the lot. How was that possible? He'd been so certain Alex Graham was dead.

He quickly realized that he'd failed in Tennessee. There was some irony to the fact, given that his client had failed to put the payment in his account. It almost balanced things out. Almost.

Victor wished he could call the client and give him the news. Except the client had gotten rid of the cell phone thinking that would be the end of it.

Victor had little to go on. Just the sound of the man's voice—and now Alex Graham and Samantha Peters. Victor had planned on using the woman Alex Graham and Samantha Peters had visited at the hospital—Caroline Graham. But now that wouldn't be necessary. He waited in the darkness outside the hospital. Something told him that the pair would lead him to his client. Or the client would find them. Either way worked.

It didn't take that long before Alex Graham and Samantha Peters emerged, jumped into her little black number and sped off with Alex driving. Victor was right behind.

Then he'd had a stroke of good luck. As he'd watched the two enter the high-rise office building, he'd decided to wait. Within two minutes a taxi arrived and dropped off a dark-haired young man.

Victor had his window down and was parked where he could hear the man talking to the taxi driver. Wrong voice. Not his client.

Victor started to get out of his car and follow the man but another car had pulled up, the driver watching the exchange between the taxi driver and the man with almost as much interest as Victor.

As the dark-haired man disappeared into the building, the other man followed, giving an order to his driver to wait. Victor would have known that voice anywhere. But it was the way the man ordered the driver to wait that cinched it.

Victor quickly got out of his car and hurried after his client, catching up to him just as he opened the office building door. The surprise on the man's face was priceless as Victor locked an arm around the man's throat and forced him inside the building. Victor wanted to hurt him right then and there, but he was nothing if not pragmatic.

"You owe me money," he whispered into the man's ear. "Quite a lot of money."

Recognition shone in the man's terrified eyes, then angry arrogance. "You bungled the job. You didn't kill them. I owe you nothing."

Victor tightened his hold on the man's throat. "The money or I will kill you here."

An unintelligible sound came out of his client. Victor, who had made few mistakes in his life, loosened his hold. Pop. Pop. Instantly he recognized the sound of bullets passing through a small caliber gun's silencer. It took a little longer to feel the pain.

Victor staggered as his client broke away turning to fire once more before disappearing into the elevator. Clutching his side, Victor slumped to the floor. He could only watch as the elevator doors closed. His pained gaze went to the numbers lighting up above the closed elevator doors.

It wasn't until the light stopped at 4 that Victor forced himself to his feet.

Alex could see Presley in Brian's office but he couldn't be sure where Samantha had gone. He stayed back in the shadows watching Presley at the computer, then at the printer. Where the hell was Samantha?

He heard the elevator doors open down the hall. Someone else in the building? His father? Or Brian? Or both? Alex knew he had to make a move as he saw that Presley had heard the elevator doors and knew someone was coming, as well.

Crouching down, Alex readied himself for when Presley came out the office door. He'd jump him and pray the man didn't have a gun.

But after a moment, Alex realized his mistake. He peeked through the office window. No Presley. And yet he hadn't come out this door.

While Alex had forgotten about it, Presley obviously had known about the secret panel that opened between Brian's office and the one next door. Where the hell was he now?

No Samantha, either.

Nor, he realized, did he hear anyone down the hall. And yet someone had gotten off the elevator.

With a curse, he realized that they had all gone through the back way into Brian's private inner office.

Alex reached for the doorknob. It refused to turn. He was locked out. But what scared him most was that Samantha was locked inside. Somewhere. Agent or not, she was in danger. Maybe more danger than she knew because she still wanted to believe in Presley Wells's innocence.

Samantha had been ready to take Presley Wells down. Like Alex, she had expected him to head for the main office door which would have given her time to come out from behind the chair, aim the weapon and take him by surprise.

Instead, he had touched a panel on the wall next to the printer and then melted into the opening that suddenly appeared, leaving her two steps behind.

Just seconds before that, she'd heard the elevator doors down the hall, heard footfalls. More than one set.

She hurried over to the panel that had closed behind Presley and felt on the wall where she'd seen him do the same. The panel slid open soundlessly and she stepped into the cool darkness, her gun raised.

She heard voices somewhere in front of her. Then a pop followed by a crash. Her heart in her throat, she hurried forward, leading with her weapon.

The first thing she saw was the body on the floor. "Presley?" As she stepped forward she saw that the man wore a pair of dark chinos and a polo shirt. Presley had been dressed in a work shirt, jeans and denim jacket.

As she moved to see the face of the man on the floor, she heard a sound behind her. Just as she recognized Brian Graham sprawled facedown, she was jumped from behind. A strong hand wrestled the gun from her fingers and shoved her. She stumbled and almost fell over Brian on the floor.

Turning back toward the darkness of another adjoining office, she saw Presley. He held her gun in his hand as he locked the door behind them. "So you know who I am."

She stepped back, bumping into the desk. She pretended to use both hands to brace herself on the desk, while she mentally tried to remember if she'd seen anything within reach that she could use as a weapon.

"Easy," Presley said. "Let's not do anything crazy, okay?" His voice had the same gentle, slightly Southern drawl she remembered. He had another weapon stuck in the waistband of his jeans. This one had a silencer on it and she knew it was what she'd heard just moments before.

"You shot Brian?"

"Actually, he tried to shoot *me*," Presley said. "You don't believe me." He stepped closer. "I love Caroline. But I think you know that."

Surprisingly, she believed him. She did know. "So this is just about money."

"Just about money?" He laughed. "You and I both know people have killed for less."

"Do you really think you can get away with this?"

"For Caroline's sake and our baby's, I sure hope so."

Brian stirred on the floor, groaning as he worked his way into a sitting position, his back against the wall.

Presley hadn't pointed her gun at her. But although he held it pointed downward, it wouldn't take much for him to raise it and fire at either her or Brian.

"I have proof what Brian was up to." Presley patted the breast pocket of his jacket.

Brian swore. "He's lying. He's a con man. His name is Presley Wells. He's here to clean out my accounts."

Presley let out a humorless laugh. "I would be too late for that. The accounts have already been emptied. I would imagine Caroline's trust fund is also empty. Caroline thought she got away with your PDA clean but you were on to us, weren't you?"

"What is going on?" Samantha demanded, looking from one man to the other but all the time worrying about where Alex was. And what he would do next.

"Brian discovered who I really was and came to me with a deal," Presley said. "A scam to bilk his father out of more money. Brian said he had an investment that was too good to pass up, but risky. His father would never go for it. Unless it looked like it came from me. C.B. liked me. Of course C.B. wouldn't go for it unless Brian gave his stamp of approval."

"Don't listen to him," Brian said rubbing the side of his head where Presley must have hit him. Samantha couldn't tell if Brian was really hurt or just biding his time, waiting for Presley to let his guard down.

"If all this is true, then why didn't you go to C.B. with it?" she asked Presley.

This time his laugh was sincere. "Brian would have told him the truth about my…background and then who do you think C.B. would have believed? So I went along with it, pretending I was in it for the money."

"Like this isn't about money," Brian piped up. "You think anyone is going to believe your story? Your word against mine. There is no evidence that I was in on any of this."

Presley smiled and shook his head. "No, you made sure you'd covered your tracks. But the only reason I went along with your so-called deal was that I'd discovered you'd been siphoning off Caroline's trust fund account. I couldn't prove it. Until tonight. I found what I needed to put the nail in your coffin. I found proof that you made an attempt to pay a hired killer to get rid of me." He patted the papers in his pocket.

Brian, Samantha noticed, looked worried. "There isn't any…" His voice trailed off as if he'd just remembered something he'd overlooked.

Samantha jumped at the sound of a loud boom just outside the office door as if the door had been rammed by something heavy.

"No!" Samantha cried as she saw Brian launch himself at Presley. Presley raised her gun as if to fire, but it was knocked from his hand as a man came barreling into the room.

She caught only a glimpse of the man but she recognized his size and shape. The man who'd been following her and Alex? The hired assassin who'd tried to kill them in Tennessee?

"You think you can double-cross me?" the big man bellowed at Brian. "Are you crazy?"

Brian grabbed her fallen gun and pointed it at the man and yelled, "You're fired!"

Two explosions boomed in the office. Two quick shots. Brian's shot went wild, burrowing into the wall over the big man's head. Samantha wrested the other gun from Presley and fired. Hitting the big man in the leg.

But he didn't go down.

"Drop your gun! FBI!" she yelled, the gun aimed at the big man. "Drop your gun!"

Out of the corner of her eye, she saw Alex. He had something in his hands. A fire extinguisher.

The big man hadn't seen Alex but her biggest fear was that he would. As the man started to turn, Samantha's finger twitched on the trigger.

The man swung around. Samantha fired but the bullet that buried itself in his chest seemed to have no effect. The big man raised his gun, pointing it at Brian. "I always finish what I started."

Alex swung the fire extinguisher. It made a loud crack as it struck the big man's skull. Presley charged the big man, stepping into Samantha's line of fire. Samantha shoved Presley aside, but not before the big man got off two shots. Alex swung the fire extinguisher again, this time the sound more of a sickening thunk followed by the heavy thud of a body hitting the floor.

"Bri, oh hell, Bri," she heard Alex saying as he bent over his brother.

Samantha was moving, first making sure that Presley hadn't been hit, then kicking the big man's gun out of his reach just in case he wasn't dead. But when she checked, she found he wasn't breathing.

She could hear sirens in the distance. Alex didn't seem to hear them, didn't seem to notice as he stripped off his shirt and pressed it to Brian's gaping chest wound.

She'd called the team against Alex's wishes. She'd had to. She hoped some day he would understand. Unfortunately everything had happened too fast. The team hadn't had time to get there. Maybe things would have gone differently. Or maybe not, she thought, looking down at Brian.

Brian was lying on the floor sobbing, his words barely audible. "I'm sorry. I just lost control of everything. I didn't know what to do. I had to stop Dad from finding out." He looked into Alex's face. "Everything just got out of control, you know?"

"Yeah, bro, I know," Alex said.

Samantha knew. She looked around the room. Presley was sitting on the floor looking sick, as if this wasn't what he'd wanted to happen, even though Brian had paid the big man on the floor to kill him. To kill all three of them.

"Don't tell Dad what I did," Brian said. "Promise me, you won't tell Dad."

"I promise," Alex said. But even as he said the words, Brian's eyes dimmed then went blank. His hand dropped from his chest. Alex let go of the shirt he'd pressed to the wound, then reached up gently and closed Brian's eyes.

When he looked over at Samantha, his gaze was filled with pain. Slowly, he rose and stepped to her. She felt a surge of warmth flow through her as he pulled her into his arms.

"Thank God, you're safe," Alex said against her hair. "Thank God."

Epilogue

"I still can't believe this," C. B. Graham grumbled as he reached for his drink on the table beside his chair.

Alex saw that his father had aged. C.B. seemed smaller, frailer, definitely chastened. C.B. had put all his money on Brian, so to speak. And Brian had caved under the strain.

"Go ahead and say it. I know what you're thinking. That I put too much pressure on my children. That I'm responsible for everything." C.B. stared down at his drink. "That if I'd been a better father…" His voice trailed off as he looked up at Alex, tears in his eyes. "I could have lost you all."

Brian had gotten in too deep, come up with a scheme to cover it up and involved Presley. Because of his background, Presley had felt he had to find proof against Brian before he could go to anyone with what he suspected.

"I still can't believe Brian hired a killer." C.B.'s voice faltered. He swallowed and gripped his glass for a moment before taking a drink.

Alex glanced out the window. It had gotten dark and now all the lights in the garden twinkled. From somewhere, he heard music. The house felt alive again with Caroline back home.

"There's been enough blame," he said "Caroline is doing great. The doctor said her recovery is going well, she'll be back on her feet in no time."

C.B. nodded. "It's nice having her here." At her father's request, Caroline had agreed to recuperate at the house—but only if Presley would be allowed to move in, too.

"I want you to get to know him," Caroline had told C.B. "That's the deal. Take it or leave it."

C.B. had grudgingly taken it.

"She's going to marry that man, isn't she," he said now.

Alex nodded, smiling a little as he thought of his sister's fiancé. Caroline had been right. Alex liked Presley. Alex just wished his sister and Presley had trusted him enough to come to him when they'd suspected what Brian was up to.

But Samantha had taught him to put the past behind him. He couldn't change what had happened. All he could do now was look to the future. And what a future it could be.

"Presley reminds me of you," C.B. said and took a swallow of his drink.

Alex looked at his father, not sure what to say. As C.B. looked up from his glass, Alex felt the full weight of the old man's gaze. "I know I let you down when I wasn't interested in taking over the family business..."

"No, not that," C.B. said with a wave of his hand. "You and Presley, you're both stubborn, pigheaded and have to do everything your own way. Invariably the hard way."

The last thing Alex wanted to do was argue with his father. "If that's supposed to be a compliment, it's not coming off as one."

His father laughed, a wonderful sound after all the pain they'd been through. "I'm trying to tell you that I admire you."

Alex stared at his father.

"The truth is you always were so damned much like me."

"Thank you," Alex said uncertainly.

C.B. laughed. "That definitely wasn't a compliment." But the pride he heard in his father's voice made him ache.

He looked at his father and saw something he'd missed for years. Grudging respect.

Is this what Brian had seen? Is this why Alex and Brian had never gotten along? Brian had tried so hard to please their father. While Alex hadn't tried at all for his father's respect or love, Brian had tried too hard. Brian had risked everything for it—and lost it all. How sad that Alex hadn't seen how much Brian had been struggling with that insecurity until after his brother's death.

While it had been Brian's scheme, Presley had invested the money he'd received from both Brian and C.B. and invested it in his companies. C.B. was going to make a sizable sum. Brian would have, too, had he lived.

Brian had been buried in the family cemetery on

the property. Most of what had really happened had never surfaced. Not much of an investigation followed the shootings. Alex knew he had Samantha to thank for that. The police had just been happy to finally have the notorious Victor Constantine and the impeccable records of his kills. Looking for Constantine's clients would keep them busy for years.

There was a tap at the door. "Am I interrupting?"

Alex motioned Samantha into the room. C.B. lit up at the sight of her. She went straight to the old man and gave him a kiss on the cheek, then came over to settle into the seat next to Alex. He couldn't believe what just seeing her did to him.

"How's my favorite wedding planner?" C.B. asked, all smiles now.

"Just fine." She glanced at Alex. He gave her hand a squeeze.

Alex had realized something over the last week. Samantha was her own woman. And that was what had made him fall in love with her. He knew now that he wouldn't have tried to change her for anything in the world. He loved her and while her "second" job might scare him, he had every faith in her abilities. Just as she did in his.

"I was upstairs talking to Caroline and Presley about their wedding," Samantha said.

C.B. frowned. He'd come a long way over the last week, but he was still a curmudgeon at heart. He still wanted his only daughter to marry another blue blood.

"They've decided to postpone it until Caroline can walk down the aisle," Samantha said.

"If she waits too long, she'll have the baby in the middle of the aisle," Alex joked, excited about being an uncle. Even more excited about someday being a father. "You'll have to plan a joint wedding-baby shower."

Samantha jabbed him in the ribs with her elbow.

"I guess there is no talking her out of it," C.B. said and took a drink, but Alex could hear more than acceptance in his father's tone. "Well, there is the baby and Caroline obviously loves the man. Presley does seem to be good with money and it will be my first grandchild."

Alex smiled to himself, seeing his father's delight at being a grandfather. C.B., he thought, just might make a wonderful grandfather.

The door opened and Presley Wells stepped in with a roll of paper.

"Pres," his father said. The two men looked at each other, mutual acceptance and admiration growing between them. Presley Wells was the last man C.B. had wanted for his only daughter. And yet that was the man she'd chosen.

The fact that C.B. had let Presley move into the house with them said it all. Yes, Alex thought, his father was learning the fine art of compromise. It was something to see.

"That the condo project you've got there?" his father asked Presley.

"I'm thinking of making a few changes," Presley said, spreading out the plans on the table as he sat down across from C.B. "Want to take a look and see what you think?"

It was just a matter of time, Alex thought watching the two of them, before Presley Wells would be running the Graham empire.

Alex saw his chance to escape and slipped out of the den with Samantha in tow. They ran across the courtyard at the back of the house, laughing and falling into each others arms. They'd had so little time to be entirely alone over the past week.

But they were alone now and Alex planned to make the most of it. The night was warm, the garden lush. Lights flickered overhead. He could hear the soft murmur of the waterfalls, the gentle splash. The air was scented with the perfume of many flowers now in bloom. Everything couldn't have been more perfect.

"It is so beautiful here," she said as she turned to look out over the gardens.

He wrapped his arms around her, never wanting to let her go. And to think there'd been a time when he'd thought he'd never be able to live with the fact that she was an agent.

But they both had dangerous jobs that they loved. They'd both chosen their own paths in life. And those paths had led them to each other.

Love, he realized, could conquer all.

Samantha snuggled against him, filled with a sense of joy at just being in his arms. His mouth felt warm as he nuzzled her neck, his breath tickling her skin. She felt safe. She felt loved. There was no greater feeling, she thought, as he drew her closer and they looked out on the gardens and the night.

They'd been through so much but it seemed to have made them stronger. It had definitely brought them closer.

Now if only there could be a break in the Sonya Botero kidnapping. The team was still investigating every avenue, following up on every lead, but still no word. Every day, they waited for the kidnappers to contact either Sonya's father or her fiancé, Juan. But still nothing.

Samantha wasn't giving up and neither was the team. She would just work harder on the case, praying there would be a break. Praying Sonya was still alive.

"Samantha?" Alex turned her slowly in his arms to face him. She looked up into his eyes and felt her heart begin to pound as his mouth dropped to hers in a soft sweet kiss. Then he drew her back to look at her.

She'd changed so much since she'd met him. She no longer wore the boxy suits. She no longer hid from her past or the girl she'd been. With Alex, she felt beautiful.

Presley Wells, for all the mistakes he'd made in investigating Brian by himself, had proven to her that there were men in the universe who were good and loyal and worth loving. And Alex Graham was one of them.

"Do you hear that?" Alex asked cocking his head and grinning as he drew her closer. Music moved on the breeze from the open terrace doors.

She smiled up at him as he pulled her into a slow dance, their bodies fitting together perfectly. She could feel the beat of his heart against her breast, hear his breath quickening as she touched her lips to his warm flesh just above his shirt collar.

The song ended and she realized that he'd danced her over to a stone bench beside a fountain. Caroline said the house should be filled with flowers and music and love.

Samantha couldn't agree more. Otherwise a house was nothing but an empty shell. Just as her heart had been before Alex.

Alex. He brushed a kiss over her lips. She breathed in his scents mingling with the fragrance of the garden, the water of the fountain, the uniquely south Florida smells. The night felt magical.

Her heart began to beat a little faster as he gently lowered her to the bench. And just like in the movies, he dropped to one knee in front of her, his eyes locking with hers.

"Samantha Peters, wedding planner and secret agent, will you marry me?" he asked, his gaze never leaving hers.

She swallowed, tears welling in her eyes as she smiled at him. "Oh, Alex."

From his pocket, he pulled out a small black box and held it out to her. Her fingers shook as she opened it and saw the diamond ring nestled in velvet.

"I never dreamed I could be this happy," she said, tears burning her eyes.

"Should I take that as a yes?"

"Oh, yes!"

He laughed, took the ring and placed it on her finger. She looked down at it, then up at him. The next thing she knew they were in each other's arms, holding each other tightly as if neither ever wanted to let go. She knew he had to be thinking about how close they'd come to losing each other.

Both knew because of their jobs, it could happen again. They'd made a silent pact to live every day as if there was no tomorrow.

"You know my father is going to want us to have a big wedding here," he said.

She smiled and tilted her head. "Would you hate that so much?"

He laughed. "Yes, but I'd do it for you. For my father." His eyes locked with hers, his bright in the twinkling lights that Caroline had asked to be strung in the trees of the garden the day she moved back in.

"My secret weapon soon-to-be spouse," he whispered. He said it with a kind of awe.

"You didn't tell your father, did you?"

"About your secret life?" Alex smiled and shook his head. "He's only just accepted the fact that I'm a fireman. Anyway, I don't think his heart could take it."

She laughed softly, smiling as she cupped his jaw with her palm and looked into those wonderful eyes of his.

Alex pulled her closer. "There are some things, sweetheart, that should be our little secrets."

* * * * *

"Chelsea, what's going on?" Johnny clutched his cell
phone to his ear and at the same time he sat up and turned
on the lamp on his nightstand.

"That man…that man is here. He tried to b-break in."
The words came amid sobs. "He…he was at my back
d-door and breaking the gl-glass to get in."

"Hang up and call Lane," he instructed as he got out
of bed.

"I…already called, but n-nobody is here yet."

Johnny could hear the abject terror in her voice, and an
icy fear shot through him. "Where are you now?"

HIEXP0522

"I'm in the kitchen."

"Get to the bathroom and lock yourself in. Do you hear me? Lock yourself in the bathroom, and I'll be there as quickly as I can," he instructed.

"Please hurry. I don't know where he is now, and I'm so scared."

"Just get to the bathroom. Lock the door and don't open it for anyone but me or the police." He hung up and quickly dressed. He then strapped on his gun and left his cabin. Any residual sleepiness he might have felt was instantly gone, replaced by a sharp edge of tension that tightened his chest.

Don't miss
Closing in on the Cowboy *by Carla Cassidy,*
available July 2022 wherever
Harlequin Intrigue books and ebooks are sold.

Harlequin.com

Love Harlequin romance?

DISCOVER.

Be the first to find out about promotions, news and exclusive content!

 Facebook.com/HarlequinBooks

Twitter.com/HarlequinBooks

 Instagram.com/HarlequinBooks

Pinterest.com/HarlequinBooks

ReaderService.com

EXPLORE.

Sign up for the Harlequin e-newsletter and download a free book from any series at **TryHarlequin.com**

CONNECT.

Join our Harlequin community to share your thoughts and connect with other romance readers!
Facebook.com/groups/HarlequinConnection

HARLEQUIN

Heartfelt or thrilling, passionate or uplifting—Harlequin is more than just happily-ever-after.

With twelve different series to choose from and new books available every month, you are sure to find stories that will move you, uplift you, inspire and delight you.